STORM CLOUD RISING

JASON LANCOUR

WANDERING BEAR CREATIVE

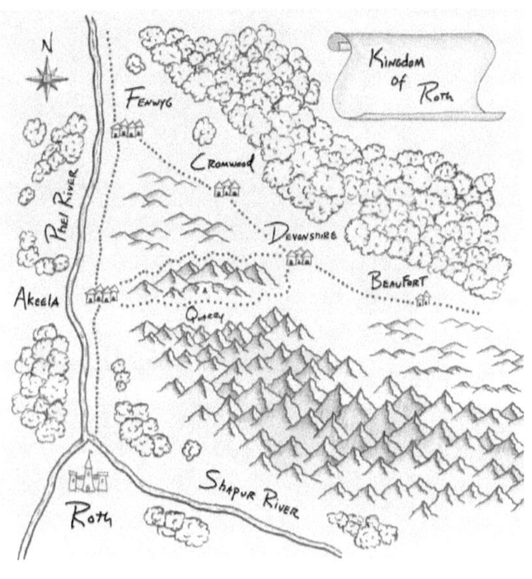

The North-Eastern
Territories of the
Kingdom of Roth

CONTENTS

Lankaran Calendar

Throughout this book, I reference days of the week and months of the year. Distinguishing dates will become important as the narrative unfolds. While I have every confidence that, if motivated, you'd be able to figure this out on your own, for your convenience, I have chosen to describe here the workings of the calendar system used in the world.

The planet of this fictional world has a slightly elliptical orbit with an axial tilt similar to Earth's. The experience of the four seasons is similar, spread out across a 364 day year.

The new year is celebrated on the first day of spring. Each season is divided into three months; each month is divided into three, ten-day weeks. The days of the week are named thusly: Firsday, Seconday, Thirday, Forthday, Midweek (a day of rest for some), Sixday, Sepday, Ethday, Ninday, and Endweek (a day off for most).

The first month of each season is broken into two parts; two regular weeks, one special holiday for either Equinox or Solstice, and then one regular week. Therefore, the first month of each season is 31 days.

The names of the months follow a patterned naming convention that you can see here. The Spring months are Cyndwyn, Eilfer, and Turadver. Summer months: Cyndmur, Eilmur, and Turadmur. Autumn: Cynddum, Eiltum, and Turaddum. Finally, the Winter months are Cyntur, Eiltur, and Turaddur.

PROLOGUE

The wind rushed out of Corelan's lungs as he landed hard on his back. He slid a few feet through the mud from the force of his opponent's blow, rolled to his side, and struggled to his feet.

"Haven't had enough beating yet?" the Ialu taunted. Corelan just shook his head. Given that there were four of them dishing out the beating and only one of him to collect it all, the statement was hardly fair, but there was a lot about the situation that was unfair, and Corelan wasn't one to fret over small details. The Ialu stepped forward, a splash of fresh mud obscuring the intricate tattoos emblazoned across his bald head. Corelan edged forward, fists raised, careful to keep a sharp eye on his opponent's companions. They stood to either side and behind, effectively surrounding him, but they seemed content to let the Ialu do most of the fighting. So far, they had only stepped in when Corelan seemed to be getting the upper hand. The Ialu circled slowly to his left, cautious of Corelan's superior reach.

While Corelan stood well over a head taller than the man, the Ialu outweighed him by at least fifty percent, as was normal for his people. In fact, the tallest Ialu that Corelan had ever seen stood no taller than his nose. Which, incidentally, was throbbing intensely from the force of the Ialu's enormously powerful blow, also typical for his people. The Ialu rushed in suddenly, arms sweeping around to encircle Corelan's waist in an obvious attempt to bear him to the ground. Corelan dropped to one knee and opened his arms as well as if to meet the force of the rush head-on, but at the last moment, extended an elbow into his opponent's face. The Ialu reacted with enough time to turn his face away and receive the brunt of the force on a bony portion of his skull, inflicting little harm. The moment's distraction was all Corelan needed. He ducked his head beneath one of the Ialu's thick arms while simultaneously reaching out to grab the Ialu's wrist with one hand. Corelan grabbed the Ialu's shoulder with this other hand and pivoted around behind him, passing under his arm. As the force of the Ialu's charge drove him past, Corelan twisted his arm into a locking position just as the Ialu's chest thumped into the ground. Corelan put a knee into the small of his back to assure that he would stay there. Despite the near-perfect execution of a classic grappling technique, Corelan now had three significant concerns – the Ialu's companions.

The first to react was a black-skinned C'thûn. Roughly equivalent to humans in size and stature, the C'thûn range in coloration from a cool grey to black as the night sky. A tribal people, the C'thûn keep mostly to themselves with the occasional exception of merchants or artisans. And warriors. The latter could easily be discerned by their prominently displayed tribal sigils. The C'thûn who came charging at Corelan now was evidently a warrior – given the intricately carved bone talisman that dangled freely on a leather cord around his neck. Corelan simply pivoted to the opposite side of his pinned opponent, placing the Ialu's immobilized arm between himself and the onrushing C'thûn. At the last moment, the C'thûn balked, realizing he was about to hyperextend and likely dislocate his friend's shoulder. Corelan took advantage of the hesitation by diving over the Ialu and crashing bodily into the C'thûn's knees. The C'thûn fell over backward to protect his delicate joints, allowing Corelan to roll across his body and plant the back of his elbow squarely and firmly in the C'thûn's face. Corelan hopped to his feet and rushed the Ialu's second companion without waiting for him to react. This one was human, thickly built, and tall. Also, fortunately for Corelan, a touch slow. Corelan caught him with a simple, quick jab to the chin and followed up with another to the solar plexus. He doubled over, wheezing. Corelan spun to face the third, also human, just as the Ialu was regaining his feet.

A drop of rain splashed off of Corelan's forehead as he sidestepped his opponents. The C'thûn struggled to his feet as the human rolled over to his hands and knees, still coughing. He glanced around the muddy alleyway. A small crowd of vaguely interested townsfolk had gathered, and it seemed a few had placed some modest bets and were perhaps anxious to wrap up their wager. One even ventured a verbal protest about the current delay but was silenced by an annoyed look from the muddy-faced Ialu. A town guardsman had also arrived, but apparently, he was involved in the betting and could not interfere due to a clear conflict of interest.

The combatants paused for a moment to size each other up as the rain began to grow in intensity. Corelan glanced at the rear door of the tavern, where he had been peacefully enjoying a drink only a few moments ago.

"Well?" Corelan asked.

"Do you take back what you said?" the Ialu asked.

"I told you I have no idea what you are talking about!" Corelan responded, annoyed that stepping out for a smoke could deteriorate into a street fight so rapidly. But this was Roth's Old Section, and he could count himself lucky no one had pulled steel yet.

"You said our lady friends were whores!" the Ialu bellowed. Politeness is central to the sensibilities of Ialu society. Any perception of rudeness can be taken very seriously – especially when whiskey was involved.

"What?" Corelan paused, bewildered. "No, I didn't," he answered, dropping his guard. He laughed, despite his miserable state. "Is that what this is about?" The Ialu returned a puzzled look. "I was asking about your *horse*." Corelan pointed to the animal that had originally garnered his attention. The Ialu turned to look at the beast in question. The animal had pulled free of his tether and was now freely wandering the street, searching for a tasty nibble.

"Oh," the Ialu responded. He jerked his head toward the street, and one of his fellows dashed off to recapture the animal. A quick survey of the rapidly dispersing crowd told the Ialu that the young ladies whose delicate honor he had sought to defend had also wandered off. After a moment's contemplation, the Ialu spoke. "Well, in that case, buy you a drink, friend?"

The four of them proved to be rather accomplished drinkers as well, and only with colossal effort was Corelan able to overcome them on that front. Hours had passed since his newfound companions had admitted defeat, and he now sat virtually alone in the closing tavern trying to determine if the pounding in his head was more from fists or from the excessive amounts of whiskey that had just been consumed. Corelan shrugged as he conceded the irrelevance of the question.

A crashing sound snapped him from his reflection. The barmaid bent to retrieve a fallen earthenware mug, sighing heavily. Corelan turned his gaze back to his own mug resting on the table in front of him. A full minute passed before he could focus his eyes on the vessel, forcing him to come to a familiar conclusion. "I'm drunk." His gaze lifted to take in the dusty tavern. The dim light from the struggling lanterns fell on the few patrons who had not yet left. Maybe they had nowhere to go either. A man in disheveled, worn clothing snored loudly as he slept in a drunken stupor in a dark corner, tightly clutching an empty mug as if planning to use it to fend off the impending hangover. Another man stood wobbling by the bar as he dug tenaciously in his pockets on a divine quest for the silver coins he had just dropped on the floor. The bartender mopped the remains of a long night's carousing from the bar as the tired barmaid resumed placing the chairs on the tables after uprooting a thoroughly soused regular. The cacophony from the previous night seemed to echo through the now quiet tavern. A glance around the bar informed him that he was likely the last remaining individual who would be able to find his way home tonight. Or was it this morning?

"One more victory," he muttered to himself.

His gaze fell back once again to his table. The somber light of a sputtering candle fell on the multitude of empty mugs that littered the table's battered surface. Corelan's vision swam in foggy circles, making an accurate count of their number impossible. Maybe he wouldn't get home tonight after all.

"Well fought, my soldiers," he said too loudly. He lifted his mug to his lips to salute their bravery. When did that happen? He wondered, gazing at his empty mug. He then wondered if he should be wondering that. The barmaid spared him a piteous glance and went back to sweeping the floor. As he pondered the wisdom of getting one more for the road, the quiet was broken by the dull thud of a man hitting the ground outside, too drunk to ride, falling off his horse for the third, and what seemed like final time. Poor chump. He thought. Poor chump indeed. He laughed quietly at himself and lifted his empty mug halfway to his lips. He stifled an oath into his empty mug and began searching his pockets for a smoke.

"Corelan." A man's voice broke the quiet.

Someone was speaking. This is not the time of day for speech. Time for a good smoke, though.

"Corelan, I've been looking for you."

Corelan looked up. A slim man in dusty street clothes stood beside his table, frowning down at him. They looked at each other for a moment, and Corelan resumed his search. The man sat beside him, sparing a glance for the field of glass and earthenware that decorated the table.

"Corelan, you look like hell," the man said in a slightly softer tone. Corelan scratched his face. The rough stubble of several days' growth scratched back. He ran his fingers through his dark, unwashed hair, dislodging a chunk of dried mud, and after a moment, he silently agreed with the newcomer.

"Corelan, you in there?"

"What do you want, Jiam."

"Were you in a fight?" he asked with exasperation in his voice.

"Just a little, uh, miscommunication."

Not wanting to dignify that statement as legitimate by responding, Jiam frowned and went on. "You're a wreck. You can't keep on like this. Listen, what you need is..."

"Don't tell me what I need!" Corelan snapped. The room wobbled suddenly, and Corelan clung to the table for support.

"Corelan." Jiam leaned forward on the table. "I can't say I understand, but she..." Corelan's eyes shot open and locked onto Jiam's face. He leaned forward, gripping the edges of the table.

"Don't. Even. Start." Corelan's voice held a dangerous edge. The two stared at each other for a long, silent moment.

"What do you want me to say?" Jiam asked, throwing his hands in the air as he leaned back in his chair.

"How about leaving it alone?"

"I'm just trying to help, you ass!" Jiam retorted.

"Help? What the hell do you know about..."

"What is that?" Jiam interrupted. "Is that your lucky silver crown?" He gestured to the coin on the table.

"What if it is?"

"You are *not* going to spend *that* coin on a bar tab." Jiam pushed the coin across the table toward his friend. "I've got this." He began to dig into his pocket. Corelan stewed in silence for a moment. "Are you that broke?" Jiam asked.

"I'm between jobs. You know that."

"Read this." Jiam smacked a sheet of parchment to the table. Corelan winced at the sudden sound. He looked at the page from across the table, making no move toward it. Instead, he turned to stuff his hand in his jacket pocket, remembering his quest for smoke.

"Another job?" Corelan asked, not looking at his friend. His hand closed around a mangled stub in his pocket, and he slowly pulled his treasure forth. They both looked at the sad little wrap of leaf, bent and torn, spilling tiny tobacco leaves. Corelan chuckled slightly and looked at his friend. "You got any smokes?"

Jiam sighed wearily. "Why can't you smoke a pipe like everyone else?"

"Mine are more convenient."

"Then smoke a normal cigar."

"Too heavy tasting. I like the little ones and so do you. I've seen you buy them."

"Will you at least read the flier?"

Still not moving toward the parchment, Corelan replied, "Where'd you get it?"

"What does it matter? Look, you haven't worked in..."

"I know..."

"You are starting to owe me more money than friends should owe..."

"I know..."

Jiam changed his tone. "Listen, I'll make you a deal. Just answer the ad..." Corelan shifted uneasily. "Just answer it. There is a meeting on

Forthday at the Boar's Tusk Inn. Just be there. Listen to what they have to say. Give it a chance. All I am asking is for you to be there."

Corelan fell silent and dropped his gaze to the table, studying his mangled cigar.

Jiam hesitated for a moment, then continued in a softer tone. "Go to the meeting. Listen to them, and you don't have to pay me back."

Corelan looked up sharply, his pale eyes intense. "That's a lot of money."

"I know." Jiam produced an intact tiny cigar from his pocket. "Say you'll answer it."

Corelan reached for the offering, but Jiam pulled it back, arching an eyebrow. A moment passed. "Okay. Just gimme the damn thing."

Jiam hesitated, exploring his friend's face for a moment. Corelan took advantage of the pause to snatch his prize from Jiam's fingers. Jiam settled back into his chair, wearily studying his haggard friend. Corelan lifted the candle from the table to light his cigarette, his face momentarily lit by the puff of flame. He inhaled slowly, closing his eyes and easing back into his chair. As he slowly released the smoke, he made eye contact with Jiam. "I promise, okay?"

Jiam stood, pushing the flier across the table. "Meeting is a sunset. Do you think you can be presentable that early?" Corelan gave a sardonic nod. "Bathe?"

"What are you, my mother? I'll be there. And I am still going to pay you back."

As Jiam turned to leave, the first rays of dawn were just beginning to illuminate the street outside with a pale gray glow. "What time does this place close?"

"Never, that's why I like it." They stood, and Jiam threw an assortment of coinage on the table. "C'mon, I know a great place you can buy me breakfast," Corelan said, clapping his friend on the shoulder. The two walked out into the street, lightly stepping around the unconscious form huddled at the bottom of the steps.

* * * * *

Lena never liked the Free Blade's Guild. Life as a mercenary was hard enough without the interference of an institution dedicated to promoting those without enough talent to promote themselves. Even the name irked her. Free Blades. Better to call it honestly. Mercenaries. And they certainly were not free, in either sense of the word. Hired blades – that was all they were, nothing more, even though only half actually carried a blade at all. Maybe less than half, she thought as a white-bearded man in a silver-trimmed velvet robe strode past. He carried himself with such bearing; he clearly felt himself equal to any in the inner ranks of the Wizard's Circle. Another man, a black-skinned C'thûn, leaned against a wall reading a slip of parchment as he absently flipped a dagger with his free hand. Despite the relative safety of the guild house, located squarely in the middle of Roth's uptown district, everyone here still came dressed in all of their weapons and armor. Call it a form of advertising, she thought, resting her hand on the hilt of the broadsword hanging from her belt.

Fortunately, the business that brought her to the Free Blade's Guild headquarters in the heart of the city of Roth was that of collection. The morning sunlight streamed in through the tall windows and fell gently on the throng within, bathing them in its soft golden glow. People of all statures busily walked back and forth across the brightly lit guild house on missions of varying importance to the survival of civilization. Some stood in small groups discussing some piece of intrigue or perhaps haggling over hidden treasure (the location of which they alone knew). People from all across the world could be found here.

Across the room, she spied a grey-skinned C'thûn studying a gigantic wall map, his black eyes absorbing some minute detail. His hands were clasped politely behind his back, not far from the foot-long knives that hung from either side of his wide leather belt. A pair of thick Ialu, bristling with weapons, crossed the room engrossed in conversation, their heavy boots thudding on the clean-swept floor planks. One of them ran a tattooed hand across his bald pate as he made momentary eye contact with Lena. Standing near a doorway, a slim gray-haired woman was dressed in red robes trimmed in yellow, indicating her membership to the Psychic League. She spoke quietly to a pair of swordsmen, whose weapons and armor matched perfectly, suggesting enrollment in some private military organization.

Everyone here had their own politics, backgrounds, and hidden agendas, but one fact united them all. Each was there looking for work. Lena absently ran her fingers through her shoulder-length golden hair as she turned to study one of the many bulletin boards. Advertisements, job offers, and other miscellaneous postings cluttered the board, most citing the need for Guild membership.

Wanted: Capable fighting men and women to protect a merchant caravan through the wilds on its journey to Bowie. Guild membership, mandatory. No good. Besides, Bowie was a boring town. Another grabbed her attention, reading; Reward - 10,000 Pheldian silver crowns for any information leading to the recovery of the lost princess of Pheldi... she stopped reading. This was old news and a dead end as far as she was concerned. She sighed heavily. Maybe the next board would have something. A loud clank of armor to her left announced the arrival of unwanted company. She did her best to project disinterest.

"You sound displeased," a robust male voice intoned. So much for disinterest. She turned to glare at the intruder. A tall figure wearing armor of steel bands encircling his torso smiled down at her through a well-oiled mustache. His dark eyes glittered beneath his bushy eyebrows as he took in her form. Lena often forgot that even in her steel plate armor, most men in this occupation found her appearance to be quite appealing. In more conservative parts of the kingdom, a man might prefer a softer, more rounded, and demure woman. An athletic, independent (and possibly dangerous) woman might be seen as something of a scandal. Here though, her appearance tended to attract the sort of fellow who seemed compelled toward conquest. A woman who clearly knew her way with a broadsword was an emotional challenge that buffoons like this could scarcely resist. She fingered the hilt of her sword. He puffed out his large, shiny chest. "Looking for work?" he asked as he settled his gauntleted hands on the hilt of the polished tapered long sword hanging at his waist.

"I'm sorry, were you speaking to me?" she asked innocently.

"Why, yes, I was."

"Don't," she snapped, the ice in her voice matching the color of her eyes. The large man sputtered with wounded pride as she turned sharply to face the board. A soft chuckle followed the man as he clanked away. Lena turned to face the newcomer.

"Maxton still in his office?" the newcomer asked, brushing a length of pale hair from her large, expressive, violet-colored eyes. The woman was Selyr. In traditional Selyrian culture, the female is the dominant sex, filling nearly every role in society. The men stay at home and tend to the children and the household, although that stereotype was either beginning to break down or was gone entirely in most large cities. Selyr children are raised in a society filled with magic. Every Selyr Lena had ever met knew at least one minor spell, and most knew much more. A large percentage of the Wizards Circle (the top wizards, psychics, and other such users and casters of magic in the world) were either full-blooded Selyr or at least given some Selyr heritage. There was some measure of debate about whether simply being Selyr gave one a superior ability to learn magic or if it was more a product of their upbringing.

"Yeah," Lena replied, glancing toward the closed office door. "Been waiting out here for almost an hour."

"He's good for it, isn't he?" she asked.

"Pevma... Don't start that again." Lena turned and leaned on the wall. "Zahra vouched for him, and that's good enough for me." As if to confirm Lena's faith, the office door across the hall opened. A man in his later years, balding slightly, stuck his head into the hall and searched around for a moment. Lena gestured toward the man with a smile, and the two approached the door.

"Sorry to keep you ladies waiting," he began as they entered the room, exchanging places with a rough-looking pair of fellows dressed in black enameled armor. He waited until the door clicked shut behind them before continuing. "Just finished negotiating a deal with… well… never mind." Maxton sat behind a slightly overlarge desk and gestured to the two chairs in front of it. "I understand you have a document for me?"

"Yes, the package was delivered safely to the address on this receipt." Lena produced the page from her satchel and handed it to Maxton as she sat. He studied the page for a moment and smiled to himself.

"Excellent," he responded. "I recognize the signature here. Everything is in order, as I knew it would be. Zahra always finds me the best contractors." He tucked the receipt into a drawer. "Lucky for me, you were in Nephron at the right time."

"As it turns out, sir, we were hired to deliver the package by a mutual acquaintance, Professor Kristaad Durwyn," Lena added. "We just happened to be working as caravan security for Zahra at the same time. The Professor also asked me to deliver this letter to you personally." She placed a sealed envelope on the desk in front of Maxton. He lifted it and studied the seal before sliding it unopened into a desk drawer.

"Durwynn. Interesting." He studied the two women sitting across from him for a moment, his face unreadable. "Well, I suppose we must address the important things first." He plopped two heavy sacks of coin onto the table in front of his visitors. "Your payment for a job well done. I appreciate your discretion and professionalism."

"Thank you, sir, for the opportunity," Lena offered with a smile, taking the purse of coins as she sat.

"And while you rightfully count your money, allow me to bend your ear for a moment." Maxton turned to a small document box on the table behind him and began to shuffle through it, muttering lightly to himself. Lena upended her coin purse onto the desk in front of her and started to stack coins. Pevma raised a thin eyebrow.

"I thought you said you trusted him," she whispered with a half-smile. Lena shrugged. Trust only goes so far.

"Ah. Here we are," Maxton said as he placed a sheet of parchment on the desk between them.

"What's this?" Lena casually asked as she glanced at the page.

"Another job, if you're interested. Any friend of Durwynn is a friend of mine." He sat in a worn-looking stuffed leather chair and produced a small pipe from a vest pocket. "There is a preliminary meeting this Forthday."

Lena lifted the page for a moment and read the handwritten text: *Wanted: Several brave individuals willing to undergo danger to fulfill a quest. Substantial payment. Only experienced applicants need apply. Boar's Tusk Inn, Forthday, 7 PM. Ask for Kudakaan.*

"Do you get a cut?" Lena asked, tossing the page back onto the desk.

"Me? Oh, not this time." He paused from attending to his pipe to offer the page to Pevma. "Just doing a favor for some associates and passing it along." Pevma scanned the page for a moment.

"Sounds interesting, but I have a prior engagement," she said.

"What about you?" he asked Lena. She stacked the last coin. Correct sum. She paused. Her current schedule was painfully empty. Sure, she had a stack of cash in front of her, but with no permanent home and no job prospects on the horizon, her financial status was still shaky at best.

"I don't suppose your associates mentioned how much the job is worth, did they?" she asked, knowing full well she intended to go to the meeting. No reason to appear too eager, in case Maxton talked to his friends between now and Forthday.

"No idea, but it seems like it could be a lucrative contract." He smiled. "And before you ask, I don't know what it is about either," he added with a wink.

"I guess I could go to the meeting. No harm in checking it out." She lifted the page and scanned it once more. "Mind if I hang on to this?" she asked. Not that she needed it. There wasn't much on the page, and she had already memorized the details. Taking it out of circulation did, however, reduce the potential competition for the job.

"Be my guest." He gestured with a bit too much flourish as Lena scooped her coins back into the sack. "I thank you, ladies, once again for a job well done, and I wish you luck on your further ventures." They stood. The door closed behind them with a click, and they walked together through the lobby to exit onto the granite tiles of the guild house patio.

"Interesting." Pevma nodded toward the page as she leaned on the stone rail overlooking the city of Roth.

"Possibly." Lena regarded the page for a moment before slipping it into her satchel. "Did you see Maxton's necklace?"

"I saw he was wearing one," Pevma answered. "I'm not current on the subtleties of men's fashion."

"The pendant was the symbol of the Knights of Maudex," Lena explained. "I recognized it from one of the Professor's tattoos. He was also a member." Pevma perked up at the mention, glancing around the sparsely populated patio before responding.

"Are you familiar with the Knights?" she asked.

"Vaguely," Lena answered. "They are engaged with world affairs, politics, and such if my memory serves me." Pevma gave a cryptic smile and nodded in response. "Do you think this might be Knight's business?"

"Maybe, maybe not," Pevma replied with a shrug. "You never know with those fellows. If this was serious, though, they'd likely have one of their own involved."

"I'll keep my eyes open."

"You stayed out of trouble so well last time; I'm sure there is nothing to fear," Pevma added with a sardonic grin.

"Of course," Lena laughed. "You sure you won't join me?"

"As interesting as it sounds, I actually do have another engagement." The Selyr moved forward to embrace Lena in a hug. "I wish you luck."

Lena bid her farewell as they parted and watched the other woman disappear into the crowd, likely never to be seen again. Lena stood alone for a moment on the patio, watching the crowd swirl through the carved wooden doors of the guild house. People tended to vanish from her life just like that – swept in by the winds of fate, swirled around in a storm, and then blown in a different direction, gone forever. Lena turned toward the stairs leading down into the city, squinting slightly against the hard light from the cloudless sky. There was a bit too much whiskey in this town currently, and she had a mind to correct that.

* * * * *

High Marshal Welton adjusted his jacket for the fourth time, ensuring the golden seal on his left breast was plainly visible. Servants scurried aside as his long strides carried him through the gray stone corridors of the palace, barely being spared a glance as he whisked by. He thought back to a time (was it that long ago?) when he was the one bowing to those of stature as they strode by on missions of importance to the kingdom. Now, as Captain of the King's Marshals, he need only defer to those who possessed a hereditary title. And of those, only the Dukes of the four Protectorates and the royal family themselves held any real power.

An aged serving woman dusting some artifact in a forgotten alcove spared him a shallow curtsy as he passed. He returned a sour glare for her lack of proper respect. He did not spend his life rising through the ranks of his king's armies to reach the most exalted position attainable by those of common blood to be snubbed by a mere servant. If he were not in a hurry, he might have spared the time for a lecture on proper respect, but the urgency of the king's summons had been quite clear.

He turned the corner and vigorously assaulted a set of stairs. Although age had stolen the color from his hair, it had not yet sapped the strength from his limbs. He had spent too much time on the training grounds and battlefields of his kingdom's army to relent from the weight of a few years. As he reached the top of the stairs, he paused in front of the great oak doors to the council chamber to adjust his coat and sword belt another time. Silently taking pride in his ease of breath after such a quick climb, he composed himself and knocked.

"Enter," a voice from within responded. With a slight push, the doors swung silently inward to reveal the king's council chamber. The throne may symbolize the king's authority to the common man, but this room was the real seat of power in Roth. This was where nearly all of the important decisions were made, where Welton D'Mark, High Marshal of Roth, did his finest work. He glanced around the room, taking in the numerous banners of allies and fallen foes, tapestries depicting one battle or another, and the massive oak table that commanded the center of the room. The afternoon light pooled reverently on the bare floor as it streamed in through the wall of precious glass that looked out over the city – a magnificent sight, which still occasionally gave him pause.

Welton's gaze took all of this in quickly and efficiently. His attention shifted to the only other man in the room; King Andarius, ruler of Roth, the so-called jewel of the northern kingdoms. Andarius seemed to fill the space with his presence, dominating attention by simply *being*. He stood at the end of the table, leaning casually on the table's edge as he read a single page on its surface, yet simultaneously he seemed to radiate power. This was a trick Welton had never quite mastered, and it irked him. The king wore fairly simple clothing, as he would on those days when state affairs kept him from the public eye. This fact did not sit well with Welton either. This king, who rose to power by mere right of birth, who had everything handed to him from day one, who simply walked into his lofty position, shunned the finer benefits of his title openly. While Welton, who fought and bled for every inch of his rise to power, never hesitated to take pride in his accomplishment by displaying his status. No matter. Things were as they were. There was no higher he could climb. For now.

"Welton. Stop daydreaming and read this." Andarius had a way of making even the simplest request seem like a moral imperative. Welton crossed the room and lifted the page from the table. The king eased himself into the large chair at the end of the table. Welton scanned the page, taking note of every detail. After a moment, he looked up. Andarius had fixed his steel-gray eyes on him, using that bold kingly stare that Welton could still not quite meet. "What do you think?" he asked. This was a common game they played; a test of observational power. Andarius would often ask questions with no context or explanation, so one would have to answer truthfully, not knowing what he wanted or expected to hear. It also made you explain yourself. At this game, Welton was a master. Time to show off.

"This is an ad. Like those commonly found in the Free Blade's Guild or other such places. It solicits mercenary work, legally, I might add, according to your law. It was generated by hand, implying narrow circulation. There are nearly no details concerning the nature of the work, possibly used to generate curiosity among its target audience. It conveys, therefore, an air of secrecy, which those in that business cannot seem to resist. This secrecy may be used merely to entice, or it may be that the nature of the work is less legal than it may seem." He paused to take a breath, laying the sheet on the table's smooth surface.

"Anything else?"

"Yes, my liege. Two points. It cites Forthday as the meeting time. Without a specific date, this Forthday is implied. That fact suggests that this flier has been in circulation for fewer than ten days, thereby lending some degree of urgency to its business. Secondly, and perhaps the most important detail, is the contact name. Kudakaan. This, I do believe, is the security advisor for one Duke Pendor, next in line to the throne after yourself, the royal prince, and the Archduke Dornibyn. Were this legitimate business on behalf of Duke Pendor, one would imagine that he would use his name and position to attract the top local talent. That this message originates from such a lofty position and possesses such an air of secrecy suggests that your newly instated Treaty of Lords may be in jeopardy.

That we are here speaking of it suggests that you feel similarly." Welton finished with a smile.

"Very good, Welton. Those were my thoughts exactly." Andarius sat comfortably in his chair, absently running a hand across his graying temple. "Next question. What should we do? Ideas?" This was the part Welton liked the least. Whatever he suggested, Andarius would make it seem as if he had thought of it himself, usually dismissing it with a 'my thoughts exactly' or 'that's what I was thinking.' This time, however, Welton felt entirely in control, perhaps because he knew things the king did not.

"I recommend we infiltrate this meeting to answer the ad. Anyone we send will experience firsthand what transpires and report their findings to me. This way, we do not offend Pendor by challenging his motives publicly, and, in the off chance that there is a breach of the treaty, we will have proof."

"Perfect. Make it so." Andarius spared him one of his famous grins, displaying the charm that won him the hearts of his people, charm that Welton deemed an inappropriate breach of reverence. "That is why I like you, Welton; you so reliably read my mind, I often wonder that I am necessary." Andarius laughed and clapped him on the shoulder as he rose from his chair. "Now, about other matters. The king of Pheldi has sent us another message concerning the disappearance of his daughter..."

* * * * *

This could be it, Daelyn thought. My big break. Or, this could be IT. The end of my life.

Wondering which, she walked slowly behind the man with the lantern, hardly noticing the dampness and cold of the underground passage. The lantern creaked faintly as it swayed in the man's trembling grasp, throwing its feeble light out into the thick darkness. The two walked silently on, their little pool of light gliding through the dark corridor, mostly unnoticed by the insects which scrambled along the walls, living their insect lives, oblivious to the politics that surrounded them. As they walked, the man would occasionally pause, as if he meant to speak, but then turn away silently, unwilling to break the oppressive silence. Frankly, Daelyn was glad. She didn't know the man well and had no desire to know him better. Sure, they worked together, but that didn't go very far toward amiability in this business. In fact, she couldn't think of any members of their little family that she would trust over a complete stranger. Oh, well. That was just the nature of the business. She ran her hands unconsciously over her black tight-fitting clothes, finding discomfort from the lack of weaponry that the impending meeting required. She could not remember the last time she was without at least one small knife. She felt almost naked.

This discomfort, however, was far outweighed by the consequences of breaking the one iron-clad rule; when you visit the Master, no weapons. Period. Her long dark hair usually fell loosely around her shoulders, but today it was restrained in a tight, neat braid. Unspoken rule. Visit the Master; look sharp and professional. And that she did. She didn't mind the hoots and whistles she received on her way through the chapter house today, nor did she mind the openly hungry stares she had received from this unctuous man who now served as her guide. Sometimes that was part of the job, like any other. Often, she could curtail the attention with a fiery look or a curt comment, or, if the job required, she would entice with a slight sway of her hip or a meaningful look shot over a shoulder from her lovely dark eyes. All part of the job, but now her eyes were fixed on the corridor ahead. This was business, and they both knew it. Going to see the Master of the Underground was a rare and sometimes fatal occurrence. If he said "jump," you said "who," no questions asked. Hesitation could be read as contemplation of disobedience. Disobedience was, of course, treason, and then... She would prefer not to think of the penalty for treason.

Without warning, the corridor terminated in a large iron-bound door. This was it. The man shifted his grip on the lantern and gently pulled a thin rope that hung by the door, ringing a bell somewhere within. Behind that door lay the center of power for nearly every successful lawbreaker in this and many other cities. Thieves, whores, beggars, cutthroats, assassins, money launderers, drug dealers, smugglers, and any other individual who lived beyond the law called him their boss or their enemy. She had seen what happens to those who call him their enemy. He ruled a vast empire, imposing a twisted but rigid order on the lawless. She presently thought of her own minuscule role in this dirty world and wondered if all her choices leading her to this door were the right ones. Probably not, but probably those choices allowed her to live long enough to be standing here. Too late to second guess herself now anyway.

"You're on your own from here, sister," the greasy man muttered and promptly turned to walk back down the hall, quickly leaving her in complete blackness. After an eternal moment of silence, a broad-shouldered man in thick black leather opened the door from within. He wore a short, wickedly curved sword at his waist and moved as if it were a part of his anatomy. An exception to rule number one; if you are one of the Master's bodyguards, you go armed everywhere, even to bed. Not that this man needed the blade to be dangerous. Nor did the other bodyguard who stood rock still by the fireplace.

That was Kragj'vak, the Master's personal bodyguard. The firelight, which served as the room's only illumination, fell on his seven-foot frame and played across the tight-knotted muscle that bulged beneath his red-scaled hide. His eyes were veiled in shadow now, thankfully, for his cold reptilian stare chilled the blood of even the most staunch-hearted. The ends of his inch-long razor teeth poked out of his massive jaw, suggesting a desire to crush and rend flesh and bone alike. He was a Chull, a monstrous race of people known for belligerence, massive strength, and a strong desire for battle and glory. A wide, curved blade of enormous proportions was slung over his broad back, a blade that had ended the lives of a good many of the Master's enemies. Kragj'vak was a killing machine, without a doubt, and was unswervingly loyal to the Master. There was no question that if the Master wished it, she would die on the spot.

She tore her eyes away from the giant to face the far more dangerous man she called Master. The light from the fire outlined a high-backed chair sitting in front of a massive black desk. The chair's occupant was veiled entirely in shadow. This was a good sign, she thought. Not many lived long after seeing the Master's face. After a moment of uncomfortable silence, he spoke.

"Your reputation precedes you. I am proud to have such a talented and lovely young woman in my employ." His voice was rich in tone and nearly vibrated with power.

"Thank you, Grand Master," she stammered.

"Yes, the thanks are all mine, for, without my training and grace, you would be nothing. Let us not forget that."

"Of course, Grand Master."

"Do you know why I have summoned you, Daelyn?"

"No, Grand Master," she answered quickly. Her mind raced. She was terrified, and he knew it.

"My friends tell me that our good King Andarius is doing something he doesn't wish anyone to know about. Being a naturally curious person, I would like to know what that is." He chuckled lightly. "I like to stay current with events in this fair city of ours. My friends also tell me that our fair king is sending one of his friends to answer the advertisement you see on the desk before me." He paused. Daelyn cautiously reached for the page, hesitant to move without specific permission. She lifted it slowly and waited for further instruction. "You too shall answer. Use all means at your disposal to determine the identity of the king's agent, the nature of his mission, and the nature of the mission outlined on the flier without compromising your cover. You will use the name Daelyn; you will be an archer and swordswoman from Toctil, so practice your accent. None but we in this room know of your mission. Make reports through our network directly to me. Encode them using a three-character variable, using the word 'bloodthirsty' as a key. I shall send you further instructions in response to your reports. You are dismissed."

Daelyn was handed a lantern and silently ushered out of the room, her mind reeling. Never previously having had a meeting with the Master, she wondered if it was a good one. Well, she was still breathing, so it wasn't a *bad* one. Her mind raced as it absorbed and categorized the details of the meeting. A three-character variable, she thought. This was secret indeed. A variable character system uses one keyword as a basis for shifting letters around within the primary message to make sense out of what seems like nonsense. It was a complex system, with many "ifs," but deciphering was essentially impossible without knowing the keyword or how many characters were shifted. It was rarely used, however, due to its cumbersome nature. Bloodthirsty as a keyword just gave it a particularly nasty touch. She also thought it strange that she would use her real name. Perhaps he feared magic might come into play. She suddenly remembered the page in her hand. She stopped in the hall and held it close to the lantern, reading it slowly. After memorizing the message word for word, she fed its corner into the lantern's flame. After a bright moment, no evidence remained of her mission save a pile of warm ash. She scattered the remains with the toe of her boot before continuing on. This was big.

CHAPTER ONE
FORTHDAY
24TH OF TURADMUR

An Ialu rode through the gray evening, occasionally stopping his short-legged mule and peering at the wooden signs in front of the shops and businesses along the narrow, twisting street. A light fog had set, throwing a slight chill across the city, and muffling the sounds of the idle streets to an oppressive quiet. He sat solidly in his saddle, occasionally adjusting the fit of his leather jerkin over his broad chest. He unconsciously shifted the haft of the long horseman's axe that hung by his side, testing its freedom.

The streets of Roth's Old Section were laid out haphazardly – crisscrossing almost randomly, winding around one another, some streets ending abruptly, for no apparent reason. Others wound on endlessly as if to follow the path of some giant drunken snail. These buildings had been built, destroyed, and rebuilt countless times, such that the architecture of a dozen generations could be found on a single city block. The long sloping eves of one wooden building stood in stark contrast to its squat brick neighbor. Here, intricately carved wooden latticework adorned the sprawling porch of an antique home. Its windows framed by wrought iron and ivy, the house stood as a grand testimonial to an age past. There, the clean lines of a modern stone structure stood out sharply from a leaning, rickety shack that barely stood next door.

All manner of goods and services could be had here; some legal, some not. All advertised with equal zeal. This was the heart of the Old Section. The local officials had long ago adopted the position that while crime could never be fully stamped out, it *could* be contained. Many things were tolerated here that would be swiftly punished elsewhere in the city. Most of the criminals in Roth were aware of this understanding and therefore chose to practice their trade primarily in the Old Section. This arrangement preserved the status quo by keeping the nice parts of town nice, while the criminal element could remain fat and happy where they were. This also made the Old Section a somewhat dangerous place at night. The Ialu glared sharply at a passer-by. He would be no easy prey.

After a few turns down these mostly deserted streets, he stopped in front of a boarding house for travelers. He studied the front of the building. The large wooden structure appeared tired from the weight of too many years and too few repairs. Several horses were hitched to the rail along the front, huddling together, seeking comfort from the gloom. A deserted porch encircled the building, adorned with an eclectic assortment of chairs and benches, all appearing less than trustworthy. All of the windows of its three-story height were shuttered tightly, and those on the first floor wore iron bars as well. He turned in his saddle and surveyed the surrounding buildings, all in similar states of disrepair. Satisfied, he dismounted, and after hitching his stubby mule alongside the horses, he climbed the few stairs to the porch and went inside. He spared a final glance to the street, weighing the security of his armor and effects stored in the packs on his mule's back. Smokey's penchant for kicking strangers who ventured too close seemed security enough for tonight.

The inn was furnished sparsely with mismatching furniture strewn about haphazardly in varying states of disrepair. The front room apparently served as a meeting room, dining hall, sitting room, and lobby. The bedraggled head of a long-dead boar jutted crookedly from a mounting plate directly over the door. A large fireplace cast its flickering light across the room, twinkling off the rows of bottles and jugs standing on a shelf behind a bar, which sectioned off a portion of the wall in the rear of the large room.

A few armed men, all humans, milled about absently in the front room. The Ialu felt their eyes on him as he strode into the room. If they were pretending to be anything other than security, they were doing a poor job indeed. A door along the rear wall marked 'Private' sealed off another section of the building. A second door led from behind the bar into what was probably the kitchen. Along the left wall, a staircase climbed into a dark hallway. At the bottom of the stairs, a thin, gray-haired man stood behind a short counter looking down at this newcomer with a somewhat disdainful expression across a large beak of a nose. The Ialu shook the damp from his cloak and brushed a few drops from the top of his hairless scalp. The Ialu people, men and women alike, were all naturally hairless from head to toe. This could be perceived as either a blessing or a curse depending on the climate. On damp nights like this, such a characteristic felt more like a blessing.

"Is this the Boar's Tusk Inn?" The Ialu asked. The man behind the counter simply nodded. He took a few steps forward and continued. "I am looking for a man named Kudakaan." At the mention of this name, the older man seemed to spring to life.

"Ahh, the meeting. Your name, sir?" The man was all smiles now.

"Murzahd," the Ialu replied, his dark eyes casually roaming about the lobby. The innkeeper raised an eyebrow, expecting more.

"Murzahd Churdaku, of the *Pesh uk Daka* Clan," he elaborated. "I am at your service." The innkeeper was clearly no expert on Ialish culture, or there would have been no need to announce his clan affiliation. The tattoos clearly identifying his family, clan and tribe were displayed prominently where they belonged on the inner surface of his forearms. Given that this was a peaceful meeting (supposedly), Murzahd had his sleeves unlaced and rolled back in proper Ialish tradition. Occasionally humans in the service industry took the time to know the basics of Ialish tattoo lore but remembering in what section of town he was, Murzahd quickly forgave the innkeeper's ignorance. His eyes completed their examination of the room and returned to the tired face of the human.

"They are waiting in the back room," came the answer. The man behind the counter then gestured a little too grandly to the door in the rear. Murzahd nodded thanks and crossed the room, running a tattooed hand across his smooth jaw as he once again tested the haft of his axe. Conscious of the armed men behind him, he paused in front of the door. His gaze fell on the sigil of Zadarsti, the Ialish god of luck, tattooed on the back of his left wrist. He was not as superstitious as his people had the reputation of being, but a little homage never hurt. He cleared his mind and pushed the door open, one hand on his weapon.

The room was crowded and dimly lit, furnished with a few short tables and cabinets along the dark paneled walls. A long meeting table dominated the center of the room. A single lantern hung in the center of the room, shedding its orange light on the motley collection of strangers that occupied nine of the ten chairs surrounding the heavy oak table. A well-dressed man, just past his middle years, stood proudly just past the head of the table, the weak light from the lantern overhead glinting off of the hilt of a bejeweled rapier that hung from his finely tooled leather belt. A cloak that cost more than Murzahd would care to guess hung neatly from the man's shoulders clasped at his throat by an overly large gemmed brooch. His jet-black hair neatly framed his clean-shaven face, which viewed Murzahd with only a hint of distaste.

Unfazed, Murzahd lifted a rumpled leaflet from his pocket. "Am I late?" he asked as he closed the door behind him and approached the table.

"No, not at all," the man replied. "We were about to begin. Do sit down anywhere you like." Murzahd rounded the table, approaching the unoccupied chair at the opposite end of the table, carefully studying its nine occupants.

In front of the regal speaker, at the head of the table, sat a somewhat lanky man in rugged brown and green leathers. His weather-beaten face was bent toward a stack of documents piled on the table in front of him. He studied these intently, his gray eyes only once flicking toward Murzahd. A wooden staff with both ends bound in iron leaned against the wall not far behind him. By his posture and position at the table, Murzahd guessed that this man worked with the rich gentleman.

To the right of the outdoorsman sat a younger woman, who leaned forward, elbows on the table, hands clasped impatiently in front of her slightly frowning mouth. Her shoulder-length golden hair was tied back neatly, though he noted it would impede the use of a helmet. Her ice blue eyes stared at him, urging him to move quickly to allow the meeting to begin. She wore armor of a few large metal plates with a padded gambeson beneath. Murzahd was familiar with that particular design principle. The gambeson served as protection on its own, but the metal plates could be (relatively) quickly strapped on top for heavier engagements. It sufficiently protected the body's vital areas yet still gave considerable freedom of movement. An excellent choice for long deployments in the field but not too heavy for a warrior of her stature. A sheathed broadsword hung on the rear of her chair. Murzahd noted from its position that she was probably right-handed.

Beside her sat a man dressed in armor of small overlapping metal scales, as was favored further east. Though, from his darker skin tone, Murzahd would have placed his heritage from the far south. He smiled congenially as he absently fiddled with a toothpick. His black hair was still damp, probably from the night fog. He glanced at Murzahd for a moment, spared a nod, then turned toward the blonde beside him, smiling and striving to make eye contact.

The woman sitting next in line lounged back comfortably in her chair, arms crossed beneath her breasts, silently observing the group. Luxurious curls of long, black hair framed her face. To Ialish sensibilities, most humans were thin, and she was thin for a human, but perhaps in a way that human men preferred. Murzahd shrugged, dismissing the differences in cultural preferences. She wore black, tight-fitting clothes, with a black cloak folded over the back of her chair. A longbow with a quiver of arrows lay on a short table behind her. She noticed him observing her, and she slipped into a wide grin and winked at him.

At the corner, a large man sat slightly away from the table, still as stone, his face impassive. A black patch covered his left eye; his other eye locked a cold gray gaze onto Murzahd and quickly scanned every detail, lingering for just a moment on the clan sigils on his forearm. His massive chest was protected by pale-colored armor that looked to be made from the hardened, scaly hide of what had to have been an enormous beast. A dark blue cloak of expensive cut fell over his broad shoulders, clasped at one side by a large red jewel. Across his knees lay a Velkasian greatsword – a blade far too large to be worn at the hip. Large, cryptic runes adorned the surface of its scabbard, and small gemstones and carvings decorated the hilt. His hand rested with dangerous ease on its well-worn grip. He sat casually yet also seemed to be on the brink of sudden movement. Murzahd decided that this was likely the most dangerous man in the room.

A short, wiry man in his middle years sat at the end of the table opposite the rich gentleman. He wore no armor and was armed with only a large knife. His loose-fitting tunic concealed his build, and he sat still and silent, his blue eyes sparkling with keen intelligence. Murzahd found his function hard to estimate.

On the corner, his back to Murzahd as he walked past, loomed what had to be one of the largest men he had ever seen. (And, in the thirty years he has walked this earth, Murzahd had seen more than a few large men.) A single one of this fellow's arms looked larger than Murzahd's thigh – and Murzahd, like all of his people, was thick limbed himself. The man's hair was cropped to a finger's breadth, and his massive frame was barely contained by what was probably enough fabric to fashion a comfortable tent. The broad expanse of a double-bladed axe heavier than most children leaned against the back of his chair. His function was obvious.

To this man's right sat a short, skinny man, barely past his youth. His light hair was cut very short, as was common to many military organizations, but he wore no armor, nor did he carry any visible weaponry. He was slight of build, hardly taller than Murzahd himself, and he doubted the man could present a physical challenge to anyone here, including the women. Murzahd wondered at his function until he saw a small red stone pin, ringed in gold, and carved into the shape of a four sided pyramid – the sigil of the Psychic League, fastened to the high collar of his simple leather jacket. He looked around patiently, waiting for the meeting to begin

Beside the youth was a man who seemed out of place in this collection of obvious mercenary folk. He wore no weapons or armor. His disheveled, wrinkled clothing showed much wear. He was unshaven and looked as if he was recently awoken from a too-short nap. He slouched in his chair, puffing on one of those tiny cigars that have recently become so popular, appearing bored.

Murzahd rounded the table and sat in the vacant chair at the end, near the outdoorsman at the head, adjusting the position of his axe as he sat. The chair was built for humans, and his feet barely touched the floor. He glanced around the table to see if anyone was foolish enough to find that amusing. The regal man spoke.

"It would appear as if we now have a full house. Let me begin by introducing myself. I am the Duke Riskin Pendor, and this is my associate, Kudakaan." He gestured to the outdoorsman sitting in front of him. "I would like to thank you all for attending this meeting." Murzahd schooled his face to stillness as he gauged the reactions of the others around the table. A duke? That would explain the security detail in the front room. "Perhaps we should proceed with introductions," the duke went on. The thin man at the opposite end of the table lifted his hand slightly to gain the duke's attention. "Yes?" The man stood.

"Not to sound rude, Your Grace, but could we first define the term 'substantial' concerning payment?" As he spoke, he produced a flier from the folds of his jacket and gestured with it slightly as he placed it on the table in front of him. Duke Pendor paused for a moment, his face unreadable, then resumed with a smile. There is always one who fancies himself a talker. Murzahd resolved to keep an eye on this one.

"Of course, naturally." The duke paused again to draw out the drama of the moment. "I trust one thousand silver crowns, each, is substantial enough?" He smiled triumphantly. The scraping sound of a chair sliding on the wooden floor emanated from the opposite end of the table. The one-eyed man had stood and was collecting his cloak around him. Pendor looked at him expectantly. He fixed an intense pale-eyed gaze on the duke.

"Not worth my time," he spoke flatly.

"It is more than enough for the task at hand."

"Then I bid you good evening." The large man hefted his greatsword and strode through the door, closing it behind him. Interesting, Murzahd thought. After a moment, the duke spoke again.

"I trust that sum is satisfactory for the rest of you?" Nods of assent and mumbles of agreement rippled through the group. "Good. Now I believe we were introducing ourselves. Let us start at this end of the table." He gestured to the blonde woman beside him. "Also, I would like to be confident my money is being well spent, so, a little about yourselves as well." He pulled a stool from the corner and sat, folding his arms, donning a disarming smile. "Please, begin." She stood slowly and began.

"My name is Lena Sullivan; I am a freelance blade for hire. I only fight for causes I believe in." She looked Duke Pendor straight in the eye as she spoke. "I was trained in eastern style fencing in the city of Pelkin by master Garis Shelnaav; I've also trained in the Pheldian Fighter's Academy for five years." The significance of these statements registered on Pendor's face as an approving arch of the eyebrow. Either qualification would have been sufficient in Murzahd's mind. Having attended both of these schools would make her talented indeed. Or a liar.

"Very, nice. Thank you, Lena." She looked at the others, making eye contact with each before she sat. The happy man beside her stood, adjusting his metal scale armor.

"I'm Qazulin Muracala, from Kannoc, but my friends call me Qaz," he began. A large iron hafted war hammer hung from a thick leather loop at his belt. "I am extremely talented in nearly everything I do, but I specialize primarily in magic."

"Magic?" the young psychic asked in disbelief.

"Why do you say that? Is it the armor?" Qaz replied. "People always seem to expect a white beard, a robe, and a pointy hat with stars and moons on it. Mages bleed just like everybody else. This keeps my skin together." He suppressed a chuckle.

"If you're such a good mage, what's with the war hammer?" Lena asked, tapping the iron-bound haft as she spoke.

"Oh, this is just backup. In case things get out of hand." He put his hand on the heavy metal head of his hammer as he spoke. She returned a look of frank skepticism. "It's hard to cast a spell while somebody's trying to poke you with something sharp. I am occasionally forced to use my friend here…" He patted the war hammer at his side. "…to persuade people to stand still long enough to be properly magiced."

"Are you a Mage Guild member?" The thin man at the end of the table spoke again. He voiced his question quietly, studying Qaz. Good question. Definitely someone to keep an eye on.

"What? Oh, no. I was trained there; you kind of have to be, but I opted out of joining. Kind of gives me a little more freedom if you know what I mean," Qaz finished with a grin.

"So, what area of magic do you practice?" the thin man asked again.

"I haven't specialized. I have a knack for healing and light magic, but like most mages, I use all prewritten spells." Qaz chuckled lightly to himself. "Heck, if I could write my own spells, I wouldn't need this job." He shot a look at the sour-faced man at the head of the table and received a blank stare for his trouble. "Guess that's it," he finished sheepishly. He sat quickly and turned to look at the dark-haired woman beside him. She looked back at him, then smiled and rose slowly, brushing a coil of hair aside as she stood.

"Daelyn Keroll. I'm from Toctil. And I'm an archer." She folded her hands in front of her and looked at Pendor. Her voice had the slight lilt of the distant southern city.

"Perhaps, you could tell us a little more," he said.

"I can hit an apple at twenty paces every time. I'm also not too bad with a sword." She blushed slightly and sat. Not much for conversation, this one, Murzahd thought. Reliably hitting an apple at twenty paces is a respectable shot, though. The thin man nodded to Daelyn, stood, and cleared his throat.

"I would like to start by saying that it's a pleasure to be among such distinguished company. My name is Jack Ripley, and this is my associate, Uglor." He gestured to the enormous man beside him. "Before we go any further, Your Grace, I wonder if you could elaborate a bit on the nature of this job. I would hate for all of this time to be wasted if things don't work out." He paused for a moment and looked imploringly at the duke.

"Of course, Mr. Ripley. Your concern is worthy of note. This involves the recovery of some stolen property. I was hoping to finish our introductions before delving further into the subject."

"Right. I didn't mean to imply anything negative, but I was just concerned because we don't do assassination or seek and destroy missions. Please accept my apologies." The duke gave a regal nod and gestured for Jack to continue. "As I was saying, I am Jack, and this is Uglor. We work very well as a team. I do the talking, and he does the walking, so to speak. I feel we will be valuable assets to this team in several ways. Uglor can contribute much with his sheer size and strength. Not to insult the fighting men and, uh, women of this group, but I think his particular style of fighting is underrepresented here. He would complement the already accomplished fighters quite well. As for myself, it would seem, at a glance anyway, that perhaps someone with a more subtle edge would round this group out quite well." He leaned casually on the table. "Any questions?" The blonde swordswoman, Lena, leaned forward, waving her hand slightly.

"Jack, is it?" He nodded. "Uglor, I understand. But it is not quite clear to me what you do." She leaned back in her chair, folding her arms. Jack broke into a wry grin.

"Are you asking for a demonstration of my skills?" He looked at Lena, then to the duke.

"If the duke has no objections," she responded.

"By all means. I would like all of us to be comfortable with each other," the duke stated, shifting his weight, his interest showing. This *was* getting interesting, Murzahd thought to himself. Jack smiled further and stepped back from the table, pulling a small knife from the folds of his jacket as he turned and began to round the table toward Lena. He twirled it deftly between his fingers as he approached.

"Miss Sullivan, I will beg your cooperation for this little demonstration." She pushed her chair back further as he strode up next to her. She scrutinized him warily as he leaned forward to place the knife gently on the table in front of her. "Now, what do you see here?" he asked, resting his right hand on the table and leaning slightly over her shoulder as he spoke.

"A knife. What's your point?"

"My point, pardon the pun, is that while you were watching this knife," He nodded toward the table. "You did not notice this one." In his left hand, resting on the back of her chair, he held another small knife to Lena's throat, edge safely outward. She froze. A sudden, silent tension fell on the room. "Do be careful. It's sharp." He held it there for a moment, expressionless, then pulled it away and placed it on the table beside the first knife. As soon as the blade was away from her throat, Lena spun out of her chair and stood, facing Jack, anger clearly burning in her ice-blue eyes. Uglor stiffened suddenly and began to rise. Perhaps this was getting a little *too* interesting. A moment passed while everyone fingered their weapons and eyed the door. The duke took a breath as if to speak, but Qaz spoke first.

"Hey! That's my knife!" He pointed at the second, smaller blade on the table.

"That is my other point," Jack said. He retrieved his own blade from the table and returned to his seat. Qaz scooped his knife off the table with a slight sense of wonder on his face, examining it as if doubting that it was really his. The duke spoke.

"You make your case effectively, though it lacks the subtlety you spoke of earlier. I would ask the rest of you to avoid demonstrations of this nature. Thank you, Mr. Ripley. You may sit down now," the duke finished with a sharp tone, implying that there was no room for further discussion. He looked at Lena, who softened her glare only slightly, before sitting as well. The feeling of tension began to drain from the room. "Uglor, do you have anything to add?" Uglor snapped his gaze from Lena to the duke, startled slightly. He paused for a moment, then silently shook his head. "Then I believe you were next," Pendor continued, gesturing to the slim youth.

"Ah, thank you, Your Grace." The youth stood. "My name is Tim Spade, and I am a member of the Psychic's League. I have no intention of demonstrating anything at this time." Silence. "That was a joke." Tim flushed slightly and turned to Pendor. Murzahd was sure the others in the room were thinking the same thing he was at that precise moment. Duke Pendor took the liberty of sharing their common thought.

"Could you describe for us, Mr. Spade, the exact nature of your relationship with the League?" the duke asked. He studied Tim intently, clearly concerned.

"Sure. I am a fifth-tier member. That is as disassociated from the League as any psychic can be. I prefer to make my own decisions. Like Qaz here." He gestured toward Qaz, who responded with a smile and a nod.

"But you are a member, and therefore subject to their rules," the duke continued.

"Well, anybody trained as a psychic has to join; everybody knows that. It is just to protect the art. At my level, you can pretty much do as you please, just so long as you don't make the League look bad. If you are worried about my loyalties, rest assured, I can't be recruited for League business or pressed into revealing any secrets or anything. There aren't many rules for the likes of me," Tim finished and looked around the room. He was met with looks of discomfort and unease. Qaz, however, gave a reassuring nod and turned to the duke.

"I'll vouch for him. Being in an associated field of study, I am familiar with this subject. The League only has compulsory membership to protect itself. The Mage's Guild toyed with the idea, too, not far back. No offense to Tim, but the League doesn't care about little guys like him. They just want to make sure the big boys like Solomon and Komec don't get out of hand and make being a psychic unpopular. It's all about job security. I've had to deal with a similar situation in my own way. I wouldn't worry." With this statement, the room relaxed a bit more. Murzahd added Tim's name to the list of people to watch closely.

"Any areas of expertise?" Jack asked. Murzahd shifted his eyes to look at Jack.

"I focus primarily on the perceptive aspects of the art," Tim answered. "Sensing auras, other people's presence, information gathering, and that sort of thing."

"Any talent with pyrokinesis or telekinesis, perhaps?" Jack asked again.

"I have studied both, actually, but to be honest, psychokinetics are not my strong suit."

"Not wanting to pry," Jack continued. "But what about psychic control?" Murzahd scrutinized Jack closely. This man seemed to know a thing or two about the varying disciplines of the Psychic League. He then turned to Tim. The very notion of psychic control made him, and most people, quite uneasy. The thought that someone could compel you to do their will with no more than a look was frightening indeed.

"Control?" Tim asked, his eyebrow raised. "Oh, no. The League keeps a tight rein on that. Nobody outside of the second tier even gets to study it at all. Anyone proficient is automatically part of the inner tier." He smiled, trying to be reassuring. "Nothing to worry about there." Murzahd looked closely at Tim as he sat. This Tim fellow may be handy to have around, he thought.

Tim turned and poked the man next to him. The man turned and looked at Tim for a moment, a slightly amused expression on his rough face. He stifled a yawn, then turned to speak to the duke, keeping his seat.

"I've been a martial arts instructor for several years," he mumbled. The Duke's eyebrow rose slightly.

"Your name?"

"Sorry. Corelan."

"Family name?"

"Devin."

"What is the name of your school?" Pendor asked. His tone was colored with a slight air of mistrust.

"Er. Well, it wasn't *my* school. I was a senior instructor for my master teacher. It was his school."

"Was?"

"Oh. Yeah. I have since moved on. I've been doing private consulting work more recently." Corelan produced a rumpled page from his pocket and dropped it on the table in front of Kudakaan. "I, uh, brought a list of clients." Corelan gestured vaguely to the page. "You'll see a few recognizable names on there." Pendor examined the page for a moment then went on.

"You taught Sir Harkem Carlune?" the duke asked with an arched eyebrow. "That's the captain of Roth's city watch."

"Yeah, I did a weeklong workshop kinda thing," Corelan explained, still slouching. "What did they call it... non-lethal conflict resolution or something. It was after the incident. Where that guy got killed..."

"An unfortunate incident indeed," Pendor interjected.

"His name was Ricket Faulk. He was innocent," Corelan added.

"I'm aware. Thank you, Mr. Devin." Pendor dismissed further comment with a gesture toward Murzahd. Corelan snorted quietly and swallowed whatever he was going to say in response. Without waiting for a queue, Murzahd stood and cleared his voice.

"I know we are all anxious to get on with things, so I'll make this quick. My name is Murzahd Churdaku, and I am a member of the Free Blade's

Guild and the Ialish warrior Clan of the Northern Fist. I am fairly well-rounded; I fight well, I am a good outdoorsman, and I've done my share of covert work. I have been in this business for eight years, and I still have all of my limbs. I guess that speaks for itself. Thank you all." With that, he sat and glanced around the table. The blonde swordswoman, Lena, was politely scrutinizing his tattoos, focusing on the section reserved for his combat achievements. Perhaps she knew a bit about Ialish tattoo lore. They exchanged a nod and turned to the duke.

Pendor paused for a moment collecting his thoughts. He stood and approached the table, standing behind Kudakaan, who sat still as a stone through this entire discourse.

"Unless anyone has objections to working with one another," He paused, looking first at Lena, then Jack. "I will continue. What I require first is an understanding that this is a clandestine undertaking. Once you sign on, there will be no talk of this whatsoever with anyone outside of this group. Is that understood?" Murmurs of agreement rippled around the table. "Good. Please be patient as I describe some background to this situation. A man of power such as myself will always have enemies. This is the way of things. This does not mean I have committed some crime against these individuals, nor does it mean I am clean of all sin. When one is forced to make decisions for the good of the people, some will suffer. It is an unfortunate inevitability. Most are understanding of this fact. They grumble quietly, then go on. Others are less noble. Mr. Devin, do, please try to remain awake." Corelan opened his eyes.

"I was listening. You did what you had to do, and some people got their feathers ruffled. I get it," Corelan responded flatly. The duke glared at him for a moment longer. "Your, uh, Grace," Corelan finished awkwardly.

"If you would at least try to convey a sense of interest, it would be appreciated. Thank you," Pendor replied with a snort. "As I was saying, some of my opponents have banded together and have managed to steal something very important. Every nobleman is given by the king himself a golden disk, about the size of one's palm, imprinted with the seal of his house. Due to its magical nature, this disk cannot be falsified or duplicated. It is used for nearly all official business – from sealing legal documentation to ceremonial use at important meetings. I cannot function as a noble of this realm without it. It was kept in a magically sealed box that none but I and a few select others could open. This box has been stolen. All of those with the ability to open this box have been accounted for, so I am confident the thieves do not presently have access to the disk. However, it is only a matter of time before they discern a way. I need that disk. I cannot approach the king with this problem without my title being held in serious jeopardy. You will retrieve this box for me. You will not try to open it. You will speak of this to no one, even after your task is complete. This is your mission," the duke finished. As his last few words echoed off the dark wooden paneled walls, silence filled the room. After a moment, Jack spoke.

"Begging your indulgence, Your Grace, it would seem that an object of this importance would be worth more than the previously mentioned sum." Jack idly drummed the surface of the table with his fingertips.

"I have intelligence concerning the location of the box and the thieves. You are not required to confront the thieves. You are not required to do your own investigation. It is a simple matter of retrieving it. The task does not call for a larger sum. However, I do appreciate your point."

"Begging your further indulgence, why then hire us to retrieve it? Why not have your own men do it?"

"This theft may have been committed by members of my house. With outsiders such as yourselves, I can eliminate possible further breaches in security." Pendor's voice took on a flat tone.

"I'll do it," Lena spoke. She turned a challenging look to the others.

"I'm in," Tim echoed. After a moment, Daelyn agreed also.

"I have a few questions, if I may," Jack said. "Could you could tell us more about these thieves?"

"I hesitate to share any sensitive intelligence that I have with anyone not yet in my employ. Surely you understand."

"Perfectly understandable. I was also wondering about the terms of payment."

"Of course. You will receive half now, as a retainer, and the other half when the box is returned to me. If you fail the mission, or for any other reason do not complete it, either through voluntary or circumstantial reasons, half of the retainer will be returned to me immediately. The other half you will keep as compensation and to aid your forgetfulness that this meeting ever occurred."

"Those papers in front of Kudakaan. Are those contracts?"

"Yes, they are. This helps protect both you and me."

"Contracts made, of course, without your official seal."

"Yes. And still legally binding, I might add."

"But not binding to the Duke Pendor."

"Correct." The duke had resumed his cautious, restrained tone.

"Then binding to whom?"

"My associate Kudakaan, who in this case acts as my legal representative."

"I see." The others who had spoken earlier had lost a portion of their zeal. Doubtful glances were exchanged across the table. The duke spoke again, using a lighter tone.

"I realize that all of this may seem very mysterious to some of you. However, you must understand that this is only due to the covert nature of this operation. I cannot reveal too much until I can be sure that this will not get back to the perpetrators of this crime. We only have one chance at this, failure at this stage will render my present information useless, and more drastic measures will have to be taken. I don't want it to come to that."

"Gotcha, chief. Sign me up." Qaz rapped his knuckles on the table for emphasis.

"How long do we have to think about this?" Corelan asked.

"I am afraid I need to know right away," Pendor replied

"You say we get two-fifty, even if we fail?"

"Yes," Pendor answered hesitantly.

"Then what the hell. I'm in."

"Another question, Your Grace," Jack said.

"What is it, Mr. Ripley?"

"Traveling expenses. Is that out of pocket, do we get a *per diem*, do we get a compensatory sum on completion... how does that work?" The duke stifled a grimace. Yes, very bold this Jack.

"I will take care of your reasonable expenses; food, lodging, and such. Any expenditure above what is necessary will be your own responsibility. Any other questions, my doubting friend?"

"What about incidentals? Say, I find a buried treasure while looking for your box. Would you lay claim to it because I was working for you at the time, or is it mine because I found it?" Pendor released an exasperated sigh.

"You won't be finding any hidden treasure. You will be focused on locating my lost property. But if you happen to stumble across something of value, you may keep it, provided doing such would not interfere with the task at hand. Is that all, Mr. Ripley?" The duke frowned at Jack.

"My apologies, Your Grace. I was only trying to get these sundries out of the way beforehand. That should just about do it. If I could get a look at one of those contracts..."

"Kudakaan, if you would please." Still not having spoken a word, Kudakaan stood and circled the group, distributing the contracts around the table. He placed a bottle of ink in the center of the table and a pen beside it. Without reading, Corelan scooped the pen from the table and signed, passing the contract to Kudakaan.

"You said half now?" he asked. Pendor eyed him cautiously and motioned to Kudakaan, who turned to a large oak chest in the corner of the room. As Kudakaan counted the money out, the others signed their contracts and placed them in a pile at the end of the table. Kudakaan returned to the table and placed eight small sacks of coinage onto the table beside Pendor with a muffled clink. Silence fell, and all eyes turned toward the duke.

"Do remember that this mission shall be held with the utmost secrecy. Kudakaan shall act as my liaison for this expedition; you will take your orders directly from him. Minimize your contact with others not involved in this group. If this goes smoothly, a bonus sum may be added to your payment upon completion." He scooped a pouch from the table and tossed it to Jack. "I should not need to mention the legal penalty for breaking a confidentiality agreement." Jack held the money in one hand, silently studying Pendor. "I will now leave you with Kudakaan. I trust large denominations of coin will be acceptable. I have other matters to attend to. I bid you good evening." Pendor stood, adjusting his cloak and rapier. As he walked around the table toward the door, Kudakaan began distributing the rest of the money. Just as Pendor reached the door, Jack turned to him and spoke.

"Oh, Your Grace. One more question." Pendor paused at the door, his face showing restrained annoyance. "How do we contact you once this is done?"

"Kudakaan will handle that. Good night, Mr. Ripley." Pendor turned and closed the door behind him with a slight bang. A moment of silence held the room.

"So, when do we get started?" Lena asked Kudakaan.

"We leave tomorrow at noon," Kudakaan answered in a flat, no-nonsense tone. "Use the morning to settle your personal affairs and collect traveling supplies. We'll meet outside the city's north gate, bring your own horse. If you have no horse, buy one. Any questions, Jack?" He spoke curtly, glaring at the other man. Jack raised an innocent eyebrow and kept silent.

"Good," Lena interjected. Jack smiled falsely and stood, collecting his belongings. The others began to rise and move toward the door. In relative silence, the group moved out of the small room and into the hotel lobby. Pendor and his security men were gone.

Corelan immediately moved to the bar and slapped its surface, striving to summon a bartender. Qaz sat beside him as a round-faced sweating man in an apron emerged through the swinging door behind the bar. Kudakaan strode purposefully through the group, across the room, and out into the night without saying a word. Murzahd lingered in the doorway, silently assessing his new business partners. Jack watched Kudakaan through a front window as the other man's lanky figure quickly receded into the darkness. The fog had thickened and blanketed the dark streets in a dense white mist. The single streetlamp outside the inn shed its feeble glow, forming an island of weak light in a sea of darkness. Jack turned as Lena stepped up beside him.

"Jack," she said. He donned a disarming smile and turned to face her. "I appreciate the point you made, but I have a point to make too," she said. Her eyes glittered intensely in the orange light of the inn's few oil lamps. Uglor circled quietly around behind her. "Never, and I *do* mean never, pull a knife on me again. If you do, I'll kill you." Her face betrayed no emotion. She was simply stating a fact.

"Understood," Jack responded. "If you kill me, you will have to deal with him, though." He gestured toward Uglor's hulking frame.

"Don't bring it to that," she replied.

"No problem. We are all on the same team here.

"I'm glad we understand each other," she finished in a much softer tone. Satisfied that the conflict was momentarily resolved, Murzahd turned his attention to the others. Across the room, Corelan sat alone at the bar, already diligently at work on his second beer. Nearby, Qaz was conversing with Tim and Daelyn, gesturing grandly. Murzahd glanced through the front window to check on Smokey. The mule stood patiently along the rail beside the other mounts. Murzahd turned to address the group.

"I think we should meet somewhere first thing in the morning to coordinate what supplies we may need for the job," he stated.

"You think that," Lena replied. "See you all at noon." She walked boldly past Murzahd and went out into the night. The others approached, leaving Corelan at the bar.

"Tenacious," Tim commented.

"Indeed," Murzahd responded, torn between feeling slightly offended and slightly impressed.

"Uglor and I are pretty much self-sufficient, so unless you can think of anything else, we will see you folks at noontime tomorrow." Jack scanned the four for a response.

"Same here," Qaz echoed.

"It was a good idea, though." Jack patted Murzahd on the shoulder as he passed, walking out into the gloom, shadowed closely by Uglor.

"If anybody needs me, I'm at the, uh… whatever the name of the inn right on the town square is. With the tile roof. Room 213. See you kids tomorrow," Qaz said over his shoulder as he pushed through the door into the night.

"Great. A mage with bad memory. This should be fun. Since no one liked my idea, I'll see you all tomorrow," Murzahd said. "See you later, Corelan." Without turning, Corelan halfheartedly waved a hand in response. Murzahd stepped outside, followed by Tim and Daelyn. Murzahd descended the steps, leaving the others on the front deck. As he occupied himself with maneuvering his mule to leave, he listened as Tim turned to Daelyn.

"Buy you breakfast?" he asked.

"Breakfast?" She paused, slightly confused.

"I mean tomorrow. Tomorrow morning. Would you like to have breakfast?"

"Uh, sure." She pushed a coil of hair away from her eye.

"There is a café on Aberkahn street; Carla's, I think is the name. Meet you there?"

"Sure." She turned to leave.

"The Old Section can be dangerous. Walk you home?"

"No thanks, I can manage," she replied with a smile. "See you tomorrow, handsome." She winked at him and went out into the night.

"Nice try," Murzahd offered from the street.

"Uh… Thanks," he replied with a slight blush. "See you tomorrow."

* * * *

Corelan watched as the others pushed through the door one by one, leaving him alone in the dilapidated inn. With the final thumping of Tim's boots on the steps outside, a thick veil of silence fell on the room. He thought about his new business partners. This Jack person seemed like trouble. Lena would probably turn out to be a handful also. The others seemed mostly harmless – decent folk by his estimate, although the tall fellow who departed the meeting early left him feeling strangely uneasy.

He shook his head. Not that any of it mattered. He was not there to make friends. He lifted his third beer and drained half the mug in a single gulp. He sighed deeply, wiping the foam from his lips. Jiam was right. He couldn't go on like this. Roth held nothing for him but memories. The last thing he wanted was to remember. Corelan set his mug heavily on the bar and suddenly came to a decision he was fighting all evening. Pendor would have his hands too full to chase after him. He couldn't go to the king without a seal anyway; he said so himself. Besides, that seal was easily worth ten times what they were being paid. Chasing after a guy who walked away with five hundred measly crowns… not worth the trouble. Pendor would let him go. He was sure of it. Tonight would be his last night in Roth. Before he left, though, he had to pay Jiam a visit. A debt is a debt. He also did not want to alienate the one person left in the world he could still call a friend. It was decided. Hell, if nothing better came up, maybe he would stick by the contract after all.

"What's the difference anyway?" he mumbled. Draining the rest of his mug, he tossed a coin onto the bar and went in search of his last friend.

CHAPTER TWO
MIDWEEK
25TH OF TURADMUR

Akeela wasn't such a bad place. From the way Jack was going on, one would get the impression this was the smallest, most backward, uneducated town in all of the kingdom of Roth. Daelyn had been through this town a few times before but admittedly had never stopped. As it seemed, being on the way to someplace else was the only reason to come here. As a natural result of her also being on the way to somewhere else, she currently sat in a corner of the common room of the Four Feathers Inn, sipping a mug of ale and trying not to let Jack's pessimism about the town spoil her mood.

Being a day of rest for most businesses, this was a busy evening, and the room was somewhat crowded with groups of travelers, all engaged in their own conversations, each competing with each other to be heard. She and her companions had made good time from Roth, arriving a touch earlier than expected. As a result, they had been settled in their rooms, fed, and retired to the common room before most of this crowd had arrived. They currently enjoyed the luxury of a somewhat private corner of the room tucked in between the outer wall and the edge of the massive brick fireplace that protruded into the room. She pressed her back against the slightly lumpy pillow that softened the wall behind her and looked across the lip of her mug at the others in her group. One of them worked for the king.

Tim, the psychic, sat across from her. He had spoken little during their ride to Akeela and appeared in no hurry to change his pattern. He sat quietly and seemed content to listen to the others. Lena, the swordswoman, sipped from her red wine and chatted casually with Murzahd, the Ialu, about some historical battle (about which they both had strong and opposing opinions). Murzahd had already amassed a respectable supply of empty mugs, but being Ialu, she would have expected nothing less from him. Jack sat across from her on a short, old sofa. Uglor, his gargantuan companion was absent - looking after supplies, she believed. Jack nodded to Qaz, the mage, as he refilled his teacup. The two of them seemed content to limit themselves to tea this evening. Kudakaan, their employer, sat in a high-backed chair against the brick of the fireplace, sipping some clear liquor while he peered into a small journal, flipping from page to page as if searching for something.

Corelan had excused himself from their table some time ago and was well into his fourth or fifth whiskey. He currently found himself involved in a game of dice with a mixed group of fellows, who had the same rough sort of edge as himself, and the lot of them were making a bit of a ruckus. One of them, a C'thûn of light grey, almost foggy colored skin, kept glancing over at the table where she and her companions sat, his black eyes unreadable. Daelyn concluded that Corelan might need looking after before the evening was concluded.

Jack had been playfully cajoling Kudakaan to reveal some morsel of their plan all day as they rode and now seemed poised to mount a more serious campaign for answers. Kudakaan, for his part, had been reticent and appeared unlikely to alter his position on the subject. As if in response to her thought, Jack spoke.

"So, what's next from here, boss?" He smiled congenially, trying to portray an image of harmless curiosity.

"We head out first thing in the morning," Kudakaan answered coolly as he closed his journal. Daelyn made a mental note of the book as he slipped it into his left jacket pocket. She would need at some point to acquire it.

"Where to?"

"Devonshire."

"Ah." Jack seemed momentarily taken aback by a straightforward answer. "So, what's in Devonshire?" he asked. "Are we meeting someone? Are the thieves there?"

"I will let you know what you need to do when we get there," Kudakaan answered.

"Right." Jack paused. "So, how long will we be staying in Devonshire?" Kudakaan simply returned a flat look. "Okay. Fine. I guess I have two days to work on you," Jack finished with a smile.

"One," Kudakaan retorted with a half-smile of his own.

"Oh?"

"We will be taking the east road."

"What?" Jack sat forward in his chair. "Why?"

"It is the fastest way to Devonshire," Kudakaan replied.

"Is the east road even passable?" Qaz chimed in. "I heard it fell into disrepair because no one ever went that way."

"That's because the north road is much better," Jack said. "We can stop in Fenwyg for the night and be in Devonshire by dusk the next day. It's a safer, well-established road. Often you end up making better time, even though you aren't going straight there."

"The north road takes us significantly out of the way. It's over twice the distance."

"Well, yes, it's more distance, but it's a flat, easy road. We can travel twice as fast."

"The east road is more direct. Faster," Kudakaan retorted.

"And it runs through some pretty rough, rocky hills," Jack responded. "Sure, it's only one day to Devonshire, but you'd still have to push hard and have zero incidents. No farms along that road. If we have a problem, we are on our own. I couldn't help but notice all of our horses are wearing flat, road shoes. No good for bare rock. If any of our mounts are injured from a slip, we won't make any time."

"You can have your horse reshod if you are worried," Kudakaan retorted.

"We have *nine* horses. Reshoeing our mounts will take most of the morning. We'd never make Devonshire by your schedule."

"Jack, I'm not going to argue with you."

"Did you know there is a bandit group operating in those hills?" Jack asked

"True," Murzahd piped in. "My cousin was attacked traveling through those hills just this spring."

"So, the road *is* open then…" Qaz inserted.

"We could very likely get ambushed," Jack suggested, trying to ignore Qaz. "Now, I am not afraid of a few bandits," he added. "But it seems like an unnecessary risk to take for minimal gain, especially given…" He glanced over his shoulder. "…given the nature of our business."

"If it is too difficult, you can resign," Kudakaan chided.

"Ok, how about this? If we are in a hurry to get to Devonshire, we can take the north road just until the hills are manageable, then we cut across country to Cromwood. The forest is much thinner there; it's not a bad shortcut. We'd be in Cromwood by nightfall. We'd head out first thing in the morning and be in Devonshire by lunch. Takes only a half-day longer, and the risk is significantly reduced. Listen, I'm not trying to give you a hard time, but we were all hired for our expertise. I've traveled these roads a lot, and I strongly urge you to consider the north road."

"Jack, I have heard your suggestion," Kudakaan answered tersely. "We will take the east road. We leave at dawn," Kudakaan stated. He stood and downed the rest of his glass. "See you all in the morning." Jack glared at his back as Kudakaan crossed the room and disappeared up the stairs.

"Hmmph." He snorted. "I don't think it's a good choice."

"As you have said," Lena added. "Repeatedly."

"Personally, I agree with you regarding the best route to Devonshire," Murzahd added. "Indeed, if I had my way, I'd have us swing through the mountains to visit the ruins of the ancient Ialish stronghold of Kravzhekny. It's very close. However, Kudakaan is our captain; we must abide by his decisions. Besides, my axe is a bit thirsty." He smiled. "Hopefully, we might run into a bandit or two. Save the King's Marshals some work." He mocked a downward smash with an invisible axe and broke into a chuckle.

"What do you guys think is in Devonshire?" Jack asked.

"By tomorrow, hopefully, us," Tim answered. It wasn't until Qaz cracked a smile that Daelyn realized he had been making a joke.

"I don't like this," Jack stated. "We are all supposed to be on the same team. I understand the need for secrecy, but he will have to trust us at some point.

Just then, a curious mix of coarse laughter and cursing erupted from the other side of the room. Daelyn shot a glance toward the noise, subconsciously reaching for one of the several knives she kept hidden on her person. It seemed as though the dice game had reached a critical juncture, and there was some dispute about the finer points of the rules. She let out an exasperated sigh as she realized that Corelan had thrown the toss in question.

Daelyn glanced toward the others in her group. Lena and Murzahd had resumed their historical debate and were oblivious to the tension. Jack and Qaz, however, had noticed and were scrutinizing the escalating ruckus, both with a touch of amusement. Tim, she saw, was looking right at her. Whether he was aware of what was going on at all was unclear. Their eyes met, and she tilted her head toward the commotion, wondering if intervention would be soon required. Tim shrugged and turned to watch as if attending a play of some sort. She sighed again. Breaking up a fight between drunken fools was not how she had hoped to spend the evening.

The argument suddenly reached critical mass as the dusky-skinned C'thûn threw a sudden jab at Corelan. Quick as a snake, Corelan brushed the other man's fist aside and pivoted his hand, clamping down on the other man's wrist. He made a large underhanded half-circle, twisting the C'thûn's joint into a clearly painful position. The C'thûn gasped and sputtered while Corelan led him in a circle, applying sufficient pressure to the joint to prevent escape. All the while, Corelan held fast to his whiskey glass, never spilling a drop, much to the amusement of the rest of the crowd.

Lena had taken notice and stood with a sigh and an exaggerated roll of her eyes. Daelyn pushed to her feet as well, primarily by instinct, and extended a calming gesture to the table. No need for this to escalate into a full-on brawl by having a group of armed and excited professionals descend on the gamblers, hell-bent on enforcing several different perspectives on justice. Surprisingly, Lena relented and sat back in her seat, resuming her dialogue with Murzahd. Jack shook his head and made a vague gesture toward the ruckus as if to concede to her intention to quell the situation in her own way. Qaz merely shrugged.

Daelyn slipped through the rapidly thickening crowd of the tavern toward the combatants. Corelan and his opponent had begun to solicit the notice of the establishment's security man, a wide and densely muscled man with a fat cudgel that he now held in one hand, resting the opposite end on his shoulder. He appeared content to allow this conflict to play out for at least a moment or two longer and observed the goings-on with a faint glimmer of amusement. Admittedly, it was a slightly comical sight, Corelan leading the C'thûn in circles by his nearly hyperextended wrist, whiskey in hand, all the while politely asking for an apology. And while Daelyn doubted Corelan needed any tactical assistance in this single conflict, the situation threatened to escalate beyond the comfort level that their mission dictated.

Just as Daelyn pushed through the outer circle of spectators, a figure strode fearlessly directly into the midst of the conflict and planted himself squarely in Corelan's path. At first, from size and stature, Daelyn took this figure to be a child of no more than a dozen years, but the smaller figure brushed his long black hair away from his face revealing the black and white striped skin indicative of his heritage. The man was a Jaan (or was it a female? It was often difficult to tell the difference with Jaan, as both male and female were nearly identical in form and voice, and they themselves seldom seemed to find the distinction important). The little fellow had a somewhat masculine (by human standards anyway) bearing so Daelyn decided for the moment to privately conclude it was indeed a "he."

"Hey, tough guy!" the Jaan spoke, his thin voice barely penetrating the excited racket of the crowd. He waved an accusatory finger at Corelan in the event that there was any confusion. Corelan had halted his movement and therefore lost some of the solidity of his wrist lock on the C'thûn. An uncontrolled smirk began to spread across Corelan's face. The C'thûn started to struggle more enthusiastically, now that he had regained his footing.

"Yes?" Corelan answered, taking a slight swig of whiskey.

"You let him go this instant, or I'll punch you right in your little biscuits." He mimed a few rapid punches toward Corelan's groin. The brightly colored sleeves of his slightly overlarge jacket made light snapping sounds as the Jaan began to perform an elaborate demonstration of how he planned to assault Corelan's more delicate anatomical features with a furious series of jabs and uppercuts. Corelan and the C'thûn exchanged glances, Corelan somewhat baffled, and the C'thûn a touch sheepish.

"Uh. Sure." Corelan released his opponent, who stood slowly, rubbing his wrist. The Jaan's following words were buried under the resounding laughter of the tavern, but there was still a fair bit of finger wagging and a few more imaginary punches before the Jaan had said his piece. Corelan and the C'thûn exchanged another hesitant look before Corelan gave him a friendly pat on the shoulder and gestured to the dice to indicate that his former opponent was entitled to the next throw.

Perhaps not surprisingly, the tavern quickly returned to its previous state of drinking and carousing as if the bizarre exchange had never taken place. The dice game resumed right where it had been left, and the Jaan swaggered up to the bar and summated a bar stool with the clear intent to celebrate his dominance. Daelyn shook her head. The Jaan were many things as a people – some saw them as scatterbrained, undisciplined, and frivolous – though Daelyn would perhaps use the terms eccentric and lighthearted (and then only by human standards). But whatever they were, the Jaan were rarely boring.

By the time Daelyn returned to the table, Qaz and Jack had each excused themselves for the evening, leaving Lena, Murzahd, and Tim as the last of her companions still seated at their corner table. Murzahd was downing the remainder of his ale as Lena spoke to Tim.

"…be prepared for that possibility?" she asked.

"Of course. You see…" Tim responded. "Daelyn." He acknowledged her as she sat. "I see our new friend there is staying entertained." He nodded toward Corelan, who presently appeared to be quite chummy with the fellow who took a swing at him moments ago. Daelyn shook her head slightly and settled into her chair.

"You were saying," Lena prompted Tim.

"Yes, of course. Metal interferes with a psychic's abilities. The alchemical properties of metals prevent us from being able to focus our internal energies," he responded. Turning to Daelyn, he went on. "Lena was asking why I don't carry traditional weapons or armor."

"I see," Daelyn replied. She, too, had taken note of Tim's seeming lack of preparation for physical conflict and had surmised that he intended to simply stay out of harm's way.

"Qaz wears armor," Lena offered.

"Yes, well, his magic is different," Tim explained. "He is using his mind to manipulate *external* energies. In fact…"

"Is it just iron?" Lena asked, clearly uninterested in the fine points. "I've seen mages decked out in bronze armor before."

"Those were probably Forcemasters," Tim answered. "Iron messes with their energies too, but it's an issue with the magnetism. Anything without iron would be fine for them."

"Sorry," Murzahd broke in. "You are saying that you can't hold metal at all, or you lose your powers?"

"True," Tim answered. "The amount of metal in a small knife is about my limit. Anything more than that, and my flow is disrupted."

"Then why not carry a sword at least, and then just set it aside when you need to… psychic something?" the Ialu asked, folding his arms as if he had just scored a point.

"It doesn't work like that," Tim responded.

"Explain," Lena asked.

"Imagine you were looking at a reflection in a pool of still water. Now suppose someone throws a stone in the pool. That's the effect metal has on our powers. The surface is disturbed, and you won't be able to make out any details of the reflection. Even once the stone is gone, it still takes time for the ripples to dissipate."

"Ah," Lena answered. "Still seems like a big disadvantage."

"It can be. Tim conceded. "But not insurmountable. I've got some hardened leather armor upstairs, and wooden weapons are no issue at all. I've even seen armor made of hardwood scales, similar in style to Qaz's armor."

"Wood?" Murzahd responded, shaking his head. "Wood will crack. Wooden scale armor would fall apart with a single blow."

"I think the wood was enchanted," Tim replied. "It was a derwij who was wearing it."

"Ah. Well. I guess that's different." Murzahd conceded. "For weapons, though, I saw that little stick you had on your belt today," Murzahd commented.

"Club," Tim replied with a raised eyebrow.

"To each his own." Murzahd followed hastily. "I meant no offense." The conversation soon wandered off to more benign subjects, mainly concerning the quality of various regional ales. After it became clear no more useful information was likely to surface this evening, Daelyn excused herself and retired to her room to compose the beginnings of her first report.

CHAPTER THREE
SIXDAY
26TH OF TURADMUR

It was a gorgeous day for a ride. The perfectly blue sky showed not a single cloud. The leaves on some of the trees were just beginning to show the first signs of fall, with an occasional hint of color peeking out of the green. A gentle breeze carried the pleasant smells and sounds of the forest across the road, wafting gently through the swaying leaves. A bird whose breed Daelyn could not quite recognize chirped merrily just out of sight. The dirt road behind her stretched more than half a day's ride back to the town of Akeela, where they had spent the previous night. The route then ran another half day back to Roth, and in all this time, Jack and Kudakaan have not agreed on a single thing yet. The others rode in small groups, trailing behind the bellicose pair, engaged in their own private conversations.

Kudakaan held the lead, with Jack riding beside. Uglor and Daelyn rode just behind them. She had initially chosen to ride near the front, hoping to perhaps pry a morsel of information out of their leader. In the light of Jack's dismal failure at the same task, she reminded herself to try a more subtle approach than the one he used. Behind them, a short distance more rode Qaz – the armored, hammer-carrying mage, who munched idly on an apple as he mused over some private thought, seemingly oblivious to the tension in the air ahead. Behind him rode Lena, Murzahd, and Tim – the psychic. Murzahd was explaining to Lena some of the clan markings tattooed along his densely muscled arm. She was either interested in the details or successfully pretending to be. Tim was riding close by, wearing light armor of toughened leather as promised. A long thin hardwood club hung from a leather loop at his belt. He was busy trying not to notice that he was being essentially ignored by his two closest companions. Daelyn strove to overhear anything she could of their conversation. Any information she could gather about her companions on this mission could prove useful.

In the rear, Corelan slept in his saddle, somehow maintaining what looked to be a deep sleep and his balance simultaneously. Daelyn sighed again, trying to find an excuse to fall back and ride with the others. The argument ahead broke her train of thought.

"I just don't see how we are supposed to be able to contribute anything if we are kept completely in the dark," Jack said.

"Information will be revealed to you as needed," Kudakaan replied.

"Well, I need it. Why are we taking this road?"

"To get to Devonshire. I told you that."

"I know. Why are we taking *this* road to Devonshire? The north road is much better. Are we avoiding the north road for some specific reason – trying not to be seen?"

"This road is faster."

"And frequently hit by bandits. And runs through rough, rocky hills. We covered this last night. The advantage of the shorter distance is negated by the hazards. That is why nobody smart ever goes this way. That is why we are having this conversation."

"You are being paid to do whatever I tell you to…."

"Just tell me what we are going to do in Devonshire. Are we going to meet someone? Are the thieves there? C'mon, we are supposed to be working together." Jack threw his arms up in frustration.

"Be quiet and ride. This conversation is over," Kudakaan finished with an angry tone and spurred his horse ahead a few paces, aggressively ignoring any part of the world that had Jack in it. Jack slowed his horse a bit, reigning up beside Daelyn and Uglor.

"Do you believe this guy?" he asked rhetorically.

"I wouldn't worry about it," Daelyn offered. "He is just worried about security. Remember, he doesn't really know that he can trust us yet. What if we go running off and spread the word of this little mission?"

"Yeah, yeah. He could at least be civil," Jack grumbled. Daelyn sighed yet again. Jack's heavy-handed approach with Kudakaan was going to make her job more difficult, she thought. She turned again, still working on an excuse to part company with Jack. Behind them, Tim had finally noticed that Lena and Murzahd were essentially ignoring him and had dropped back. He had awoken Corelan, who was smoking another one of his absurd little cigars.

After another hour of riding in relative silence (discounting the occasional attempt at small talk and Jack's grumbling), Kudakaan halted and broke the team for a rest and a meal. It seemed a touch early for lunch, but perhaps his decision was made based on location rather than timing. Where the road had up until now been hedged in rather closely on both sides by dense forest, here it passed through a small clearing, edged on one side with small boulders. A few rings of stones scattered about the tall grass suggested long-dead campfires. Apparently, this was once a somewhat popular rest stop before this section of road had fallen into disuse.

As each of them milled around, securing their horses and opening their packs, Daelyn took the opportunity to study her companions more closely than she could while riding. Jack had pulled Murzahd aside and was likely venting to the poor fellow his frustrations concerning Kudakaan. Murzahd seemed to be tolerating the tirade with the characteristic politeness of his people. Lena was brushing her horse down and patting the beast on the neck as she spoke softly to the animal. Daelyn thought she had heard the animal's name was Steel, and to be fair, he looked the part; a magnificently muscled stallion with clear evidence of training and discipline. Daelyn herself wasn't much of a rider, but she did know the value of horses. Kudakaan made a sharp whistle and gestured for everyone to come close.

"Ok, everyone, listen up," he began. "I need you all to stay sharp. Let your horses rest and graze a little. There is a small stream just past those rocks where you can water them. Get some food and water yourselves." He looked over his shoulder toward the road. "I am going to range ahead to scout around. The upcoming road gets rocky, and there are a lot of boulders and natural walls. Good places to mount an ambush." He pulled a short horseman's bow from his pack and strung it up as he spoke. "Attend to your needs but stay ready to move suddenly if there is an emergency. When I return, I will whistle like this." He let out a perfect imitation of the bird Daelyn had admired earlier. Daelyn shot a look around, gauging the reactions of the others. There were nods and murmurs, and everyone continued on with their activities as Kudakaan disappeared down a small game trail that seemed to parallel the main road.

Jack watched Kudakaan slip into the woods, and as soon as the other man vanished, he slid up next to Murzahd, and the two began talking in hushed tones. Daelyn made her way over and caught the end of Murzahd's response.

"You think that's a good idea?" the Ialu asked. Jack paused as he saw Daelyn grow closer. He waved her over in a conspiratorial fashion.

"I think Kudakaan needs someone to watch his back. Very dangerous out there. I was just volunteering to help out with that." He grinned. He turned back to Murzahd. "You in?"

"Sure," he responded. "Ol' Smokey here knows to stay put." He patted his short, stout mule on the shoulder. Due to their own shorter legs, the Ialu tended to prefer shorter mounts, choosing either particularly stubby mules (or the occasional hinny) or a specific breed of horses bred specifically for their needs, the *velni* horse. However, the surefooted nature of a mule was a better choice for this terrain.

"How about you, Daelyn?" Jack asked. "Feel like helping out our friend Kudakaan?" As Jack spoke, she saw Tim slipping quietly away between two large boulders, not far from the mouth of the trail Kudakaan had taken. Daelyn stifled a curse. She had been searching all day for an opportunity to make progress, and now she had to choose between two.

"Would three of us make too much noise?" Murzahd asked.

"I'll stay here," she offered. She didn't want to get on Kudakaan's bad side by getting caught disobeying orders this early. Besides, she would interview Jack and Murzahd separately later to see if their stories matched. That might be worth more than anything they actually saw. Jack said a few words to Uglor before he and Murzahd slipped off quietly down the trial after Kudakaan. Daelyn made her way toward the opposite side of the clearing, moving causally in the direction she had seen Tim go. Lena stood by her mount, fitting the metal chest guard over her padded gambeson and adjusting the buckles along her ribs. She wrinkled her brow as she saw the two men disappear into the woods.

"Where are they going?" she asked.

"They are making sure Kudakaan will be okay out there in the scary woods all by himself," Daelyn replied with a sarcastic smile.

"Really? Not enough trouble in the world; they gotta go looking for it?" Lena rolled her eyes and turned away from the trail.

"You're getting ready for it, though," Daelyn observed, nodding toward Lena's armor.

"There's a difference between prudence and recklessness," Lena responded.

"True." Daelyn paused for a moment, studying the other woman. She needed to start making progress on her mission. "So, Lena, do you do a lot of this sort of thing?"

"Jobs like this one?" Lena asked. "The last few jobs I did were either caravan or personal security. Oh, and occasionally delivering an important package using my utmost discretion." She added with a wink. "The whole mystery element to this one is a new twist, but honestly, I don't care that much about the politics behind it. I'm done with all that."

"Done?"

"I… uh…" Lena stammered. "What I meant was …" Lena took a breath and regained her composure. "I was involved in the politics of royalty a long time ago. It's all a big game to them. They only see you as a footman in a game of elements. You know the game?" Daelyn nodded. "I'm not a game piece. I try to stay clear of that world."

"I hear you," came the answer. As she considered the other woman's response, Daelyn felt the wheels spinning in her head. The likelihood that Lena was the king's agent seemed less. A Royal Marshal would have a better cover story planned and rehearsed. Lena's slip seemed very genuine. However, it *was* a slip that would lead a suspicious person astray, so a truly talented agent might deliberately slip in the wrong direction to cover her tracks. Damn this double-thinking industry paranoia.

"What about you?" Lena asked.

"Discreet security usually," Daelyn responded with her own rehearsed backstory. "Sometimes a wagon carrying something important escapes notice if its security people don't look like security people." Lena nodded in reply.

"Speaking of security, I suppose we should organize a defense in case trouble finds us." Lena gestured to the others who gathered close in response.

"What's up?" Qaz asked. "Are we missing some people?" He looked around, counting silently.

"Jack and Murzahd are doing some scouting of their own," Lena answered as she finished the buckle on her forearm guard. "I think we should be ready if we run into a problem. If trouble comes, it will be from that direction." She pointed to the road ahead. "After we are settled with the horses and our lunches, Qaz, you and Tim collect the animals and lead them off, out of sight just around that bend. Find some low ground; try to hide that monster Uglor is riding. Daelyn, you will conceal yourself behind those bushes right by the road; bow ready. Uglor, Corelan, and I will take position in this high grass and lie low. If things get ugly, Daelyn, you will shoot as well as you can, then get out of the way. The three of us will take the center while you and Qaz watch our flanks. Tim, no matter what, don't leave the horses. Where's Tim?" She looked around.

"Oh, he's…" Qaz offered, looking around "…I think he's… I dunno."

"I think I saw him head over toward the stream. I've got to refill my canteen anyway. I'll find him and let him know the plan," Daelyn offered. Lena nodded and began digging in her saddlebags. The others scattered a bit and went about their own tasks. Daelyn made a show of producing her water canteen and made off toward the boulders where Tim had slipped away a few moments ago. She adjusted the fit of her black leather jerkin and sword belt, discreetly checking on her hidden throwing knives. Tim had a bit of a head start, but she was confident she could track him and remain undetected.

Daelyn paused as she rounded a large boulder, listening intently. The ruckus of someone moving through the forest whispered faintly ahead. She slipped along quietly, stepping on rocks and roots to avoid making sounds of her own. This section of forest was thinly blanketed with relatively few scattered dried leaves. That fact, combined with generous patches of soft grass, smooth rocks, and moss, made the task rather easy for someone with her skill. She closed in on the sound of movement and caught sight of a figure moving through the trees. She paused, crouching down behind a tree. It was Tim. He stopped, looked around as if checking to see if he had been followed. She took a sharp breath. What was he up to? He turned away and faced a large tree, unbuckling his belt. She turned away with a slight chuckle as Tim relieved his bladder. She shook her head with amusement, laughing at herself for so readily creating some sinister motive for a man to slip off alone into the woods after riding all morning. She shifted her weight to slip quietly away when she heard voices away to the left.

"Who's there?" Tim asked, his voice a loud whisper. She heard his belt buckle clank as he hurriedly refastened his trousers. Daelyn deliberately made a few rustle sounds, hoping to project the impression that she had just arrived.

"Tim, is that you?" she asked. "It's me, Daelyn."

"Yeah, I know," he offered as he stepped closer. "I sensed you just now." He blushed a moment.

"Oh, yeah, sorry…" she began. "I wanted to respect your privacy…"

"No worries. We're both adults." They stood close enough to whisper. "Did you hear the other voices ahead?" he asked.

"Sounded like it came from over that hill," she offered. With a nod, he followed her as they quietly ascended the slight rise. The sound of voices talking became more distinct. As she and Tim approached the crest of the hill, the conversation (though she could still not quite make out the words) grew in intensity. Several other voices joined in. She looked at Tim. "You can sense people when they are close, right?" she asked.

"Yes." He nodded. "Feels like there are quite a few over there. Over a dozen, at least. Maybe these are the bandits Jack was warning us about." He turned to move closer to the top of the hill, crouching low. Suddenly the sound of steel clanging on steel rang out. Voices shouted.

"Shit." She reached over her shoulder for the bow that wasn't there. She swapped a worried look with Tim as he pulled the slim club from his belt. She drew her slender sword. They raced to the top of the rise to see the fight unfolding below. Kudakaan and two complete strangers were running hard back toward their encampment with well over a dozen armed men hot on their heels. One of the strangers was wounded already, the bloodstain on his arm spreading rapidly between his fingers as he ran.

"What do we do?" Tim asked, his breath short from exertion and anxiety.

"Too many for the two of us to hit head-on." She shook her head, silently cursing her choice to leave her bow behind. "We slip in behind them. See what we can do." She waited for a beat longer and rushed down the far side of the hill, trying to minimize the sounds made by crashing through the forest. The attackers ran past as she and Tim gained the small trail that had led Kudakaan here. "Keep up, but don't get seen," she warned Tim. "If they turn on us, we will be cut off from our friends." Tim nodded. "Let's go."

To stay on the narrow trail, the supposed bandits were spreading out into nearly a single file line as they raced through the woods. Incoherent shouts and curses and the sounds of bodies flying heedlessly through the scrubby underbrush helped conceal the noises she and Tim were making as they strove to keep up with this mad chase through the forest. The pursuit through the trees lasted only a moment or two longer. Daelyn skidded to a halt, reaching back to restrain Tim as the group of men fanned out suddenly. They had chased Kudakaan and the two strangers into the small stream that wound through the woods, and the trio was blocked by a steep embankment. They were forced to turn and face the attackers.

The closest bandits rushed in to attack without a word, blades drawn. The wounded stranger was cut down almost immediately as he struggled to bring his own weapon to bear. Kudakaan whirled his iron-bound staff in swooping defensive action, keeping his immediate opponents at bay for the moment. Numbering close to twenty, the bandit group began to spread out in the stream bed to surround Kudakaan and the second stranger who stood nearby, sword in hand. Daelyn paused, caught in a moment of hesitation. If she and Tim attacked the men from behind, they might disturb their ranks enough for Kudakaan to either climb the embankment unharmed or otherwise escape the entrapping formation. She and Tim might also seal their own doom by having nearly two dozen bandits turn to attack them, cutting them off from any reinforcement.

"Daelyn…" Tim began in a hushed voice. His thought was interrupted by a rapid blur of motion from her left. A knife whistled out of the trees and lodged itself into the shoulder of one of the bandits, followed quickly by another. The second knife struck a glancing blow across the man's skull as he stumbled backward in surprise. Murzahd burst into the fray from the nearby underbrush and, with a vicious low swing of his axe, he shattered another bandit's leg. He whirled his weapon around in a rapid arc and finished the man with a second stroke before he hit the ground.

"Now!" Daelyn hissed to Tim as she rushed forward to engage. She still wasn't sure this was the wisest decision, but it was the only choice that had presented itself. She took a few running steps toward the bandits who had not yet taken notice of them and jabbed the closest in the back with the point of her sword. He wore a thick, toughened leather jerkin. While the tapered point of her blade easily penetrated the man's thin armor, as he spun in surprise, the leather twisted, entrapping her blade for a brief moment, thus preventing her from delivering a killing strike. The man shouted in pain and alarm, stumbling sideways to tumble onto his hip in the shallow stream. Daelyn managed to keep hold of her sword hilt as he fell but lost all the momentum of her charge.

Tim had angled to her right and cracked another bandit on the side of the head as he ran past, stunning the man momentarily. Daelyn followed behind him and slashed at the same fellow, angling her strike toward his leg as his guard had lifted instinctively in response to Tim's attack. Her blade bit a deep wound into his thigh as she ran past. Tim kept running, circling around the right side of the bandit group into and the stream, smacking another bandit on the elbow, causing him to drop his blade. Daelyn lunged at another bandit, but the group had responded to the influx of attackers and what had been an orderly formation disintegrated into a whirling melee.

Murzahd flailed brutally with his axe, having felled another bandit and presently had several others scrambling to defend themselves against his wrath. Kudakaan had taken advantage of the chaos and accounted for another of their foes. The bandit lay motionless, face down in the shallow water. She couldn't immediately see Jack but was fairly certain he had opened the attack with the thrown knives. In the last few seconds, she and her companions had managed to kill or injure six of their opponents, but they were still faced with at least half again their own number.

Several of the bandit group had turned to face her and Tim, bringing weapons to bear in defensive postures as they looked around wildly, attempting to size up the new threat. Kudakaan rushed past them without pause, followed closely by the stranger. The bandits were beginning to coalesce into a group, and here in the stream bed, they had enough room to maneuver and coordinate their attacks. It was time to get the hell out of there.

Daelyn and Tim wasted no time turning and running after Kudakaan, sloshing through the ankle-deep water of the stream with the bandits hot on their heels.

As they rounded the edge of the embankment, Kudakaan immediately angled back onto the dry ground, heading straight back to their encampment. Daelyn lost sight of Murzahd (and never did see Jack), but she was confident they had come to a similar conclusion about the prudent course of action. Though they had lost the game trail and were now heedlessly crashing through the underbrush, Kudakaan chose his path through the bracken with as much prudence as haste would allow. Daelyn heard shouts and curses from the pursuing force as they became entangled in thorny vines or stumbled over fallen branches.

She and her companions managed to maintain their distance ahead of the bandits, and with the racket that everyone was making as they charged through the woods, Daelyn hoped that her remaining companions had enough forewarning to be combat-ready once their new guests arrived. As they burst into the clearing, she looked around wildly. No one was visible. This was either a very good or a very bad thing. In either case, she needed her bow. She spied the horses gathered near the forest edge opposite the road, clustered near one of the large boulders that rimmed the north side of the clearing. She angled her trajectory toward the horses, able to add speed now that she was on open ground. She snatched her bow from the strap on her saddle and turned to assess the situation as she hastily strung her weapon.

Kudakaan, the stranger, and Tim had stopped near the center of the clearing. Murzahd had caught up with them, and the four turned to face their foes. There was still no sign of Jack. The bandit group began to encircle her companions, delivering indistinguishable taunts and threats. She had just fitted an arrow to the string and was drawing the shaft to her cheek to provide her response when Uglor and Corelan descended upon the bandit group from behind, leaping from their hiding places amongst the boulders. Uglor charged in from her right, gripping his monstrous axe in one hand and bellowing at the top of his lungs as his long powerful strides bore him down on the fray.

A bandit turned to engage him but was smashed aside by a massive shoulder and flung into a bush several paces away. Without pause, Uglor crashed heavily into the bandit's south flank. With a tremendous upward swing, he sent a man spinning through the air in a spray of blood. He moved like lightning, flailing madly around with his axe like it weighed nothing, his foes scattering like frightened birds.

Corelan leapt from atop a large rock, hit the ground in a tight ball, and rolled to his feet in an instant. He ducked under a bandit's sword slash and smashed bodily into his bewildered opponent sending him to his back, his sword disappearing into the long grass. As the bandit tried to stand, Corelan skipped forward and shot his foot out, smashing into his opponent's neck. He rolled aside, clutching his ruined throat as he struggled vainly to breathe. Daelyn arched an eyebrow. Her doubts about Corelan's qualifications vanished.

Murzahd leapt forward without hesitation and took two strides to close with a bandit as he swung his long axe. The weapon bit deeply into the man's chest, and he collapsed like a sack of bones. Chaos erupted as everyone moved at once. Kudakaan also sprang into action, his staff a blur as he charged into the thick of the fray. Bandits raced everywhere; some converged on their opponents, and some appeared to run about randomly. Daelyn sent an arrow after a bandit near the edge of the fray. She scored a hit, and the man fell, a feathered shaft protruding from his shoulder.

Just then, Lena rocketed past, riding Steel at full gallop with her sword held aloft. Before Daelyn could blink, she bore down on the center of the fray, her sword dropping in a clean arc to send a bandit sprawling in a spray of blood as his companions desperately dove aside. The combat area dissolved into complete disarray as the combatants strove to adjust to this new threat. Daelyn drew another arrow and searched for an open target. Movement atop one of the larger boulders caught her attention. Qaz stood atop the stone, seemingly frozen, his hands held aloft. He gestured sharply, and the air between his hands began to ripple like the heat of the summer sun distorting the air above a rise of hot road. He moved as if collecting the distortion, almost as one would roll a towel into a ball. With another sharp gesture and an unrecognizable shout, he hurled the mass of swirling… whatever it was, at a hapless bandit. The rolling distortion engulfed the man, and he fell into a fit of uncontrolled twitching with a surprised shout. He collapsed into the tall grass, flailing about as if caught in a seizure.

While she and her companions had fared quite well thus far, the superior number of the bandit group was still a troublesome factor. A pair of bandits were pressing Tim hard. He gave ground liberally, retreating slowly toward the forest as his opponents slashed at him. Another pair of bandits had spotted Daelyn and charged her position, hoping to close with her before she could shoot. She released her arrow, aiming low in case her target tried to duck under her shot. Her guess proved accurate as the bandit bobbed directly into the arrow, taking him near the collarbone. He cried out and fell in a heap.

Daelyn tossed her bow aside and pulled her sword free, bringing it to guard position as the second bandit closed into range. One of the bandits facing Tim apparently decided his compatriot could handle the smaller man and turned his attention to Daelyn. She counted herself somewhat proficient at swordplay (at least in an even fight) but fighting two opponents who both outweighed her was worrisome. Even a very skilled swordsman would find those odds difficult. Behind her opponents, she saw Tim's adversary lose patience and leap forward to tackle the smaller man. They fell into a jumble of flailing limbs. Tim would have to handle his opponent on his own. She had more pressing concerns.

The two men she faced moved in cautiously, slowly spreading to either side of her. A third still lay on the ground struggling with the arrow wound to his shoulder. She initiated the conflict, lunging toward the bandit who had initially rushed her, slashing at his head with a cross-body motion. The bandit lurched backward and fell, tripping over his injured companion's prone form, and fell to the ground. She immediately turned away from them and deflected a thrusting attack toward her midsection from the other bandit. She allowed his motion to take him forward as she stepped right past him to deliver a backhanded swing at his exposed spine. He spun and lifted his blade to parry, deflecting her attack, but the momentum from his charge took him a step away from her. She stepped back a few paces to distance herself from both men.

Without hesitation, she lunged forward again, stabbing quickly toward her closest opponent while stepping to one side, placing him between her and the second bandit, who had regained his footing. He parried her attack and countered with a wide, cross body slash, swinging his large, heavy sword with both hands in a blatant attempt to overpower her. Rather than try to block the attack head-on, she stepped back just out his reach, giving up ground. She had learned a long time ago that when ground was unlimited, it could be given freely.

The other bandit, armed with a slimmer, faster blade, moved around his companion, circling to her left. She stepped back further, circling toward her right to keep the two men lined up and therefore unable to attack her simultaneously. Her primary opponent swung again in a massive downward chop, forcing her to give more ground. Just as she shifted her weight, the other bandit lunged forward, stabbing with the point of his thin blade toward her leg. He had read her body motion and chose the leg to which she had just shifted her weight. She could not react quickly enough, and the bandit scored a cut across her thigh. Luckily, he was too far away to inflict mortal damage, but the wound was long and would bleed a lot.

It also showed this bandit to be more of a thinker than his companion. She shot a glance to Tim, who was wrestling with his opponent on the ground just inside the tree line. He would need to handle his own situation for the moment. Her two opponents exchanged glances and cautiously moved in opposite directions, trying again to encircle her. She frowned and sidestepped away from them, moving back in Tim's direction. Constant motion was the key to survival in situations like this.

The bandit armed with the heavier sword initiated another downward chop, swinging a bit in front of her in an attempt to cut off her retreat. She spun on her rear heel, rolling away from the attack which whistled past her to vent its fury into the dirt. As she turned, she shifted her sword into her left hand, and with her right, she pulled a small knife from her sleeve. In a single motion, she let it fly toward the other bandit who had injured her. It struck him low in the abdomen just as he was stepping forward to stab her again. She continued her spinning motion and extended her sword to attack the first bandit, swinging toward the back of his neck in a crosswise motion as his motion carried him past her. He ducked clumsily, barely avoiding the unexpected attack, and lost his footing in the loose foliage of the forest floor.

Just then, the second bandit completed his attack, tearing into her arm with the point of his blade. He stumbled forward, clutching his wounded belly, and drew his sword back for another strike. For a moment, Daelyn thought she was doomed.

Both bandits were within striking distance and stood on either side of her. She turned toward the wounded bandit and kicked him in the hip as he brought his weapon to bear. He stumbled again and fell over, sprawling on his back in a shower of leaves with a cry of surprise and pain. She lunged forward, trying to ignore the crawling sensation in the middle of her spine she felt from turning her back on her other opponent. It just couldn't be helped.

She stabbed forward, trying to skewer the fallen bandit where he lay before the other man killed her from behind. The fallen bandit twisted his wrist, bringing his thinner, lighter blade around in a quick arc above his body to deflect her attack off to his side. The point of her sword buried itself in the earth inches away from his torso. He moved his feet in a sudden scissoring motion and clipped one of her legs right out from under her. She, too, fell to the forest floor. He rolled over with a growl and seized her by the throat. He squeezed with the ferocity of a crazed animal. She pulled another knife from her boot and jammed it between his ribs. His eyes opened wide, and he gasped in pain and surprise. She stabbed him again. He grunted and released his grip, rolling off to one side. She stabbed him a third time in a finishing strike. She rolled to her feet, snatching her sword from the ground, and spun to face the last bandit.

He was pumping his legs as if running like mad, his eyes open wide in stark terror as he floated a few inches above the forest floor. Tim knelt on the ground a few yards away with one arm extended toward the hapless bandit. His prior opponent lay on his back in the dirt beside him, rolling on his side, clutching his profusely bleeding nose. Tim's hand was clutching the empty air, and his face was twisted with effort as if he wrestled with lifting an invisible weight. The airborne bandit struggled uselessly for a moment more. Daelyn took a hesitant step closer. Tim dropped his arm suddenly and fell forward, catching himself with his hands on the ground. The hovering bandit also fell and wasted no time bolting off into the forest, his eyes wide with stark terror.

"Tim!" Daelyn shouted a warning as Tim's former opponent regained his feet and kicked the psychic in the back of the head with a stomping motion. He pulled a fat-bladed dagger from his belt and moved in for the kill when Daelyn's thrown knife caught him in the chest. He grunted and staggered back. He looked up in a fury, clutching his wound, and looked rapidly around his feet, searching for his fallen sword. Tim was struggling to his feet as Daelyn moved to retrieve her bow. The bandit read her intention and surmised that he could not reach her before she could reach her bow. He fled. The fellow she had shot a few moments ago had apparently also fled, leaving her and Tim unmolested for the time being.

Fiery pain radiated from the heavily bleeding wound in Daelyn's leg. As waves of dizziness flickered through her head, she realized that she must stop to dress her injury, or she would soon pass out. Daelyn left her bow where it lay in the clearing. She limped toward Tim, ripping her already torn sleeve free to form a makeshift bandage.

She glanced around the clearing. Murzahd was pressuring his last remaining opponent into a slow retreat, their savage blows ringing loudly through the trees. Closer by, Corelan was engaged in conflict with two bandits. He dodged their blades with surprising agility, but their coordinated attacks and longer reach kept him from an effective counterattack. Qaz was loosening the war hammer from his belt and moving to descend from the rock to render aid. She struggled beside Tim and pulled him to his feet by the arm.

"Are you okay?" she shouted. Tim nodded woozily, shaking his head to clear his mind.

"Are you?" he asked weakly. Blood ran freely from her wounds and trickled off her elbow. She grunted and turned to appraise the rest of the fight. Murzahd had pushed his opponent deeper into the woods, such that the two were barely visible through the underbrush. Twenty or thirty yards away, Uglor stood by the edge of the clearing, his torso a bloody mess. He fought two bandits simultaneously, still shouting as he thrashed about ferociously. They dove and dodged wildly, staying just out of his reach.

Of the stranger, there was no sign, but sounds of conflict rang out from the trees. Unidentifiable bodies lay motionless on the ground. Lena was heeling her horse in a tight turn, driving bandits like cattle, untouchable on her battle-trained steed. A few bandits hovered on the fringes of the battle, possibly considering the wisdom behind exercising the better part of valor. It seemed that the enemy was about to be routed. She sat heavily on the ground just inside the tree line and began to hastily bind her leg wound, receiving another wave of agony for her efforts.

The last bandit facing Kudakaan turned and fled, heading directly toward Daelyn and Tim. He looked back at the fight over his shoulder as he ran, clearly having no idea he was running headlong into two more enemies. Tim stepped into his path, brandishing his slender club, perhaps hoping to ward him away from his injured companion. The bandit, running at full tilt and looking behind him, instead proceeded to crash bodily into Tim, their heads colliding with a loud thunk. Tim was sent flying to his back and landed against a tree stump in a flurry of fallen leaves. The bandit, however, who outweighed Tim by at least fifty percent, staggered only for a moment and lurched past the two, bolting off toward the deep forest. Kudakaan leapt after him with a loud shout, clutching his staff close to his body as he ran.

"Tim! Are you all right?" she shouted. He rolled around for a moment on the ground and waved in her direction in vague response. She let Kudakaan chase after the man alone. Her leg injury would only slow her down and handicap his efforts. She crawled over to where Tim lay on the forest floor. His eyes rolled around in his head as he struggled to gain focus.

Qaz dropped to the ground to confront the bandits engaging Corelan, standing with his feet planted wide. His war hammer dangled from the long, thick leather loop on his wrist. With his other hand, he hurled a dagger that struck one of the bandits in the chest handle first, bouncing harmlessly to the ground. The stricken bandit turned to face Qaz with an almost amused look. Corelan dropped low and swept his leg in a wide arc close to the ground, clipping his opponent's legs out from under him. He fell out of sight for a moment behind the tall grass, and Corelan pounced on his prone form, also disappearing from view. His arm rose and fell twice.

With an irritated look, Qaz moved his hands almost together, just in front of his abdomen, one over the other. The air between his fingers shifted again, this time forming a dull green glow. The bandit facing him was clearly no longer amused and rushed to close the distance, hoping to overtake Qaz before he could finish his spell. Qaz lifted his hands as if to hurl his rapidly forming conjuration at his foe. The bandit, realizing he would be too late, skidded in the loose leaves of the forest edge, striving to angle away from the mage. Suddenly, an arrow protruded from Qaz's left shoulder. He staggered back with a surprised shout and fell out of sight to the ground between two boulders. The green light rapidly coalesced into what looked to Daelyn like a mass of watery oatmeal, falling to the dirt in an unceremonious splat, where it sat steaming harmlessly.

Daelyn quickly scanned the clearing, searching for the source of this new threat. A man stood atop a tall boulder with a longbow in hand. He drew a second arrow to his cheek. The bandit who had already turned away saw none of this and ran right past Qaz and his magic goo, fleeing into the open forest. Daelyn shouted a warning to Corelan as she pulled the half-conscious Tim around behind a tree. Another arrow zipped from the top of the boulder, tearing a gash through Corelan's sleeve as he dove to one side into the underbrush.

The last of the bandits in the open field spun and raced away, with Uglor hot on his heels. Daelyn lost sight of the pair as they rounded the edge of the boulder. Lena turned in her saddle, now painfully alone and exposed in the center of the clearing. She charged Steel forward, toward the cover of the boulders, leaning low and to one side, taking partial cover from the horse's bulk. The man atop the boulder took aim and released. The arrow took her horse squarely in the neck. It stumbled and fell, the momentum of the charge sending it and Lena tumbling across the ground. She rolled several times and crashed face-first into the side of the rock, her armor clanking loudly against its hard surface. She rolled onto her back and was motionless.

Daelyn looked about the clearing in dismay. The tides of battle had just shifted back in the bandits' favor. The archer had them all pinned. Qaz lay bleeding somewhere behind the rocks. Thirty or so paces away, Corelan was trapped behind a tree and a small bush, struggling to conceal himself within its meager protection. Tim had lapsed into complete unconsciousness, and a sizeable bloody knot was forming on his forehead. Lena had not yet moved since she hit the rock. Daelyn herself was still bleeding freely from her injuries. Of Murzahd, Kudakaan, and Uglor there was no sign. He had still not seen Jack since before this whole thing had begun. Lena's fatally injured horse twitched and whickered faintly.

The man atop the stone was leaning forward, looking for Lena. He pulled another arrow from the leather case at his hip and fired blindly into the undergrowth where she had fallen. The arrow stuck into the dirt a few inches from her head. Daelyn searched wildly for her bow. It lay several paces away in the exposed clearing, impossible to reach without being shot, even with both legs intact. The archer loosed another arrow toward Lena. It glanced off of the stone above her body and shot off into the woods. Daelyn ground her teeth in frustration.

Corelan popped up from his meager cover and hurled a stone at the archer. His throw was short by several yards. The thrown rock made a faint cracking sound as it bounced ineffectually off the boulder's surface. The archer turned his attention back to Corelan and buried an arrow in the tree near his head. Corelan huddled down behind the foliage. There was not enough coverage, and both he and the archer knew it. Corelan made eye contact with Daelyn and motioned grimly for her to run. She hesitated, then gasped as the realization of what Corelan was about to do dawned on her. Corelan shifted his weight to his heels and readied himself to leap. She shook her head at Corelan, urging him to wait. An arrow whizzed past and spent its fury into the ground near Corelan's foot. He frowned back and pointed at Tim mouthing the words 'Get him out.'

She struggled to lift him onto her slim shoulders. The archer noticed her movement and shifted his attention toward the pair. Corelan shouted to distract him and leapt into the open field. Daelyn clenched her fists in impotent anger as she turned to run clumsily through the trees, a wounded and unconscious Tim on her back. She staggered after only a few steps, swiftly realizing that even unburdened and unwounded, there was little chance of escape. She stumbled over a root and went to one knee, barely keeping hold of Tim's body. A scream broke the natural sound of the forest, and Daelyn winced as she struggled to her feet, silently thanking Corelan for his sacrifice and vowing to do her best to keep it from being in vain. The scream, however, continued for longer than she would have thought and abruptly terminated with a dull thump. She staggered onward a few steps.

"Daelyn. Stop. It's over," Corelan shouted from behind her. She turned hesitantly. Corelan stood in the clearing, a few yards from the twisted form of the archer. She looked up to the top of the boulder. Jack stood there, a long knife in his hand, looking down at the dead bandit in the dirt below. Jack's shirt was bloodied and torn, but it was unclear if the blood was his own.

"Check on the wounded," Jack shouted down from the rock. "I will look for the others." He backed away from the edge and disappeared from view.

* * * * *

Her eyes fluttered open, and then the pain hit her. Daelyn tried to sit up, but it seemed her bones had somehow turned to lead. Hard. Cold. Lead. She let her head drop back onto the rolled cloak that had found its way beneath her skull and tried to focus her eyes.

"Hey there. You were starting to worry us," a man's voice said. She moved her head, much more slowly this time, and brought Tim's smiling face into focus. He wore a large bandage around his head. Over his left eye, a small red stain decorated the torn cloth.

"Aaugh, what the hell happened?" she mumbled. Her tongue felt thick and only reluctantly obeyed her wishes.

"You passed out from blood loss," Tim offered. "Lie still and rest for now." He spoke in a soft tone, trying to be reassuring. He was unsuccessful. She was lying on her back on the grass at the edge of the clearing turned battlefield. She looked past him. The other members of her group had gathered around and were tending to their injuries. A short way off, a shirtless Uglor sat patiently on the ground while Qaz and Jack worked to bandage the multiple cuts and slashes that decorated his already heavily scarred chest. In the shadow of a tree nearby, Kudakaan crouched beside Lena. She sat leaning on the trunk as he tried to examine a knot on her head, dabbing at it with a damp cloth. She shied away, apparently insisting that she was fine. Corelan milled around in the woods, wearing a bandage tied around his arm. He smoked another one of his tiny cigars and occasionally stopped to examine something on the ground. The sun bathed Daelyn in a warm glow, and a gentle breeze wafted the unpleasant smell of death past her nose.

"Where is Murzahd?" she asked. Tim's cheer fell. He looked away and swallowed, seeming to be at a loss for words.

"He didn't make it," he said after a moment.

"What happened?" Daelyn asked. Murzahd seemed one of the more capable fighters in their group. Odd that he would fall after they had routed their enemies.

"I'm not sure. He got separated… I wasn't there."

"I see," she said. A wave of sadness rippled through her. She wondered at her reaction. She had lost many companions before, most of which she had known for much longer. It was a part of the business. Why would this be any different? It must be my injuries playing on my emotions, she thought.

"Yeah. He was a good man," Tim said. Perhaps that was the difference. She shoved the thought aside. "Listen, I want to thank you for…" he started.

"Forget it." She cut him off. "You would have done the same. Now, help me up," she said.

"Qaz said you should lie still until…"

"I don't work for Qaz. Now help me up." With her head spinning like a top, she found it particularly difficult to maintain the light Toctillian accent she had been asked to assume. She hoped if anyone noticed, they would chalk it up to her being thick-headed from her injuries. Tim took her arm and eased her gently into a sitting position. The forest wobbled and faded momentarily. Maybe Qaz had a point. She took stock of her injuries, carefully testing the movement of her injured arm. She was surprised to find it as mobile as it was.

"Qaz did some magical healing on you," Tim commented. "He would have fixed your arm up completely, but he only had so much magic to go around." She gently ran her hand over her leg wound. Aside from a dull, aching stiffness, all trace of the injury was gone. She had heard of magically healing wounds but never personally experienced it until now.

"How is your head?" she asked.

"Me? Oh, I'm fine. Didn't need anything." She looked past him. Corelan had finished his survey of the battleground and offered Lena a metal pocket flask. She took it and downed a large gulp. Kudakaan stood and exchanged some words with him before heading over to speak with Jack. Lena offered the flask back to Corelan, but he waved it off and crossed the road, approaching Tim and Daelyn.

"We are heading back to Akeela," Corelan said, crouching down beside them. "We lost some horses, and…" He hesitated, looking away for a moment. "…Murzahd didn't make it." He paused, searching for something appropriate to say. After a moment of awkward silence, he just nodded and stood, walking away toward the rest of the group. Daelyn was certain she saw him slip something into his pocket. She eased herself into a standing position, unconsciously accepting Tim's offered arm for assistance.

"I want to talk to Kudakaan," she said, moving in the direction of the other men.

"Maybe we should just…" Tim began, trailing off as it became apparent Daelyn would do whatever she wanted, regardless of his opinions. She walked slowly, favoring her injury, though the caution was born more from a profound weakness she felt to her core rather than the injuries themselves.

Jack and Kudakaan were at it again, engaging in what seemed like a heated discussion in an almost whisper. Daelyn could not quite discern the words as she approached, but from what she could tell, she almost did not want to. The conversation died as she walked up beside them. A few paces away, Corelan ignored the awkward silence and nodded cordially to Qaz, who looked up and smiled as he bandaged Uglor's wounds.

"What's our status?" she asked.

"A few injuries. None serious. We lost Murzahd, though," Kudakaan answered tersely.

"Did anybody see what happened?" she asked.

"He and I got separated from the rest of you," Kudakaan began. "We were faced off with a remaining pair of bandits when a third attacked from behind, just as Murzahd was finishing his opponent." Kudakaan stood rock still as he spoke. "Murzahd was fatally injured but managed to defeat his attacker before he fell. My back was exposed. He saved my life." Daelyn shot a glance toward Lena. The other woman sat a short distance off, leaning on a tree with her eyes closed. She clutched Corelan's pocket flask in one hand.

"Brave man," Tim added.

"How many got away?" Daelyn asked, turning to the others in the group.

"Nobody got a clean headcount," Jack answered. "We were all scattered around, but no matter whose account you consider, more than a few escaped into the woods."

"What of the two strangers?" she asked. "It looked like there were two other guys that weren't part of the bandit group.

"Both dead," Kudakaan replied. Daelyn shot a glance at Tim. He was studying Kudakaan with a blank look on his face. Maybe he was doing his psychic whatever.

"But who were they?" she followed. "They were fighting against the bandits too."

"Maybe just travelers in wrong place at wrong time. I suppose we will never know. What did you find?" Kudakaan turned to Corelan, changing the subject.

"Not much," Corelan responded. "I'm guessing they hadn't scored in a while. Not much cash or supplies. Really just the weapons and armor they carried."

"Horses?" Jack asked. "We are down a few mounts. It would be helpful to salvage something."

"I went up the road just a little. Looked like they might have had some mounts stashed, but the stragglers probably grabbed them on their way out." Corelan paused to take a short drag from his tiny cigar. "Didn't seem prudent to wander off too far on my own."

"Did you find anything else?" Kudakaan kept his stone-faced composure. Cold man, Daelyn thought.

"No."

"You were thorough?" Kudakaan asked.

"Yeah." Corelan looked back at Kudakaan with a raised eyebrow. "Were you expecting a mound of treasure?"

"What's our next move, boss?" Qaz asked, cutting off Kudakaan's retort. He still crouched beside Uglor, tending to his wounds in a more traditional fashion – with some kind of poultice and cloth bandages.

"We head back to Akeela."

"Not forward?" Jack asked cautiously.

"With this delay and short on mounts, we won't make Devonshire before dark." He shifted his gaze, scanning the tree line. "We don't know how many bandits escaped or if they have additional forces elsewhere. It's foolish to go on."

"Right then. Back to Akeela," Qaz butted in, cutting off whatever Jack was going to say.

"Saddle up." Kudakaan ordered flatly. Corelan turned away to tend to his horse. "Jack, you and I will finish this conversation later," Kudakaan added. Qaz stood and stepped back from Uglor.

"All done, big guy. I can finish patching you guys up with some more magic once I've rested a bit." He unconsciously massaged his shoulder where he had been struck by the arrow. A blood-stained bandage bore a stark testament to his injury.

"I think he blames me for what happened to Murzahd," Jack said to Qaz as Kudakaan crossed the clearing toward Lena.

"He is an ass," Qaz said. Jack smiled reluctantly. "I blame the bastard who killed him. C'mon." Qaz gathered his things and walked over to his horse. Jack turned to Uglor.

"You done resting yet?" Jack extended a hand to help his friend to his feet. Daelyn supposed it was more of a magnanimous than a practical gesture. Uglor took his hand but stood on his own. Jack sighed deeply.

"I hate this crap. When we get done with this job, remind me to retire." Uglor simply smiled and patted Jack on the shoulder.

Daelyn sighed as well and grunted as she stumbled toward her own horse. Retirement was beginning to sound like a good idea.

* * * * *

The trip back to Akeela was a quiet, somber journey. In the chaos of the battle, she and her companions had lost three horses. Tim's mount had panicked and fled into the woods, and Murzahd's mule, Smokey, was missing as well. Corelan suspected that one or both had been stolen by fleeing bandits. Lena's stallion, Steel, had to be put down and the poor woman was clearly quite broken up about it despite her attempts to hide the fact. The injured were mounted on the remaining horses, and Murzahd's body was covered in a blanket and draped across Uglor's saddle. With several of the group afoot, they had reached the town after dark and had to rouse the town's only innkeeper from a peaceful sleep to arrange for rooms. The sight of Murzahd's body and the numerous bandages adorning the others in the group dampened his temper. Kudakaan had spoken to him quietly, and a few moments and a glittering handshake later, they were moving their things back into the *Four Feathers*.

Kudakaan, Jack, Uglor, and Corelan sat alone in the inn's small common room. Lena had insisted on being at this meeting also, despite being told to rest. Tim, Daelyn, and Qaz all reclined in their rooms upstairs. A fire burned brightly in the fireplace, throwing a warm light on the overstuffed chairs and couches that crowded this small, pleasantly furnished room. Corelan had been unable to procure any whiskey before they sat for this impromptu meeting, and he found himself regretting the lack.

"Sorry, maybe I missed it when you first explained, but please, one more time," Lena insisted. "Who were those guys?"

"Like I said before, I don't know," Kudakaan answered. "I ranged ahead as a general precaution and ran into those two fellows on the trail. All I could get out of them was that they were on the run from some bandits. The next thing I knew, we were under attack."

"Well, I guess it's a good thing you had friends nearby to help you," Jack commented.

"Friends that should have been doing what I told them to."

"We heard shouting," Jack offered.

"Nevertheless." Kudakaan frowned. He jabbed the fire with poker and sat silently for a moment. "We leave town first thing tomorrow," he finally said.

"Absolutely not," Jack responded. "There are too many injuries. Qaz needs to rest fully before he can heal us all back to full capacity. We all heard him say that. If we go out on the road in this condition, we are asking for more casualties." He folded his arms and leaned back on the couch, glaring at Kudakaan.

"I think Jack is right," Corelan added. "I can walk fine, but you saw Tim. Poor guy was about to pass out when we got here. Daelyn too."

"Lena?" Kudakaan looked at her, his face unreadable.

"If we are injured, we will just travel slower," she answered. "Plus, we need to acquire more horses, re-supply, and take care of Murzahd's body. I vote we wait a day. It will end up the same either way." Kudakaan stewed silently for a moment, his forehead creased with vexation. The occasional crackling of the fire was the only sound in the room.

Jack broke the silence. "What plans do we have, if any, concerning our approach to the legal aspects of recent events?" Kudakaan raised an eyebrow. "Do we intend to make the local authorities aware of the pile of bodies we just left in the woods?" Jack went on in a hushed voice.

"I don't think that is within the best interests of the security needs of our mission," Kudakaan answered.

"What about the guys who got away?" Jack persisted. "Like we said earlier, nobody got a clear headcount, but possibly as many as six of them got away. What if they have something to say?"

"It's unlikely our adversaries will look to the local authorities for justice," Kudakaan responded.

"Nevertheless," Jack went on. "Don't you think our situation could put us in a bit of legal jeopardy?"

"Duke Pendor should be able to smooth out any troubles that may arise as a result."

"Should?"

"Remain focused on our job," Kudakaan answered. "I will handle the larger issues. As for the condition of our wounded, we will see how things look in the morning." He spoke coldly. "Dismissed." He stood and curtly turned his chair to the fire, grabbed the poker, and began jabbing sharply at a log.

Corelan looked at the somewhat stunned faces of his companions. The meeting had apparently ended. The others rose slowly and left Kudakaan stewing in the room. Corelan bypassed the stairs and wandered through a wide doorway into the tavern that adjoined the inn. It was deserted. All of the chairs stood on tables with their legs pointing to the ceiling like some miniature, solemn forest. A single lantern burned on the bar, illuminating the edge of the room in a weak pool of flickering light. He found his way behind the bar and pulled down a bottle of Velkasian whiskey. Fighting for your life had a way of making a man thirsty. He rooted around under the bar for a moment, found a glass, and unstoppered the bottle.

Lena walked in a moment later and pulled a stool off a table, her boots clunking heavily on the floor. She wore a deep blue jacket over a brown tunic and black work pants. Corelan put another glass on the bar as she sat down opposite him.

"What's a nice girl like you doing in a dump like this?" he asked as he poured her a shot.

"Taken to stealing whiskey, have we?" she asked. She drained her glass in a single gulp as he filled his own. "And who says I'm nice?"

"This goes on Pendor's tab. Reasonable expenses and all." He drained his glass. She pulled his flask from her jacket and placed it on the bar.

"Forget something?"

"Ahh, there you are." He filled their glasses before retrieving his lost companion. "Not bad whiskey. Velkasians know their stuff."

"So I've heard," Lena responded with a half-smile.

"You okay?" Corelan asked. Lena had been uncharacteristically quiet after losing her horse.

"It's tough," she answered, her eyes glittering in the low light. "Steel and I had been through a lot. I lost a friend today." She lifted her glass in silent salute. Corelan felt a familiar tension rising in his chest. Not now. Don't do this now. Force the darkness back down. He concentrated on breathing.

One breath at a time. In. Out. One more. "Enough of that," She spoke suddenly. "New subject. You don't do this very often, do you?"

"Uh, yeah." Corelan pounded the last of his whiskey and felt the warmth of the liquor pushing the darkness away. "Kinda obvious, huh?"

"I'm not one to tell people what to do, but you might want to consider carrying a weapon of some kind."

"Probably not a bad idea," he conceded.

"Are *you* okay?" she asked him. "Was that the first time you ever had to kill anybody?"

"Not the first time." Corelan fought for composure. "But yeah, the whole mercenary thing is new to me."

"Can I offer you a tip?"

"Certainly."

"No more hero shit," she suggested. "Daelyn tells me you were going to take an arrow so she and Tim could escape." The lamplight reflected in her pale eyes as she studied him intently. He looked back at her for a moment. Her hair was still slightly damp from the hasty bath she had somehow managed to find. She studied him in return, looking as if she were trying to solve a tricky riddle. Hmpf. Riddle indeed.

"Not trying to be a hero," he mumbled. He was pinned down and likely going to die anyway; he might as well, in the process, give somebody else a shot at getting out. No heroism there.

"Well, it's either that or you've got some kind of death wish," she chided playfully. Corelan swirled the whiskey in his glass and glanced at the mark painted on the side of the bottle.

"This stuff is from Jamis," he answered. "Not my favorite. They use a lot of rye up there, and this one came out a little edgy. Not to discount rye whiskeys as a whole." He put the bottle down without looking at her. "I like the stuff from Haldonna or Kannoc much better." He threw his head back and drained his glass. "A lot of drinkers in Kannoc. Big military town."

"Okay then," she laughed. "Die on your own time; just try not to get me killed while you're doing it."

"Not trying to die either." He forced a chuckle. "The city wall back in town is high enough to do the job. No reason to get anyone else involved."

"That's dark."

"It's a dark world."

"Well, thanks for stealing me a drink." She finished the rest of her whiskey and set the glass on the bar. "Just think about carrying a weapon, and no more hero nonsense, okay?"

"I'll restrain myself," he joked. Corelan watched as she put her stool back on the table and left the room. He sat in silence for a moment, staring into the darkness. Death wish? Certainly not. His glass shattered against the far wall before he realized he had thrown it. He stood quietly, leaning on the bar, listening to the blood rushing in his ears, his arm tingling slightly from the sudden movement. "*Are* you certain?" he asked himself. He inhaled slowly and deeply to calm himself.

"I never much cared for whiskey myself either," Jack spoke from the shadows. How long had he been standing there? That's the problem with small towns, no privacy.

"So, what do you usually drink?" Corelan asked as he refilled his flask.

"Honestly, drinking has never agreed with me. I usually avoid the stuff completely." Jack leaned on the bar. "Got a question for you." He dropped his voice slightly and leaned closer. Corelan took another deep breath, forcing his mood to change. Jack probably had just walked in anyway. He gestured for Jack to continue. "How do you feel about this job so far?" Jack asked, his eyes glittering slightly. "Anything that strikes you as odd?" Corelan studied Jack for a moment, then reached into his pocket and dropped a heavy gold ring and an envelope onto the bar. "What's this?" Jack asked.

"Found this stuff after our recent… encounter," Corelan answered. Jack picked up the ring and studied it.

"Looks like a signet ring." He tested the weight in his hand. "Heavy gold. Expensive. I don't recognize the house." He set it back down on the bar.

"Odd?" Corelan asked, gesturing to the ring.

"Yes indeed. Odd that a thief would keep such a thing instead of selling it."

"Odd that he would keep it in his pocket."

"Agreed."

"Odd that this would be the man who managed to kill Murzahd," Corelan stated. Jack's eyebrow rose at this revelation.

"What of this envelope?" Jack asked.

"Found it on another guy. One of Kudakaan's so-called strangers."

"What is this symbol on the front?" Jack lifted the sealed envelope to examine it more closely. A wax seal bearing a pattern of four interlocking rings held the missive closed. The surface was otherwise blank. He shook the envelope slightly and held it against the lantern light. The material appeared to be paper, but it had a strange heavy feel, almost slick and leathery. Impossible to tell what was inside.

"Don't know." Corelan shrugged. "Should we have Tim see if he can psychic anything out of it?"

Jack looked at the envelope for another moment, his eyes glittering. "Maybe we take a peek inside ourselves first," he answered with a wink.

"Go for it."

Jack examined the wax seal closely one last time and pressed on it. Nothing happened. Corelan watched as the other man struggled to break the wax.

"Having trouble?" Corelan cracked a half-smile.

"It won't break." Jack pressed it against the corner of the bar. "This is not an ordinary envelope."

"Clearly." Corelan gestured for the envelope. He took the missive, examined it for a moment, then placed it on the bar. He lifted Lena's heavy whiskey glass and pounded the corner against the seal. Not even a mark. "Ok. Well, I dunno what to tell you." Corelan handed the envelope back to Jack, who produced a short knife from his belt.

"There's more than one way to get into a letter." He attempted to slip the point of the knife into a crack either under the seal or along the seam of the paper. No luck. Jack ground his teeth in frustration and tried to slice through the paper with the sharp edge. Still nothing, He stabbed the point of the knife repeatedly into first the seal and then the body of the envelope itself. Not a mark was made.

"Looks like a secret." Corelan shrugged.

"Definitely sealed with magic somehow," Jack stated, offering the envelope back to Corelan.

"Naah. You keep it." Corelan waved it away.

"You sure?"

"I don't want it." Corelan shook his head, trying and failing to care about the mysterious indestructible envelope. "Don't know what any of this means." He gestured to the ring and the envelope. "Just more trouble. Probably has nothing to do with us," Corelan sighed. He took a swig directly from the bottle and offered it to Jack. He waved it away. "What do you think?"

"Not sure." Jack examined the symbols on the ring's face again. "We are sent on a secret mission under circumstances that to me seemed fishy. Duke Pendor says he was looking for professionals to complete a job, but he automatically accepts any and all takers. Wouldn't he at least have a set number of contractors in mind? Or some minimum qualification?" Corelan smirked unconsciously both at Jack's subtle comment on Corelan's apparent lack of qualifications and at his euphemism for mercenaries. "We undertake this noble quest but are kept totally in the dark by our supposed leader. On the way out of town, we take a bad road that everyone avoids with good reason. On this bad road, our illustrious leader has a burst of intuition that he should range ahead, happens to run into two complete strangers, one of whom is carrying a magically secured secret letter. Stop me when something seems strange," Jack added sarcastically.

Corelan stoppered the bottle and put it back on the shelf.

"The bandits had dismounted. If they were chasing the two fellows, then why dismount? Not much for supplies and hardly any cash either. Not even enough coinage to buy one meal for the lot of them. But one guy has a gold ring stashed in his pocket, which could feed them all for a month. This is the one who killed our man. Or so Kudakaan says because he was the only one who saw Murzahd fall. Never mind the mysterious indestructible envelope."

"What are you getting at?"

"Nothing." Jack leaned back. "I was just stating the facts as I saw them." Jack pushed the ring back toward Corelan. "At least hang on to this. You found it, so it's yours. Could probably get a reasonable price for it somewhere."

"Okay." Corelan scooped the ring from the bar. "You really think this job has gone bad already?"

"Maybe I am just letting my personal distaste for Kudakaan color my perception. Hell, it could be nothing. Did you mention your… findings to our boss?" Jack asked.

"Didn't want to bother him," Corelan smirked.

"Agreed. The man is far too busy for such trivial matters," Jack agreed. "What are your thoughts concerning the other members of our little troop?" He gestured with the envelope as he slipped it inside of his jacket.

"Would you prefer to keep this between us?" Corelan asked as he tossed the ring from one hand to the other.

"Maybe it would be better not to burden any of them with such distractions." Jack waved his hand as if shooing away a pesky fly. "Sometimes, we can learn a lot by keeping a card or two up our sleeves."

"Yeah. No problem." Corelan shrugged. He was still somewhat surprised at himself that he hadn't turned and walked away from this job yet. Jack nodded and pushed away from the bar, heading back toward the inn. "Jack," Corelan spoke to his retreating back.

"Yeah?"

"Thanks."

"For what?"

"The last bandit. He had me."

"Life is a toss of the dice. Sometimes you win. Sometimes not. We won this time. That's it."

"Yeah. Well, thanks anyway." Jack smiled and left the room, leaving Corelan in dim silence. He looked at the whiskey splashes on the bar for a moment, then brushed them away with his sleeve and put the ring in his pocket. Maybe it was time to go. This was getting far too hairy. He was reasonably sure that the others could get along just fine without him. He would have to wait for a good opportunity to leave, probably when they were too involved in something to chase after him. Maybe he should wait until everyone was in full health. After that, then I'll bail, he thought. He stoppered his own whiskey flask, slipped it into his pocket, and snuffed the lantern.

Chapter Four

Sepday

27th of Turadmur

"The problem with morning is that it always comes so *early*."

"Shut up, Qaz."

"What time did you get to bed, Corelan?"

"Shut up, Qaz."

"Geez. Relax."

"I can't. Someone won't shut up."

"It is well past noon."

"I don't remember asking the time."

"We are having another meeting. Kudakaan says everyone needs to be there."

"You can fill me in."

"Come on. Get up. It's a beautiful day, the sun is shining, the birds are singing, little butterflies are fluttering all over the place, heavenly music is playing, flowers are blooming everywhere, beautiful women are dancing naked in the streets…" Corelan opened one eye. Qaz sat on a stool beside his bed, fully dressed in a clean white cotton shirt and brown pants, smiling at him with his freshly washed and shaven face. "Thought that would get you. Come on."

"I'll be down. Don't wait," Corelan mumbled. Qaz frowned and reached for his bed covers. "Ever had any bones broken?" Corelan asked.

"Okay, okay," Qaz said. "Five minutes. I don't want to listen to Kudakaan any longer than I have to. If you are late, I'll turn you into a toad." Qaz left the room loudly, like everything else he did. Corelan sat in bed for a moment as the last remnants of his dream faded from memory. He scarcely remembered his dreams, but when he did, they were always bad. That was why he preferred to avoid dreams altogether with the help of his little friend.

"Where are you anyway?" he asked as he rummaged through his rumpled jacket. Finding his flask, he pulled out the cork with his teeth and sipped lightly as he pulled on a shirt of questionable cleanliness. He made his way downstairs and shuffled around the corner to the small common room. The others were all seated around a low table, crowding onto the couch and chairs that lined the walls of the room. Kudakaan stood by the fireplace, clearly annoyed. Corelan wondered if he had ever seen the man when he was not annoyed at something. At least he could give Kudakaan a break from being irritated by Jack.

"Oh, thank you so much for deciding to join us." Acid nearly dripped from Kudakaan's tongue.

"All in a day's work. I like to be helpful. You may begin," Corelan said as he plopped down on a rickety wooden bench by the wall. Kudakaan fairly boiled at the remark. Fine. Boil away, jackass. As Kudakaan swallowed his anger, Corelan could see Tim struggling to keep a straight face.

"The purpose of this meeting is to address several points," Kudakaan began after a moment of vigorous swallowing. "First, Qaz and I have examined our group's injuries. He has healed those who have needed further attention. We are now all at full capacity. However, his professional opinion is that one more night's rest is required to let your bodies regain their strength. We can't afford to proceed in such a weakened state. I have devised an adjustment to our planned schedule to allow for this. We leave tomorrow at dawn to Devonshire along the quarry road." Shock registered on everyone's face at once.

"My apologies Kudakaan," Jack said. "But I could have sworn you just said we would be taking the quarry road."

"I did."

"But that…"

"Don't argue," Kudakaan snapped. Jack fell silent, striving to maintain composure. He went on in a restrained tone.

"I think, as we all probably do, that an explanation is in order."

"Why not along the same road as last time?" Lena asked. "It's roughly the same distance. The bandits are beaten." Kudakaan's face seemed to be chipped from stone.

"There are bound to be more bandits," he responded.

"Explain," she demanded.

"Why not take the north road, through Cromwood? No bandits, well-traveled… makes sense." Qaz spoke around a mouthful of apple. Where did he get the apple? Corelan's stomach growled.

"The north road is too long, and we are behind schedule already. I missed a meeting in Devonshire today. A hard ride along the quarry road leaving at first light can put us there by nightfall," Kudakaan said. Corelan wondered why no one was addressing the primary issue.

"I think what everyone is concerned about is the fact that the quarry road runs right through the heart of Troll country." Jack rose as he spoke, standing on the opposite side of the room. Scratch that last thought, Corelan mused privately.

"Our schedule dictates the need to take this road."

"You'll be a lot more than two days late for your meeting if you're dead," Jack commented.

"The Trolls won't be a problem," Kudakaan answered. Corelan looked around the room. No one else believed it either.

"What is the problem with Trolls?" Daelyn asked. "Some of my best friends are Trolls." Qaz snickered. "No, really," she added.

"This is a lot different," Tim spoke up. "While you may have met a Troll or two who has abandoned his cultural heritage, they are far from typical. The Trolls we would be riding towards are what they call *Thulkhagg Loha*. I think it means great kings of the earth, although some simplify the translation to just Rock Troll." Tim lifted a hand to indicate he was about to get to his point. "They are as different from any Troll you have met as I am. They even call the Trolls that you may have befriended 'fallen ones.' These Rock Trolls are a society unto themselves, with their own language, customs, and beliefs."

Corelan shifted his attention from the spider slowly making its way across the ceiling to look more directly at Tim. This part was news to him too. The only thing Corelan had known (as did anyone who traveled much) was that if somebody took the quarry road, they would almost certainly be killed by Trolls. One didn't really need to know more than that. Tim went on. "Rock Trolls live out in the wilderness and uphold the old ways. In their cultural tradition, the eldest males are the warrior caste.

They live solely for battle and conquest - like the Chull, only less chaotic and glory-minded. Best guess is that there are about a thousand or so living in the mountains up that way. No way can we take that road. It's suicide."

"The last significant battle against Trolls was more than a hundred years ago. There may be no one left up there," Kudakaan said in a dismissive fashion. "They also have no reason to do us harm."

"No reason?" Tim shot to his feet. "Do you have any idea why that quarry shut down when it did?" Kudakaan folded his arms and glared at the shorter man. "Rock Trolls object very strongly to the destruction of their land. Those mountains are sacred to them. So when we humans started pulling their mountains down to make paving stones for our muddy feet, they were outraged." Tim spoke passionately, looking Kudakaan right in the eye. Corelan wondered if Kudakaan was remembering what people say about making psychics upset. There was a saying – something about kissing a rabid dog on the lips.

"We did not come here for a history lesson."

"Well, it would seem you need one," Tim went on. "When they found out what we were doing up there, they came in and killed everyone in the mining town."

"Thank you, Tim…"

"Then, of course, that was like a declaration of war, so we came back and sacked their villages while all of the warriors were away." The fire burning on the small hearth behind Tim flared up suddenly. Corelan found himself growing tense.

"We? That was Balsheega the Terrible. Generations ago. He was eventually beheaded, if you recall," Kudakaan retorted casually.

"Yes, but not by Trolls, and not for any of his crimes against them. No amends have ever been offered for those atrocities.

"That is enough, Tim."

"So, despite the change in human leadership, the cycle of blood grew…"

"Make your point, Tim." Kudakaan's voice held a bit of heat. Corelan sat forward on the bench. This might prove to be an exciting meeting after all. Tim took a deep breath and continued in a more controlled tone.

"My point? There is a good reason people now get their stone elsewhere. That land belongs to the Trolls, and we will most certainly *not* be welcome." Tim sat and sighed deeply. The fire in the hearth returned to its normal size. Corelan let out the breath he had been unconsciously holding. No one burst into flames, no exploding heads. He almost felt disappointed.

"That land belongs to the king of Roth," Kudakaan responded.

"Tell that to the Trolls," Tim muttered beneath his breath.

"If I may ask," Jack began. "Do we have a plan to deal with the Trolls that we may encounter? If not, I suggest we use a different plan than the one we used on the bandits."

"Trolls are reasonable people."

"Have you ever tried to reason with three hundred pounds of angry muscle, waving a small tree over its head, hell-bent on your destruction?" Tim asked.

"Trolls are like anyone else. They will do what is most profitable," Kudakaan answered coldly.

"Can I ask what the hell any of this means?" Corelan interjected. This meeting was going nowhere, and he was getting hungry.

"What it all means is this." Kudakaan had lost his icy tone and spoke with genuine anger in his voice. "We are taking the quarry road to Devonshire. There is no room for discussion. Anyone who will not be joining us can give me your two hundred and fifty silver right now and talk to this town's constable about breaching an official contract. I refuse to explain myself any further. You all work for me and will do as I say. Are there any questions?" Corelan lifted his hand. Kudakaan locked a furious glare on him.

"We leave at dawn?" he asked.

"Yes," Kudakaan replied more calmly.

"Great. I'll see you then. I'm hungry." Corelan stood and walked into the tavern next door. He was unsure if he meant to leave toward Devonshire with the group in the morning or by himself in another direction at the time of his choosing. He had all night to decide anyway.

"Any other questions?" Kudakaan asked the group. He was met with silence. "Then you are dismissed. Anyone with injuries, see Qaz."

* * * * *

Jack watched Corelan walk past into the adjoining tavern without looking back. For some reason, he enjoyed the other man's lack of subtlety. Refreshing. Corelan also had a valid point. It was definitely time to eat. He stood, looking over at Uglor, who was nearly always hungry.

"Jack. Come here for a moment," Kudakaan said. Jack paused and motioned for Uglor to proceed without him. Uglor headed toward the front door, in the direction of the sandwich shop they had spied during their previous stay here. Most of the others had decided to follow Corelan's lead on this pressing new topic and followed him into the adjoining tavern. Jack walked over to Kudakaan.

"Yes?" He suspected that he knew what was coming but decided to pretend otherwise.

"Yesterday, I instructed you to stay with the others when I ranged ahead. You didn't."

"Begging your pardon, sir, but you instructed us to attend to our needs," Jack answered. "I felt like I needed to watch your back." Kudakaan surprisingly swallowed his ire.

"Ok. Then where were you yesterday, when the fight was thickest? I saw everyone contributing but you," Kudakaan asked in a low controlled voice.

"I don't participate in pitched battles. I thought I had made it clear at our first meeting that isn't how I work." Kudakaan opened his mouth to respond, but Jack lifted a finger. "Hear me out. Please." Kudakaan grudgingly nodded. "You may recall a well-placed knife when you had your back to an embankment." Kudakaan nodded again. "That is how I add value to a conflict. Once the situation with the primary body of bandits had moved into the purview of the fighters in our group, I had little else to contribute." Kudakaan looked down at the smaller man, his face sneering with contempt. "You may not approve, and frankly, I don't give a damn."

"Did you know that there were actually three bandits with longbows?" Jack asked. "No?" Kudakaan squared his shoulders, losing some of his resolve. "I took care of two of them in the woods before they ever got to you. Quiet, knife work. If I had done what you are suggesting, and jumped into the primary conflict, then all three archers would have swooped in on you, not just the one. I would have been already dead in the melee, and the archers would have cleaned out at least two or three more before it was all over with," Jack finished, crossing his arms. "If you want to blame me for what happened to Murzahd, then I can't stop you. Believe what you want. I don't care." Kudakaan looked down at him for a few moments before he spoke.

"I need you to obey my orders."

"I have no problem with following orders, so long as I can trust the source," Jack answered.

"I need you to cooperate."

"Cast me in the proper role, and I'll make you proud," Jack followed.

"I need you to hold your tongue. If you have a problem, approach me privately. We need harmony in the group."

"Done." Jack extended a hand. Kudakaan hesitantly took it. "Believe it or not, I do want this to work," he finished with a smile. "So, what are the plans for the rest of the day?"

"Qaz is going to send for the Guild to collect Murzahd's body," Kudakaan responded. "They will contact the family and make funeral arrangements. Those in need will acquire some fresh horses and supplies. The injured will rest and recover." Jack nodded. "Also," Kudakaan continued. "Given that we have a deceased body with us, and this is known to several outside of our group, I have decided to leave a statement with the local sheriff. I will craft the conversation in such a way as to properly balance our legal obligations with our need for privacy. I don't want him sniffing at our heels investigating Murzahd's death."

"Sounds reasonable," Jack replied. "Once you have a story concocted, it seems prudent to share any… alternate perspectives on yesterday's events with the rest of us." Jack lifted a finger to stay Kudakaan's objection. "Our stories should match in case the sheriff gets bored and wants to investigate further." Kudakaan nodded begrudgingly. "Regarding this afternoon, Uglor can help you manage the supplies if you need him."

"Excellent."

"Then, if that is all, Uglor and I will get something to eat, and then he will find you." Jack watched Kudakaan's retreating back and felt a light touch on his arm. Jack turned with a forced smile on his lips.

"Hello, Tim."

"Hi, Jack. I am concerned," Tim began.

"If it's about the Trolls…"

"It's about Uglor." Jack's smile quickly faded.

"What about him?"

"As soon as Trolls were mentioned, he got very nervous."

"What makes you say that?" Jack asked. He did not like this line of questioning.

"I am a psychic, remember."

"Go on."

"He got profoundly worried. He nearly panicked. It was so strong I got caught up in it myself."

"What are you asking me?"

"Is there something we should know here?" Tim asked hesitantly. Jack's face went blank for a moment, lost in thought. He looked around and lowered his voice.

"I won't go into detail because frankly, it isn't any of your business, but I will tell you this." He wet his lips. "Uglor has some Troll blood in him."

"That explains a few things," Tim responded. "But wait a sec, Rock Trolls don't traditionally intermarry. Very concerned about the purity of blood," Tim went on, confused slightly.

"Exactly. You fill in the rest. I'd prefer you keep this to yourself also."

"If we meet some Trolls…"

"Let's hope we don't."

"Hmm. Thank you, Jack." Tim turned away and went out the front door, no doubt to see if he could catch up with Daelyn to include himself with her lunch plans. Jack frowned and headed toward the street to catch up with his friend.

* * * * *

Corelan, Qaz, and Lena had occupied a table against the far wall of the tavern and sat in relative silence, waiting for their lunch to arrive. Fortunately, the ale they had ordered had come out quickly enough, and the three had found a moment to relax. Corelan spared a glance at the large wood and brass nameplate above the bar. *Dargram's Tavern.* Dargram must serve a decent meal, he thought as the lunch crowd had filled the place near to capacity.

"So Qaz," Corelan tipped his chair back on two legs, leaning against the wall of the tavern, soliciting a creak of protest from the battered wood. "I have been meaning to ask, what exactly can you do?"

"What do you mean? With magic?" Qaz responded, pouring himself a mug of ale.

"Yeah." Corelan took the pitcher from his companion and filled Lena's mug. "It's never been clear to me."

"What hasn't?" Qaz asked.

"Like, what is the difference between what Tim does and your magic?" Corelan pushed the newly filled mug across the table toward Lena and went to fill his own mug.

"I've got one too," Lena added, lifting her mug with a nod of thanks. "I have known a few people in the Derwij Conclave. I got the impression their magic has to do with nature, but I'm not sure what the deal is. Is that fundamentally different from what you do?" Qaz smiled and took a long pull from his mug, thinking.

"Do you want the quick and easy answer?" he asked. Corelan sighed. He knew the alternative was probably going to take a while. He waved at the serving girl across the crowded and dusty tavern and gestured to their nearly empty pitcher. She nodded in response.

"Do you actually have a quick and easy answer?" Lena asked with a sarcastic grin.

"No," Qaz admitted.

"Then give us the long one," Corelan said. He wasn't going anywhere just yet anyway, and the mental exercise might do him good.

"I promise I'll keep it as short as possible," Qaz lied. "There are four basic schools of magic," he began, leaning forward on the table. "First, you've got standard magic, or wizardry, which is what I do. It is subdivided into two categories, wizards and mages, but I'll get to that in a minute." He paused to sip his beer.

"You are a mage, right?" Lena asked. "As opposed to a wizard."

"Correct," Qaz answered. "You have Psychics, like Tim. And then there are the Derwij, which, as Lena has mentioned, base their magic on the forces of nature. Lastly, there are the Forcemasters, who manipulate raw magical energy." Corelan took a sip of his own ale, absorbing the information.

"So, what is the difference?" Lena asked.

"I'm getting to that," Qaz responded. "Roughly speaking, the primary difference between the schools of magic is in their sources of energy and how the energy is manipulated. Without getting too deep into magical theory, I'll start by saying the world around us is made of seven elements – four substances and three energies. These can, to varying degrees, be controlled by the power of the mind."

"Whose mind?" Corelan asked.

"Anybody, really," Qaz answered.

"I thought you had to be born with a special gift or something," Lena responded.

"Well, yes and no." Qaz made a vacillating gesture with his hands. "Some people are born with more aptitude, but anyone can learn if they try hard enough."

"Explain," Lena asked.

"It's like anything else. Take fighting, for example. You have a guy like Uglor who is born with obvious advantages in a fight; he's bigger, stronger, better reach, and so on. For him, learning to fight is easy. Then you take a smaller guy, like a Jaan or an Azrak." He gestured to a striped-skinned Jaan across the tavern, who was sitting at a table nearby. His short legs swayed energetically beneath his chair, almost reaching the floor. "They can learn to fight as well as anyone else; they just have to put in a lot more effort and training."

"Ah. I see," Lena said. "So, what you are implying is that if I practice and concentrate hard enough, I can make things happen?" She asked, skepticism clearly showing in her voice.

"It's not that simple," Qaz responded. "Direct manipulation like that takes too much energy. Nobody has that kind of mental prowess."

"I thought that was how it was done back in the day," Corelan added. He had read a history book somewhere that described all kinds of seemingly impossible things and attributed them to magic.

"That was before the Backlash," Qaz explained. "The Old Magic was kind of like that. You could achieve certain magical effects essentially through sheer force of will. People *used* to be born with that kind of ability."

"But not anymore?" Corelan asked.

"It was a hereditary trait, and when the Backlash occurred, everyone who could use magic that way died."

"Causing the First Apocalypse," Lena added. "Everything that used magic stopped working if I remember my history lessons."

"Exactly," Qaz said. "Back then, magic was the backbone of society. Nearly everything ran on magic in some way. Take the famous floating cities…"

"What the hell is the Backlash?" Corelan asked, trying to get back on topic. He, of course, had heard the fables of ancient floating cities like every other child. He expected Qaz to have accepted them as fables like most reasonable adults.

"Oh, sorry." Qaz shrugged. "Direct manipulation of magical energy transcends the boundary between the substantial and insubstantial realms. Especially when you tie off a chunk of energy for a permanent application. It causes tension on the barrier, and eventually, over the course of centuries, the accumulated strain grew to be too much, and the barrier snapped. All energy returned to its natural state in one big bang, and it was lethal to anyone in contact with the other realm."

"Okay, you completely lost me," Corelan admitted. "Insubstantial what?"

"Sorry." Qaz shrugged. "Would you prefer I avoid heavy Magic Theory?"

"I don't even know what that means, but yes," Corelan answered. "And never mind." Corelan dismissed his question. He got the gist of it, if not the details. Even if the details were based on childhood fairy tales.

"So, hang on, if everybody that knew magic died, how come people can still do magic?" Lena asked. This was getting complicated. Corelan looked around the tavern, searching for the barmaid, who owed them a pitcher of ale.

"Well, everyone that could *directly* manipulate magic died. Except for… you know what, never mind him. For the most part, the people who survived were those poor unprivileged few who had to do it the hard way," Qaz explained.

"What do you mean?" Lena asked.

"The way we do it today." Qaz lifted a hand. "I won't burden you with the technical explanation, but we essentially leave magical energies in the insubstantial… uh, the world of magic… and use their effects indirectly."

"Lost again," Corelan added, draining the last of his ale. He spotted the barmaid approaching with a fresh pitcher in hand. Ahh, come to papa, he thought.

"It doesn't really matter, and it brings me to the difference between wizards and mages, which I believe was part of your original question anyway."

"Indeed." Corelan bit off a curse as the serving girl placed the pitcher on another table beside them and turned away without sparing a glance.

"The majority of magic practitioners are what we call mages. Granted, some of them get all high and mighty and call themselves sorcerers or whatever, but the word 'wizard' is reserved by the Guild for people who have taken and passed certain tests." Qaz glanced over his shoulder, searching the tavern for the missing barmaid.

"She is working on it," Lena interjected. "Get back to the point."

"Right." Qaz nodded. "To invoke magic, the vast majority of the time anyway, you are casting a prewritten spell. Somebody else, a wizard, sat down and figured out how to make something happen and worked out a formula to do it consistently. The mages of the world rely solely on the spells that they can buy, beg, or steal to get anything done."

"Is it like a bunch of magic words or something?" Corelan asked.

"Sort of," Qaz responded. "With proper training, the words can be associated with complex mental processes, which would then manipulate the energy flows. A string of words would serve in place of the mental exercise and therefore cause the effect. Words alone won't do it. You have to know what they mean." Corelan scratched his head, unsure what any of that meant.

"So, your magic is limited to those spells you have in your possession?" Lena asked.

"Exactly."

"So, if you could get your hands on a big stack of spellbooks…" Corelan began.

"Well, we don't really use books so much anymore."

"Oh?" Lena asked. "Why not?"

"A wizard doesn't like to have the sum total of his abilities all written down where anyone can come along and read it. Writing out a spell is labor-intensive and prone to more potential errors. Plus, a lot of the words, pardon the pun, are difficult to spell."

"Okay, well, what do you use instead of books?" Corelan asked, wondering how a person could devise a word that no one can spell.

"We use spell gems." He produced a pouch from his pocket and pulled out a small, semitransparent blue stone about the size of a hazelnut. "Like this." Lena squinted and gazed at the stone intensely.

"May I?" she asked, extending her hand.

"Sure." Qaz handed over the stone.

"So, how does this work?" she asked, examining the stone closely.

"You hold the stone up to your eye and let some light shine through it," he explained. Lena held the stone close and peered at a nearby window.

"All I see is blue," she stated.

"Well, with training, you can see a pattern of lines or shapes. The shapes are like words, and a mage can read them."

"So, it's like your own language," Corelan stated. The barmaid caught his eye as she approached their table with a frothy pitcher.

"Yes, but words aren't made of letters. Each word has its own pattern."

"Then why not just draw the shapes out in a book? Seems pointlessly complicated to embed them in crystal," Lena stated, still peering through the stone.

"To be quite frank, spell books are really heavy. The words to the spell you are holding in your hand would take several pages to write out, and to carry all the spells I have in this small pouch would require a pretty large volume. It's just not convenient for travel or field work to carry around a stack of heavy books."

"How can you fit that much writing into a tiny crystal?" Corelan asked.

"As you spin the gem, different patterns and be seen, and the shapes themselves are three-dimensional," Qaz stated, sparing a congenial grin for the young serving girl as she placed the ale on their table. "Saves a lot of space. You could try to draw them out on paper, instead of writing the words out phonetically, but drawing three dimensional shapes in two dimensions is more difficult to render accurately and more prone to subjective perception."

"Oh." Lena handed the stone back to Qaz. "Still seems like books would be easier."

"So, in answer to your question Corelan, no."

"Which question?"

"If I got my hands on another mage's collection of spell gems, would I have all of his powers."

"Why not?" Corelan asked. He lifted the pitcher and began to distribute its contents.

"Some spells are more difficult to invoke than others. Some require more power than I can control. I might not recognize all of the characters in the spell. A lot of reasons." He took his newly refilled mug from the table and paused as he took a long sip. "But if you find a stash of spell gems, it is quite likely that you will be able to use at least a few."

"What do you mean by more power?" Lena asked.

"Using magic is in a lot of ways like exercising any other part of your body. In the short term, it makes you really tired. But, in the long run, the more you do it, the stronger you will become."

"Okay, that is the first thing you said that makes sense to me," Corelan admitted.

"Now, Qaz, I have seen people use magic dozens of times, and this is the first time I am hearing about a spell gem," Lena said, taking on a scolding tone.

"You don't need the gem to invoke magic, just to learn the spell," Qaz explained.

"So, once you have the spell, why keep the stone?" Corelan asked.

"You need to be sure you are getting the spell one hundred percent correct," Qaz stated gravely. "A slight error could have…" He trailed off, searching for the correct word. "…unforeseen complications. It is important to refresh the mind as often as possible."

"I see," Lena said. "So, you never explained the difference between being a mage and a psychic."

"Well, I can't speak with absolute authority on the subject, but I can lay out the basic differences."

"Does the answer involve the use of the word 'insubstantial'?" Corelan asked.

"No." Qaz laughed.

"Then go ahead."

"A psychic's powers are divided into three categories."

"Is there going to be a quiz later?" Corelan asked. "I can't help but feel like I am back in school." Lena very nearly choked on her ale.

"No quiz." Qaz laughed. "And you asked. The three categories, I think they call them realms of the psyche or something, are Psychokinetics, Divination, and…" He paused, scratching his head. "Well, I forget the name of the third, but it is like psychic combat."

"Hold on," Lena interjected. "I thought some psychics could control people with their minds."

"Oh yeah," Qaz replied. "I guess that makes four." He shrugged, dismissing Lena's flat look. "So anyway, Divination is the stuff that creeps people out. Like reading minds, or knowing things for no reason, getting impressions, and so forth. Psychokinetics involves using the power of the mind to either move things or set them on fire."

"Hold on, this psycho-kina-whatever; moving things or setting them on fire? That sounds like two totally different powers to me," Corelan responded.

"Yeah, me too, but I'm told they are actually quite similar in practice," Qaz said.

"So, you really don't know that much about psychics," Lena stated.

"No, not really," Qaz answered with a shrug.

"Then skip it. I'll ask Tim later," she stated.

"Fine. What else?" Qaz asked.

"So, what about these forcemaster people?" Lena asked. "I worked with a forcemaster once guarding a merchant caravan for a month, but we were never attacked, so I didn't get to see anything."

"Forcemasters directly manipulate chunks of raw energy," Qaz began.

"Didn't you just say a minute ago that nobody can do that anymore?" Corelan asked. His head was beginning to hurt, causing him to regret having broached the subject in the first place.

"Well, nobody can do that and get anything really intricate done. And it isn't the same thing anyway."

"You need to explain that a bit more," Lena stated.

"Forcemasters have a short list of things they can do with their magic. Most of it involves blasting energy around in bursts. If a mage's powers are like a surgeon's scalpel, then a forcemaster's are like a wood axe. Only so much you can do."

"Ah," Corelan replied. "Still seems like you are contradicting yourself."

"The energy *they* use is already on the material side of the divide between realms. To explain further requires the use of the word insubstantial," Qaz offered. "And, I haven't even touched on the seven elements."

"Then save it."

"So, here's a question." Lena set her mug down on the table and looked Qaz squarely in the eye. "If forcemastery is so limited, why does anybody lean it?"

"Two reasons." Qaz smiled. "It is *so* much faster than magic. A forcemaster can fling a bolt of energy at you in the blink of an eye. Some even combine it with swordsmanship to give their blades a little extra punch. We mages just can't cast a spell that fast, no matter how simple." Lena nodded as she absorbed the statement.

"You said there were two reasons?" she asked.

"Oh yeah, and number two, if you want to chop down a tree, would you rather use a scalpel or an axe?"

"I see." Lena sat back in her chair and lifted her mug to her lips. Corelan got the impression she regretted never having seen her forcemaster friend in action.

"So that leaves the Derwij Conclave, which I know very little about other than their magic, as Lena has already stated, involves the manipulation of natural forces, like trees and plants and weather and stuff." Qaz made a dismissing gesture and took a long pull from his mug. Corelan looked at his own mug and suddenly felt a need for something a bit stiffer. Some Velkasian whiskey, perhaps. "Does that clear things up for you guys?" Qaz asked.

"Clear as mud," Corelan responded, pushing himself up from the table. "Remind me to never bring it up again." He drained the last of his mug in a single gulp and let the conversation drop as their food arrived. Whiskey was definitely in order. Kudakaan had instructed them to relax after all.

By nightfall, Corelan found himself returned to the bar in Dargram's Tavern (now thoroughly relaxed) sitting beside Jack, who had some catching up to do, relaxation-wise. Corelan had spent most of the afternoon milling around the small town, wandering aimlessly. Lena had tried to assemble a group to go horse shopping with her, but he had politely declined. If Kudakaan wants us to rest, then that's just what I'll do, he thought. It had been a perfect day for a stroll. A cool breeze offset the warm afternoon sun perfectly. He had spent a good portion of his idle time relaxing on his back in a grassy field just outside of town, gazing at the sky, watching the clouds drift by. Jack, however, had wasted his time today mentally struggling with the large tangled puzzle that had materialized out of what had started out to be a straightforward (albeit fishy) job. The only conclusion Jack was eventually able to share, though, was that he needed more information, and none would be forthcoming until they got on with things. Jack shook his head and sighed, sipping the beer he didn't want, grimacing slightly at its bitter taste.

"Damn. I guess you aren't a drinker," Corelan said. He had insisted on buying Jack a beer, citing Kudakaan's explicit orders to relax.

"Well, thanks anyway," Jack offered, pushing the mug away from him. "So, do anything interesting or constructive today?"

"Other than napping in a field?" Corelan asked. "I made the gross error of asking Qaz to explain the world of magic."

"How did that go?" Jack asked with a half-smile.

"Not quickly enough."

"Learn anything?"

"Nope." Corelan finished his own beer and looked longingly at Jack's abandoned mug.

"Go ahead. You bought it." Jack shifted on his barstool, turning to face the tavern's occupants as Corelan seized the abandoned mug and downed the remainder. The bar was getting crowded and noisy. Travelers from all walks of life had made their way to this tavern from the adjoining inn.

"Okay. Out with it," Corelan suggested.

"Sorry?" Jack asked.

"Something is on your mind. You do this wrinkly eyebrow thing when you are about to say something important."

"Fair," Jack conceded. "I'm just trying to make sense out of taking the quarry road. Even if it is a tiny bit faster, we still aren't in Devonshire before dusk. And if he's in that much of a hurry, why agree to waiting the day here?"

"Maybe he is just an idiot," Corelan joked. "Your eyebrows are still bunched up. You've got more."

"Kudakaan left town," Jack said. "Uglor and I were organizing supplies in the stable and noticed his horse was gone. He left almost immediately after our meeting and still hasn't returned as of an hour ago."

"Huh." Corelan scratched his unshaven chin. "You think he went back to Roth for some reason?"

"Possibly," Jack responded. "It matches the timetable."

"I'm not sure that I care, though." Corelan appreciated Jack's dedication to analyzing everything, but in all honesty, he didn't really care what Kudakaan was up to, so long as he intended to pay out the contracts as promised. Jack arched his neck as he spied a plate of roasted potatoes gliding past in the hands of a young serving girl.

"I'm definitely going to need those potatoes," Jack announced. Corelan tried to follow the path of the heavenly roast through the room but found his gaze landing on a pair of lovely young Selyr women sitting at the end of the bar. Their slightly tilted green eyes scanned the room, possibly looking for stimulating conversation. Perhaps Akeela wasn't such as sleepy little town after all. Jack hopped off of his stool.

"I should have expected to find you here, Corelan," Lena said, having appeared out of nowhere. "Oh, hi Jack." Jack looked back toward the kitchen.

"Hello, Lena. Say Corelan, why don't you buy Lena a drink. Excuse me."

"Where is he going?" she asked Corelan, scanning the other side of the bar as he crossed the room.

"Divine quest for potatoes."

"Ooh, I saw those! They looked good."

"Uh, yeah." Corelan turned away from the Selyr women across the bar. They were trying to ignore the advances of a large red-faced man with an oversized nose. He was making that a difficult task.

"You ok?" she asked. Corelan nodded and gestured to the vacant stool. She sat and leaned onto the bar, slapping its surface sharply with her palm. The bartender looked over and nodded quickly. "So, how about that drink?" she asked. Corelan set his beer on the bar.

"What will it be, pretty lady?" the bartender asked. He wiped a glass with a white cloth and stashed it beneath the bar as he spoke.

"A Whiskey Warhammer. And save the pretty lady crap."

"You got it." He turned to Corelan. "Sir?"

"One more of these. And hers is on me." The bartender fell to his appointed task.

"How was the rest of your day?" Corelan asked.

"Qaz and I went to the Free Blade's Guild chapter house here in town to see about Murzahd's body," she answered solemnly. "His clan didn't have any representation here, but the Guild should be able to contact them."

"Clan?" Corelan asked. He knew Ialu had a complex hierarchy but not much beyond that.

"He was Fist of the North," she stated. "You didn't know that?"

"We didn't talk much."

"You don't talk much to anyone," she added. "He was also a Knight of Maudex, but I think his clan affiliation takes precedence." She read the blank look on Corelan's face. "I spent some time among Ialu. Another fellow I knew took some time to explain their tattoo lore. You can learn a lot about someone if you pay attention."

"Okay. I'm paying attention now," he began. "You said he was a Knight or something?"

"The Knights of Maudex. Are you familiar with them?"

"Isn't that like a social club where a bunch of guys drink beer, wear funny hats, and come up with secret handshakes?"

"Really?" Lena shook her head, brushing a lock of hair behind her ear. She wore a loose white cotton tunic that was so immaculate that it had to be new. She smelled faintly of lavender soap. "There is a lot more to it," she said.

"Do tell."

"It's a quasi-military organization with members in nearly every major city. They concern themselves with current affairs and politics, and if you weren't rolling your eyes right now, I'd tell you more." Her icy blue eyes regarded him with their usual challenging look. The bartender arrived with their drinks, placing them down with a smile.

"Sorry," He offered. "The word 'politics' automatically turns my brain off."

"When is it ever on?" Lena asked. She folded her arms and crossed her legs, tapping the heel of her boot on the wooden stool. She gave him a smirk across the lip of her glass. Just then, the red-faced man stumped over and lurched to a sudden and wobbly halt, standing and breathing loudly beside Lena. He swayed slightly, reeking of cheap whiskey. He leered at Lena, his eyes drifting in and out of focus.

"Say, that's a pretty little outfit you got on," he slurred. "Can I talk you out of it?" He chuckled in amusement at his own razor wit. Lena fixed a cold gaze on him, sizing him up.

"You seem very confused. Are you lost?" she asked.

"Huh?" The man wobbled and shot his hand out to stabilize himself on the back of Lena's stool. She leaned away from him and uncrossed her legs, placing one boot on the floor.

"Beat it," Corelan said, putting his hand on the man's forearm. Lena gave him an angry look.

"I can handle this, thank you," she said tersely.

"It's okay…" Corelan began.

"Back off," she said, looking Corelan straight in the eye. She was clearly angry about something.

"You heard the lady," The man jerked his arm free. "Back off." He shot his arm around Lena's shoulder and pulled her roughly into his hairy chest. "She is with me." Lena shifted her weight on her stool to get both feet on the ground and began to pull away. The man turned to smile at her and therefore did not see Corelan's fist connect squarely with his jaw. His head snapped backward, and he staggered several steps back.

Corelan stood dumbfounded, staring at his own hand, equally surprised. The punch happened instinctively as if his fist had decided to begin making his own decisions and act independently of Corelan's wishes. The man shook his head to regain his focus.

"Corelan!" Lena shouted.

"I… Uh…" Corelan looked around wildly as if someone with a reasonable explanation was standing close by, waiting for the proper moment to rationalize what just happened. The copper-haired man that Corelan had just inexplicably punched found his bearings, and his face began twisting in a rage.

"Big mistake, little man," he growled. He lunged at Corelan, grasping with both hands toward his throat.

"Dammit," Corelan muttered to himself. Definitely my fault this time, he thought to himself. As his opponent strode forward, Corelan splashed the contents of his newly filled beer mug into his face and brushed his attacker's arm away, closing off his attack and diverting the force of his rush away to the left. The crowd parted swiftly. A woman screamed as the large man toppled heavily into a table of highly displeased patrons.

"Corelan, what the hell!" Lena yelled at him, but he found himself preoccupied with the entirely unjustified fight his own hand had started without him. The larger man threw several wild punches, swinging with the wide, clumsy motions of a drunk. Corelan gave ground, easily evading the slow attacks, drawing the man toward the front door. A pair of burly men rushed out from behind the bar and fought the crowd toward the conflict. Corelan dropped back further, drawing his opponent into ever-increasing boldness, bringing them closer to the tavern's front entrance.

Both doors had been propped open to let the cooler evening air wash through the establishment. As Corelan backed toward the threshold, he planted his feet suddenly and seized the other man's wrist as he reached the apex of another clumsy punch. Corelan rooted his stance and pulled his opponent toward the door, placing his other hand behind the shoulder. He pivoted in place, sending the large man through the doorway with all their force combined. He managed to take one desperate step before flailing helplessly through the air, over the steps, and down into the dirt of the street below.

"Corelan! Stop!" Lena grabbed him by the arm and spun him to face her. "What the hell is wrong with you!" She was livid. He himself had little notion of what just happened. He stood silently in the doorway, his heart thumping loudly in his ear as he looked at the stunned faces of the tavern's patrons who gaped back at him. It seemed that someone else had just gone completely mad and taken off running, leaving Corelan alone to explain. What the hell *was* wrong with him? He looked at Lena, who had a hand full of his sleeve balled in her fist. He moved his mouth, hoping an explanation would fall out and he could find out himself what the hell just happened.

He heard himself mumble something incoherent. Think man! Say something! With an exasperated curse, she put both hands on his chest and shoved him, sending him backpedaling through the front door onto the porch. He stumbled on the steps, half falling to the dirt street where he landed on his back with a solid thump. She burst through the door, taking all three stairs in one stride. She closed on him and knelt on his chest, seizing a fistful of his rumpled shirt.

"I can take care of myself," she hissed through tightly clenched teeth. She pushed him down and stood. Corelan could hear her growl with frustration as she stormed off down the street. He propped himself up on his elbows and shook his head to clear it. Of the red-faced man, there was no sign. Four beefy hands clamped down on his arms and hauled him to his feet. Corelan found himself eye to eye with two very large and very displeased employees of Dargram's Tavern.

"I've got it from here, gentlemen," a voice said. Jack slid up beside Corelan, smiling. "This irate young troublemaker is a friend of mine. We were just leaving."

"He has to go to the constable," one of them said.

"Oh goodness, I didn't realize you were police officers." Jack put up his hands defensively. "I guess we have to go to the station to straighten this out."

"We aren't cops," the other said.

"Oh?" Jack arched an eyebrow.

"No, we work here," the taller of the two added, jerking a thumb toward the tavern.

"You aren't policemen?" Jack asked again, leaning forward slightly. Corelan looked to the ground, trying to remain as unobtrusive as possible. He wasn't sure where Jack was going, but he seemed to have something in mind.

"No." The taller man looked questioningly at Jack.

"Then how can you justify arresting my friend?" he asked them.

"We aren't *arresting* him. He started a fight."

"In the bar?"

"Yes, in the bar! You saw it."

"Need I point out that we are no longer in the bar?" The tall man looked around the street. His face twisted slightly as he struggled with this concept.

"So?" he cleverly retorted.

"So, you have no jurisdiction. You have to let him go."

"What?"

"Inside the tavern, you are security men. If he goes back into the bar, you can take him to the constable. Out here, you are regular citizens." Jack looked at the men and shook his finger at them in a scolding manner. "You can't go around town taking people to the authorities any time you want, now can you?"

"Uh, no… but…"

"So, you have to let him go."

"But…"

"But nothing. If you're not going to let him go, then we should *all* go to the constable, and you can explain how you have decided to spontaneously deputize yourselves. You can explain that he apparently isn't doing his job well enough, and he needs your help to round up troublemakers. You can tell him that you will be arresting random people off of the streets and hauling them off to jail on a whim." Jack put his hands on his hips. "Come on. Let's go. I would like to hear what he has to say to that." The two men let go of Corelan's arms. He stood quietly between them, wondering how in the hell that had worked.

"Just take your friend home, and don't come back," the shorter of the two said. As they walked back into the bar, Corelan scanned the dark, night streets for the red-faced man. There was still no sign. Jack sighed deeply.

"Wow," Corelan said, brushing dust from his sleeves.

"What the hell is your problem!" Jack shouted. Corelan took an involuntary step back.

"That guy…" he trailed off. Honestly, he had no idea.

"That guy, what?" Jack asked. Corelan did not answer. He felt like he had only watched the incident, and someone else had gone berserk and assaulted a stranger for no good reason. "Yes, that guy was just a drunk jackass, but that does not entitle you to punch him in the face! Are you some kind of psycho?" Jack lowered his voice slightly. "You will not do anything like that again, do you understand?" Corelan looked at the ground, his face hard, lost for a moment in thought. It had never been this bad before. He turned away and began to walk down the street. "Hey, we are not finished." Jack took hold of Corelan's shoulder. Corelan's arm whipped a tight circle around Jack's, throwing his grip off. He pressed his palm into Jack's chest and pushed him to the ground. He continued walking off without looking back or saying a word. Jack sat on the ground where he fell, waving the dust from his face, muttering to himself.

* * * * *

Daelyn gently sprinkled fine sand on the paper to absorb any excess ink. She looked over the page she had just spent the last two hours encoding. Three-character variable indeed; what a colossal pain. She really did not have much to report. She knew they were headed to Devonshire. There was supposed to be a meeting, but she didn't know with whom or why. They had been in a fight with bandits for no apparent reason. Nobody liked Kudakaan. These were the facts. She had nothing but hunches and suspicions regarding who the king's agent might be. Probably not Corelan; the man just didn't seem to care enough. Murzahd was dead, so if it was him, it didn't matter much now. As for anybody else, it was still pure conjecture.

She folded her report and slid a stick of sealing wax into the candle flame. As she sealed the message closed, stamping her own mark into the hot wax, she looked around the small room she shared with Lena. The two narrow beds sat to either side of the small writing desk, at which she now sat. Their things lay in neat piles at the foot of each bed. She looked out of the window in front of her into the night streets. She felt the faint twinge of guilt as she encoded directions on the envelope, using a standard Underground cipher instructing for it to be directed straight to the Master's desk. Was she betraying these new friends?

"Companions," she said softly to herself. "Travelling companions only." A knock on the door disturbed her reflection. She stood quickly, slipping the message into the folds of her jacket, which hung on a peg by the door. She smoothed the front of her skirts and grimaced inwardly. She hated skirts and dresses of any kind. They were impractical and made moving cumbersome. She reminded herself of the role she played, and this choice for casual fashion helped sell her cover as a Toctillian citizen. She crossed the room and cracked the door slightly. Tim stood in the hall, hands clasped politely behind his back, smiling with a boyish grin. Let a man see a pretty face and a coy smile, and his tongue would flap in the breeze. Not that anyone's tongue flapping so far had been worth listening to.

"So, uh, have you eaten dinner yet?" he asked. She smiled inwardly. Tim really was a nice fellow, very genuine. She opened the door fully and leaned on the frame, tilting her head slightly.

"Not yet. Have you?" she responded, slipping back into her accent.

"Not yet. I was wondering…"

"I'd love to." She retrieved her jacket, conscious of the letter in the pocket. "Where shall we go? Downstairs?"

"The tavern? I thought I saw a small café on the other end of town. The tavern might be too rowdy." He paused for a moment, then hurriedly added. "Unless you want to go to the tavern."

"The café would be wonderful," she replied. She folded her jacket over her arm and closed the door behind her. As they strolled the few blocks to the café, she chattered idly, asking Tim what he had done that day.

"I slept a good portion," he replied. "Qaz told me after he healed my head that it would make me tired. That was the understatement of the week."

"Oh, I know," she added. "I slept like a baby almost all afternoon. I had to force myself to get up and get dressed to avoid ruining tonight's sleep." She yawned to emphasize her point, wondering if Tim thought her as silly as she felt. "Do anything else?"

"I had to buy a horse and replace my travel supplies. Kudakaan paid for the goods and mumbled something about helping with the cost of the horse, but I'm not hopeful. After that, I looked around town for a library, hoping to find some literature on the customs and behavior of traditional Rock Troll tribesmen, in case we run into any, but this town isn't exactly a crux of higher learning. They have exactly one dozen books, half of which are fiction, three of them are written in Archaic Lankaran, a language no one here can read, and the remaining three are…" He caught himself for a moment. "Are about as boring as I am." He looked at the ground sheepishly.

"Oh, stop, you." She poked his arm. "That was probably the only constructive and useful thing any of us did today." As they walked past the shops and businesses lining the street, she scanned the signs and windows, looking for a specific mark. She finally saw it painted on the window of an antique shop. The mark of the Underground was painted in the four corners of the window, mixed in with and disguised as mere decoration.

"Oh, I just love antiques!" She rushed to the window and cupped her hands around her eyes, looking inside. A sign hung crookedly in the darkened window, indicating that the store was closed. If she was correct, there would be a man inside, sitting in the dark where he could not be seen. Tim walked up beside her.

"I think they are closed," he offered.

"I know. I just want to look." She turned and looked across the street. "I wonder if there are any more antique shops." As Tim turned to look also, she let her jacket fall to the ground. She knelt, and as she retrieved it, she slipped the letter out of her pocket and under the door. She stood just as Tim was turning back. Perfect execution, she thought to herself.

"What's wrong?" he asked, a concerned look on his face.

"Nothing. Why do you ask?" She donned her most innocent face.

"You were nervous for a second."

"Do I seem nervous now?"

"No."

"Then it must have been nothing. You *were* hit sharply on the head recently." She giggled. Sometimes the most enjoyable part of undercover work was the acting. She occasionally wondered if life had put her on a distinctly different course if she would have had success in the theater.

"I suppose so. Shall we continue?" As they walked away from the shop, the man inside strained to catch the rest of their trailing conversation. After silence returned, he waited for a complete count of sixty before he silently crossed the room and retrieved the page the woman had slipped beneath the door. He quickly retreated from the light and brought the message into the rear room. A lone candle lit the dusty, cluttered closet with barely enough light to see. The man held the page up to the light and saw the wax seal and encoded wording on the front. He recognized the encoded address. Whatever this was about, it was important.

"Damn," he muttered to himself. He was not looking forward to a late-night ride into Roth. It looked as if it might rain tonight. He pulled on his jacket, grumbling. When duty calls, one must answer. He buckled on his sword belt as he walked through the back of the store.

"Going to the city," he shouted up the stairs. "Watch the shop."

"Go bugger yourself," came a gruff reply from the darkness.

"I love my job," he mumbled as he stepped into the alley. He turned to lock the door, humming to himself. It definitely smelled as if it would rain. His heart lurched at the sudden shuffle of footsteps behind him. He spun to face his attacker, but he knew it was already too late. His hand was only halfway to his blade when the pain ripped into his side. As he struggled vainly to breathe, part of him coldly admired the perfect execution of the stabbing – right between the ribs, through the diaphragm. He knew right away that he was a dead man. The force of the attack had slammed his head into the stone wall and knocked him off of his feet. As he lay on the cold ground, he struggled to turn, to at least see the face of his murderer before death collected him. Warmth flowed out of his body, and the ground spun.

A man mechanically searched him, his hands efficiently discovering each of the hidden pockets he had sewn into his clothing. Very professional, he thought. He fought to open his eyes. As his killer found the message this woman had written, he, at last, forced his eyes to focus one last time. The assassin sat balanced on his heels and examined the missive carefully before slipping it into his own jacket. He wore a black cloth tied to cover the lower portion of his face, but the makeshift disguise did nothing to hide his snow-white eyes. That makes you a Ygazi Assassin, deep in the throes of the bloodspice, the man thought. The assassin looked down and saw his victim gazing back at him.

"Sorry, chap." he offered. "Nothing personal." Small comfort that was. At least he wouldn't have to ride to Roth tonight in the rain. He spasmed as he tried to laugh at life's cruel joke. "At least you've got a good sense of humor about the whole thing." The killer offered, misinterpreting the man's last laugh. He stood and looked around the alley. "You should have been more careful," he went on. "Wolves wander these streets."

Ah, so it *is* you. He thought. The Wolf. At least I was killed by the best. He felt his feet being lifted as he was dragged away. He admired the stars for the last time. Death came.

CHAPTER FIVE

ETHDAY
28TH OF TURADMUR

"You heard me, didn't you?" Jack whispered. "I said this was a bad idea from the start."

"What does it matter now?" Qaz whispered back.

"Good point." Jack looked ahead at Kudakaan, who stood on the trail beside his horse, speaking softly to the dozen or so heavily armed Trolls that had materialized suddenly from the rocks and bushes surrounding the road. Uglor and the others sat on their horses a short distance behind, shooting nervous glances into the dense forest on either side of the trail. Jack took advantage of this pause to examine the Trolls. They stood in three neat rows, effectively blocking off the trail ahead. All were dressed in animal hide of various origins, hardened in some cases to act as armor. No two were dressed identically, nor were they armed uniformly. A few held stout spears; others, massive clubs. Some bore enormous axes, similar to the monster that Uglor carried. One Troll, possibly the leader of this group, stood directly in front of Kudakaan, his massive arms folded across his enormous chest. Hardened animal hide covered most of his body, and a sword that likely was taller than Tim was strapped across his broad back. His head was shaven bare, save for a narrow strip of short spiky black hair which ran across the top of his head, terminating as a short braid at the base of his skull. His nutty brown skin showed signs of prolonged exposure to the sun. He glared down at

Kudakaan threateningly across his broad nose. Kudakaan spoke with him, gesturing slightly. Jack would have given his left eye to hear their conversation. Well, maybe not an eye, but a finger certainly.

"I don't think they want to kill us," Tim offered. Qaz looked at him strangely.

"Why do you say that?" he asked.

"Because we aren't dead."

"Not yet, anyway," Jack added. He looked at Uglor. He sat in his saddle, rigidly looking straight ahead. Jack could see the tension in his shoulders. This was not good. "See if you can read anything from them," he suggested. Tim nodded. His face went strangely calm, and his eyes took on a faraway look. Jack turned in his saddle. Behind him in her full armor, Lena sat on her horse, gripping the hilt of her sword tightly, looking all around the trail for more hidden Trolls. She seemed tense but in control. Daelyn sat beside her, clothed in her usual black, hands folded neatly on the pommel of her saddle, in a deliberately calm, non-threatening manner. Corelan slouched in his saddle to the rear, looking for all the world as if this were a mere inconvenience, like waiting for the ferry. Neither Corelan, Lena, or Jack himself had said anything about Corelan's outburst from the previous evening, and surprisingly, Kudakaan had nothing to say about the issue either. Only Tim had seemed to be in a decent mood today; no doubt it had something to do with Daelyn. The man was clearly smitten.

"They are hostile. No news there," Tim whispered. "Some are slightly surprised that we are dumb enough to try to take this road. I get the impression they are scouts or guards, and this sort of thing doesn't happen that often. Some of them have less of an idea what is going on than we do." He leaned in toward Jack slightly. "It is hard to read with so many of them standing together like that. If I could get closer…"

"Don't worry about it," Jack said. "What about our people?"

"Doing okay. Uglor worries me a bit, but you know him better than I do."

"What about Kudakaan?"

"That is an interesting…" Jack cut him off with a sharp gesture as Kudakaan mounted his horse and rode back to the group. Behind him, the Trolls were moving away down the road.

"They are going to grant us passage through their land," he announced.

"And here I thought I was a smooth talker," Jack replied with a smile. "How did you swing that?"

"I appealed to their avaricious nature," Kudakaan replied with a smirk. Lena and the others closed in.

"So, you bribed them to abandon their beliefs," she said with a frown. She seemed almost disappointed that she wouldn't be killed by an overwhelming force of hostile Trolls.

"Bribe, shmibe, nobody's dead," Qaz offered. She shot him a dark look.

"Let's move, people," Kudakaan snapped. Jack shook his head as he spurred his horse. This was still no good. He looked over at Tim. *"Later,"* he mouthed silently. Jack looked over his shoulder at his companion. Uglor looked at the ground, lost in thought.

He spurred his horse to ride abreast with Kudakaan. The slight squishing sound of the horses plodding through the mud from last night's rain was the only sound that broke the calm, humid air. They rode down the center of the path, which began to cut through the rocky hillside, forming steep walls on either side of the road. The road was hewn out of the bedrock, probably to facilitate moving large stone blocks from the quarry ahead. Just as they fully entered the man-made canyon, a small contingent of Troll warriors closed in behind them around the mouth of the corridor. They now had Trolls in front and Trolls behind with nowhere to run. Jack looked up at the rim of the hill and saw the silhouette forms of a few soldiers looking back down at him. Trolls in front, behind, *and* above. This was definitely not good.

"So, what's the plan now, boss?" Jack asked.

"We talk to the chief," Kudakaan replied curtly.

"We? You mean you. This is your plan." Jack paused for a moment. "I hope you brought enough petty cash for this."

"That is the other thing I need to speak to you about."

"Need to borrow, huh. No problem." Kudakaan eyed him warily. "What, surprised? I'm sure you will find my interest rate very reasonable." He smiled. Kudakaan suppressed a chuckle. There was something to be said for this cooperation thing after all. As the path continued up the mountainside, the walls climbed higher and higher around them. The road twisted as it ascended the mountain, switching back on itself, leaving a chasm to one side and a sheer rock wall on the other. After an hour of hard climbing, occasionally dismounting to lead their horses, they crested a ridge, and the path opened in front of them onto the floor of a high valley. On the opposite side of the valley, slightly obscured by a thin haze, the stark gray of the abandoned quarry stood like an ugly scar ripped across the pristine mountainside. Jack looked around warily as they rode onward through the stunted conifer trees that occupied the valley floor. The road curved along to his right, away from the quarry toward a low pass in the valley walls, likely leading toward Devonshire. As he rode along the path, Jack spied several dark openings dotting the surface of the sparsely grown, rocky mountain walls. They emerged from the scrubby forest into a clearing occupied by a dozen or so lodges and huts. One large cave-like opening stood gaping like a giant mouth in the wall of stone a few hundred yards past the rough village. The Troll soldiers dispersed into the village as they reigned to a halt. More troops came from the huts and cave to meet them, bringing the number of soldiers milling around the small village to well over a hundred.

"I didn't know there were mines up here also," Jack said in a hushed voice.

"Neither did I," Kudakaan answered. Tim reigned his horse in beside the pair.

"No wonder the quarry was abandoned," Jack commented. "No way could you dig this many Trolls out from tunnels like that. Hell, a handful of troops could hold these caves almost indefinitely."

"It's not a mine," Tim added. "At least not originally." He paused in response to his companion's blank stares. "This is Kravzhekny. The Ialish Stronghold." Jack nodded in response.

Murzahd had mentioned something about it previously. "I didn't realize it was so close," Tim went on. "As it turns out, the history of this site is quite interesting. Corelan and I were just yesterday…" He trailed off and looked around uneasily. A number of Troll warriors had circled around behind them and milled around the mouth of the road. "I am getting a bad feeling," Tim said. The Troll, who Jack had labeled as the leader of the small band, approached the group accompanied by two bulky soldiers.

"Quiet, you two," Kudakaan whispered. "Dismount," He commanded the group in a louder voice. They eased down from their horses as the Troll came to a stop in front of Kudakaan. He stood easily a head and shoulders taller than any of the humans present, save Uglor.

"You will come with me into the mountain," he said. His deep, rich voice held the exotic flavor of a strange accent.

"What of the horses?" Kudakaan asked.

"They will remain outside." He folded his massive arms. One of the warriors behind him gripped the haft of an enormous steel studded club. He glared at the humans with open hostility.

"*Dou maka ne failla. Sho dwonja!*" he growled.

"The half breed must remain as well," the leader spoke, gesturing to Uglor. Jack winced. This was probably not the ideal way for things to unfold.

"I will leave my horses in your trust, but my people stay together." Kudakaan looked defiantly at the Troll. Jack felt the tension level rise. He fingered his dagger and looked at Uglor, who stood rock still, his eyes fixed on the horizon. The Troll captain glared back at Kudakaan for a moment before speaking in a level tone.

"So be it. Come. Now." He turned away from the group and headed for the mouth of the tunnel. Kudakaan motioned for the group to follow. The warrior who had spoken earlier voiced a loud protest and was silenced by a sharp word from the leader. Qaz leaned in to speak softly to Kudakaan.

"Are the horses going to be all right?" he asked.

"They should be. He gave me his word that no harm would befall us. Unless."

"Unless what?" Jack interjected.

"He didn't say."

"Great," Qaz responded. "Well, if you need me to take care of things, just let me know," he finished with a half-grin. Jack looked at the intricately carved façade, hewn from the solid stone foot of the mountain as they approached. A pointed arched opening carved to resemble the interlocking branches of a pair of trees decorated the mouth of the cave. He paused briefly as he passed through the entrance to admire the exquisite craftsmanship and spied the distinctive patterns of Ialish script amongst the carvings. This was definitely the work of Ialish hands. *Maybe I should sit down with Tim for that history lesson, after all,* Jack thought. *That is – if we survive.*

They walked to the cave entrance and strode into the darkness without pause. Two soldiers bearing torches approached from deeper in the cave, throwing a feeble but welcome light across the ribbed vaulted ceiling. A word and a nod were exchanged, and the five Trolls walked ahead into the dark tunnel. The cool, damp air of the cave felt refreshing after standing out in the dusty air of the valley, Jack thought as he dropped back to walk alongside Uglor. A half dozen more Trolls followed the group into the tunnel. The relative silence was broken only by the shuffle of footsteps on the dusty stone floor and the crackling of the torches. Jack looked around at the group. He was not usually one to worry. But then, he was not usually one to go down a road that clearly led to a large encampment of hostile seven-foot-tall, bloodthirsty warriors either. The two Trolls in the lead of their little parade were arguing tersely in their own tongue. Jack did not like the sound of it. Qaz dropped back and spoke in a low whisper.

"If I say 'now,' cover your eyes tightly for a few seconds. Pass the word." He stepped ahead to remain abreast with Kudakaan. Jack looked at Uglor, who nodded, and turned to Tim, who walked a step behind. Before he could relay the message, Tim spoke.

"Jack…"

"Not now, listen…"

"Not now, but any minute," Tim spoke over him. Jack looked at him carefully.

"What…"

"These soldiers are boiling. They are right on the brink. I think they're going to…" The column stopped abruptly at an intersection. The soldiers turned to face Kudakaan. Without warning, the angry warrior from before swung his club at his head. Kudakaan desperately tried to lift his staff in time to deflect the blow, succeeding only in absorbing some of the force. The attack smashed through his block and glanced off of the side of his head, sending him staggering back into the wall. He sunk to the floor and was motionless.

"NOW!" Qaz yelled. Jack lunged forward, clamping his hand over the eyes of a very surprised Tim. He closed his eyes tightly just as a loud snap reverberated through the hall. A bright orange glow blazed against his eyelids as he heard the surprised yelps of the dozen Trolls that escorted them. As the flash of light dissipated, he opened his eyes. Chaos spread through the hall like wildfire. Everyone moved at once. All of the Trolls had been blinded by the light and were now swinging their weapons about madly. Qaz hunched down under the attacks and was running back toward the group. Tim pushed Jack away and looked around, bewildered. Uglor, who had heard the warning as well, pulled his enormous axe from his shoulders and turned his back to the wall. Corelan had pushed Lena to the ground, and the both of them groped about blindly on the floor. Daelyn knelt in a corner, dagger drawn, futilely rubbing her eyes in a desperate attempt to regain her vision. The Trolls bellowed like madmen, smashing into the walls and each other. They shouted incomprehensibly at the top of their lungs in their own language.

"Move!" Qaz yelled. Uglor uncoiled like a spring. He shot forward toward the entrance swinging his axe as if he meant to carve a path to freedom. Jack pushed Tim forward and turned to face Qaz.

"Get Daelyn!" Qaz shouted. "I'll get Kudakaan!"

"Dammit!" Jack shouted as he rushed forward to scoop Daelyn to her feet. As he grabbed her arm, she lashed out suddenly with her dagger.

Jack threw his guard up defensively and fell backward as her blade traced a thin line across his forearm. She lunged forward and pinned him to the ground, straddling him and stabbing down with her knife. He grabbed her wrist, stopping the point of the blade inches from his eye.

"Daelyn! It's Jack!" he shouted. She rolled off of him and spun to her feet. He leapt up, grabbing her hand. "Let's go! Now!" He pulled her forward into the wake of Uglor's bloody trail. He looked around wildly. Uglor was ducking and weaving through the blinded Trolls as they swung madly at their unseen foe. Several Trolls lay on the ground, killed or grievously wounded either by Uglor's axe or each other. Qaz desperately tried to weave through the swarm of flailing wood, flesh, and steel to reach Kudakaan's prone form. Corelan and Lena had crawled off down the hall deeper into the cave.

"Tim! Take her," Jack shouted, pushing Daelyn's hand into Tim's. "Get out!" He turned back to help Qaz. The Troll leader bent to seize Kudakaan by the shirt, and after groping about for a moment, grabbed hold and lifted his unconscious body to his shoulders. He began to carry him off down a side tunnel as the other Trolls smashed about in the dark. Jack grabbed Qaz by the collar.

"Leave him! There is nothing we can do!" He heard shouts and the tramp of boots from down the hall. "More are coming! We have to go, now!" Several Trolls had backed away slightly, rubbing their eyes and shaking their heads slowly. One peered intently at one of the fallen torches, which were the hall's only source of illumination.

"It's wearing off," Qaz said. "They won't fall for it again. Go, Jack. I'll get Corelan and Lena."

Qaz ran down the hall, flattening himself against the stone wall, as he passed the retreating Trolls.

"Good luck," Jack muttered. He turned to run after his companions toward the sound and commotion ahead, passing the fallen bodies of several Trolls. The sound died off as he drew closer, filling the tunnel with an eerie silence. He slowed as he approached, just able to see the glow of daylight spilling into the tunnel mouth from around the corner. He stopped just inside the shadow of the corner and peered out. The camp was engulfed in motion. Nearly fifty warriors had amassed themselves and began racing toward the cave entrance. Jack looked around wildly for a place to hide. The floor of the tunnel was smooth and featureless. There was nowhere for even a mouse to hide. He turned to run back down the tunnel when a large hand clamped down onto the collar of his shirt. He slashed blindly with his dagger and struck empty air. He was lifted off of his feet and up through the ceiling.

"What the…"

"Shhh…" a voice urged him. Jack's eyes adjusted to the sudden darkness. Tim and Daelyn crouched beside him on the stone floor of another dark corridor. A small square hole in the floor opened up into the hallway below. Uglor released his shirt and patted him on the shoulder. Jack leaned forward slightly to peer into the tunnel below. A moment later, the band of warriors rushed past into the mountain. After they had gone, Jack looked around at his companions.

"Thanks. I'm not sure I would have been able to handle quite that many at once," he joked, striving to peer into the darkness of the upper passage.

"This looks like a defense measure," Tim offered. "I've seen holes like this in a few castles. You dump nasty, heavy, or pointy things on people through the hole."

"Thought so," he replied. "You okay, Daelyn?"

"Yeah. Vision is still a little blurred. What happened?"

"Qaz threw some kind of magical flash of light to temporarily blind everybody," Jack said as he rolled back his sleeve.

"Well, it worked," she said. "Where's everyone else?"

"We got separated," he replied as he tore a strip of cloth from his ruined sleeve. "Qaz, Corelan, and Lena were forced deeper into the cave. Kudakaan got dragged off. Nothing anybody could do."

"Sorry about the arm," Daelyn offered as Jack wound the makeshift bandage around the gash in his arm.

"What do we do now?" Tim asked.

"We get the hell out of this cave," Jack replied.

"Shouldn't we help our missing companions?" Tim asked.

"What do you propose we do?" Jack asked. "Fight the whole mountain? None of us are getting out of here by force of arms. We either sneak out or talk our way out."

"Yeah, but…" Tim began

"But what? How are we going to help them sneak out? More of us in there just draws more attention. And I don't know about you, but I am disinclined to open negotiations with our Troll hosts at present. We can address our long-term strategy later," Jack answered. "Right now, we can't help anyone but ourselves, if that."

"Were no good to them if we're dead," Daelyn offered.

"I hate it, but there is truly nothing we can do to help them at the moment. We aren't out of the woods ourselves yet." Jack knelt by the hole and listened.

"Tunnel," Tim corrected gravely. Jack shot him a sour look. He paused for a moment and stuck his head down through the hole. He looked around and pulled himself up.

"Looks clear. I guess they all rushed in. We had best get moving." They dropped through the hole one by one. Jack peered out into the valley as the others huddled along the inside wall of the tunnel. A strange quiet hung in the air outside. There was no movement at all in the small collection of huts. Their horses stood where they had left them, tied to a horizontal bar near the mouth of the road.

"This is too easy. I don't like it." Jack edged forward into the mouth of the cave. "Daelyn, where's your bow?"

"On my horse."

"Well, that simplifies things. Watch my back." He stepped out into the sunlight and walked casually to the nearest building. A thick blanket of silence covered the village. Jack darted into a shadow and stood still as a stone, his back flat against the hewn log wall of the lodge. Something felt wrong. Jack knew he was being watched. It was one of those feelings he could not quite put his finger on, one of those indescribable perceptions he could only attribute to experience. The thing that bothered him most was that these feelings were always right. He looked around the small village. There was no motion or sound to suggest that he was anything but alone here. He slipped silently around a corner. The horses stood peacefully, tied to a post only a hundred or so paces away across open flat dirt. A short length for a casual stroll, but under these circumstances, it was a vast distance. Jack gritted his teeth. There was really little else he could do.

"Time to gamble," he mumbled to himself. He stood from where he crouched in the shadow and strode out into the open. He walked casually over to the horses and began to untie them one at a time. He expected at any moment to hear an alarmed shout or the crunching of gravel as Troll soldiers rushed forward. The only sound was the vibrant chirping of a nearby bird. Jack lifted himself easily into his saddle and urged his horse forward at a slow walk, leading the other horses behind. He fought the urge to kick his horse into a gallop, knowing that if someone was watching and for some reason unaware of what transpired in the cave, running would be a sure sign that something was amiss. He stopped just in front of the mine entrance.

"Mount slowly. Like you are in no hurry," he told the others. He casually shifted his gaze across the valley. There was still no sign of anyone. It still felt wrong.

"Is someone watching?" Daelyn asked quietly as she mounted her horse.

"Don't know. Let's move. Nice and easy," he responded. "Leave the other four horses. Our friends are going to need them once they get out." They reigned their horses around and walked toward the path carved through the hillside. Jack's eyes darted around, looking for the source of his uneasiness. He felt the other's apprehension as they walked cautiously across the clearing.

"Sense anything, Tim?" Tim lifted a finger, gesturing for a moment's quiet. They walked along in silence for a moment more.

"The cave is swarming with turbulent emotion. I'm not getting anything from out here except for the four of us." Tim looked back at the huts and shrugged. "If there is anyone out there, they are *masking*."

"Masking?" Jack asked.

"Some people can learn to mask their aura. It's a way of hiding from a psychic," Tim responded, still glancing around between the buildings.

"Could a Troll learn that?" Jack asked.

"It's possible. Though, in this circumstance, unlikely."

"Nothing for it then," Daelyn added.

"True." Jack nodded toward her. "What about the scout contingent at the other end of this road?"

"Too far to tell," Tim answered. "When we get closer, probably once it is too late, I'll be able to tell."

"Well, do the best you can." Jack turned to Daelyn. "Got that bow ready?" She nodded. "Okay, let's see what happens." He spurred his horse forward.

* * * * *

Corelan peered over a stack of barrels down the dark corridor. He strained to hear the sounds of the retreating boots of the Troll soldiers. He cursed himself silently. If he had trusted his instincts last night and left the group before dawn, he'd be clear of this mess. But unfortunately, his preference for multiple nightcaps left him in bed until Qaz woke him in the dim pre-dawn quiet. Too late to make a discreet exit. As the sound faded away, Corelan whispered to the others.

"I think they are gone," he said. He dropped back down behind the barrels with the others. "Okay. Now what?" They hid in a small niche along a corridor used to store supplies. The hooded lantern they had just stolen threw its weak light across the small corner of the storeroom, flickering slightly as he crouched beside it. The lantern's cover was nearly closed, letting only a trickle of light escape.

"I'm guessing our first step might be to get out of this cave," Qaz offered. He dabbed a wet cloth on the large knot that decorated his forehead.

"Brilliant," Lena snapped.

"Glad to be of help," he responded, leaning his head back on the barrel behind him and closing his eyes.

"How's the head?" Corelan asked.

"Nothing serious," Qaz replied unconvincingly. "If that Troll had any idea where I was standing, I would be about ten inches shorter now." He gently fingered the bloody lump on his head. "Lucky he just caught me on the backswing."

Corelan puzzled at the other man's sense of luck. Seems like 'lucky' would have been to not get hit at all.

"Can you do any magic?" Lena asked.

"Not for a while. I tried a few minutes ago, and I thought my head was going to split open." He examined the cloth. "Stopped bleeding, though."

"Anybody have any idea which way is out?" Lena asked. Qaz shook his head. Corelan shrugged. "Me neither." She sighed deeply. "Let's look at our options. If we sit still, eventually, we will be discovered. On the other hand, if we wander around aimlessly, we could be found even sooner. I suggest we sit tight for just a short while to give the Trolls time to settle down. It's a safe bet that once they have run around for a while, somebody will call a meeting. When they are all in the same place, that would be a good time to do some exploring to find our way out of here. Plus, it gives our directionally-challenged master mage here time to reassemble his skull." She gestured to Qaz with a thumb.

"Challenged?" He opened his eyes and grimaced.

"You could have made it out," she responded.

"And leave the two of you in here to have all the fun with the Trolls?"

"It would have been smarter. No need for three of us to be trapped in here."

"With both of you blinded, you would never have made it." He broke into a sheepish grin. "Besides, it was my fault you were blinded in the first place."

"Good point," Corelan said.

"Very good point," Lena added. "How about some warning next time? If everyone knew what was coming, we might have all made it out." Her voice took on an aggressive edge as she glared at him fiercely. Her eyes glittered in the weak light.

"Actually, I was just starting to…" Corelan cut him off with a sharp gesture and stood suddenly. Lena snapped the lantern closed, plunging them in total darkness. A tense moment passed as Corelan peered into the darkness. He felt a touch on his leg. He stood motionless as someone rose to stand beside him.

"Anything?" Lena's voice whispered into his ear. He felt her body brush slightly against his as she stood close. He forced himself to concentrate and pulled away slightly.

"I thought I heard something," he whispered back.

"Let's give it a minute or two," Lena responded. She leaned on the barrel beside him close enough to whisper without the sound traveling. Her other arm crossed behind him to rest on the wall. She moved in closer. She whispered in a low tone; seemingly to avoid Qaz overhearing as much as the Trolls. "You could have gotten out too. Why didn't you?" She spoke softly, without her usual brusque tone. His mind reeled. He forced down the familiar hollow feeling that crept into his chest. She drew back slightly as he turned to respond.

"What makes you say that?" he breathed into her ear. She turned back to him.

"Don't play games with me. You were all the way in the back. Closest to the exit." He suppressed another shiver as her soft breath tickled his ear. "How did you find your way up to the front where I was?"

"I don't leave my friends behind." *At least not when they are in danger, anyway.* Corelan forced down the nagging voice in his head that suggested the whiskey may not have been the only reason he didn't leave last night.

"You were blind. Helpless. What did tell you about that hero crap?"

"What are you getting at?" he whispered a little louder. Her body tensed suddenly as a cough echoed from down the corridor. The sound was followed by the soft shuffle of two sets of booted feet clomping down the hall. A dull glow began to emanate from down the hall as the footsteps grew louder.

"Trouble," Lena whispered.

Corelan crouched behind the barrels in tense silence as the footsteps grew louder. Two Trolls approached from the corridor adjoining the small niche that concealed the three humans. The Trolls talked to each other quietly in their own brusque language. Corelan could, of course, not make out the words, but their tone implied they were in a sour mood indeed. As the Trolls drew closer, Corelan could begin to see the faces of his companions by the light of their lantern. Lena sat on her heels with one knee on the ground gripping the hilt of her sword tightly, giving the impression of a cat about to spring. Qaz seemed to be locked in a deep state of concentration, focused on some inner vision. His face broke suddenly into a painful grimace as his concentration shattered. He looked back at Corelan and shook his head. *I never much trusted magic anyway,* Corelan thought. His attention shifted to the Trolls.

They were close now, close enough to smell. Lena wrinkled her nose as the acrid smell of unwashed and active bodies filled their little alcove. He could hear the dirt scraping under their boots and the creaking of their hardened leather armor. The pair came to a stop directly in front of the barrels that hid the human intruders. Corelan held his breath. A Troll placed his lantern on top of the stack, and he and his companion lifted a crate from the far side of the niche. Lena jumped slightly at the loud crash made by the crate as it was dropped on the floor. Corelan struggled to see between the barrels, trying in vain to see what the Trolls were up to. All he could see was the corner of the crate they had moved. Sweat trickled down his forehead and across his jaw. He had seen danger before, but this time more than ever, a violent, bloody death seemed like a very distinct possibility. He wondered if he shouldn't be more afraid. Shouldn't a normal person be quaking in his boots right now? It wasn't that he felt particularly brave. It was something else. Something more apathetic. He felt a sudden shock as he realized that he just might not care. That thought alone disturbed him more than the prospect of being killed and forgotten deep inside a mountain in the middle of the wilderness.

The Trolls continued in a more casual conversation, oblivious to the tension just footsteps away. Corelan heard the familiar pop and slosh of a bottle being uncorked. The wooden crate creaked loudly as one of the Trolls sat on it. He looked at Lena, who rolled her eyes. Looks like we are going to be here a while, he thought. The Trolls sat and joked and drank for what seemed like an eternity. During a particularly loud rumble of course laughter, Qaz leaned over to whisper in Corelan's ear.

"If all the soldiers are this slack, we should have no trouble finding our way out of here," he whispered. Corelan suppressed a grin as Lena glared sharply and gestured for them to be quiet. A few agonizingly long moments later, their revelry was broken by the sound of a horn being blown deep within the cave. The Trolls rose slowly to their feet, grumbling in their own language. After a few tense moments, darkness and silence filled the storeroom, and the three were once again alone.

"Well, Lena, there is your meeting," Corelan whispered. Dim light suddenly bloomed into the darkness as Qaz unhooded the lantern. Lena stood quickly, brushing the dust from her thighs and stomping the circulation back into her legs. Qaz stood slowly, wobbling slightly.

"Let's get moving." She adjusted the fit of her sword belt. "You okay, Qaz?"

"Nothing a bucket of rum wouldn't cure." He smiled weakly as he gestured to the corridor. "This is your plan; I'm following you." She took a slow step forward, straining to hear any sounds of movement from within the cave. Corelan could feel the silence wrapping around them like a blanket. She listened for a moment more, then gestured wordlessly and moved forward into the cave. Corelan chuckled to himself sadly. *I really should have left when I first had the notion*, he thought.

* * * * *

The Four Feathers really wasn't a bad place. Under ordinary circumstances, Daelyn might have enjoyed her stay. It was just that this was the third time in a short number of days she had checked in to the very same inn, not to mention the fact that the last two times, she and her companions were returning from a thorough beating. The innkeeper was surprised to see them – again – and had made available some rather pleasant rooms on short notice. She would have to remember this place if she traveled through Akeela again. Just, hopefully, not tomorrow or the next day.

She looked around the tavern that adjoined the inn. She had learned that in this very same tavern the last time they were in town, Corelan had assaulted another patron for no good reason, earning himself a lifetime ban from the establishment. She had not been present at the time, so no one would recognize her or Tim, but Jack had apparently smooth-talked the security men out of contacting the sheriff. If they recognized Jack, they let on no sign.

Dargram's Tavern was doing brisk business tonight, and the crowd was bustling quite noisily. Jack and Uglor shared a round table with Tim and herself, each quietly idling over the remnants of a well-cooked meal, lost in their own thoughts. Tim stared into a candle that sat in the center of the table, absently extinguishing and re-igniting it repeatedly with the flick of a finger. She sipped on a generous portion of red wine and mulled over what had happened so far. She would have to compile another report for the Master soon, and she needed a theory. Unfortunately, the identity of the king's agent was still a complete mystery to her, and, given her current preoccupation with staying alive, deeper investigation of the subject had become a lower priority.

"So," Tim spoke first. Jack looked up, tried to crack a grin, failed, and returned to his tea. Uglor sat still and quiet as ever. Tim looked at Daelyn. "Any thoughts on our situation?" he asked.

"Not really," she answered. "Nothing useful anyway." She shook her head sadly. "We just can't go back for them. It's suicide."

"I hate it too," Jack added. "I just hate it, but we don't even know if they are still alive." Tim nodded, dropping his head.

"But we don't know that they are dead either. I am deeply worried, and I don't feel right about turning away," Tim said, frustration showing clearly on his face.

"I feel the same way," Jack replied. "I am certainly open to options on how we can help them. If there is something we can do, I'd be all for doing it. Any ideas?"

"We can't just leave them behind," Tim said after a moment of silence.

"I agree." Jack paused, collecting his thoughts. "Here is how I see it. There are three distinct scenarios. Worst case, they are all dead. Best case, they also escaped and are currently outside the cave and on their own. The third possibility; they are alive but still trapped in the cave." He counted the options on his fingers. "If they are dead, we can't help them. Now, if they have escaped the cave, you will recall that the only way to get to that valley is through the narrow pass."

"With the high walls," Tim commented.

"And the sheer drop," Daelyn added.

"Exactly. If they are out, then they are on one side or the other of that pass. If they are on this side of the pass, then all is well. If they are on the other side, we can't help them. If the pass is guarded, then *no one* is getting through. I don't think the king's army could get through." Jack sat back in his chair and sighed. Tim lifted a finger to protest, but Jack held out a restraining hand. "If they made it out, and they came this way, and the trail was open, they would be here by now. The fact that they have not arrived in Akeela yet tells us that they didn't go this way, either because they couldn't or because they went the other way. There is only one road through the valley, and it goes toward Devonshire."

"That's what I would do," Daelyn added in her slight lilting Toctilian accent. Mimicking accents was one of her specialties. Once she put it on, it came naturally – without thinking. She once had an undercover assignment that had her maintain the hurried twangy clip of a Nordican islander for almost two months. That assignment had ended with nearly a full dozen people, two of them Nordicans themselves, convinced she was born and raised in Lodin.

"So that leaves us with the third possibility. The complicated one," Jack went on.

"They are trapped inside," Tim said. "They would need help."

"Any rescue plan would involve going back to the mountain, and there is no realistic way that ends well. We would never get through the pass."

"It was open when we went through earlier," Tim offered.

"Are you willing to bet everyone's life that it is still unguarded? And even if it was, or if we managed to find another route…"

"There isn't another route," Daelyn interjected. She had already understood Jack's thought process and agreed. However, she still wanted Tim to reveal some more of his thinking, hoping to make progress on her actual assignment. "You saw those mountains. Without a road, unpassable."

"So, we just leave them to die?" Tim asked.

"How are we going to assault that cave complex?" Jack asked gently. "If we somehow miraculously managed to even get there alive, we have no intel on the cave layout, no information on the Trolls' distribution or numbers. The likelihood of a successful operation with no information, no time to plan or recruit new help is pretty much zero. And we don't even know if they are still there. As much as I hate to say it, there is just nothing we can do. We just have to hope they are still alive and, if they already haven't, that they can find their own way out," Jack finished with a black look on his face. Tim silently nodded.

"It's strange, though…" Daelyn began.

"What's that?" Tim asked.

"The Trolls. When we escaped, why were there no Trolls guarding the pass?"

"Strange indeed," Jack replied. "At the far end of the road, they would have been too far away to hear any alarm. They would not have moved in to assist…" He shook his head. "You're right. It doesn't make sense."

"Maybe everyone came through the pass to the village with us and were already outside when everything went down," she suggested. A man just past his middle years in a gray riding cloak caught her eye where he sat across the tavern at the bar. His gaze slipped away as he turned to sip from his mug. He looked somewhat familiar. She could not quite place him, though.

"Possibly. They clearly moved away from the pass for some reason. I don't think we are going to know what it was," Jack responded. He took another sip of his tea. "I suppose now would be a good time to discuss our next steps."

"What are you suggesting?" Tim asked.

"Everybody in our group knew we were headed for Devonshire," Jack began. "If our friends got out of the cave, I'm guessing they went that way. If they didn't, we can't help them. I propose we go on to Devonshire and hopefully meet them there."

Daelyn looked back at the man in gray. He was gazing absently into the large fire that flickered brightly on the massive stone hearth that formed the entire far wall. The reasonable part of her mind told her that this was the third time she had been in Akeela in the space of four days, and it was only to be expected that some of the faces would begin to look familiar. Another part of her mind insisted that she had seen this man before, in Roth perhaps. She let out an exasperated sigh as her memory refused to cooperate. She reminded herself that it was not unusual for men to look at her, and his actions were in no way suspicious. She shoved the thought aside, determined to think about it later since presently there was nothing to be done anyway.

"We should leave them a note or something here with the innkeeper," Tim suggested.

"I have to disagree." Jack shook his head. "Something has been extremely fishy about this project since day one, and I would hate to give whatever opposition we may be facing too much information by leaving a clear trail. And besides, I don't think they are going to come this way."

"We will be taking the north road, right? We could leave a message along the way," Tim offered. Jack turned to Daelyn.

"What do you think?" he asked. She thought about the too-familiar man across the bar and had to agree with Jack's line of thought.

"I think Jack is right about this," she said. "Our people will probably figure out what to do." If they are still alive, she thought. "Besides, they may have Kudakaan with them, and he knows more than we do. It just isn't worth the risk."

"What are our plans once we get to Devonshire?" Tim asked.

"When we were last sitting idle in Akeela, I took the liberty of doing a little investigating. We were supposed to meet a man named Walsh K'thaam at a specific address; I have it written down. The only problem is that we will be a few days late."

"Investigating?" Daelyn asked.

"I, uh, acquired some of Kudakaan's notes..."

"You stole information from our boss?" she asked.

"Stealing is such an ugly term."

"You stole." She suppressed a grin at the irony of her accusations but seeing how he or Tim reacted might shake loose some insight concerning her primary mission.

"Yeah, well, if I hadn't, we wouldn't have any clues at all. Just be thankful I am willing to set aside my personal honor for the greater good," Jack responded. Tim snorted loudly.

"You think we should meet this Walsh person?" Tim asked. "What then?"

"I suppose that depends on how the meeting goes."

"What exactly does that mean?" Tim asked again.

"It means… we'll see." Jack turned to Daelyn for help.

"We will just kind of have to play it by ear," She offered.

"That's our plan?" Tim asked.

"Well, it's *a* plan," Jack answered. "The beginnings of a plan anyway. I was hoping this could be a forum for open discussion. Does anyone have any other ideas?"

"Not really." Tim shrugged and smiled weakly. Daelyn shook her head. It wasn't much of a plan, but it was all they had. She sipped her wine and glanced across the tavern. The man in gray had left.

"I am going to call it a night," Jack stated. "I was hoping we could get up and get moving first thing. It's a long ride to Devonshire, and we're already late. I think," he suggested as he stood. Tim stood as well, mumbling something about being tired also.

"I am going to finish this," Daelyn said, lifting her wine. "I'll see you fellows first thing in the morning." Jack, Uglor, and Tim excused themselves and moved through the tavern to the adjoining inn. She shook her head again. This job was not going well. She would not want to disappoint the Master. It was unusual for anyone who had to survive the experience.

* * * * *

"Next time, we listen to Qaz," Corelan whispered. Lena turned to glare at him. "He did say this tunnel went the wrong way." Lena held up a finger to silence him. Not that it was necessary. Qaz could barely make out Corelan's whisper over the racket made by a hundred or so Trolls conversing and milling around. They had traveled down a randomly selected hallway until it had terminated into this large room ahead. Just as they had turned around to head back, several dozen Trolls approached from almost every direction simultaneously. Lena had pulled them behind this curtain at the last possible moment.

Corelan sat back on one of the sacks of grain that were piled behind the animal hide curtain, which served to partition this small storage area from the rest of the room. It also served as the only separation between them and the congregation of Trolls in the vast meeting hall only a few feet away. Lena turned away to peer between the curtains. Qaz leaned forward from the other side of the alcove.

"No sense in worrying about it now," Qaz whispered, giving Corelan a reassuring pat on the knee. Lena turned back to them and slumped to the floor. "What do you think?" Qaz asked, his voice barely audible above the din. She leaned forward, gesturing for the two of them to move closer. Although Qaz had placed a magical spell on the alcove to dampen any noise they would make, none of them felt comfortable with risking any sound that was not absolutely necessary.

"There are two soldiers, just outside of the curtain, blocking the hallway we came in through," she stated. "If they move forward a few paces or so, we can probably slip out behind their backs."

"Just like that?" Corelan asked.

"Everyone's attention will be on whatever is going on at this meeting. It should work."

"What if there is someone else at the other end of the hall?"

"Let's just try to stay positive," Qaz interjected. Corelan shook his head and leaned back. *We are so dead*, Qaz thought. He cursed silently. If only he knew how to cast the *Invisibility* spell, they could walk out right through the middle of the meeting, and none would be the wiser. He knew the basic principle – bending light around yourself – but theory and practice were two very different things. Now was certainly not the time to experiment. Corelan swallowed his next sarcastic comment as a hush settled into the room. The three humans looked at each other apprehensively. Qaz held his breath as an intensely quiet moment oozed past. He fully expected the Trolls to come bursting through the curtain at any moment, demanding to know whose heart was pounding so loudly. Lena rose ever so slowly and turned to face the curtain again. The only sound that could be heard was the quiet breathing of the legions of Trolls that stood just on the other side of the curtain. Qaz shot a glance at Corelan. He sat on the floor, leaning casually against a sack of grain, his arm resting on the pile beside him. Qaz wondered what it would take to make this man look nervous. Corelan spared him a cynical shrug, then turned to Lena.

She had her back to them and had leaned forward onto the sacks in front of her, slowly reaching toward the curtain. She paused, her fingertips inches away from the cloth. She looked back at the two men. Corelan shrugged again as if to say, "why not?" Qaz motioned for her to continue. She moistened her lips and turned back to the curtain. Qaz held his breath as she slid her finger slowly into the seam of the curtain. She paused yet again, then parted the cloth a fraction of an inch, moving her eye closer to the curtain.

An insufferably long moment of stillness and quiet passed. Qaz fully expected his heart to leap out of his chest through his throat, hop over the curtain, and explode violently. When it did not, he decided to exhale slowly instead. Without pulling her eye from the curtain, Lena suddenly began to gesture eagerly, waving her arm back and forth toward the curtain. What she was trying to say, Qaz had no clue, but it seemed important. He looked over to Corelan. The other man was already moving toward the opposite corner of the curtain to have a look for himself. As Qaz began to move to the near corner of the curtain, a sudden single drumbeat reverberated through the room. Qaz froze in mid-movement. Silence. If that was their signal to attack, they are certainly making a horrible job of it, he thought. Another drumbeat boomed into the silent room. Both Lena and Corelan were still glued to the curtain. Qaz scrambled quietly to the cloth and peeked through.

A group of nearly two hundred Trolls was amassed in the center of the large round room.

Every one of them stood in rapt attention, facing a raised platform on the opposite side of the chamber. A huge gaudy throne stood in the center of the platform, its surface covered with furs, the trodden battle flags of fallen enemies, a few skulls, and other such things a Troll king would deem appropriate for such a monstrosity. Beside the throne, two fat bronze braziers burned a pungent-smelling wood. All around the room, enormous torches blazed, throwing a flickering orange light across the eager faces of the three hundred Trolls in the room. A thin gray haze from the flames hung in the air, swirling slowly toward the ceiling thirty or so feet above their heads.

Another drumbeat drew Qaz's attention toward the throne. Just behind it, a large Troll (of course, they were *all* large) smashed a mallet down on the enormous kettle drum in front of him one last time. All eyes were locked on the front of the room. Qaz edged open the corner of the cloth slightly to steal a glimpse down the corridor just beside them. Two Troll soldiers stood solidly between them and freedom. Lena was right; those Trolls would have to move before he and his companions went anywhere. Qaz turned his attention back to the front of the room.

A deafening cheer went up as three figures emerged slowly through a curtain behind the throne. The figure in the center grabbed his attention like an owl snatching up a mouse. Standing a full head taller than everyone in the room, he had to be nearly eight feet tall. Instead of the narrow strip of short hair that decorated the heads of many of the warriors, a full mane of snow-white hair fell past his enormous shoulders. His scarred, weather-beaten face looked to be chipped from stone, but even from this distance, Qaz could feel the unbridled rage that seethed rabidly in the man's gaze. The hardened hide of some large, thick-skinned beast protected his immense chest. A single red stone slung from a simple golden chain was the only mark of regality he wore, but the absolute authority with which he carried himself left no doubt that this was the king of the Trolls. He strode forward without pause, bearing a scabbarded great sword in one hand. He paused at the edge of the platform, silencing the uproar quickly with the sheer force of his gaze. Qaz was spellbound by the power and fury of his presence. The king eased himself into his throne, resting the sword across his knees. Only after a moment of stillness could Qaz tear his eyes from the king to evaluate the other two figures that had emerged with him. One was clearly a warrior of significant standing. He bore himself with no less assurance than the king, and Qaz could see some resemblance in their faces. A prince perhaps, if Trolls used such terms. Probably a warband leader. Definitely family, though. He stood beside the throne with a look of equal furor blazing in his black eyes. A blade of tremendous proportions was strapped across his back. He folded his huge arms across his chest and glared at the congregation.

Qaz suppressed a chuckle. *I now understand what a Jaan feels like*, he thought. The third figure appeared to be a mystic or an elder of some kind. Undoubtedly, this fellow was an extraordinary physical specimen in his youth, but the weight of a rather significant number of years had dulled his edges and stooped his shoulders slightly. He leaned on a staff that looked like a small, uprooted tree, lopped off eight feet from the ground. He was wrapped in dull gray robes and adorned with small stones, feathers, and other things Qaz could not identify from this distance. His skull was shaven clean, save for a ring of long silver hair that circled around the back of his head. He peered about the room, eyes glittering with unreadable emotion. Qaz could sense some gift of magic in him. If this fellow could, in turn, sense the spell that Qaz had laid on this alcove, they would be very dead, very soon. He shuddered. Too late now.

The younger warrior held his fist aloft and yelled something in the Troll's harsh guttural language. Four hundred pairs of eyes turned toward the back of the room. Two soldiers entered from a hallway across the room, dragging a third figure between them. Qaz did not need to see the third man's face to know it was Kudakaan. He pulled away from the curtain to exchange a worried look with Lena. She shook her head grimly, echoing his thoughts, and turned back to watch. The Trolls dragged Kudakaan through the crowd and pushed him to the floor in front of the platform. Silence fell as he struggled slowly to his feet. Qaz was slightly surprised that the sheer power of the trio's gaze did not scour the flesh clean from Kudakaan's bones. He composed himself somehow and began to speak.

"Sir, I can explain…"

"SILENCE!" the warrior shouted, the anger showing clearly in his voice. He shook his fist at Kudakaan. "Thulcandra the Great does not wish to lower himself to speak with a dog such as you! Therefore, in the name of my king, I, Sharak

Bazeen, war leader of these great people, am forced to soil my tongue with your speech." He lowered his voice straining for composure. "You will not speak to my king. You will not look at him. You will not move your eyes from mine. You will not speak unless bidden to do so. When I ask a question, you will answer without hesitation, or your tongue will be ripped from your body and fed to my dogs for contemplation of a lie. Do you understand me?" He glared at Kudakaan, clearly wanting to tear him limb from limb with his bare hands there and then.

"Yes, sir, I do," Kudakaan meekly replied.

"Good." Sharak turned to the king, exchanging words in their own tongue. He turned back to Kudakaan. "The king wishes to know why you were late."

Qaz was so shocked by this question that he completely missed Kudakaan's reply. Late? We were expected? His mind struggled to categorize this information. He pulled back from the curtain for a moment. Lena was locked intently onto the conversation taking place in the throne room. Corelan sat on the grain sacks, his usual complacent, almost bored look being replaced by one of acute concern. Sharak spoke again.

"The money you promised. Where is it?" Sharak stood with his arms folded across his chest, arms that reminded Qaz of the roots of some gigantic tree. A very angry tree, if there was such a thing.

"We were attacked by bandits and forced to alter our plans. I beg your indulgence to remember that it was never agreed to bring the money here." Kudakaan wet his lips, his gaze never faltering from Sharak as Thulcandra spoke to his war leader.

"Do you even know why you stand before us, broken and bleeding, instead of eating with us at table?" Sharak went on. "Do you even know of the grave offenses you have committed?" He gestured wildly, letting his anger take hold.

"I…" Kudakaan began.

"You must not." His tone softened slightly. "For if you knew, surely you would not have dared to show your sniveling face in our land."

"Sir, I must assure you…"

"Silence!" Sharak's eyes glittered dangerously. "I did not bid you speak." Sharak turned away as Thulcandra spoke again to him; all the while, the king stared at Kudakaan as if he were examining a succulent morsel on his plate before devouring it.

"Because you are weak and stupid, I will explain to you the reason for your pathetic state. You have offended Thulcandra in four ways. You arrive late. This tells us that you care little for your appointments with our great king. This says you deem yourself more important than our great king. In this way, you have offended us." He folded his arms again, glaring down at Kudakaan.

"You bring armed men into our midst. Humans, yet! What need have you of armed men? Do you trust us so little that you need bodyguards? Do you have such small respect for our ways that you disregard the wars we have fought with these men to bring them among us, into our heartland? You say that our great king is not worthy of trust. You threaten the security of our families by bringing strangers to our secret home. You say that our great king is weak and will stand meekly by while you dishonor the deaths of our ancestors by bringing our enemies to our door and asking us to bring them into our home! In this way, you have offended us." Sharak was beginning to lose control of his rage. He clenched his fists repeatedly, gesturing toward Kudakaan. It seemed all that stood between Kudakaan and a bloody violent death was a few feet of thin air. Sharak's voice shook with anger as he continued.

"You bring a half breed before us. One who has sullied the blood of our ancestors with your own. One whose every breath is an insult to our proud lineage. You bring armed women… Women! Before us. It is forbidden for a woman to touch a weapon, yet you bring them to us, women who have to audacity to not only touch a weapon and wear armor like a man but to look a man in the eye when he is armed. This says you care nothing for our ways. That you feel we are beneath you, that we, in our own home, should strive to be more like you; you who rape the sacred land, you who spoil the earth with your…" Sharak, clearly on the brink of violence, was interrupted mid-sentence by Thulcandra clearing his throat. The war leader sputtered a moment more, then continued in a more measured tone.

"What have you to say for yourself, human?" Kudakaan took a measured breath, then spoke. This had better be good, Qaz thought.

"I first must extend my thanks for your gallantry in permitting me to live thus far. Your grace is beyond compare." Kudakaan dared a quick glance at the king, then continued. "I must beg your indulgence; I offend out of ignorance, not malice. Through my own fault, I fell into circumstances beyond my control which kept me from our very important meeting. All the while, it pained me to know that I was dishonoring your grace by my delay. I, therefore, rushed here as quickly as I could in a vain attempt to rectify this grave insult. I only took the time needed to secure a greater amount of gold with the fond hope of mending this offense." Sharak's shoulders relaxed a slight bit.

"Unfortunately, in my haste to correct my error, I committed a greater error. I failed to learn your ways sufficiently, and by blind ignorance, offended your great king and people by neglecting the proper presentation of my gift to you and your people." Kudakaan's face took on that calculating look Qaz recognized.

"Gift?" Thulcandra spoke. This shook Kudakaan visibly. He apparently had not anticipated having to deal directly with the king.

"Yes, your grace." Kudakaan now spoke directly to the king. Sharak observed quietly. "The women were meant as a gift to you and your men." Qaz heard the hiss of a sharp intake of breath from Lena, a few feet away. He hoped no one else heard it.

"How so?" Thulcandra spoke. His voice held no emotion, but its deep, rich, commanding tone demanded an immediate response.

"I assumed, perhaps wrongfully, and if so, I humbly beg your forgiveness, but I had assumed that it would do your grace honor to have human women as slaves and objects of pleasure." Thulcandra slowly leaned forward in his throne. "I felt it would show greater respect for your people than for my own by sacrificing to you our women who, as you know, we foolishly hold so dear to us. If I was wrong, I fear I must again beg your understanding." Kudakaan dropped to his knees in supplication. A gesture Qaz thought may have been a little over the top. The king leaned back into his throne. His massive hand played slowly across the handle of his gigantic blade. Likely the sword was as tall as the human standing before him, and all that would be necessary to kill this man would be to simply drop the weapon on his head, the sheer weight of it being more than sufficient to do the job. The mere sight of such a fearsome weapon had to be unnerving, and Thulcandra knew it. He stroked the handle for a moment more as if contemplating a use for it.

"It is not foolish to care for one's women," he began. "They are the wellspring of life, the lifeblood of a people. Our code requires protecting the women of the tribe above all else." Kudakaan winced slightly at his miscalculation. Thulcandra went on. "Though you are clearly a fool, your gesture does not go unnoticed. As the women are now gone, it is of little importance. We will speak no more of it. What of the men you brought? I would hope your judgment is not so poor that you believed they were to serve us the same?" A ripple of coarse laughter echoed through the hall. Qaz suppressed a chuckle of his own. That the king was making a joke was a very good sign for Kudakaan. This point was not lost on the prisoner either.

"The men were aiding me as I sought to complete my end of our bargain, nothing more. I never had any intention of bringing them here. Circumstances being what they were, I was forced to bring them along…"

"How much do they know?" the king interrupted.

"Nothing. I have told them nothing," Kudakaan replied. "That is why I could not send them ahead of me and come alone, as we had agreed." He licked his lips. Looks like he is about to gamble, Qaz thought. "I took the chance that bringing them here would be a lesser offense than sharing our secrets with them. If I have erred, please accept my humblest apologies. I only sought to serve your interests to the best of my limited ability." He hung his head as if in ultimate shame. Bravo, Qaz thought.

Thulcandra studied the man before him quietly, coldly watching the perspiration and blood drip from his head. Qaz had no idea if Kudakaan's words had any effect on the Troll whatsoever. Thulcandra sat impassive as a stone. Qaz sincerely hoped he would never have the opportunity to have a conversation with this king of Trolls.

"What of the half breed? Such an obvious insult, even one as daft as you could not ignore." With that statement, Sharak shifted and appeared as if he was about to speak. Thulcandra silenced him with a gesture. Kudakaan cleared his throat and began.

"Again, I find my ignorance painfully revealed. It now seems obvious that one of such physical stature could never be fully of human stock. I should have realized that no mere human could be so powerful, that such strength could only come from your noble people. I am a blind fool for not seeing that on my own. If I had been able to see, certainly I would never have ventured such an insult to you and your people."

"He killed some of our warriors; with the aid of your sorcery, of course," Sharak interjected. He glared down at Kudakaan as if expecting retribution on the spot.

"When the deal is finished, I will hand him over to you. I do not wish to stand in the way of justice." Kudakaan stood as he finished as if rising to accept a task. Qaz shook his head with distaste. He could understand saying what he did earlier to save his own hide, but now he was making promises they would certainly expect him to keep. He looked back into the room, hoping more would be said about the mysterious deal.

"About our bargain," Thulcandra spoke. Qaz wondered for a moment if the king could read his thoughts. An awkward moment of silence followed until Kudakaan realized that was a question.

"If your lordship is still interested, I suppose it stands."

"What of the extra gold? You spoke of more gold," Sharak asked. It seemed that Sharak was torn between killing Kudakaan now to vent his frustration and pursuing the more profitable bargain.

"Ah yes, with much debate amongst my superiors, I have secured half again as much as what was originally promised. If this is not sufficient…"

"It will suffice," Thulcandra spoke with cool, regal authority. Whatever the sum was, from the reaction of the five hundred or so warriors in the room, this was a big step. "We will continue as if none of this had occurred. We will keep the coin and horses you had with you when you came, as you no doubt intended those as gifts. The plan will proceed. Afterward, we will accept the half breed as recompense for your crimes. I have spoken."

Thulcandra stood suddenly. The room fell eerily silent. Qaz held his breath. "What say you, man?"

"I am truly humbled by your wisdom. Not many leaders can see past injuries to their name to do what is best for their people. If only my people were also led with such wisdom, perhaps we would not have such an unfortunate history." Qaz winced as the level of tension in the room rose a notch. Kudakaan sensed his error and quickly went on.

"My man will meet your warriors just outside of the town we call Devonshire in five days. He will bring the gold. Everything else will be the same," he finished using the tone he usually saved for Jack or Corelan. Getting cocky? Qaz wondered.

"No," Sharak interjected. He did not see the look on Thulcandra's face, or he would most likely have fallen silent. "You will be there in person. And you will bring the half breed." Sharak obviously disapproved of Kudakaan's tone.

"I cannot be there. I have to attend to my end of the bargain. If I am in Devonshire, I cannot assure that things will go smoothly."

"I do not trust you," Sharak began. "How will we know your man?"

"He will be the one who does not run away."

"I do not like it…"

"Enough." Thulcandra raised his hand, holding the sheathed sword aloft as a reminder to all those present of who was in charge and why. "It will be as you have said, human." He lowered the sword and went on. "I do not need to tell you the penalty for betrayal. As much of a fool as you are, you are not *that* foolish. It will be done."

Qaz suddenly felt a hand on his arm and nearly leapt through the curtain. Lena's hand clamped over his mouth, silencing his cry of surprise. Once his heart began to beat again, he gave a calm nod and she removed her hand. Corelan was standing by the curtain near the far wall, peeking out toward the soldiers that had been blocking their escape. Qaz began to ask, but Lena cut him off.

"They moved," she whispered. "Let's go." Qaz nodded silently. Corelan looked back and nodded to the pair, motioning for them to come closer. Qaz could hear the conversation continue in the background. Part of him (a tiny part) wanted to stay and hear the rest of the details. That part was silenced by the much larger part that would prefer to continue breathing. Corelan peered once more through the curtain and suddenly slipped through the opening. No reaction came from the Trolls. Qaz gestured for Lena to proceed. She frowned and pushed him toward the curtain. He slowly and carefully parted the cloth. The soldiers had moved several paces forward and were now standing facing away from them, intent on the exchange in the hall. No other Trolls were facing this direction.

He looked toward the connecting corridor only a few yards away. It seemed immeasurably distant. He looked back into the hall. There had to be six hundred Trolls in there, he thought. Corelan poked his head out from around the corner and motioned for Qaz to come. Qaz shot a glance back to the Trolls. They were still facing the other direction. All they had to do would be turn slightly while he was walking past, and they would all die. Lena poked him from behind. He took a deep breath, hoping it would not be one of his last, and slipped through the curtain.

Chapter Six

NINDAY

29TH OF TURADMUR

Daelyn brushed a few crumbs from her lap as she leaned back in the grass. She stretched lazily, looking behind her down the road back toward Akeela. It truly was a spectacular day. The direct sunlight was only a little too hot, but a cool breeze occasionally gusted through the trees, bringing with it the fresh smells and sounds of the forest. She had lived in the city her entire life and had always thought the forest seemed so serene. She wondered if she would ever be able to enjoy a day like this without all of the nagging doubts, fears, and suspicions that were constantly brewing in the corners of her mind. She tried to think back to a simpler time, a refuge of peaceful childhood memories that most people took for granted, but she again came to the sad realization that her life would always be complicated. It always has been, and it always would be.

She tried to dismiss some of her misgivings as "industry paranoia" – a term she had often heard when talking with her associates in the Underground, but her instincts told her no. Instincts were also touted as the ultimate finder of truth in her business. Today her instincts told her the man she thought she recognized yesterday in Akeela was someone to worry about. The man's face again came to mind.

"Lunch not sitting well?" Tim asked. She turned to smile at him. It was her only way of throwing him off balance to keep him from sensing too much. It was clear that her smiles had a particular special effect on Tim. She hated to manipulate him like that. He actually was a rather likable fellow. She reached over and touched him on the arm.

"No, it's nothing really," she responded.

"Nothing at all?" Tim asked with an arched eyebrow. She smiled.

"I just don't like how this job is turning out so far," she responded.

"I think I know what you mean." He nodded solemnly. "Something isn't quite right." He wrapped the remaining heel of bread from their lunch in a cloth and brushed the crumbs from his hands. Daelyn looked around the small clearing beside the road where they had chosen to take their lunch. She would need to start pursuing information more actively if she was going to learn anything worth reporting. Jack was rearranging his supplies in his saddlebags, sitting on the ground amidst a respectable assortment of equipment. Uglor stood a short distance off, gently grooming his horse, gingerly picking a burr from its mane with his fingertips. She could see his lips moving slightly as he spoke softly to his mount. She hadn't realized he had such an affinity toward animals.

"So, Tim." She shot a sideways look at Jack to reconfirm their privacy. Tim looked up with an arched eyebrow, clearly sensing her change in tone. "If you don't mind my asking, why did you take this job originally?"

"What do you mean?" he asked. "Aside from the money?" She nodded. He wrinkled his brow, thinking. "I suppose I was drawn in by the element of mystery." He shrugged. "How about you?"

"The phrase 'substantial payment' got me," she answered. "How did you hear about it, though? Was it posted at the Psychic League downtown?" she asked, trying to keep her tone as conversational as possible.

"No, A friend of mine at the Free Blade's Guild passed it along," He answered. "Why do you ask?"

"If I can figure out Pendor's thought process, maybe I can make some sense out of this mess," she replied truthfully.

"I see." Tim sat up straighter as he engaged with the idea. "If the flier was posted at the League, that suggests that Pendor was actively seeking a psychic for the team."

"Something like that," Daelyn explained. "If I was putting a team together to track thieves and recover stolen property, I would definitely want a psychic on board. But if I was up to something more nefarious and had something to hide, I probably wouldn't."

"Pendor still hired me, though," he pointed out.

"Maybe it would have been too suspicious to hire everyone *except* you."

"You folks mind if I interrupt a moment?" Jack asked. She turned and looked over her shoulder.

"Not at all," Daelyn answered. "What's up?"

"Uglor and I were discussing our travel plans, wanted to see what you two were thinking. We've got two options. We can stay on the road the whole way to Devonshire. If we don't dally, we can hit Fenwyg by nightfall. We'd stay the night there, head out first thing, and pass through Cromwood on the way to Devonshire. We'd arrive by nightfall, Endweek," Jack explained.

"When you and Kudakaan were arguing earlier…" Daylen began.

"Arguing? It was just a discussion," Jack explained.

"Sure. Didn't you suggest cutting across the hills to save time, though?" she followed.

"That is option two. We'd get there sooner but going off-road has some inherent risk."

"We would need to be careful in Fenwyg," Tim interjected.

"Oh? Why is that?" Jack asked.

"It's the hometown of a particular duke that we all know," Tim answered.

"Pendor is in Fenwyg?" Jack asked, his brow wrinkled.

"It's the seat of the North Protectorate. He's a duke," Tim explained. Seeing the blank expressions on his companions' faces, he went on. "You know the security of Roth's surrounding areas is relegated to the four protectorates, right?"

"Well, yeah, sure. Who doesn't?" Jack answered sarcastically. Tim arched an eyebrow. Seeing Tim's hurt expression, Jack went on. "Sorry, I'm not originally from Roth."

"Well, the point is…" Tim began. "I did some investigating when we were first hired, and I learned that Pendor's estate is in Fenwyg. Since he is a duke instead of an earl or a baron, that means he is the Protector, and living in Fenwyg makes that the seat of the Protectorate."

"Okay. Good to know." Jack looked at Daelyn for support. She shrugged.

"I thought the security of outlying areas was under Duke Dornibyn," Daelyn stated.

"Well, he's the *arch*duke. There is only one of those," Tim answered. "Dornibyn's seat is further east, in Elrynth. The East Protectorate has the largest number of towns under its wing, hence the 'arch' honorific. Plus, he's related to the king." Looking at his companion's faces, he stopped. "Okay. Well, just never mind."

"Tim," Jack started trying to suppress a grin. "It *is* valuable information. I think it helps us decide. I was already inclined to skip Fenwyg and make for Cromwood today. Uglor is a very competent outdoorsman, and I'm confident we can successfully navigate the off-road segment. I'm also concerned about our friends who may need assistance and might be in Devonshire already. I'd like to get there sooner than later. Knowing our duplicitous employer lives in Fenwyg with his own loyal armed forces, and we are traveling without his agent, who may be dead, just solidifies the decision in my mind. Do either of you object to going off-road?"

"I think I'd prefer to skip Fenwyg also," Daelyn answered.

"Good. If we are persistent, we can make Cromwood before dark and turn back southeast toward Devonshire the next morning. We should be there by midday on Endweek. Saves us half a day. Tim?"

"Sounds good to me," Tim responded. Daelyn nodded and stood as the others moved toward their horses. She felt as if a piece of the puzzle in her mind was beginning to resolve itself. The Master was having her use her real name, probably because he feared magic or psychic detection. Tim was a psychic. Tim hasn't done much for decision making, but he tends to ask 'why' a lot. If the king were sending someone to investigate people's business, it makes sense to send a psychic. None of this was enough for her to be sure of anything, but at least now, she had a slight suspicion. She felt a bit of surprise as she found herself hoping that she was wrong and Tim did not work for the king. After all, if he was a covert investigator, why tell the truth about being a psychic? Daelyn forced the thought out of her mind. Why should she care? She had to stay objective. This was just another undercover job - wasn't it?

* * * * *

A distant part of Corelan's mind knew it was a dream. It was always like that. That same part of him knew he would dream it again. Knowing never seemed to help. He needed to get there. Somewhere up ahead – somewhere in the city. He knew it was important. Nothing else mattered. He trotted through dark, deserted streets, thoroughly lost, with the feeling of urgency weighing on his mind. Nothing was familiar. The flat, cold, gray stone of the buildings looked identical to the buildings a block away. Or had he walked in a circle and was back to where he started? He studied the façade of a large structure, looking for a distinguishing feature he could use as a landmark. His mind felt numb and unreceptive. As soon as he would memorize a crack in a wall or an upturned paving stone, the thought would slip away, and he would be left wondering what he had just seen.

There was no time to stand idle, gazing at architecture. Time to move. He turned a corner to face a locked gate. The key had to be somewhere. Certainly, someone was in charge of such things. Where would a man keep a key? Faceless strangers slid by, fading into the grey. None of them would know, surely. Likely, the key would be kept inside somewhere, perhaps inside the door that he had just passed. Corelan turned to retrace his steps, approaching the plain wooden door. It wouldn't budge. His muscles felt weak. If he had a tool, a pry bar perhaps, he could open the door. He thought back to a smithy he remembered seeing a block past. He trotted back further, searching for the blacksmith shop. There! He ventured inside. The room was deserted of people, but Corelan spied a collection of tools and iron wares on a table in the dark corner. He rooted through the tools, searching for a prybar. Horseshoe. Hammer. Raw bar stock. Nails. Frying pan. Broken fragments of an iron gate. The pile seemed to go on forever. No pry bar, nothing he could use. Perhaps the blacksmith was close.

He wandered toward the rear of the shop, searching for a sign of someone, anyone that could help. He heard faint voices coming from underneath the floorboards. Someone was below. He wandered further into the building, searching for a way downstairs. He rounded one corner after another, growing more deeply entangled in this warren of dark corridors and locked doors. Certainly, there had to be some way to get downstairs.

He ground his teeth in frustration. He was getting nowhere and desperately needed to be across town. If only he could find a way downstairs. He tried another door. His body felt made of lead. He could barely remain standing. If only he could summon enough strength to open this door, he could make his way downstairs. With colossal effort, he demanded his body respond, and he felt the door handle budge. Finally! The door swung open to reveal a closet of brooms. Dead end. He tried to cry out in frustration, but even his voice was paralyzed. He struggled to breathe. Something was covering his mouth. He fought for air. His hand shot to his face and found a hand covering his mouth. His eyes sprang open.

"Corelan, wake up!" Lena hissed. He sat up and looked around. Blackness still filled his vision. He had no idea where he was.

"What…"

"Shhh! You were dreaming. You started thrashing around and moaning," she whispered, leaning in close. His dreaming reality and the reality in which he now sat exchanged places. As the fear faded, his memory returned. They were still lost in the cave, trapped under a mountain with countless hostile Trolls. Much better.

A low light bloomed forth as she unmasked the lantern. The small delicate flame danced precariously on the wick, throwing its feeble light across the left side of her face, bathing her skin in a soft orange glow.

"Do you remember…" He waved her into silence and nodded. Once they had found themselves free of the Troll meeting, they had wandered around aimlessly for several hours, winding deeper and deeper into the cave, ducking and hiding, until what had to be well after nightfall. They found what looked to be an abandoned storeroom, possibly from a time before the Trolls even occupied this mountain and had decided to lay low and get some rest. He looked around.

This complex network of tunnels and chambers they had found themselves trapped in was the culmination of the diligent effort of Troll, man, Ialu, and nature. Before Fate had stuffed him into this rather uncomfortable position, he had a rather in-depth discussion on the history of the area with Tim. Well, actually, it was more of a monologue, with Corelan paying only half a mind, and only that half just to be polite. He now wished he had given the man more attention as he strained to remember the details. Based on Tim's little history lesson and a few things he had heard previously, he felt he had a basic grasp of the general story. This cave, it seemed, only started out as a cave.

Some time ago, two thousand years or so (Tim had given the specific date – was it 1034 or 1043?), a group of Ialu, having just fought in a big war or something, relocated to this part of the world. They found this cave and embellished upon it greatly, carving the natural stone formations to be more conducive to the demands of an active society. They added to the cave, chiseling more chambers and passageways out of the solid rock, carving the engineered arched corridors with evenly spaced living stone pilasters they had seen on the way in. Sometime later (the date was sixteen something), the Ialu became involved in another war that went badly for their allies. Tim had made a point that the Ialu technically didn't lose, but they were forced away from their stronghold. Afterward, the place sat empty for about a century or so.

That was how the humans found it, and, after clearing out the goblins and other riff-raff who were squatting in the place, they proceeded to carve up the mountain in a fairly crude fashion, converting the underground complex into more of a mine than anything else. Their work was evidenced by quick, sloppy cuts into the stone, supported by a thick wooden post and lintel system. After the humans began the open pit quarry just down the road, the Trolls stepped in and threw everybody out. Since then, the Trolls have been making minor improvements over the portion of the complex they actually used while letting the parts they did not use fall into disrepair.

Corelan remembered asking how big the whole thing was, and apparently, at least according to Tim, nobody knew. Ialish records from the time are scarce since "the incident." Tim seemed to think that Corelan knew what *incident*, and Corelan, not wanting to encourage further dissertation on history (a subject in which he had little more than passing interest at most), allowed the misconception to thrive. However, the existing Ialish records indicate the natural portion of the cave ran very deep and was never fully explored before they were called to arms. The human records that were available were sketchy at best. They seemed more interested in material wealth than archaeological exploration, primarily providing statistical information on mineral output, the status of workers, and such. It seemed they never even bothered to fully map the Ialish portion of the cave. The rock Trolls, of course, did not share whatever archives they had, so little was known about their contribution to the site.

The room they were presently in seemed a human addition. The walls were roughly hewn stone, supported by a thick aging wooden post in each corner. The posts supported a square frame that ran along the edges of the room. Several fat logs sawed into halves formed the lintels that spanned the ceiling of the crudely built chamber. Corelan had expressed concern regarding the load-bearing capacity of wooden beams that (if Tim's history lesson had been properly absorbed) were well over 1500 years old. Qaz had examined the beams briefly and concluded that the wood was "enhanced" by derwij magic. Corelan wasn't sure how much faith would choose to place in centuries-old magic, but as Lena pointed out, the room was still standing, and they had nowhere else to go.

Although the structure still seemed to be functional, Corelan would hardly term the effect 'cozy.' A few fragments of wooden crates and one dilapidated barrel barely held together by rusted iron bands (all from the current century) were all that occupied this small dusty room when the three of them had stumbled in during the painfully oppressive darkness of the underground night. The only reason they had chosen to rest here was that someone had the sense to block off this eyesore with a stout wooden door.

Qaz lay sprawled on the dusty floor, his head propped up on his rolled cloak. He slumbered deeply, oblivious to the world. "You okay?" Lena asked. The memory of the dream had slipped slowly away, leaving only a vague impression of unpleasantness.

"Sure, I guess so. What time is it?" He already knew the answer.

"I haven't the faintest notion. I guess you guys have been sleeping for a few hours." She looked away.

"A few hours? You were supposed to wake me after one hour so you could get some rest too."

"Yeah, I know, but I wasn't tired." Corelan raised an eyebrow. "Honestly. I was sitting here thinking about what we overheard." She clenched her jaw unconsciously.

"So, what do you think?"

"What the hell is Kudakaan up to? What kind of deal do you think he had with these Trolls? It just doesn't add up." Corelan thought for a moment before he answered.

"Maybe the Trolls were supposed to act as some kind of backup, to do it the hard way, in case we fail. A dozen or so Trolls could probably take a small village or even a heavily armed caravan."

"Thought of that. I don't think that's it. Sounds like he arranged for this way in advance. Before we got tangled with those bandits. He couldn't have solidified anything with the Trolls anytime afterward. He has to have something else in mind." She studied him in a way that made him uncomfortable.

"Maybe it's got nothing to do with us. Hell, maybe it's got nothing to do with Pendor either. I mean, Kudakaan could have something going on the side."

"He talked about arranging more money. With whom? From the reaction of the Trolls, it sounded like a lot. I'd bet a double crown that someone else higher up is involved. It almost has to be Pendor." Double gold crown? That was Pheldian currency; Pheldi was the only city he knew of that felt the need for such a monetary increment.

"I thought you were from Pelkin," Corelan asked.

"What?"

"Never mind. You have a good point...." he began

"Why did you ask me where I was from?" This caught him completely off guard, as seemed to be her habit. Come to think of it, this seemed to be the habit of most women.

"I, uh, thought you said, in the meeting, that you were from Pelkin," he stammered. "There was a fencing academy or something." Corelan put up his hands in an unconscious defensive gesture. She looked back at him, her face resolute.

"I didn't say where I was from."

"Well, I must have misunderstood then."

"So why did you ask me just now?" He looked back at her, astonished. Why was this such a big deal?

"It's just the thing you said... about the, uh... double crown." She still had an unexplainable intensity to her gaze.

"What about it?" she asked. Corelan was stunned. Usually, when he would cross a woman in some way to solicit this kind of reaction, he would at least have some vague notion of what he had done.

"Okay. Never mind." What has gotten into this woman? He asked himself. "You don't seem to want to talk about your past. I don't want to talk about mine either, so I get it. I won't bring it up again." Corelan finished with a little more heat in his voice than he intended. Lena softened.

"Sorry," she offered.

"Sure. It's fine. Really." He took a deep breath. "We were talking about Kudakaan."

"I was thinking about what he said about Daelyn and me."

"You mean the gift thing?" he asked. She nodded. The thought of such a thing brought back a wisp of the cold from his dream. He shuddered. "I'm sure he was only saying that to save his own neck."

"I'm not so sure. I mean, after learning about this whole Troll deal, whatever it is. We could have been played for fools all along. I wouldn't put anything past Kudakaan; not now." Corelan rubbed his jaw. The prickly stubble of a forgotten number of days' growth reminded him that he could use a long, hot bath.

"I have to disagree." he offered. "If he had always intended to trade off women for… those purposes, he could have hired unskilled labor much cheaper, on less convoluted terms. I don't see why he would hire talented fighters at top dollar to trade them off for… that." A burning fury he could never quite fully contain began to build within him. He forced it down.

"You okay?" Lena looked genuinely concerned.

"I'm fine," he replied flatly. Her face told him she clearly doubted that. She went on.

"One thing is very clear. We have been deceived. There is no disputing that." Corelan nodded in agreement. "We signed on to this job… You sign onto *any* job with an understanding of trust. He clearly broke that, so I in no way feel obligated to fulfill my end of the contract. When and if I see Kudakaan again, I will get answers, one way or another. This I promise you." She had a glint of cold determination in her eyes; a look that Corelan had come to learn was never far away. She stood, restless. She unconsciously clenched her fists by her sides and began to pace. Corelan secretly reminded himself not to get on her wrong side. At least not again.

"Have you reconsidered your policy on carrying a weapon yet?" she went on. "I've seen you fight; I know you're skilled, but I don't like anybody's odds when facing multiple armed Trolls emptyhanded."

"You can take me weapon shopping once we are out of here," Corelan conceded. She had a good point. This mercenary business was proving itself to be quite different from self-defense in the streets of Roth.

"Deal."

"I have an idea," he said. She came closer. "How to get out of this hole." She sat.

"Should I wake Qaz?" she asked.

"Nah." He shook his head. "I could tell his head was killing him when he laid down. Let's let the boy rest so if we need him, he can start pitching fireballs or something."

"If he can." Her voice took on a cynical edge. "All I have seen him do is make a big flash of light. And alternate between flirting with Daelyn and myself."

"Well, he did heal us up a time or two," Corelan offered. She still did not look impressed. "Anyway, it seems to me that, by trying to avoid the soldiers patrolling the halls, we have let them push us into the far corners of the cave." She leaned forward, interested. "I am thinking, if we can shadow a group of Trolls who know where they are going, we might get closer to an exit." She looked back at him, expressionless. "The way I see it, we are like a mouse trapped in the corner of a room. If we don't come out from under the sofa, we will eventually get eaten by the cat."

"That could be one of the most brilliant or most stupid things I have ever heard. I can't decide which." She smiled mischievously. "Either way, it takes guts. I like it." He was saved from further comment by the sound of Qaz shifting around.

"Okay, who put the dead squirrel in my mouth?" Qaz mumbled as he sat up.

"Back amongst the living, I see," Lena chided.

"I thought I might come back just to help you kids along." Qaz yawned with such force, Corelan half suspected his jaw might unhinge itself. "What day is it?" he asked. "Is it still Ninday?"

"I have no idea. Maybe," Corelan answered, looking at the crumbling ceiling. "Does it matter right now?"

"I usually study my spells on Ninday," Qaz answered.

"Do you have enough light in here for your gem thingies?" Lena asked.

"Uh, not really."

"But plenty of light for a spellbook," she suggested.

"The book that would be far too large to carry around all the time? That book?" Qaz sat up defensively.

"Then sounds like study time will have to wait," Corelan suggested.

"Guess so." Qaz stood and twisted his torso, working out the kinks earned from sleeping on a stone floor.

"We have some pressing issues on our schedule anyway," Lena followed.

"I thought of an idea for that," Qaz said.

"We did, too," Lena said.

"Okay, shoot." Qaz rubbed one eye with such vigor, Corelan feared for its safety.

"We follow the patrols out."

"That's dumb," Qaz replied with the half-smile that seemed permanently attached to his face.

"Oh?" Lena replied. Corelan thought it odd she would be defensive over an idea that wasn't even hers.

"It was my understanding we wanted to *avoid* the Trolls." He looked at Corelan for support.

"Don't look at me; I think it's a great plan. Pure genius." Corelan winked at Lena as he spoke.

"So, what's your brilliant idea?" Lena asked.

"I know a spell that tells me which way is north."

"How is that useful here?" she inquired.

"Well, we know Devonshire is east of the quarry. We just follow the tunnels east."

"What if the exits are all to the south or west?" Lena countered.

"Okay. Good point. Maybe not the spell, but I have a better plan anyway." Qaz smiled and looked as if he was about to reveal a morsel of supreme enlightenment.

"And?"

"Always turn left," he responded with solemn dignity.

"Huh?" Lena apparently felt no pressure to pretend it made sense.

"It makes sense," Qaz explained. "If you always turn left, you will, in essence, trace the entire wall." He yawned again. "At some point somewhere, the wall is connected to the exit. It can't fail." He smiled.

"What if you are on an inside wall?" Lena asked. "You could end up going in a huge circle." Qaz wrinkled his forehead.

"Then turn right?" he offered. Lena responded only with a flat look. Qaz smiled sheepishly. "Okay, that idea stinks too. I guess we'll go with your plan."

"Well, let's get on with it," Corelan suggested, standing and rubbing circulation back into his legs. The others stood and began to stuff themselves back into their armor. Qaz wasn't shy about asking for help. His armor of overlapping metal scales had been hastily dumped into a heap as soon as they agreed upon a rest. The leather cords that secured the thing around his body had gotten badly tangled, and he only became aware of his situation after he had the monstrosity halfway around his shoulders. It took him and Corelan nearly twice as long to properly suit up as it should have with a single, patient person working alone. Lena watched the men struggle with the armor with an expression exactly halfway between amusement and irritation as she calmly and professionally donned her own dual-layer protection. She tightened the final lace of her steel thigh guard several minutes before Qaz belted his war hammer around his waist and declared himself ready.

"Don't say it," Qaz muttered as Lena bit off the comment she had spent the last five minutes preparing. They collected what little else that had, and within moments they were stealing along quietly down a dark tunnel lit only with the weak light slipping from the crack in Lena's hooded lantern.

This portion of the cave, dotted by numerous cobwebs, seemed to Corelan as if it had been completely abandoned for quite some time. A thin blanket of dust covered the smooth stone floor of these long-forgotten passageways. Faint impressions made by tiny rodent feet occasionally decorated the floor, leading Corelan to turn at one point and observe their own tracks, plainly visible, trailing off into the darkness behind. He shrugged. At least we won't get any more lost, he thought.

They would stop at the occasional intersection and peer intensely into the dark, striving to sift through the murky blackness for some clue as to which path was true. Qaz had suggested turning left at every opportunity until Lena rounded on him and just stared darkly until he promised to be quiet. In the end, they resolved to take whichever path seemed the least dusty.

Corelan surmised that this portion of the complex was of Ialish fashion. The corridor floor was even, smooth and straight; the stone ceiling arched and strong. When they passed through a natural portion of the cave, a wide path had been cut, leading plainly ahead through the original rock formations. Where cuts had been made through solid stone, intricate representational carvings decorated the walls and thresholds. Corelan could only imagine what this place had been like when it was inhabited. It was large enough to house hundreds – likely thousands of Ialu. The dancing shadows thrown by Lena's lantern seemed like ghosts of the past, flitting and darting about on the edges of his vision. This place made him uneasy, yet at the same time, inspired a sense of wonder.

The three wandered for hours before coming across signs of habitation. They rounded a corner and found a stout wooden door blocking the end of the corridor. Pale orange light leaked out from beneath. Lena dropped to a crouch and lowered the lantern's flame to emit a mere trickle of light. Corelan took a step past her and motioned for the others to remain where they were. She gave him a look of protest, but he reached over and tapped the metal of her shoulder guard, raising his other finger to his lips. She would make a racket indeed trying to creep about in all that metal. He turned away before she could respond and slid silently up to the door.

He stole a glance back at his companions. Lena had drawn her sword and was crouched low, her back flat against the wall. Qaz peeked around the corner above her head. He smiled and urged him on. Corelan pressed his ear to the wooden door. Silence. He crouched to the floor to try to see beneath the door, but the crack was just too small. No help there. He ran his fingers along the door's edge and found the hinges. They were dry and held traces of rust. Corelan guessed this door was rarely used and, therefore, would likely resist opening. He turned back to the others and gestured to indicate that the door opened toward himself into the hallway. He pointed to his ear and shook his head.

Qaz and Lena whispered to each other for a moment. Lena stood and crept to the door, only making a few soft clanking sounds as she approached.

"Let's do it," she whispered. Corelan shrugged. Why not? "Open the door but stay behind it." She spoke softly, spinning her sword to loosen her wrist. Looking back to Qaz, she gave him a thumb's up sign and positioned herself in the center of the tunnel, standing solidly planted with her sword drawn. This lady is nuts, Corelan thought. He looked back at her. She nodded. He took a deep breath and grasped the door handle. He swallowed once, breathing deeply to calm and energize himself as he was taught. He firmed his grip on the handle and planted his feet, grounding his weight. Taking one more deep breath, he turned to Lena and nodded. She nodded back.

He lifted and dropped his weight suddenly, focusing his entire energy into one quick jerk. The door resisted for a fraction of a second, then popped open. He opened the door slightly with two backward steps and braced it with his left shoulder. He had opened the door about a third of the way. He looked back at Lena, who was locked into a low fighting stance. The shadow of the door split her face evenly. Half was illuminated from the room's light, and half fell into deep shadow. Still silence. Her expression was serious but not alarmed. She shifted slightly to see more of the room and motioned for him to open the door further. He pulled back slightly, still bracing the door. Lena stood up out of her stance and cautiously approached the doorway, sword pointed defensively. Corelan opened the door a bit more to allow her space to pass. She glanced at him briefly and entered the room cautiously. As soon as she passed, Corelan moved from behind the door and looked into the room.

The chamber was round – nearly fifty paces in diameter. Thick wooden beams, supported by four posts, held the ceiling roughly twelve feet overhead. Lena had slipped around the corner, offering him an unobstructed view. A sturdy wooden table, surrounded by four chairs, stood in the middle of the dirt floor. A large lantern sat on the table, its light complemented by a dozen or so torches that hung in regular intervals along the hewn stone walls. Without looking back, he motioned for Qaz to approach. Qaz arrived a moment later, accompanied by the unmistakable sound of someone in armor trying to move quietly.

"Hold here; I am going in too," Corelan told him. He poked his head into the room. Lena had moved off to his left, slowly making her way to a door on the far side of the room. To his right, the wall was sectioned off by a row of iron bars stretching from the floor to the ceiling. This was some kind of prison, perhaps. Heavy shadows fell into the cell, making it difficult to discern its contents from a distance. Corelan looked back at Lena. She had her ear pressed to the room's only other door. Qaz had poked his head into the room and was trying to look everywhere at once.

Movement to his right grabbed Corelan's attention. Something was in the cell. He froze. A figure materialized out of the shadows. Corelan snapped his fingers twice. He heard Lena spin rapidly behind him. The figure approached the bars. It was a man somewhere in his middle years, dressed in tattered, filthy shreds of now unrecognizable clothing. A long, dirty, untrimmed beard covered his dirt-stained face. He placed his hands on the bars of the gate and looked at the three intruders. Corelan waited for a tense moment, wondering what to do next. He heard Qaz mumbling softly behind him. The prisoner spoke.

"Hello, my friends." A smile of surprisingly clean teeth suddenly split his dusty face. Corelan looked back at Lena for a moment. She stood behind the swing of the far door, sword ready. She looked back and said nothing. He turned back to the prisoner.

"Uh. Hi," he replied.

"I am thinking they will be back soon." The prisoner spoke with a slight accent, somewhat reminiscent of peoples further south.

"The Trolls?" Corelan asked. He wondered how he ended up being the group's spokesman.

"Yes." He nodded calmly. "I am hoping you can let me out of here before that, eh?" Lena stepped closer to stand beside Corelan.

"We, uh, don't have any keys," Corelan offered. He really had no idea what to do. The thought of just leaving this man here to the mercy of the Trolls did not sit well with his conscience. On the other hand, trying to find a way to free this man, a total stranger, and escape this cave with him on the loose certainly complicated an already unfavorable situation.

"He is probably locked up for a reason," Lena whispered.

"It is my thought that if the Trolls found you sneaking about such, you might find yourself locked up as well, pretty lady." The prisoner smiled and nodded to them.

"He has got a point," Corelan said.

"What if they threw him in there for murder or thievery of something?" she offered.

"Oh, my dear sweet friends, you judge me too rashly…" the prisoner began. Corelan turned back to him.

"Would you excuse us for just a moment…" He took hold of Lena's arm and began to move toward the door they had entered through.

"Marcis. Marcis Shelvala is my name." He smiled again.

"Thanks, Marcis," Corelan answered over his shoulder. Lena pulled her arm free and walked with him. "Certainly, we can't leave him here…" he began.

"Why not?" she asked. "If we try to break the lock on that cell, the noise would certainly bring half the Trolls in the mountain down here." She folded her arms across her steel breastplate. "Do you know how to pick a lock?"

"Uh, no, but…"

"Then how exactly do you plan to get him out of the cell anyway?"

"Maybe Qaz can magic it open…"

"I am thinking they will be back any moment now…" Marcis piped up.

"Quiet!" Lena hissed. Marcis fell silent with a very hurt look on his face. "Corelan, your need to rescue everybody is getting out of hand. This makes four."

"Four?"

"Count 'em."

"Look, any enemy of the Trolls is a friend of ours," Corelan said. "And we are currently very low on friends." She opened her mouth to protest, but he held a stern finger aloft. "If we leave him here, it is a certain death sentence. You might as well run him through yourself." He did not want to admit, though, that he still had no idea of how to get the man out of the cell.

"Well, whatever we do, we had better do it fast," Qaz added. "This doesn't seem like a place that is likely to remain deserted for long."

"You may wish to free me now. I think I hear them coming…" Marcis interjected.

"I said quiet!" Lena snapped.

"No, woman. I said I think I hear them coming." The room fell very suddenly to dead quiet. Corelan whirled to face the far door. The sound of heavy booted feet could now quite clearly be heard coming down the hall. For a brief moment, his heart stopped. Lena drew her dagger and tossed it to Marcis.

"You start it. We'll back you up," she whispered. Qaz ducked back into the hallway as Lena grabbed Corelan by the arm and followed, hauling him through the door.

I suppose she decided to help, after all, he thought. She pushed the door almost closed and waited, sword drawn. Corelan opened his mouth to speak just as the sound of the far door crashing open broke the sudden silence. After an insufferably long moment of quiet suspense, a gruff Troll voice rang out.

"Human." Silence followed. "We heard speech. Who were you talking to?" Corelan felt pressure in his chest. He exhaled slowly as he realized he was holding his breath.

"Why don't you and your two friends come in here and ask me politely?" *So, there are three of them. Smart.* "Well, answer me, you son of a motherless goat!" *Not wasting any time, I see.* Corelan thought.

"What!" came the response. Corelan heard the sound of keys rattling and someone crossing the floor rapidly. "You will pay for that, human!"

"Churok!" another voice yelled. It followed with a string of Troll speech that sounded like a warning. Corelan looked at Lena. She had her sword drawn and stood ready to jerk the door open. Marcis spoke again.

"I see your friends are not as eager to die as you, Churok. They stand away, in fear of me." *Giving us their positions in the room,* Corelan thought. *This Marcis is a clever fellow.*

"They simply do not wish to have your blood soil their boots." The sound of squealing iron announced the opening of the cell door. "Now, human, you will die slowly. What are you smiling about? Are you so eager to die?" Corelan reached to nudge Lena, but she was already in motion. The door crashed open, followed by three grunts of surprise. Lena rushed across the room in four quick strides, charging toward the taller soldier furthest away to avoid crossing in front of Corelan and Qaz. The two warriors in the room spun rapidly. The Troll in the cell – Churok, Corelan assumed – turned to face the three intruders with wide-eyed amazement.

Lena's opponent took a step backward, struggling to free the broad axe strapped to his back.

A moment before he brought it to bear, she closed in on him, slicing his belly open with a vicious slash. He bellowed loudly as he fell forward, his hands still fumbling to free his axe. She sidestepped his falling body and severed his head with a downward, backhanded stroke.

The Troll facing Corelan was armed with a spear and wasted no time hurling it directly at his chest. Corelan flung himself to the ground mid-stride, hitting the ground in a roll. A solid thunk announced the spear burying its fury in the stout wooden support beam just behind him. As Corelan rolled to his feet, the Troll whipped a short thick blade from its scabbard at his side and slashed downward as if to split his attacker in two. Corelan lunged closer and reached forward to meet the Troll's swing with both hands. He grabbed hold and pushed the Troll's wrist to one side, allowing the force of the attack to carry itself down and away. As the soldier struggled to maintain his balance, Corelan stepped to the Troll's side, smashing his other elbow to his opponent's ribs. The soldier grunted and planted his weight, shifting as if to pull his weapon hand free from Corelan's grasp. Corelan moved with the warrior's arm, twisting the Troll's wrist and stepping around behind himself as he did so, completing the circular motion with his hands. Corelan felt something pop in the soldier's wrist as he fell over backward, landing with a thud on the ground beside him. Corelan smashed a booted heel into the Troll's temple, pulling him into the strike with his ruined hand. The Troll went limp.

Corelan whirled around, stepping away from the soldier, taking in the rest of the scene. Churok had turned away from Marcis, who had taken the opportunity to plunge the dagger into the Troll's side. The two had fallen to the cell floor, and now Marcis was scrambling to stab the Troll again. As he brought the dagger up, Churok rolled, bashing his elbow into the prisoner's face. Marcis tumbled across the cell, the dagger skittering across the floor. Churok, his face a mask of rage and bloodlust, rose slowly to his feet, favoring the wound in his side. Lena took a step toward him as he reached for the huge sword that hung at his hip. Before anyone could act, a grapefruit-sized ball of orange and white sizzling flame streaked through the air past Corelan's shoulder and took Churok full in the face, carrying him several paces toward the wall before he fell. He hit the floor without a sound and was still.

Corelan spun around as Qaz lowered his arms. A thin trail of wispy smoke led from his right hand to the cell. Corelan stood motionless for a moment, unsure what to think. Lena stared at Qaz as if she had never seen the man before.

"What?" Qaz asked.

"Uh, nothing," Corelan replied.

"Let's move," Lena said, entering the cell. "Now."

Qaz moved to the opposite door and peered out into the hallway beyond. Corelan entered the cell behind Lena, who knelt beside Marcis, helping him to his feet. The acrid smell of burnt flesh filled the room. Corelan avoided looking directly at Churok and stepped around the body to retrieve Lena's dagger.

"You okay?" she asked Marcis. He smiled weakly and nodded.

"Thank you for saving me, my friends. I am forever in your debt."

"Thank us when we are outside," Lena replied curtly. "Lena. Corelan. Qaz." She pointed at each of them in turn. Marcis nodded and stepped out into the room.

"You good?" she asked Corelan.

"Fine. This yours?" He offered her the knife.

"Thanks." She took the blade, wiping it clean with a rag, before sheathing it. "Qaz?"

"It's quiet," came the reply. Qaz had his head stuck through the far door and was peering out along the hall.

'Good." She stepped out of the cell into the room, pausing beside the Troll's spear where it still quivered slightly from being buried in the wooden support post. "Corelan?" She gestured to the weapon.

"That's Troll size, it's really too long…" He trailed off in response to her raised eyebrow. "Fine, it will do." He tugged the weapon free of the post and tested its balance.

Lena gestured toward the underused door they had originally entered through. "Come on. This won't go unnoticed for long." Marcis had retrieved the small, stout blade from Corelan's fallen foe and was testing its heft.

"I must disagree, my new friend. We should go this way." He pointed to the door the Trolls came through. Lena sheathed her sword and adopted a posture Corelan could only describe as scolding.

"And why is that?" she asked. Corelan could tell she was already beginning to regret this man's rescue.

"Because, my lovely friend, this is the way I came in." He smiled and gestured toward the door. Corelan paused at this comment.

"You know how to get out of here?" Lena asked.

"Yes. Who would enter a cave of Trolls and not…" Marcis realized where that was going and wisely chose to let that line of thought die.

"Are you sure?" She took a step forward, a look of mistrust on her face.

"I have had a bit of time to think about it, no?" he responded as he strapped on the Troll's sword belt. Lena looked at Corelan. Sure, why not, he thought. He shrugged to echo that thought. Marcis dropped his newfound blade into its scabbard. "So, my saviors, if you will allow, I shall lead you to safety." He gestured grandly to the door as if he were about to lead them on a tour of Pheldi's Imperial City.

We are so dead. Corelan thought.

* * * * *

Daelyn looked across the table at Tim, watching as he painstakingly blew the steam from his teacup. The man seemed entirely absorbed with this task, content to sit and puff his cheeks until his tea was the perfect temperature, all of life's stresses set aside. Uglor's wilderness navigation skills had proven to be flawlessly accurate, and they arrived in Cromwood ahead of their schedule with two hours of daylight to spare. He and Jack had chosen to take their dinner in the common room of their inn, and while Daelyn felt duty bound to join them and engage in yet another circular discussion of their tactical situation, she simply could not bear to spend another evening in a dark tavern surrounded by raucous townsfolk.

After a long overdue visit to the bathhouse, Daelyn felt almost human again. Tim had spied this outdoor Selyrian teahouse on their way in, and, in the light of spending another evening listening to Jack over-analyze things, she agreed to dine here with Tim in the open air instead. They now sat at the far end of one of the long communal tables that filled the brick-paved courtyard of the teahouse, sipping their teas as they nibbled on a fresh loaf of bread and awaited whatever soup the chef had decided to make today.

The sun had finally relented its dominance of the sky and slipped behind the horizon. An elderly Selyrian man was painstakingly making his way around the patio, affixing lanterns one at a time with a long hook to a web of hemp rope crisscrossed overhead. Tim gestured to the stubby candle on the table between them. A flame sprung forth from the wick.

"A light for the lady?" he said with a sheepish smile.

"Show off," she chided him.

"It's the most I can do," he responded.

"Don't you mean least?"

"Well, honestly, right now, it's the most." Tim looked away and sighed. "I haven't reached my threshold with psychokinetics yet."

"Sorry?" Daelyn asked.

"Oh. I don't want to bore you with magic talk."

"We could sit here in silence and stare at each other instead." Daelyn kept the bite out of her sarcasm to spare the man's feelings. He smiled.

"Okay, well, the strength of a psychic's psychokinetic powers is relative to their emotional intensity at any given moment," Tim explained.

"I've heard something like that," she replied.

"With experience, though, a psychic can learn to draw to their full potential with a calm mind. It's called finding your threshold," Tim explained.

"I see." Daelyn shifted her gaze for a moment as a Selyrian woman in a blue velvet jacket entered the courtyard accompanied by a hulking black-scaled Chull. His reptilian eyes quickly scanned the other patrons as his companion spoke to the proprietor. Daelyn turned back to Tim.

"I'm tired from traveling, relaxed from this lovely tea, and in a good mood, so I haven't got a lot of fire in me right now, so to speak," he explained.

"So, if I reached out and slapped you in the face, would you be able to conjure more?" Daelyn asked.

"If *you* slapped me," Tim chuckled. "I'd probably just wonder what I did to deserve it." He noticed the Chull across the patio. "Now, if he slapped me, it would be different. If he slapped you, I'd probably be able to chuck him over the wall just by looking at him."

"Protective, are we?" she asked with a smile. Daelyn noticed the Selyrian woman and her Chull companion making their way across the patio, moving toward where she and Tim sat. The Selyrian gestured to the communal table and smiled.

"May we join you?" she asked, speaking directly to Daelyn. The Chull stood silently behind her, delicately holding a tray with an iron teapot and cups. A massive war hammer hung from a loop on his belt.

"Of course," Daelyn responded, gesturing to the bench beside them. As the two sat, the Chull spared a toothy smile and a nod for Tim.

"I am Athala and this is Svarka," she said. "We are pleased to share a table with you." Athala smiled congenially as Daelyn introduced herself and Tim. "How is the soup here?"

"It looked like rice and mixed peppers in a vegetable broth. I'm looking forward to it," Daelyn answered.

"A proper Selyrian recipe." Athala nodded in approval. "I'm sorry, Svarka; I did warn you."

"It won't be the first time." He rasped an almost hissing chuckle. "I apologize, my new friends; as you may be aware, we Chull only consume meat, so I will not be joining you in your delicious soup. Tea, however, is another matter." He poured tea into everyone's cups wearing the inherently disturbing toothy smile of the Chull.

"Are you travelers?" Athala asked.

"Merchants. Passing through town," Daelyn answered quickly before Tim could spoil their anonymity. He smiled in a controlled fashion and sipped his tea. "Yourselves?"

"We are on the trail of a dangerous criminal," Athala replied.

"You're King's Marshals then?" Tim asked.

"Not Marshals, per se. The king's justice has posted a generous reward for the capture of one Feren Kippux." Athala spoke in a slightly hushed tone.

"Don't coat it with honey," Svarka interjected. "We are bounty hunters," he added, draining his tea in a single gulp. She gestured in concession.

"What did this Kippux fellow do?" Daelyn asked.

"Murder and such." Athala shook her head. "Terrible crimes. He is worth five thousand silver crowns, dead or alive." Daelyn raised an eyebrow at the sum. Terrible crimes indeed to be worth that much. "I don't suppose you have heard anything?" Athala asked. "We'd be happy to share some of the reward for information that leads to his capture."

"I'm afraid we don't know anything about any murderers," Daelyn answered. Athala nodded to her in understanding, essentially ignoring Tim, as was typical in traditional Selyrian culture. Men were best when quiet and submissive.

"We are too busy buying and selling," Tim interjected, perhaps sensing the dismissal. "Shoes. We are selling shoes," he added. Daelyn restrained herself from looking directly at him.

"This tea is lovely," Svaka chimed in. "But I am afraid I must seek food that is more suitable for my needs. I think I smell a grill close by." He raised his scaly snout to sample the air. "I bid you a good evening, my friends." He rose and excused himself with a bow.

"Stay out of trouble," Athala scolded him. He donned a mock hurt expression and turned away without responding. "I mean it," she said to his retreating back. "Chull." She turned back to the table. "Always interesting to travel with."

A young Selyrian serving boy arrived at their table with a pot of soup and three bowls. Athala dismissed him with a pat on the head. The conversation turned to more mundane subjects, and, after a few failed attempts at joining in, Tim resigned himself to being a quiet observer of the conversation rather than a contributor. After finishing their second pot of tea, Athala excused herself, citing concern over Svaka's ability to behave himself properly. Once the table was exclusively theirs again, Daelyn turned to Tim.

"Shoes?" she laughed.

"What?" He put up his hands defensively. "If we need a cover story, next time, let me know in advance, so I don't say something stupid like we are selling shoes." He sounded almost hurt, but he also seemed to be having trouble containing his own mirth.

"It's fine," she assured him. "You're just a terrible liar. Next time let me do the talking."

"You did that part just fine."

"Oh, get over it." Daelyn waved him silent. "You men do that to us all the time. It was just your turn." She lifted an eyebrow at him, inviting a challenge. While her comment was certainly justified, given that she was pretending to be Toctillian, it was doubly so. A "proper" Toctillian woman sitting among men would likely not speak a word.

"Fair," he conceded. "I apologize. To nurse my bruised ego, allow me to settle the bill."

"I think you've missed something here," she suggested with a wry grin. Tim laughed out loud. To hear a genuine laugh was refreshing. "Besides, I think our friend Athala has already paid for us all." Daelyn gestured to the pile of coinage their recent dining companion had left on the table before departing. As they walked back toward the inn, Daelyn felt herself analyzing the evening. Tim seemed quick to engage with their dining partners on the subject of the King's Marshals. Was he afraid they would recognize him as one of their agents? But then again, he genuinely seemed to be lousy at improvising a cover story, which suggested that covert work was not his forte. Unless he was pretending to be clumsy to throw her off. She dismissed the circular thought pattern and decided to simply enjoy a cool evening stroll through town. Maybe someday life would be simple. Just not today.

CHAPTER SEVEN
ENDWEEK
30TH OF TURADMUR

"Well, what now?" Lena asked their newfound friend. Marcis turned away from peering down the hall to face her. He shrugged and smiled. Past him, at the mouth of the dark tunnel, the silhouette forms of a half-dozen Troll warriors stood out against the bright moonlight of the night sky. Lena wasn't sure why she was surprised to see it was dark out. It was nearly impossible to keep track of time in the oppressive blackness of the cave interior, and while she had initially thought they had been inside for only a day, it now seemed more like two. She felt she could get a better idea of the time once she could see the night sky. Her stomach rumbled faintly to inquire if perhaps her throat had been cut, and that was the reason no food was coming through. She forced the thought away to concentrate on the situation.

"Let's just run for it," Marcis suggested. Qaz and Corelan adopted identical looks of disbelief.

"Are you suggesting we simply run past six heavily armed and armored Troll warriors out into the night?" she asked him. She fought to keep from raising her voice past a whisper. If the soldiers at the end of the tunnel heard them, this discussion would very quickly become pointless.

"Sure," he responded. "They are looking to keep their enemies out, not in, no?" Marcis answered. He had to be mad. The confinement in the Troll prison had driven him mad. That had to be it.

"Well, what then?" She had to put a stop to this crazy talk. "We just run until we are out of bounds, and they turn back? This isn't a game of toadhop, you know." Lena stabbed an accusing finger in his face. Behind Marcis, she could see Qaz trying and mostly failing to suppress a grin.

"Surely we will lose them in the darkness."

"This is their territory. They know these woods; they live here. None of us have any idea where to go." She looked at Corelan for support.

"She has got a point," he added.

"Ah, but that is where you are wrong, my lovely young friend." He raised a finger. "I know this country as I know my own face." He smiled. "Besides. What choice have we?" She leaned back against the bend in the hall that hid them from the Trolls at the end of the tunnel. She thought about this tactically. They were only a few hundred paces from the exit with only six soldiers between them and escape. A quick dash just might put them past the guards and out into neutral territory with much greater freedom of movement. There was nowhere to hide here in the hall; if they turned away, they would have to retreat further into the cave. That was unacceptable. None of them had any idea where another exit might be. As much as she hated to admit it, this really was their only option. When life offers you but one choice, you seize it with both hands.

"Qaz." She took him by the arm to get his attention. "Can you hit them with another one of those flash-of-light things?" she asked.

"Not from this distance." He turned to look around the corner. "I would have to get about halfway there to be sure to blind them all."

"How long would the blindness last?"

"A minute. Maybe two."

"Good enough. Let's go for it." She unsheathed her sword. "Qaz will casually walk down the hall." He raised an eyebrow at that. "We will follow a short distance behind. Our goal is to be quiet. Once they see you, Qaz, run in only as close as you need to hit them with the light." The men stood in a small arc around her, watching silently. She went on. "Marcis, when you see Qaz raise his hand, you shut your eyes, cover them with your hand if you have to." He nodded. "Once the light fades to a safe level, Qaz, give a quick whistle…"

"I can't whistle." He smiled sheepishly.

"Then shout. It doesn't matter. Once he gives the signal, we run out. Stay together no matter what." She made eye contact with each of them to be certain they understood that point. She had seen too many examples of a good plan going bad because people did not act as a group. "Marcis. You lead once we get into the woods. Remember – stay together no matter what. If anyone gets separated, we are not coming back, so don't wait around." She ventured a peek around the corner. The Trolls were still milling around by the cave entrance. "Any questions?" Three heads shook in unison. "Then let's do it. Qaz?"

"Thank you, my dear." He donned that goofy grin that had become his trademark and straightened his armor, puffing out his chest and lifting his chin as if he were about to step out on stage. She shoved him forward. She watched him, wincing involuntarily with each echoing footfall of his boots as he strode down the hall. Corelan took a step to follow, but she placed a hand on his chest. Not yet, she thought. He backed away, almost avoiding her touch. She was not sure what was going on with this fellow. She knew the effect she had on men. She could see it in Qaz and some of the others in the group, but Corelan – he was hard to read. He clearly had some things going on, but hell, don't we all? She forced the thought away. Time to focus on the task at hand.

Qaz had gotten about a third of the way down the hall. None of the Trolls seemed to have noticed him yet. All they had to do was turn and look. She stepped forward, and without looking back, she motioned for the others to do the same. She felt her heart pounding with each step she took toward the cave mouth. Surely, they would turn. Qaz reached the halfway point. He slowly raised his hand as if stretching.

"Get ready," she whispered. One of the Trolls heard Qaz approaching and turned to peer into the darkness. Lena took another hesitant step, then clamped her eyes shut as she saw Qaz's hand drop suddenly. The Troll shouted. Qaz said something incomprehensible, and suddenly a brilliant orange light tried to burn through her eyelids. She heard a clamor of surprise from the soldiers guarding the tunnel as they were affected by the spell.

"Let's go!" Qaz shouted as the light began to fade. Lena's eyes snapped open, and she looked around rapidly, taking stock of the situation. The Trolls at the end of the cave were stumbling about, most rubbing their eyes trying to regain their vision. Lena leapt into motion, shouting wordlessly, clanging the flat of her sword against the steel guard on her forearm, trying to make as much noise as possible. Marcis followed suit quickly, dragging the blade of his sword along the stone wall as he ran bellowing like a madman. Qaz made enough noise by simply running in his armor. The Trolls parted quickly, unsure of what or who was attacking them and making all that clamor. They stumbled over each other, trying to free up their weapons to fend off the army of mages and lunatics that were somehow pouring out of their own cave. The four dashed past the Trolls into a small clearing in the woods. Lena's heart sank as she saw seven more warriors running from a small hut off to one side of the clearing. Qaz skidded to a halt and raised a hand. Tiny points of light began to flicker between his fingers as the soldiers brought their weapons to bear. Without slowing, Lena grabbed hold of his collar and yanked him toward the other side of the field. Marcis and Corelan raced past without pause.

"Hey…" Qaz began. The lights faded from his hand.

"Not here!" she shouted, dragging him to a run. "There is a whole mountain full of them! Run!" She slammed her sword into its scabbard and tore off after Marcis and Corelan, not waiting for the clever quip that was sure to follow. In seconds they were racing through the dark woods. Marcis had somehow spied what had to be a small game trail, and they were plunging headlong into the forest depths. The moonlight barely lit the path ahead. She slowed slightly. It would be rather pointless to miraculously escape capture by a mountain full of angry Trolls only to break your neck running blindly through the woods. Unseen twigs and branches whipped across her face and clutched at her hair and armor as she raced ahead. The sound of the soldiers crashing along behind them was unmistakable. The Trolls were definitely in pursuit.

Corelan ran along the path about fifty paces ahead of her, spear in hand. She could not see Marcis but assumed he was ahead, leading the way. Qaz was a few paces behind, breathing heavily. Ahead, Corelan suddenly darted to the right. She followed suit instinctively and was several steps past the turn before realizing the trail had forked. She risked a glance over her shoulder. Qaz crashed through the underbrush as he careened past the turn. She slowed slightly, cursing under her breath. Her hand drifted to her sword hilt. Qaz quickly found the trail and motioned for her to continue. She stepped up her pace.

The trail split again, and Marcis took the left fork without hesitation. The path darkened as the moon slipped behind a dense cloud. She was forced to slow again. She heard Qaz's labored breathing behind her. He did not seem to be tiring yet, but she doubted that either one of them could maintain this breakneck pace in heavy armor indefinitely. Corelan was a pale, almost ghostly image on the trail ahead. She had to concentrate just to see him. For a moment, she feared losing sight of them altogether. The warriors crashed along doggedly on the trail behind them, and from the sound of it, it seemed the Trolls were gaining on them. The path twisted again, almost doubling back on itself. She nearly plowed straight into a tree as she struggled to make the turn, grabbing hold of a branch to keep from falling over. Qaz, only a few seconds behind, skidded to a halt to avoid smashing into her. Without a word, she leapt to a run, pointing the way. Four strides down the trail, she realized she had completely lost sight of Corelan. The path was beginning to weave its way down a steep hill. She kept running, slowing yet again to avoid missing any turns. A cold knot started to form in the pit of her stomach. This was not good. Moonlight suddenly flooded the trail as the cloud cover blew past. She sped up, searching the path ahead wildly for signs of Corelan or Marcis.

"I don't see them," Qaz gasped behind her as he ran. The blood pounded through her veins, her ragged breath reminding her that she couldn't recall the last time she had anything at all to eat. Much less a sip of water. They needed to escape quickly. A prolonged run through the dark forest, in their current state, being pursued by well-fed and rested Trolls on their home turf was not going to end well. She doubled down her effort to gain some distance. She could hear the sound of the Trolls shouting as they came across the switchback that almost tumbled her to the forest floor. As she ran, she caught sight of a small fallen tree, no bigger around than her wrist, lying across the path. She leapt over it a fraction of a second later. Before she could shout a warning to Qaz, he tumbled over it with a surprised shout. He sailed silently through the air for a moment before crashing face-first onto the trail. He tumbled along in the dirt and leaves for a few paces and crashed to an abrupt halt into a tree trunk. Lena skidded to a stop and ran to help him to his feet. He staggered to stand, shaking his head. He took a step to run down the trail, but she held him back by the arm.

"What…" he began.

"Shhh!" She silenced him. "Listen."

"I don't hear anything," he whispered. Silence fell over the forest like a blanket. From down the hill, she could faintly hear the sound of a small stream gurgling.

"Exactly. No one is running," she whispered. Her voice held an edge of dread. Qaz pulled his hammer from the loop at his belt and turned to look down the trail. A cloud drifted slowly in front of the moon. Based on its position, she guessed the time to be no more than an hour past midnight. Still plenty of darkness left. "Let's go. Quietly," she whispered as she pulled his arm. The cloud cover shifted further, plunging forest once again into near-complete blackness. The two took a few tentative steps along the trail. Lena dedicated every bit of her energy toward gathering each and every sound the forest made. There was no sign of either her friends or the pursuing soldiers. The moonlight bloomed forth again, revealing three Trolls standing a stone's throw away on the trail ahead, their backs turned, weapons out. She froze. Her pulse quickened. How could someone so large move so quietly? She turned around slowly. Four more Trolls occupied the path behind them. One of them was bent to the ground examining the tree Qaz had nearly felled with the top of his head. One of the others spotted them and shouted. All seven spun to stare at the two humans trapped on the trail between them.

"This is just not a good week for me," Qaz muttered. For a very brief moment, Lena contemplated a fight here on the trail. The odds — seven against two with enemies on either side — made her decision easy. Without warning, she grabbed Qaz's arm and ran off the trail, straight down the hill. With a surprised shout and very little choice, he followed. She more fell than ran, just trying to keep her legs beneath her as small branches whipped at her eyes and grabbed at her ankles. A shout from the Trolls was followed quickly by the sound of seven enormous bodies crashing through the woods. This is absolutely insane, she thought. Her foot caught on some unseen root, and she pitched forward, hitting the ground in a tight ball. She rolled to her feet in an instant, almost by accident, and continued her mad descent. She heard a loud grunt and the thudding sound of a body smashing into a tree. She hoped it was not Qaz, noting to herself that even without the Trolls in pursuit, she could hardly stop to help anyway.

Without warning, the hill ended in the small stream she had heard earlier. The momentum of her descent sent her sprawling into the shallow water with a loud splash. A split second later, Qaz came flying out of the brush face first and barely managed to halfway roll in midair, splashing on his side into the brook. She heard the sound of Trolls descending the steep hill off to either side. They would be cut off from going either up or downstream. She staggered to her feet and took a step toward the equally steep hill forming the opposite bank. With a sense of dread, she realized there was no way to ascend the hill she faced with half a dozen Trolls hacking at her heels. She drew her sword. Without the cover of foliage, the moon provided enough light to fight. This was a good enough place to die, she thought. Qaz pushed himself out of the muddy water to sit on his heels, coughing. He rubbed his eyes, trying to clear his head from the impact with the rocky stream bottom.

She strode over to him and hauled him to his feet just as the Trolls burst from the forest a dozen or so paces to either side. Had she been closer, she thought, she could have taken one or two as they fell into the stream. No matter, the end result would be the same. Taking outnumbered Trolls by surprise was one thing. Facing three times your number in battle-ready Troll warriors was quite another. Qaz brought his hammer to bear as she turned to face the three upstream.

"I've got these three," he said. All traces of his usual good humor were gone. The Trolls took a moment to gain their bearings. Two of the three she faced held clubs that resembled small, uprooted trees. The third brandished a makeshift weapon that appeared to be a flattened shovel on the end of a long pole. They took battle stances and approached cautiously. She heard Qaz begin to mumble something, hoping it was some kind of devastating battle magic. Based on her limited knowledge of the subject and what little she had seen so far, she doubted Qaz had that kind of firepower. She sank into a low, solid stance herself. If these Trolls wanted her, they would have to come get her. They approached slowly. Just as they neared the edge of what she judged to be their combat range, she heard rustling in the bushes across the stream.

"Woman! Get down!' A voice rang out of the darkness. The Trolls spun to face the new threat, and she dove toward the opposite bank. Just as she hit the water, she saw a tall bearded man in dark green step out of the underbrush a few paces away and fire a bow at her assailants. She ducked low, splashing into the deeper water in the center of the stream and kicked off of the sandy bottom, drifting only a pace or two in her armor. She stood up in the waist-deep water as chaos erupted around her.

More than a dozen armed men suddenly materialized out of the woods. Those not armed with bows or crossbows rushed through the shallow water to attack the Trolls with blades drawn. Lena was not sure who was more surprised, the Trolls or herself. Arrows streaked through the air as men and Trolls bellowed in anger and pain. The sound of steel ringing on steel echoed through the dark forest. The stream splashed angrily, pulling at the legs and ankles of the combatants who dared to disturb its journey to the sea. It was immediately apparent that the newcomers had no interest in fighting her or Qaz; they had thirst only for Troll blood.

Two men rushed past her within a pace to either side, not sparing so much as a glance as they closed in on the foes she faced alone not a moment before. The Trolls were caught by complete surprise, and two fell to arrows almost immediately. The remaining Trolls recovered quickly, tearing into their attackers with astonishing ferocity. One of the two men that rushed past her was cloven almost in two by a vicious downward stroke from the warriors. As his body fell, another Troll lunged past him, locking eyes with Lena. She immediately snapped out of the shock this surprise attack had given her, falling into the state of supreme singular concentration Instructor Narziim at the Pheldian Academy referred to as "The Spirit of One."

She was aware of the men moving up behind her to engage the other Trolls. She was aware of the second group of Trolls embroiled in a conflict further downstream. She was aware of the sandy river bottom and of the current tugging at her legs. She was aware of her own heartbeat and breathing – of every detail of her physical state. She was aware of all these things but not distracted by a single one. Both her instruction at the Pheldian Academy and her time studying under the fencing masters of Pelkin placed paramount importance on this ability to focus on the task at hand without shutting out the world. Her fencing instructor, the master Garis Shelnaav repeatedly emphasized that "Clarity of mind made the difference between good fighters and great ones."

Lena circled slowly around the soldier advancing up the stream's bank, weapon held ready. She had to get out of the deep water to gain mobility. Against an opponent with much superior reach and power, her mobility and speed were vital. The Troll smiled wickedly. An intimidation tactic, she idly thought. Just before she was on dry, solid footing, the Troll lunged forward, swinging the log he probably called a club in a wide powerful crosswise motion. The attack was slow enough to see in time to respond, but to try to bring the brutal force of such an attack to a dead stop with the obvious parry, would have been futile even for a large man. With her feet still held by the stream, she could never step back fast enough, nor could she move inside the swing for the same reason. She dropped low, catching the attack with her sword held at an angle, conducting the force of the swing up and over her head as she ducked. Bowing to the wind, Instructor Narziim would have said.

She rolled the blade in a half circle over her head and lunged forward, attacking with a downward chop. Her attacker stepped out and away, moving with the force of his deflected attack. She was now on solid ground. Somewhere behind her, a man died. Whipping his weapon around in front of him, the warrior spun around to face her and smiled again. She realized that her initial assessment was wrong. The smile was no tactic; he was simply enjoying himself thoroughly. They live to fight and die, she remembered Tim saying. This Troll did not care a whit that he and his fellows were outnumbered and very likely going to die here in this muddy river tonight. He was simply trying to take as many enemies with him as he went and relishing in the process. Part of her had to admit that it *was* a hell of a way to go.

She circled around him, both moving away from the water and looking for an opening. He stepped forward, attacking with a much shorter, faster stroke. Growing cautious, she noted. She extended a block and was nearly toppled by the force of the strike. Gods was he strong! He immediately pulled his weapon back and stepped forward, stabbing with the tip – an unorthodox move for a blunt clubbing weapon, but it nearly took her head off. As she stumbled back and away, he closed in, whipping the club around to attack the other side. Again, the force of the blow ringing on her blade rattled her bones. He attacked repeatedly, without much flair or strategy. With each bone-jarring block, she realized he was simply trying to keep her on the defensive while he bashed away at her, sapping her strength with each blow. She also realized that there was little she could do about it.

He had superior reach and more than enough power to make up for her speed. Behind him, one of his fellows fell, sprouting an arrow from the back of his head.

Further downstream, the remaining two Trolls were being pressed hard by superior numbers. A bolt of yellow light streaked through the crowd, illuminating the riverbed for a brief moment. It was only a matter of time before the Trolls would be defeated. This fact was of little comfort. She did not think she could hold this one off for much longer.

She tightened her grip on her blade, bracing herself for the shock of another devastating attack. He was now striking with short, fast motions. This, combined with the low light, made it nearly impossible for her to read his intention in time to use a more diverting defense. Her arms felt like lead, and her hands were growing numb. She fought for breath, stepping heavily, as she was slowly forced away from the group. She was expending too much energy with each block. She knew she would be dead soon if something did not change. The Troll had forced the fight across the sandbar, almost into the woods.

These men who had appeared out of nowhere were now too far away to help, even if they started running immediately. She hoped one of the bowmen… That moment's distraction nearly cost her life as a quick upward stroke glanced off of her shoulder guard. She stumbled several paces back and miraculously stayed afoot, realizing that by instinctively tucking her head, she had kept it attached to her shoulders. Master Garis taught her that there was no battle that could not be won. She found with a sense of despair that this belief was now being profoundly challenged. Her enemy sensed this somehow and smiled wickedly, as before.

She found herself suddenly angry. If Death was coming, He would have to work to take her. She would not lie down for anyone, not now or ever. With renewed clarity of mind, she realized that out here on the sand, her opponent could swing his club freely and utilize the full extent of his advantages. She had every intention of changing that. She began to give ground more freely, retreating backward, away from her newfound companions. The Troll pressed on, agreeing with that sentiment. The sound of a leaf crunching beneath her boot was like the sweetest music she had ever heard in the finest Pelkinese symphony halls. The Troll circled his weapon in a short arc to attack downward as he had been, using gravity to assist the power of his swing. There was a leafy crashing sound as the end of his weapon smashed through the low branches overhead, slowing his attack. She lunged forward, tracing a red line across his ribs. He grunted and nodded in appreciation. She stepped back further. He stepped forward, pulling his weapon back for another strike. His club crashed into a small sapling on the backswing, throwing off his timing. She lunged in again, scoring another cut.

The moonlight barely penetrated into the forest. The Troll would have difficulty seeing her, whereas she could see him rather well in silhouette. Her shoulder throbbed with a deep burning pain where the Troll had hit her. This will end soon, she thought, one way or another. The Troll was getting serious now; he lunged, stabbing with the tip as before to avoid becoming entangled in the surrounding foliage. Lena stepped aside, placing a small tree between herself and the weapon. She stabbed forward with her good arm, flinching involuntarily as the tree beside her head shuddered with the violent impact of the Troll's counterstroke. She felt her blade hit home, solidly this time, and heard a reassuring grunt from her opponent. She stepped back, expecting her enemy to fall.

He took a step back, clutching his wounded abdomen. He paused and lifted his blood-covered hand to his eyes. She could see his fingers glistening in the moonlight with his lifeblood. They realized simultaneously that he would not survive this wound. The next few moments seemed to happen in slow motion. With surprising speed, the Troll threw his club end over end at Lena. Under ordinary circumstances, this would have, of course, been a very foolish tactic. He, however, had nothing more to lose.

She fell backward, swinging her blade to deflect the enormous weapon. The tremendous force of the throw nearly sent her sword flying from her grasp. The air whooshed out of her lungs as she landed on her back on the forest floor. He rushed forward and was upon her almost before she hit the ground. Instinctively her sword came up. She felt the blade pierce his body as he forced himself forward. The sickening sound of tearing flesh confirmed that he had impaled himself on her sword. With a growl of ferocity, not pain, he seized her by the throat with fingers like the roots of an enormous oak. *What does it take to kill one of these guys?* He hauled them both to their knees. Lena stared at him in amazement as he pulled back his fist and smashed her in the face. She was three feet away, lying in a daze on the forest floor an instant later. Her head was swimming. None of her limbs would respond. Her whole body was numb. She fought to remain conscious.

He knelt there on the forest floor, with the hilt of her sword protruding from his belly. The dappled moonlight fell through the leaves across his face. The terrible light that shone in his eyes began to fade. His head wobbled as if his neck were made of rubber. He swayed back and forth as he grabbed hold of the blade that pierced his body. She could do nothing but watch. The Troll tried to pull the sword free but tumbled over backward and fell still. After a moment, the darkness began to clear from her vision. She felt a hand on her forehead before realizing it was her own. Every fiber of her body begged for a moment's respite. She forced herself to move. Leaning on a tree, she struggled to her feet and took a wobbly step toward her fallen foe. He lay motionless on his side; the weak moonlight reflected in the pool of wetness forming around his body. She fumbled at her belt, pulling forth her dagger. She could hear the sounds of the battle ending out on the sandbar. She crouched beside the fallen Troll and cautiously rolled his body back with the toe of her boot. No reaction. She grasped the hilt of her sword to pull it free.

His eyes fluttered open. Lena's heart nearly leapt out of her chest. She took a quick step back and nearly blacked out. The point of her knife trembled in her unsteady grasp as she stared in open amazement at the fallen warrior. He fixed a glassy-eyed stare on the moon, struggling to bring it in focus. His head lolled over to bring his gaze to Lena. She stood there in the woods, dagger in hand, watching the Troll breathe his last, awestruck by the power and tenacity of the Troll spirit. He smiled one last time, seeming to acknowledge her battle prowess as if to thank her for the opportunity to have been killed by a skilled fighter. Acting on its own, her head nodded back. The light drained from his eyes, and his life left him.

When she stepped out onto the sandbar, bloody sword in hand, she felt a profound fatigue set upon her. All of the Trolls lay dead in the stream. One trailed a stream of gray smoke, filling the air with the pungent smell of burnt flesh. Five men lay dead as well. Three others were gravely wounded and being tended by five other men. They were all dressed in dark greens and grays and looked as if they had been living in these woods for some time, all unshaven and rough around the edges. Qaz stood in the center of the sandbar, surrounded by men neither of them knew with a bewildered look on his muddy face. The wound he had suffered in the Troll cave had broken open again, and a thin trickle of blood snaked its way across his cheek. One of the men tending to a wounded comrade noticed her almost immediately but did not react as she emerged from the woods. Some of the others were beginning to fan out along the shore, peering into the forest. Lena had no idea what to do next. Qaz looked around at their saviors, obviously sharing her hesitation. He broke the silence.

"Thanks, guys, but we had them," he said, returning to his usual aplomb.

"Lena..." Corelan's voice rang out of the crowd. She snapped out of her daze and whirled around. The ground lurched in the opposite direction and threatened to jump up and hit her in the face. She steadied herself on the point of her sword. Corelan appeared from nowhere. "Are you okay?" he asked. His voice held an edge of concern.

"Just a little beat up," she replied weakly. He looked at her closely, plainly not convinced. Okay, a *lot* beat up. "You lost your spear." She observed.

"It was too long anyway."

"Say, Corelan," Qaz was standing beside her now. When had he walked over here? "Not to be an ingrate or anything, but are these friends of yours?" he asked.

"They are now," he responded. "Friends of Marcis before me, though." Marcis who? She thought. "Apparently, when he got captured a few weeks ago, they hung around looking for a way to get him out."

"Lucky we ran into them then," Qaz responded.

"Not lucky," Marcis interjected. Oh, *that* Marcis. She wished people would stop appearing out of the air like that. "This path is along the way to our home." Lena felt the point of her sword begin to dig itself into the pebbly sand. We are about to fall over, a voice in her head announced.

"Qaz, do you think you can use a bit of your magic to heal the wounded?" Corelan asked. He sounded much further away for some reason. It was a good idea, though, she thought. Without warning, the ground beneath her feet made good on its earlier promise and leapt up, smacking her full in the face. Now that was awfully sneaky, hitting somebody like that when they aren't looking. She heard some alarmed voices talking about someone falling down, but it probably wasn't important. Perhaps a nap would be nice right now. Yes, a short nap.

* * * * *

Corelan wondered for the eleventh time if they were all going to die that night. He forced a smile at the man handing him another mug of his long-lost, malted friend. Well, if I am going to die, I might as well have another beer, he thought. The other man smiled and plopped himself into one of the overstuffed chairs that commanded the center of the room. As near as he could tell, at least a dozen or so men were either in the house or nearby. Corelan swiveled his head toward the door as someone entered. A lanky man with a scar running across his cheek strode in from the damp night. He shook some of the evening's drizzle off of his cloak before hanging it and the short, fat-bladed sword he was wearing on the coat rack beside the door.

Where in the hell were Qaz and Lena? Two hours ago, Qaz went upstairs to check on her, and he had heard not a word since then. They had spent a good portion of the night (or was it morning?) trudging through the woods with their newfound companions to arrive at this dilapidated farmhouse several hours later. It was difficult to accurately estimate time or distance. The march had been a blur of darkness and stumbling – a seemingly endless trek through a seemingly endless forest. Lena's injuries were limited to a possibly dislocated shoulder, a concussion, and an all-around firm pummeling. No significant blood loss. While Qaz had done what he could to heal her, she lapsed into unconsciousness halfway here. A stout man who introduced himself as Ouij (he was particular about the spelling) carried her the rest of the way. Quite a feat of strength, Corelan thought. After the fight with the Trolls, he could scarcely carry himself the distance. Once they had arrived at this farmhouse, Ouij had helped her upstairs, and Qaz followed shortly thereafter. That was the last he had seen of either of them.

Corelan had been urged (ordered?) to stay downstairs and relax until somebody named Kippux or something got back from town. Since then, he had been sitting in this large, ugly chair, which at first had presented itself as also quite lumpy. As time progressed, however, the chair and his bottom had begun to work out some sort of mutually beneficial agreement. He sat amid a motley collection of benches and chairs next to a large blazing fireplace and found himself being essentially ignored. Corelan rubbed his hands together vigorously, both to stay awake and to coax the cold of the mountain stream from out of his bones.

The building seemed to once have been a dwelling for a rather large family. It now seemed to have been converted into a dwelling place for Marcis' two dozen or so friends. All of the details that make a house into a home were gone, having been replaced with stark, utilitarian furnishings. It appeared as if a good number of these men slept on the floors or wherever they could find space. That is, whenever they did actually sleep, which didn't seem like it would be anytime soon. Constructed of large timbers chinked with dried mud, the house felt solid and heavy. Or maybe it was just his eyelids that felt heavy.

As he watched the house's occupants amble around, he became more and more confident that Marcis and his friends were outlaws of some sort. All were armed in some way and had a shifty-eyed manner about them as if they were always looking over a shoulder. They talked in low voices, huddled together as if by habit. That and some of them just plain *looked* dishonest. Corelan sat up suddenly with a stark realization. It was very possible that these bandits were part of the outlaw gang he and his companions had fought earlier. Remembering that there were several survivors from that day, Corelan shuddered to think what would happen if they were recognized. The room suddenly felt once again very cold.

He looked around the room again, this time with a tactical perspective. Five armed men were directly between him and the door. At least two more were in the room directly adjacent, and he could hear at least two outside on the front porch. He decided that he would have to go through a window to have any chance of escape. He sized up some of the smaller pieces of furniture to possibly break the glass when he realized that there were iron bars on all of the windows. The grizzled man with the scar looked up from his conversation across the room and smiled as he thumbed the edge of a large knife. Returning a genuine-looking smile was one of the more challenging things Corelan had done in quite some time. Maybe I *should* start carrying a weapon, he thought. That is if I survive.

He sat in the chair, trying to think of a polite way to go look for his friends, when he heard Lena around the corner. He stood, as casually as he could manage, stretched a bit to further the illusion that he was in no hurry, and ambled around the room toward the staircase. He brought his beer mug in case he needed to smash somebody across the face with something hard. As he rounded the corner, he spotted Lena at the top of the stairs, talking with the Ouij fellow who had carried her from the river. He wore a leather vest and was showing Lena part of a massive tattoo that covered his shoulder and back. She seemed genuinely interested, and the two talked for a moment or two before she noticed Corelan standing at the foot of the stairs. She waved energetically and shook the other man's hand, apparently thanking him again for his gallantry. Enough already, Corelan thought. She came down the stairs quickly, showing no sign of having been beaten unconscious a few hours ago.

"You seem like you are feeling a bit better," he commented.

"I am completely faking it. I feel like my bones are made of lead," she replied quietly, with a big smile.

"It occurred to me that these might be the same highwaymen we trounced last week." She looked around slowly as if she had not a care in the world. "If any of those survivors are here…"

"Then we are in it deep," he finished.

"Even if this is a completely different group, I don't want them to think we are easy prey. Apparently, some of them were a bit impressed with my fight against the Troll. If they see that I can hardly stand, then they may be more tempted to try something." She fingered the hilt of the broadsword hanging at her belt. Corelan tried to decide if being feared far less than a woman bothered him. After seeing Lena in action himself, he had to agree with the assessment. He dismissed the thought as he occupied himself with more practical matters. He glanced around, noticing that the men in the room just ahead had moved off further into the house. Not wanting to draw attention by having an extended conversation in the middle of the foyer, he moved into an adjacent room. It looked like it could have once been a dining room. They sat on a long wooden bench against the wall, and Corelan rested his feet on a small stool to further the illusion that they were at ease here. A large, heavy table had been pushed into the corner, and judging by the thick layer of dust underneath, it had sat there for quite some time. A fat stubby candle sat lonely on a mantle on the far wall, throwing meager light into the dark, dusty room. Lena sat casually beside him.

"Have you seen Qaz recently?" he asked.

"I woke up just after he did some, his words, 'slightly more complicated' magic on me. Turns out I had a cracked rib too. He said he was going to go and see what he could do for some of the others that were injured in the fight." She stretched and yawned a bit too loudly. The collar of her too-large shirt fell from her shoulder, and she absently replaced it. Corelan suddenly felt flush.

"Nice outfit," he commented. She wore what was obviously a man's pants and tunic. The man who once owned these clothes was probably half again her size. Of her armor, there was no sign.

"Yeah, stylish isn't it. Mine were soaked through." She absently fiddled with the sleeve, revealing a tattoo emblazoned on her right shoulder. "Since we lost most of our own stuff with the horses, this was all they could come up with," she commented. Corelan suspected they could have done much better. He had seen at least two men who were nearly her size exactly. Very likely, the bandits thought they could get their jollies seeing her halfway falling out of clothing made for a giant. The more he thought about it, the more it irked him.

"Is that a tattoo? It looks Ialish." The Ialu reserved their stylistic tattoo art for themselves and have been known to become quite offended when an outsider mimics the style.

"This?" She favored Corelan with a glimpse of the art for a moment before covering it up with the overlarge sleeve. "It's an Ialish campaign tattoo. They are sometimes given to outsiders," she explained.

"I suppose I'm going to have to wait for that story," Corelan commented after a moment of silence. He looked out through the window into the black night. It seemed they would also have to wait until morning to leave. If they lived that long. "Is your armor handy in case we need to leave suddenly?" he asked. She covered a yawn with her hand, gesturing slightly to the doorway, placing a finger over her lips as she withdrew her hand. Corelan turned to put his mug on the bench behind him, looking toward the door as he did so. A tall man with a thin mustache had stepped around the corner and now leaned on the wall across from them. Dressed all in black, he gave the impression of a gangly panther lounging around, waiting for a rabbit to emerge from its hole. He looked at the two of them with a squinty gaze. There was not a smile anywhere near his face. Corelan tried to recognize him as one of the survivors but was not entirely relieved when he could not. A moment of awkward silence passed. Lena cleared her throat as if to say something when someone shouted outside.

Corelan stood and walked past the man in black to the window in the foyer. He heard Lena take a position behind him. Around two dozen riders charged past the few surviving posts of a low fence which probably once marked the edge of a kept yard. Four men who had been taking their ease on the front porch walked out slowly to greet them. The riders dismounted in a chaotic jumble, and nearly half of a dozen walked straight up to the front door. The man beside him spoke

"Kippux is here." He uttered the words flatly and turned away. Corelan shot a glance at Lena. Now? It seemed an odd time of the day indeed for extended road travel. She shrugged. The door crashed open as the men entered. Corelan was instantly certain that the man who pushed the door open was Kippux.

He looked around the room with absolute authority, his keen eyes seeming to absorb every detail. He was in his forties, compactly built, with dark hair and eyes. A thin ring of scrubby facial hair circled his mouth. He wore a dark, loose-fitting leather vest over a black silk shirt. The gold-plated hilt of a slender sword stood out against his black leather riding pants. He wore a thick cloak to fend off the damp night, which he promptly threw off in no particular direction. Two men carrying a wooden crate between them shoved their way into the room behind Kippux. He turned to them and glanced at their burden. "Take that to the basement," he commanded. "Now, where is my nephew?" Kippux bellowed at the ceiling. He smiled, his eyes flashing with feverish excitement. As if on cue, Marcis stepped out from around the corner behind Corelan and Lena. He had trimmed his beard and washed his face, and now in clean clothes, was hardly recognizable. Nephew? Corelan looked at Lena. She shrugged again.

"Uncle." He smiled and held his hands up in a gesture of greeting. Kippux rushed to him, taking his head in his hands, pressing his forehead to his nephew's.

"Ah, Marcis, only son of my beloved sister. However did you escape the clutches of those despicable Trolls?" He spoke with the same accent as Marcis. Someone had picked up Kippux's cloak from where it fell on the floor and was hanging it on the coat rack by the door.

"These people were kind enough to rescue me, despite great danger to themselves." Marcis gestured to Lena and Corelan. Kippux spun to face them and sized them up, expressionless. No one was moving or saying anything.

"It is a pleasure to meet you, sir." Lena offered a handshake. Kippux face split into a wide grin. He took her hand and bent forward slightly, kissing her knuckle as if being introduced to a Baroness or Lady.

"The pleasure belongs entirely to me, my lady." He withdrew himself slowly, looking at Lena with unmasked approval. Lena carried herself as if it were the most common thing for her to have her hand kissed by a stranger. Kippux turned to Corelan, who still wore a good deal of the night's mud. Corelan felt suddenly awkward. Kippux moved forward and embraced him solidly, clapping him firmly on the back. Corelan awkwardly returned the embrace, unsure if he was dealing with a sane man. "My friends. I am forever in your debt." Kippux took a step back and appraised the two, savoring the moment.

"There is a third. A worker of magic. He is tending to our wounded," Marcis added.

"Bring him here. I must thank them all!" Kippux unbuckled his sword as he spoke. "But I am a rude host! Have you eaten?" Corelan's stomach squirmed violently at the suggestion. He tried and failed to remember when he had eaten last. As if to echo his thought, Lena's stomach grumbled audibly. Without looking, Kippux held his sword aside to be taken. The thin man in black materialized out of a shadow and took the blade from his leader's hand. "Come, we shall dine. An overdue meal is certainly better than no meal at all!" He took them both by the arms and led them into the rear of the house, through a large kitchen, and out onto an expansive rear patio. Several mismatched tables and chairs were spread haphazardly across the patio. A poorly constructed addition to the house stretched off to the right. To the left, across a sparsely grown yard, a large, slightly saggy barn stood just outside of the pool of light created by the torches and lanterns that lit the courtyard. Corelan could see some men stabling their horses in the rickety structure. He now estimated that close to fifty men called this place their home. Very poor odds if things were to go sour. Where the hell was Qaz? Kippux clapped his hands twice as he seated his guests.

"Bring us food and wine," he addressed to no one in particular. After a moment or two of entirely inane conversation, four plates of food were brought out, each with a bottle of rather cheap wine. Dinner was a mixture of a scant few bits of what may well have once been a skinny bird, served with several unseasoned vegetables that were not usually served together, chopped up with chunks of undercooked potato. It was absolutely divine. Corelan spent the next few minutes trying to stuff food into his mouth as fast as possible while simultaneously trying to remain something close to polite. If that was not difficult enough at what had to near dawn, he had to act as if he was listening to whatever Kippux was chattering about as well. Not sure if he was succeeding at either goal and not particularly worried, either way, Corelan was certain, however, that he was doing a better job than Lena, who seemed to be completely ignoring the world while she completely ignored manners. After the initial surge of food-lust had passed, and the meal had been reduced to crumbs, and the four sat quiet and alone on the patio, the conversation took a noticeably serious turn.

"So, you must tell me how you came to rescue my troublesome nephew." As he spoke, he leaned comfortably back into his chair, producing a pipe and tobacco pouch from nowhere. Corelan looked across the table at Lena. This could become tricky. She looked past him suddenly and waved.

"Qaz, over here," she said, flagging him down as she spoke. Corelan couldn't help but notice her hands were shaking. She needed some rest soon. Kippux had risen from the table and assaulted Qaz with the same bear-like embrace with which he had favored Corelan. Qaz nearly toppled over. He, unlike Lena, was making no charade of his fatigue. He looked nearly ready to collapse. Kippux ushered him into a chair, just as some more wine was brought out. Qaz had also washed and changed into some borrowed clothing. Of his armor and weapons, there was no sign. He looked around the table, wearing his usual smirk despite his profound weariness. Kippux offered Qaz some dinner, and after Qaz assured him he had already eaten, Kippux sat back in his chair, seizing his empty wine cup.

"I thought I told you to get some rest." Qaz addressed to Lena. She opened her mouth to offer an excuse, but he cut her off with a raised finger and a grunt. "Women," he said, turning to Marcis. Kippux roared with laughter, pounding the table exuberantly. A dangerous fire burned in Lena's eye for a moment as she swallowed her response in the name of good public relations. *You are going to pay for that one later, my friend,* Corelan thought. Wine was poured for the five at the table. Marcis turned to Qaz.

"My uncle was just asking how you three came to be rescuing people in a cave full of Trolls," he said with genuine good humor. "You must admit, it is rather strange to be wandering about in the lair of murderous Rock Trolls, looking for people to rescue, is it not?" Qaz laughed aloud and took a deep drink of wine. As he tilted his head back, he winked at Corelan. He leaned further back than Corelan thought was necessary, then continued with the motion to topple over backward in his chair. His head bounced on the flagstones with an audible thunk. Kippux and Marcis shot to their feet. Qaz was struggling to sit up, with wine spilled all over the front of his shirt.

"Uncle? I didn't know he was your uncle." Qaz went on as if nothing had happened. Kippux stopped in the middle of helping him up.

"Gods, man! You just fell out of your chair," he exclaimed. Qaz looked around for confirmation as if this were a remarkably acute observation. Was this his idea of dodging a question?

"Ah. Indeed, I have." He put on a sheepish look. "All of this magical work takes a lot out of a guy." He rubbed the back of his head, looking for the entire world like he was wondering why it hurt. "Oh, look. I spilled wine everywhere." Kippux lifted Qaz slowly to his feet.

"You must rest. All of you." He looked concerned. "We shall talk of things tomorrow, no?" He turned to the small crowd that had gathered. "Prepare beds for our guests," he addressed his command to the entire group. They responded all at once, rushing away in six different directions. "Please, go with my men and take your rest. I shall see you all in the morning." He looked imploringly at each of them.

"Thank you for your hospitality. I look forward to tomorrow," Lena said, offering another handshake. Kippux kissed her hand again, winking at her this time. Oh please. Corelan thought. Lena took Qaz's arm as if to help him along, digging her fingers into the soft flesh on the inside of his elbow. He grimaced and rubbed his head as if fatigued. Corelan led the three of them back into the house, where they followed a dusky-skinned C'thûn up the stairs to their rooms. He gestured to two doors directly across the hall from one another and left them standing in the hall with a simple nod. Corelan watched the man go and pushed open a door, ushering the two of them into the room. Closing the door, he let out a sigh of relief.

"What the hell was that, Qaz?" Lena demanded, glaring at him. Qaz sat on the edge of one of the two beds and began to pull off a boot.

"Magic really does make you tired," he replied. "I am beat."

"What?" she responded a bit too loudly. Corelan winced and gestured to lower the noise a bit. He sat on the only other piece of furniture in the room; a short chest of drawers, sliding aside the lantern, which served as the room's only illumination,

"I had to do something to change the subject," Qaz offered.
"Don't you think that was a bit over the top?" she snapped.

"It worked, didn't it?"

"I don't know," she responded as she sat on the other bed. "Who knows what they think of us now." Corelan rose and looked out the window. It was hard to see anything aside from his own distorted reflection.

"We probably *should* rest," he offered. "They might get suspicious of your wonderful acting job if we stay up half the night talking."

"Yeah." Lena rose from the bed and half-turned away. She stopped and cuffed Qaz on the back of the head before walking toward the door.

"Hey, what was that for?" he asked as he rubbed the back of his already sore head.

"I think you know." She tried to suppress a grin. "Good night Corelan." She closed their door and entered her room across the hall. Corelan looked at Qaz and shrugged.

"Women," came the response.

* * * * *

She was on her feet with sword in hand before she knew she was awake. The intruder calmly placed a basin of water on the small rickety table in the corner of her room and ventured a half-smile. Lena shook the fog of sleep from her brain for a moment as she looked down the length of her sword at the Ialu who had brought her some morning wash water. He gestured to the door to indicate that he intended to leave and would prefer to do so without any steel in him.

"Sorry," she said as she re-sheathed her sword, only then realizing she held her scabbard in her other hand. "Perhaps it would be best to knock next time." His smile increased to about three-quarters as he shrugged. His green eyes held not a hint of concern at nearly being chopped to pieces by a half-sleeping madwoman. He nodded and left the room as if nothing had happened. Ialu were renowned for their calm demeanor, and it had always made Lena a bit uneasy. It was difficult to tell what they were thinking. She pressed her ear to the door, barely able to discern the sound of his footsteps as he retreated down the hall. Ialu were also known for being quiet in both movement and speech, despite their relative bulk. Satisfied that she was alone, she tossed her sword on the bed beside her, stripped off her tunic, and bent to wash her face in the cool water.

Painted in the bottom of the cracked porcelain basin was a faded image of a dragon fighting a lion. The lion, the official and somewhat inappropriate symbol of the kingdom of Onic, was winning the fight, which she also felt was inappropriate. She supposed the dragon was meant to represent the Black Army, or the United Army of Justice, as they called themselves. She also recalled that after their last clash two years ago, the lion lost quite plainly. In fact, only due to the city's lack of strategic value did Onic's Lion survive at all. The angle of the sun leaking in through the window hinted that morning had come and gone some time ago. A rumbling in her stomach agreed. She toweled her face dry and pulled on her borrowed tunic, just as a knock on the door gave her a slight start. She moved a step back toward her sword on the bed before asking who was there.

"It's me," Qaz replied from behind the door. She muttered vague permission to enter, and he slipped into the room as quietly as he could manage. He was no Ialu. The bright sunlight streamed into the room through the small shuttered window, illuminating the floating dust particles that seemed to own this old farmhouse. It fell right across his eyes as he stepped into the center of the room. He squinted, running a hand through his damp hair. "Hey, sleepyhead. I trust you are sufficiently rested?" he asked with a smirk.

"What time is it?"

"Sometime after noon on Endweek, I think," he replied. "I forgot to tell you that magical healing will make you a bit groggy the next morning," he added with a sheepish grin. "Your body has used up a fair amount of its own energy in the accelerated healing process. You are going to be really hungry, too, until you can replace that energy."

"Do you have your things ready to go?" she asked him quietly. She moved to the window and pushed the shutters open to let in more light. "We have wasted enough daylight. I don't want to stay here any longer than manners demand." Qaz blinked a bit at the sudden bloom of light.

"Armor is still in my room. I didn't think it polite to show up for lunch armed and armored. Which is why I came here in the first place, to tell you that lunch is on, and Kippux expects us to dine privately with him and Marcis." Qaz slid over to the window and peered out as well.

"Where is your dagger?" she asked, gesturing to the empty sheath that hung from his belt.

"Oh, I uh, lost it," he responded sheepishly. "In the fight with the Trolls. Tossed it at one of them and missed completely."

"Why were you throwing knives instead of magic spells?"

"As a matter of fact, you may recall seeing the spell of…"

"Never mind." She stopped him. Left to his own devices, Qaz would likely recap the entire affair, embellishing generously on the details. "Seen Corelan this morning?" she asked. She began to arrange her armor on the bed, taking mental note of where maintenance was needed.

"He was almost conscious when I left the room. I thought you two were competing to see who could sleep the longest." He turned back towards her and sat on the windowsill. "Hey, are you in a bad mood or something? You're not still mad about last night, are you?" She sighed unconsciously and turned to face him.

"No. I just don't like our present situation. It makes me nervous to be surrounded by people who would probably slit my throat for a silver penny." He nodded in silent agreement. She knelt and looked under the bed, searching for something she could use to pack her armor into in case a sudden departure became necessary.

"Do you think we should discuss a unified story to tell Kippux in case he has questions?" Qaz asked. She reached under the bed and pulled out a large canvas sack, which was stuffed with something, probably the clothing of whomever usually slept in this room.

"Let's try to be as evasive as possible without being rude," she offered. "If he is too insistent, tell him we were coming back from a mercenary job gone bad and got captured ourselves." She dumped out the contents of the bag – a dirty pile of awful smelling ragged clothing and shoved them under the bed without looking.

"Sounds good. I'll round up Corelan and meet you downstairs." She began to stuff her armor into the bag, pretending she did not know what was there previously.

"Be ready to go," she said without looking as he slipped out into the hall. She set the bag on the bed and, with a great deal of hesitation, placed her sword beside it. She tried once more to adjust the neckline of her overlarge tunic and gave up, still dissatisfied. A woman could earn a poor reputation wearing clothes such as these. The leather sheath of her fat-bladed dagger slapped lightly against her thigh as she fastened her belt. On basic principle, she refused to go out there completely unarmed.

A few moments later, she stepped out onto the same patio where Qaz had pulled his stunt last night. Kippux and Marcis were already seated with a modest display of fruits, bread, and cheese adorning the table in front of them. Kippux wore a tight-fitting black jacket with black trousers and boots. The hilt of his sword poked out from over his shoulder from where it hung on the back of his chair. Had it been anyone else, she may have found it perhaps a trifle cliché – the bandit leader who dresses in all black. He, however, held himself with such an air of supreme confidence; she suspected he could look serious in a jester's outfit. Marcis stood as he saw her and walked across the patio to greet her, taking her hand in both of his.

"Ah, my lovely friend, won't you join us? I trust you slept undisturbed." He pulled out a chair and gestured for her to sit. Kippux nodded slightly to greet her but said nothing. "Please enjoy this food. Would you like some tea?" Marcis poured from a porcelain teapot into a mismatched teacup without waiting for her answer. She nodded in thanks and broke off a heel of bread. Kippux had fixed her with an unreadable stare that made her very nervous. He sat silently.

Just then, Corelan and Qaz emerged from the house and were greeted and sat in a like manner. Corelan instantly noticed Kippux's subdued tone and exchanged an uneasy glance with Lena. Marcis sat after pouring tea for the two men. Qaz dove right into a very loud apple and munched happily as Kippux sat quietly observing his guests. Corelan surprised her by breaking the silence.

"So. How are things?" he addressed to no one in particular. Eloquent, she thought. Kippux face broke into a wide smile.

"Things could not be better. My nephew is returned to me, and I have made three new friends, all in one night. What a homecoming." He was all smiles. He looked directly at Lena as he spoke. She suspected he had been intimidating them just for the fun of it.

"I'm sorry, did you say homecoming?" Corelan asked. He asked as if simply making polite conversation.

"Yes. Until two nights ago, we have been many miles north of here for the past month… on… a business trip." He shot a wink at Marcis as if the other three at the table had no idea that he was an outlaw.

"So, you and all your men have been out of this area for quite some time then?" Lena asked. She suspected Corelan was thinking the same thing she was right at that moment.

"Yes. Essentially. Only Marcis and a small handful of others remained here to protect our home from thieves." He snickered at his own subtle irony. That confirmed her thought. If this bandit group was away, who did they get into a fight with days earlier? "However, it seems I have been gone long enough to allow time for my troublesome nephew to be abducted by Trolls in my absence." He glared at Marcis with an arched eyebrow. "Why do you ask? Is there some morsel of news I have missed? Do tell." She schooled her face to remain calm as she answered.

"Oh, no reason." She lifted her teacup to take a sip, trying to appear at ease. Kippux wrinkled his brow, not satisfied with her answer. Something was odd about the smell of her tea, distracting her momentarily. Corelan came to her rescue.

"Well, it's just that we have heard rumors," he began. She looked at him sharply, wary. She wondered if Qaz had remembered to fill him in on their cover story.

"Rumors?" Kippux asked. Qaz sipped his tea and looked into his cup, slightly perplexed.

"I'm sure it's nothing, but rumor has it, there is a large group of highwaymen that prowl this area…" He shrugged and smiled as if the idea were absurd. Kippux laughed out loud.

"Ha! If there were any bandits in this area, I would certainly know of it. A man must protect his interests, no?" He gestured grandly to the dilapidated farmhouse behind them. "I can assure you. No bandits have been in these woods recently. None at all." He nudged Marcis again as if sharing a private joke. Her suspicion was confirmed, which in turn opened a whole new set of concerns.

"Pardon, but is this Pheldian tea?" Qaz asked. She tried not to gasp as she realized what had been bothering her. Pheldians were quite fond of mixing dried castaguille leaf with their tea. The distinctive flavor of the somewhat bitter herb was unmistakable.

"Why yes, it is," Marcis answered. "You have a distinguished palate." *That* was what had seemed strange. She now recognized the distinctive flavor, its memory returning from her childhood.

"It is quite good." He sipped again. "And fresh." Where would a group of bandits this far south get their hands on a fresh supply of Pheldian tea, she wondered

"We are in the business of trading goods over distances," Marcis answered. For a flash, she wondered if she had spoken aloud. When he said many miles north, he apparently meant it. Kippux laughed.

"I should not leave you be for so long, nephew. With so little else to do, it would seem my nephew needed to involve himself with a mountain full of Trolls to keep occupied," Kippux addressed to the table. "My dear sister would have skinned me alive had I let harm befall her only son."

"Ah, uncle, you exaggerate," Marcis chided. Kippux replied with only a lifted eyebrow. Lena got the impression he wasn't kidding at all. "I suspect our Troll neighbors were simply displeased with our… trading post so close to their home. Perhaps they simply wished to encourage us to take our business venture elsewhere."

"You and I will discuss this in length later," Kippux replied. "I'm still not satisfied with your explanation. Perhaps out new friends will be more forthcoming. This brings us back to a topic from earlier." Kippux turned to his guests. "How indeed did you find yourselves so deep inside of a Troll's lair?" He sat back and stroked his mustache with a smile. Corelan conveniently chewed a slice of cheese at that moment and looked innocently at Lena. Qaz sipped his tea quietly. Okay. I'll field this one, she thought.

"I suppose it was a set of circumstances not unlike your nephew's," she responded.

"You too were captured?" Kippux asked.

"We managed to overpower our guards as we were being taken in, and we soon found ourselves lost in the cave." She nodded to Marcis. "In fact, your nephew rescued us in a sense. Without his help, we may never have found our way out." Marcis smiled sheepishly.

"Yes, I have heard tales of your prowess in battle, both from my men and Marcis here." He nodded with approval. She saw Corelan relax visibly as the topic moved on to more harmless things. Qaz and Marcis discussed their mutual fondness for tea, and Corelan chatted about the weather as the five ate. All the while, Lena was composing a polite way to excuse themselves and be out of this place. Although the immediate threat had subsided with the news that these fellows had not been the same bandits from before, the danger of hanging around with fifty or so thieves and possibly murderers was undeniable, especially being the only woman in what was probably a group of undoubtedly rather lonely men.

"So, my friends, what are your plans from here?" Kippux asked in a casual tone.

"I'm sorry?" Qaz asked.

"What will you do now? It was implied that you three are in the… freelance business. Do you have work for yourselves when you return home?" Qaz shot a quick look at Lena before answering.

"We, uh, have a few possibilities," he offered.

"Perhaps you would consider joining our little enterprise," Kippux suggested. Lena hoped she did not look as surprised as Qaz. Corelan nearly choked on his tea. "There is always room for talented and bright individuals such as yourselves, eh?"

"We have a small commitment to fulfill first," Lena interjected as Qaz fumbled for a proper response. Kippux sat back in his chair and shrugged.

"Perhaps another time then." He stood. "I suppose then, you wish to be along your way." Lena felt herself relax. This was going to be easier than she thought. They stood, and as they removed themselves from the table, Corelan pulled her aside.

"Who saw that coming?" he ventured. Over his shoulder, she could see Kippux speaking quietly with Qaz. Corelan noticed her expression. "What?"

"Don't look, but Kippux is discussing something with Qaz." Qaz nodded and laughed at whatever Kippux said. Marcis had left the patio and was heading toward the rear of the farmhouse. Qaz saw Lena looking at him and ventured a wink before shaking hands with Kippux and joining them. Corelan turned and acted slightly surprised as if he and Lena had been discussing something totally irrelevant. She kept an eye on Kippux, who gave her a wink of his own before following his nephew into the farmhouse. The three of them turned and began to walk back to their rooms in the rickety add-on wing of the house.

"Having trouble saying goodbye?" Corelan asked before she could.

"What? Oh, no. He was just asking if we needed any provisions for the road. I told him we did." He nodded politely at the Ialu, who held the door open for them as they entered the building. The Ialu nodded back and gave Lena an approving look before moving away on his business. A quick glance at his clan tattoo showed only a blacked-out circle. This man was forsaken by his clan – what the Ialu called 'brotherless'. Such a punishment was reserved for only the worst of crimes. Yes, the sooner they got out of here, the better.

"We'll let Corelan get the food," she said. "I haven't forgotten the beans you murdered on the road out of Akeela." Corelan nodded in assent, rubbing his stomach unconsciously.

"They weren't *that* bad," Qaz offered. "I think your memory of the experience is tainted by the sudden onslaught of armed hostiles."

"You get your things together and meet me out front," she continued, trying to avoid a debate on the caliber of Qaz's cooking skills. "Fifteen minutes?" The two men nodded. "Great." Qaz, still thinking of his failed beans, put on a slightly pouting, hurt face. She might have regretted her comment had she not known him well enough to know it was an act. She pushed open the door to her borrowed room and quickly crossed the floor to scoop up her sword and stolen bag from where they lay on the bed. She froze in her tracks.

Resting lightly atop her things was a freshly picked pink rose, still damp from the outside air. She stared at it for a moment as a few representatives of the horde of tiny dust particles that called this place home swirled around lazily in the sunbeam that fell across the center of the room. On its own, her hand strayed to the knife at her belt.

"I wish you would reconsider leaving us," a voice behind her spoke. She found the hilt of her dagger in her hand suddenly as she stepped back into a defensive posture. Marcis pushed away from the wall he was leaning on and sat on the edge of the bed, smiling in his overly charming way. When she decided to breathe again, Lena put her dagger away and stood in what she thought would be a non-threatening pose. "I do so enjoy your company," he added. It vexed her to know he had been able to surprise her in such a way. Especially since she considered herself to be in hostile territory. She could almost hear her instructor's voice berating her for carelessness. However, he probably *did* have to work fairly quickly to have beaten them upstairs.

"I am sorry, Marcis, but we really do have another commitment." She tried to sound as sincere as she dared without overdoing it.

"But you see, who would know?" He leaned forward and lowered his voice slightly. "As far as anyone knows, you perished at the hands of merciless Trolls." He smiled as if having just won an argument. She sighed unconsciously. Persistent fellow.

"I gave my word," she responded. Men usually respected such things.

"Again, who would know?" So much for respect.

"I would."

"Ahh, but you said yourself that I saved your life. What of that?" He put one hand on the bed behind him and leaned back. Lena felt her face darken. She hoped he was not implying what she imagined.

"What of it?" she asked flatly.

"In many cultures, when you save a life…" Apparently, he was.

"Need I point out that we saved your life also? And in a much more direct way. In my book, that makes us even, at the very least. Thank you, but I am afraid we must go." She folded her arms and looked down at him. His face took on the wounded puppy look that Qaz had faked earlier. To his credit, however, he did do a slightly better job of it. His eyes strayed to the rose on her bed.

"Please, Marcis, let's not make this more difficult than it needs to be; for either of us." Ordinarily, she would have said her piece and been done with it, but this circumstance demanded that they part on good terms. The rose was a nice touch, though. He sighed, then stood, donning a disarming smile.

"Ahh, well. What will be, will be, no?" He took her hand, kissed it lightly, and left the room, pausing at the door. "Last chance? No?" He shrugged and turned down the hall. Lena sighed, wondering how many more surprises the day held.

* * * * *

Corelan forced a smile as he spoke. "I'm sorry, what did you say your name was?"

"Eram," the man responded. Or perhaps boy. He couldn't have seen more than a score of summers. He looked back at Corelan with a smug expression, as if he were Lord of the Foodstuffs, and Corelan was a peasant beseeching a boon. Corelan found it difficult to take him seriously. He looked around the kitchen, hoping that there was someone else to speak to besides this Eram person. There was not.

"Okay... Eram. I'll explain it one more time. Feren Kippux, your boss, gave me specific permission to take some food from this pantry, so my friends and I would have something to eat when we leave." He looked into the younger man's eye for a glimmer of understanding. Finding none, he went on. "So, I am doing that. Taking some food. Because he offered. Hello?"

"No food is to leave the pantry, except at mealtimes. No exceptions," Eram stated as if quoting scripture from a sacred text. Corelan looked at the table between them, at the small bag he had filled with a few dry goods from the pantry and the waterskin beside it. He contemplated for a brief moment, grabbing the goods and shoving past the smaller man, his rules be damned. Wisdom prevailed.

"Did you hear anything I just said?" he asked.

"Of course. But right now, I am in charge of the kitchen, and nobody talks his way past the Rules. That is something you and your friends are going to have to learn if you want to survive here." He folded his arms and looked up at Corelan as if scolding an enormous child. Corelan took a deep breath to calm himself.

"I thought I had made it clear that we were leaving," he said. Was this boy completely daft? "Kippux offered for us to take some food. Do you remember Kippux?" He gestured with his hand. "About so tall, beard, wears black… ringing any bells?" Eram's face showed a flash of anger.

"I am not an idiot." He spoke through clenched teeth. Although sorely tempted to pursue that topic, Corelan let it drop.

"Look, I understand that you are just doing your job," Corelan said. Eram relaxed a bit. "I can't say in your circumstance that I would behave much differently. Help me out. Do you need me to pay for this? C'mon, what is it going to take to get some food out of here?" Corelan asked, hoping the 'I-feel-your-pain' approach would work since the 'this-makes-sense' approach didn't.

"Wait till dinner," Eram said, donning an irritating smirk. Corelan rolled his eyes in exasperation. Just then, a shaggy, russet-haired, hulking beast of a man walked into the kitchen, brushing right past the both of them. He went straight to the cupboard and began to root around. Eram turned slightly and spoke to him over his shoulder, keeping an eye on Corelan should he decide to make off with the disputed booty.

"Hey, Renny. Stay out of the pantry. You know the rules." He adjusted his smirk slightly.

"Bugger off, twerp. Boss wants a bite," the man responded, his back still turned.

"Okay, fine. Just say so next time." Eram turned back to face Corelan fully.

"Hey, wait a damn minute!" Corelan exclaimed. "I have been saying that all along…"

"No, what you have been saying is…" Eram was suddenly and violently forced aside by the other man, his head bouncing loudly off of the wall. Corelan looked up in surprise at the man, who, for no apparent reason, flung his compatriot to the floor. With a slow and painfully sickening realization, Corelan found himself staring up at the same red-faced man he had assaulted in a similar manner in Dargram's Tavern in Akeela several long days ago. He still had a faded bruise under one eye as a memento of the event. He stared down at Corelan, his face growing redder by the moment with a livid rage.

"YOU!" he roared.

"Uh. Renny, is it?" Corelan responded as his heart slowly sank through his chest to rest in a hollow area just behind his navel. "Good to see you again," he lied.

* * * * *

Qaz knocked lightly on Lena's door before entering. She stood in the center of the room, finishing her preparations to leave. She had packed her steel armor into a bag, donned her gambeson, and was buckling on her sword. A satchel she had stolen from somewhere lay on the bed beside her. Qaz wondered if it was actually stealing since the bag was probably stolen from a third party in the first place. To his surprise, a small pink rose peeked out from under her left lapel. Leave it to a woman, after telling everyone else to hurry up, to take the time to scrounge up a flower so she can look good. Well, it worked anyway.

"You ready there, sweetie?" he asked, knowing it would irritate her slightly.

"Uh, yeah. Just a minute," she responded distractedly. Qaz frowned at both her lack of spirited response and her seeming reluctance to leave.

"Hey, are you okay?" he asked, stepping into the room.

"I'm fine," she responded. "It just feels like I'm always leaving somewhere." She shook off whatever mood possessed her, and looked up at him, the fire back in her eye. "Let's get out of here. Where's Corelan?" Qaz opened his mouth to answer but was cut off by a loud shout outside her window. A clamor of voices and several more shouts quickly followed. It sounded as if a small crowd of rather excited people was gathering in the yard below her window.

"What the hell?" she asked. Qaz had a spurt of intuition he sometimes experienced that the answer to her first question was about to be revealed. She stepped over to the window and threw open the shutter. "You cursed son of a motherless goat!" she swore. Qaz stepped over to the window, having a fair idea of what he was about to see. A small circle of bandits was gathered around two combatants; one a huge copper-haired hulk, the other, Corelan.

"Well put," he added.

* * * * *

Corelan dove to his left, narrowly avoiding a vicious right hook. He hit the ground in a roll and came to his feet slightly behind the larger man. As he shifted his weight to move in on his opponent, a flash of sunlight glinting on metal off to his left caught his attention. He hopped away from both his opponent and whoever was pulling steel. He pondered how his personal situation could deteriorate so rapidly. Only a few moments ago, he was getting free food from the man who had saved his life, and now he was in a life and death struggle against a huge psychotic with a vendetta and lots and lots of his friends. *Do I just have bad luck?* He asked himself. As if in answer to his question, someone in the crowd tossed a large, fat-bladed knife to Renny, who caught it in midair, gingerly avoiding cutting himself. *Guess so.* There was now quite a crowd gathering in the yard to watch the fight. More than a few voiced their disapproval of this display of poor sportsmanship with loud boos. Several more shouted in satisfaction, though, with the promise that this was now going to be more than a mere fistfight. Corelan felt himself agreeing more with the first group.

"I am going to gut you like a fish, little man," Renny boasted, brandishing the knife for emphasis. Corelan sighed. *Guys who thought they were tough* always said something like that. Corelan supposed that someone with a greater gift for diplomacy might be able to diffuse the situation with a few well-placed words, though, to be fair, someone with a greater gift for diplomacy would likely not have placed himself in this situation, to begin with. He glanced around the ring of spectators to see if anyone else cared to make his day a bit more dismal. No one offered. Yet. Renny moved to close in. The larger man kept his eyes locked onto Corelan's as he approached, making it difficult to anticipate his next move. Without breaking his stride, he stabbed quickly toward Corelan's midsection, growling slightly in eager anticipation of victory. Corelan dove to the side again, rolling to stand several feet away. Renny turned and smiled.

"Not so tough in a stand-up fight, are you, little man?" Corelan frowned. The man was relatively fast. Renny approached again, more carefully this time. Corelan did not think the 'dive to one side' tactic would work a third time in a row. He ground his rear foot into the loose dirt and turned slightly to his left again, hoping to portray as if he were planning to try it again anyway. Renny stepped in, slashing with the knife in a wide arc, targeting the direction he suspected Corelan would dive. Corelan shot his foot forward, catching Renny on the forearm, just above his knife hand. With a growled curse, the knife tumbled from his grasp, landing in the dirt between them. The two looked at the knife, then at each other. Renny flexed his injured hand.

Simultaneously, they dove for the blade. Renny reached it first. He shot his other hand forward to stabilize himself as he tumbled forward.

Corelan landed a split second later, grabbing Renny's wrist with both hands and shouldering into his opponent to knock him off balance. Renny fought to his feet with a roar and pulled Corelan in closer, hoping to overpower the smaller man. He wormed his free hand around from behind Corelan, underneath his arm to grasp his throat. Figures. The big guys always want to wrestle.

Corelan kept his grip on his opponent's wrist with one hand and, with the other, pried his thumb away from the knife handle. Just as Renny began to apply real pressure to the throat, Corelan leaned forward and bent his thumb back in an unnatural direction. Renny also leaned forward from the pain from his nearly breaking thumb and unconsciously loosened his grip on Corelan's throat. Corelan stood straight suddenly and flung his head backward, smashing directly onto Renny's now outstretched nose. He heard a crunching noise as Renny fell backward, howling in pain. The knife fell harmlessly to the dirt. As Renny staggered to his feet, clutching his newly broken nose, Corelan casually picked up the knife and flipped it into a throwing position. Renny's eyes widened slightly as he realized he had lost all advantage. Blood trickled between his fingers as his eyes darted back and forth. Corelan looked around the circle as well, hoping no one would realize he had absolutely no intention of throwing away his only knife.

The other bandits erupted into a turmoil of mixed reactions. Some howled in amusement at Renny's ill twist of fate. Some coinage exchanged hands – the losers grumbling and the winners triumphant. A few of Renny's closer friends frowned deeply and strayed toward their own weapons. Corelan sensed that this situation could either turn his way or proceed downhill very quickly. There probably was something appropriate to say. He just had no idea what it was. He made as if to throw the knife, causing the crowd to flinch a bit, hoping to buy some time or shake loose a favorable reaction.

Just then, the crowd parted suddenly as two riders at full gallop crashed through the circle. Before he knew what was happening, Corelan was swept from the ground and, by pure instinct, found himself struggling to right himself on the rear of Lena's horse. As the farmhouse quickly receded behind him, Corelan muttered a word of thanks as he fought to remain on the horse.

"Idiot!" came her reply.

* * * * *

Kippux strode regally into the middle of the circle to face Renny even as the other bandits were picking themselves up, knocking dust from their clothes. Some chuckled, and some cursed. Kippux folded his arms and looked up at the larger man, waiting for a response.

"But sir, he was the one who…" Renny began, his voice distorted and nasally.

"I don't care," Kippux responded flatly, sounding almost bored.

"But sir, he…" Renny was boiling inside.

"What did I say?" Kippux dropped his casual demeanor and took on a steely edge.

"I'm sorry, sir."

"That is correct. You are." Kippux grinned.

283

"They are escaping! What should we do?" he asked.

"Your fight is none of my concern. Nor is your pride. I suggest you attend to your nose, however. You cannot afford to become any uglier." Kippux suggested lightly as if recommending a type of cheese. Renny paused for a moment, thinking.

"They stole two of your horses," he offered quietly. Kippux sighed.

"I suppose they did." He shrugged. "Retrieve them if you feel you must."

"And what of him?" Renny asked.

"Whatever happens, happens." Kippux could see Marcis squirm as if to protest. "Forget her, my nephew. Come. Let us drink while you explain yourself." He gestured to the younger man and walked into the house as the crowd dissipated. Moments later, Renny and three others rocketed past on horseback.

* * * * *

"Ladies and gentlemen, the bustling metropolis of Devonshire," Tim announced as they crested the hilltop. Jack chuckled lightly at his sarcasm. Devonshire was a small town, but to give credit, it wasn't *that* bad. They had just crested a hilltop and were now looking down at the town from the eastern approach. It was a small collection of no more than seventy or so rough, squatty buildings collected fairly evenly around the main road which passed through the center of town. It had grown large enough to warrant several cross streets and even a town square; a sizeable paved courtyard several blocks across, located near the center of town. A small stream glistened its way through the forest just to the north of town. Large pleasant-looking fields of short grass and wildflowers formed the southern and eastern borders of the town. Not an altogether unlikable place, Jack thought, but the nightlife here, if there was any, was undoubtedly slow.

"Let's pause for a moment here to discuss our plan," Jack suggested. The others reigned in their horses, and the four stopped on the hill.

"We have a plan?" Daelyn asked with mock innocence. Jack smiled and went on.

"We have an address and a name. My thought is to go straight there. Depending on the lay of the land, one or more of us will go inside and try to bluff through the contact. The others will wait outside. If things get ugly, kick in the door and start swinging."

"That isn't really much of a plan," Tim commented.

Two hours later, sitting alone in Walsh K'thaam's office, Jack found himself in reluctant agreement. Maybe they should have paused for lunch and hashed out a few more details. He looked around the room. The room's only window looked three stories down to a narrow alley, which spanned the distance to the unattractive brickwork of the four-story building next door. Somewhere outside, Daelyn, Tim, and Uglor were watching the building and waiting for a signal of some kind. One single door was the only way in or out of the room. A heavy oak desk, one of the two pieces of furniture in this drab, depressing space, occupied the center of the room. Jack sat on a dilapidated, lopsided sofa opposite the window, fighting the urge to riffle through the desk drawers.

The door opened only a moment later, rewarding his prudence. The fellow who had ushered him up here, a youngish bull of a man whose scruffy face held no glimmer of intellect, led another man into the room. The second man was older, perhaps in his forties. His dark hair was graying at the temples, and he carried himself with a degree of assurance that definitely placed him in command of the younger fellow. Jack guessed this man was their contact, Walsh. The two entered the room without a word. The man Jack suspected was Walsh took a seat behind the desk, and the younger scooted a chair from the corner, placed it in front of the desk, and pointed, indicating that Jack should sit there. He closed the door and folded his arms, leaning on the door with a sour expression.

Jack stood and stretched, knuckling the small of his back and yawning. He nodded politely to the bull-necked man by the door and approached the desk. As he sat, he wondered for the thirty-fifth time what exactly he was going to say. Walsh pulled a small wooden box of those tiny cigars that Corelan favored from the desk drawer and offered one to Jack.

"Smoke?"

"No thanks."

"Later perhaps." Walsh lit the absurd little thing from the lamp on the desk corner. "So, my associate, Grimmley, tells me you wanted to see me." Jack turned slightly to look at the younger man. He mentally went over the reasons why he didn't like sitting directly between the two of them. Grimmley smiled back, thinking the same things.

"Yes, I did," Jack began with a casual smile. "Thanks for seeing me on such short notice." Walsh blew out a thin stream of smoke and smiled falsely, gesturing for Jack to continue. For a brief second, he had no idea what to say next. So, he did what he always did in these situations. He opened his mouth and let some words fall out. "I work for Pendor."

"The duke?"

"Of course," Jack started. "*With* Kudakaan…" he followed, finishing with a raised eyebrow.

"Oh! Ha! I knew Kudakaan had too much on his plate. Not surprised he needed help." Walsh nodded to his companion by the door. "Hey Grimmley, we are expecting a pigeon from the boss. Do you mind checking in on it?"

"No prob," Grimmley answered and shuffled through the door. As the door clicked shut behind him, Walsh took a short drag from his cigar and continued.

"So, where the hell is Kudakaan anyway?"

"We had a little issue; he is dealing with the… uh…" Jack made a vague gesture with his thumb toward where he thought the mountains might be."

"The mercenaries?" Walsh offered. "I thought that was settled. Pick up the crew in Roth and head here."

"Oh, no problem with them, that's all smooth."

"And they don't know anything, right?" Walsh asked.

"Not a thing," Jack answered, almost truthfully.

"So, what's the issue?

"I'm not exactly sure what the issue is – you know how Kudakaan can be – but he assured me that he's handling it."

"Not a problem with the Trolls, is it?" Walsh looked slightly alarmed. Jack just nodded. "Seriously though, tell me something."

"There was some hostility. I don't know what it was about, but he stayed back with some of the mercenary group to handle it. I came ahead with the rest."

"Wait, he is doing it *himself?*" Walsh exclaimed. "He needs to be here! What happened to the guys that were supposed to be handling that?"

"I really don't know."

"Well, did Kudakaan meet with them or not?" Walsh seemed deeply vexed by this development.

"Have you ever tried to get solid information out of Kudakaan?" Jack threw up his hands.

"Good point," Walsh conceded with a halfhearted chuckle.

"All I know is, last time I saw him, he was there, dealing with the problem. For all we know, it's all taken care of, and he's on his way here now." Jack was deliberately keeping things vague in hopes that he didn't give himself away. "It's out of our hands at the moment anyway." Best to change the subject. "Does any of this affect our immediate business?" he asked.

"Well, our guys in Elrynth are still on schedule, no problem, but what's-his-name… Kalush is taking care of that end anyway, so that's about all I know there." Walsh flicked ash into a filthy unglazed dish.

"Good to know." Jack sat back in his chair, trying to appear relaxed. "Where is he staying?"

"Klaush? He has an apartment there I think, but he is taking all his meetings at the Dewdrop Inn," Walsh answered. Jack raised an eyebrow. "Yeah, I know, it's a dumb name, but I'm told it's a pretty nice place," Walsh answered. "Expensive, though. He had better be worth it."

"Not my call." Jack shrugged.

"We didn't want anyone to be able to connect him to Ashe," Walsh admitted. "They've got meeting rooms there and it seemed safer than going to the manor."

"Makes sense," Jack answered. "Anything to report on our end?"

"No problems so far," Walsh replied. Hmm. Not helpful.

"So…" Jack opened his hands in a questioning gesture.

"I got the hotel; everything's fine."

"What name did you use?"

"What do you mean?"

"You didn't use your name, did you? With the hotel."

"Of course not," Walsh replied, a look of mock offense on his face. "I used the captain's name."

"Yes. The captain." Jack nodded.

"Sarlo," Walsh offered, wrinkling his brow.

"Well, yeah." Jack shrugged. "Captain Sarlo. Of course." Jack turned to the door as the sound of booted feet clumping down the hall caught the attention of both men in the room. A moment later, the door opened, and Grimmley walked through, holding a small slip of paper. He handed it to Walsh without a word and picked up the cigar box, helping himself to a smoke. Walsh nodded to Jack and unrolled the message, reading it carefully.

"Hmm." Walsh's face went still. His eyes flickered to Jack for a moment before he slipped the message into the flame of the candle burning on his desk. He sat quietly as the fire spread slowly across the paper, dropping it into a tin bucket on the floor next to his desk once the flame grew too large to hold.

"Good news?" Jack asked.

"I never caught your name," Walsh stated flatly.

"Garret," Jack answered smoothly. He had picked out a pseudonym to have handy in case he got in too deep to tell the truth. He felt he was quite past that point.

"Garret," Walsh repeated. "Do you play *elements*, Garret?" Walsh asked, his face unreadable.

"Fancy a game?" Jack asked. He did not like the sudden change in tone.

"Well, let's say I opened with moving the Earth King to the gates of the Air Temple."

"Bold move," Jack answered. He did not like where this was going at all.

"Yeah. Sure is. What would the counter move be?" Walsh asked, folding his arms and leaning back into his chair. With a sudden twist in his stomach, Jack realized that he had just been given a coded challenge phrase. If he did not answer correctly, then his ruse was spent.

"There's hundreds of counter moves," Jack answered, stalling. Grimmley strode to the door and threw the latch, locking them in.

"True," Walsh continued. "But you need to tell me the right one."

"Oh. Right the *code*." Jack laughed. He hesitated for only a moment longer. A bold open would need a bold answer. "Counter move: Air wizard to match." It was a guess.

"Wrong." Walsh smiled. A bad guess, it seemed. Who opens by moving the King anyway? Walsh stood and turned to Grimmley. "This guy is a spy. I don't know if the Lady in Grey is getting involved, or who else might be poking around, but we need to be sure. Take him down to the basement. Sit on him, maybe soften him up a bit, but hold off with the messy stuff till I can get somebody professional here to skin him and find out who he is, what he knows." He turned back to Jack. "Not bad, mister. You got some good stuff out of me; too bad you won't be able to use it." He nodded to Grimmley. Jack sighed. I hate this part, he thought. He looked up at Grimmley.

"Sorry," Jack said. Grimmley's face looked confused for a fraction of a second. His eyes lit up in sudden understanding as Jack plunged his knife into the fleshy part of Grimmley's thigh just above the knee. He howled in pain and staggered back. Jack leapt to his feet, hurling his knife and pulling a second from his other sleeve. Walsh dove behind his desk as Jack's blade buried itself into the back of his chair with a solid thunk. Grimmley fell backward onto the couch, gripping his wounded leg. With his free hand, Jack grabbed the chair he had just vacated and tossed it towards the window. It smashed through the poorly constructed wooden frame, shattered the cheap glass panes with a loud crash, and showered the alley with shards of broken glass and splintered wood. The chair broke apart loudly as it crashed into a wooden trash barrel in the alley below. There is the signal, he thought to himself. Now hurry. He looked wildly around the room. Walsh was still ducked behind his desk and out of sight. Grimmley staggered to his feet, gingerly shifting his weight, testing his injured leg. Jack lifted his knife to his ear, holding it by the point as if he meant to throw. The other man crouched low, either in preparation for a dodge or a charge, Jack could not tell.

"Don't just stand there! Get him!" Walsh demanded from behind the desk. Grimmley looked at Jack, his face unreadable. He shifted his weight to his good leg. Oh, this has gotten far too ugly, Jack thought to himself.

"Don't do it, big man." He warned him, brandishing the knife for emphasis. "I don't miss." He heard shouting in the street below. Someone had seen the chair burst through the window. He hoped his friends had as well. Walsh ventured a peek from behind the desk. Jack twitched, feinting a throw at him. He ducked back down. "I can hit you in the eye from here, Grimmley," Jack warned him. "It just isn't worth it."

"He's bluffing!" Walsh yelled. "He missed me, and I was only five feet away!" Grimmley looked at Jack's knife, sticking out of the back of Walsh's chair, standing in a stark testimonial to that fact. He steeled himself for a charge. Someone in the street shouted something. Jack heard the word 'police.' Oh hell.

"I am just going to walk out of here. Stay where you are, and you won't get killed." He took a sideways step toward the door. Jack heard booted feet stomping up the stairs down the hall. This could be really good or really bad, he thought. Grimmley heard the footsteps as well. A smile slowly spread across his face. With a sense of dread, Jack realized that he was about to charge. "Don't!" he said. For an agonizingly long fraction of a second, the two stood staring at each other, motionless. Grimmley's hand shot out suddenly smacking a pile of loose papers on Walsh's desk. A cloud of swirling paper billowed into the air between them, obscuring Jack's view for a fraction of a second. He threw blindly and dove toward the door. He heard a grunt as the knife hit its target. He had not even taken a full step when he felt a snag as Grimmley grabbed the back of his shirt. Jack stumbled and nearly lost his balance as he was yanked violently backward. His breath whooshed out of his lungs as he smashed heavily into the windowsill. In a desperate panic, his hands shot out to grab hold of something to keep from tumbling out of the window completely. Grimmley lunged forward, seizing Jack by the throat, just as Jack grabbed hold of his attacker's shirt.

Grimmley had a maniacal look in his eye as he began to squeeze, forcing Jack's head further through the window. Jack could see the street below in his peripheral vision. His knife had buried itself in a fleshy portion of Grimmley's shoulder. A good throw, given the circumstances, but apparently not good enough. Gasping for breath, Jack took a firmer hold of Grimmley's shirt in one hand and reached over with his other, stretching to grab the hilt of his blade with the tips of his fingers. Grimmley growled in pain as Jack twisted the knife. He clamped down onto Jack's throat with terrible strength. Jack felt his vision begin to grow dim. He twisted the knife again. Another howl. Somewhere far away, he heard pounding on a door and shouting. He was now hanging halfway out of the window. Grimmley maintained a steely grip on his throat. A distant part of his mind told Jack he did not have long before he would lapse into unconsciousness. He felt his strength begin to fade. In desperation, he lurched forward. Taking a firm hold on the knife, he yanked it free and stabbed it toward Grimmley's neck. Grimmley released his grip suddenly and fumbled to grab hold of Jack's wrist and control the knife. Jack gasped in a sudden intake of breath as he pulled his hand away from Grimmley's grasp. He leaned out further to seize Jack's wrist. Both men came to the same sudden terrible realization simultaneously. They were falling.

The world spun as Jack released his hold on Grimmley's shirt to grab the windowsill. As the larger man tumbled past, Jack felt his arm twist. He struggled desperately to maintain his grip on the window frame. He distantly heard a loud clattering thud as Grimmley fell into the debris below. Jack hung there single-handed for a moment, struggling to regain his breath. As his senses returned, he heard shouting in the nearby street. The pounding inside had not ceased. With the broken glass of the window cutting into his wrist, he shot his other hand up and grabbed hold of the sill, pulling himself up into the window. His heart skipped a beat, and he almost slipped and fell when he saw Walsh standing in the center of the room, aiming a small assassin's crossbow at him. The pounding on the door stopped suddenly. Walsh looked at the door, then shouldered the weapon, taking aim. Jack felt the skin between his eyes crawl in dreadful anticipation of being split by a crossbow bolt. He weighed the idea of letting himself fall to the hard flagstones below rather than be shot in the face with a crossbow. Walsh smiled in an awful way.

The door behind him suddenly burst open, the frame shattering into countless pieces as Uglor's huge form came crashing through. Daelyn stepped into the gap with her bow drawn. Walsh turned his head. He held the crossbow at his waist, still pointing toward the window. Jack could see by his expression that he knew he could never bring his weapon to bear in time. Daelyn had him, and everyone knew it.

"Put it down," she said calmly. "Slowly." Walsh set his jaw with determination. By the look in his eye, Jack knew what his answer would be. He stood there for a brief moment, he and Daelyn glaring at one another. She held her bow steady, the arrow's fletching lightly brushing her cheek. Jack lowered himself slightly to present less of a target, leaving only the top of his head and eyes visible. Walsh spun suddenly, whipping the crossbow around, and dropped to one knee. Daelyn's arrow took him in the neck before he could even get off a shot. He fell over backward, gurgling his last few breaths as the crossbow rattled harmlessly to the floor. Uglor shot to his feet and crossed the room in two quick strides. He grabbed Jack by the wrists and pulled him in the window, as easily as if he were lifting a small child.

"I take it you got my signal." Jack sighed, still laboring to breathe normally. His knees buckled, and he slumped to the floor, leaning on the wall by the window. Daelyn knelt over Walsh's body. She looked at Jack and shook her head. "Dammit," he said.

"What was he thinking?" she asked. She retrieved her arrow with not so much as a grimace and wiped it on the fallen man's shirt.

"Where is Tim?" Jack asked. He pushed his way to his feet, wobbling slightly. He felt Uglor's hand take hold of his elbow to steady him.

"Outside watching for the local law enforcement," she replied as she studied the point of her arrow. She grimaced and tossed it into the corner.

"Bring that," Jack said. She looked at him questioningly. "If these guys were important enough, there might be some psychic investigation. Uglor, could you get my knife?" He pointed to the blade stuck in the chair. Jack stepped over to the window and looked out. Grimmley was nowhere to be seen. Jack shook his head in disbelief. Was the man indestructible? He hoped Tim had seen where he had gone. Of his second knife, there was no sign. He doubted they would have time to search for it. He turned back into the room. Daelyn had unstrung her bow and was peering out into the hall.

"Is there a back way out of this building?" she asked. "I doubt we will have an easy time just strolling out of here." As if to punctuate her sentiment, a bell rang out in the street below. "Speaking of law enforcement…"

"On my way in, I saw a door which probably leads out into the alley." He visually scoured the room, wishing desperately that they had time to look around for anything useful. "Let's move."

They darted out into the hall. This really wasn't a very good plan, after all, he admitted to himself.

* * * * *

Tim dropped himself heavily into the lumpy chair that lived its wretched existence in the dusty lobby of Devonshire's lowliest of inns. He looked around the room. There were a few more equally miserable chairs clustered in a crooked circle around a battered and war-torn coffee table, all facing an equally decrepit couch. Next time, I pick the hotel. He thought to himself. The few extra coins they were saving were hardly worth the "unwanted attention" that Jack claimed they were avoiding by staying in this dump. The name of the place was Ingrid's, but as of yet, Tim had seen no sign of any such person. Not that he was surprised. If he owned a wreck like this, he would do his best to distance himself as much as possible from the monstrosity.

The late afternoon light that fought its way through the filthy windows streamed through the dusty air to fall on a clock (whose accuracy was in extreme question) sitting on a mantle that Tim had already decided he would not approach closely if he had a choice. This marvel of precision proclaimed that it was a few minutes before six. This meant that either he was a little early, on time, or a little late. Since he didn't see anyone else, he decided he was early. Unless, of course, they were all late. He tried to determine if it mattered anyway and gave up. Whatever lies the clock was sowing, it *was* time to eat.

He had nothing to contribute to the upcoming meeting anyway. His day had been a waste. After executing Jack's brilliant plan early that afternoon, it was suggested that they split up and investigate or something. Tim still wasn't clear on what he was supposed to be doing in a specific sense. Jack's exact words were something like, "… let's buzz around town this afternoon and try to make something out of what we got…" Just what does that mean anyway? He asked himself.

We know there are multiple persons in Elrynth, led by someone named Kalush. We don't know if it is his given name, his family name, or some name he just made up. It would seem that Kalush does not frequently communicate with Walsh, so this may mean his rank is equal to or greater than his. Or, maybe it doesn't mean a thing. We know that amongst these fellow employees who labor for the common good in the fair city of Elrynth is a gentleman named Ashe, who has recently joined our noble cause. Again, we do not know if this is a first name, a last name, or even a real name. We know these fellows are up to something and on schedule. A fat lot of help any of that is. We know Kudakaan had a plan of unknown origin involving a meeting with an unknown party for an unknown purpose. It also seemed the Trolls were involved somehow. Great. We know that someone named Captain Sarlo is in the mix too. Captain of what, we have no idea, nor do we know how or in what capacity he is involved. We also know Walsh "got the hotel" using his name. What hotel, or where, remains yet to be disclosed.

A more detailed analysis of the facts seemed impossible due to the acute shortage thereof. It was a moot point anyway since Jack had insisted that they all spend the rest of the day walking around the town waiting for the next clue to fall from the sky. It didn't. Aside from the expected hubbub concerning Walsh's unfortunate demise, he had discovered exactly nothing useful. Tim sighed. At least he tried. The only item of note he could uncover was a general concern about the growing banditry in the area, but this certainly had no bearing on their present situation. Tim watched the hands of the clock ooze forward as he went over the newly discovered facts at hand. For the fifth time today, he wondered if they should just scrap the whole affair and go their separate ways.

The clock was now making claims that the time had passed six by several minutes. To hell with it, I'm getting something to eat, Tim thought. He stood, with every intention of going over to the inn's dining area, when Jack and Uglor strolled in through the door. Jack smiled and waved, looking around the room quickly as he always seemed to do when he entered one.

"Seen Daelyn?" Jack asked. Tim shook his head. You had better ask me if I am hungry. Tim thought.

"You hungry?" Jack asked again. "I'll buy." In a few moments, they were seated around a rickety table in the inn's poor excuse for a dining room. A serving girl who looked as tired as the business she worked for was making her languid way around the room. Tim estimated she would pass this table just as he was blacking out from hunger. His stomach growled at him.

"No," Tim said. Jack looked at him questioningly.

"No, what?"

"In answer to the question you were about to ask. No, I didn't find anything. I wasn't even sure what I was supposed to be looking for." He must have had a sour expression on his face. Jack looked as if his feelings were hurt.

"Well, don't worry about it. Uglor and I found a few interesting things… ahh, there's Daelyn." He stood and waved her over. She crossed the room and sat, sparing a nod for Uglor, who sat still and silent as ever. Jack stood and pulled up a chair from the adjoining table for her. Tim winced at his own oversight of such obvious protocol. He felt his face flush as she sat and smiled at him. She *is* a stunningly beautiful woman. It is only natural for a healthy man to react like this, he told himself.

"Hello, Tim," she said with a slight knowing smile on her face. Who is the psychic here? He stammered something back, missing the first part of what Jack was saying.

"…like I was telling Tim here." She nodded, listening intently to what Jack was saying. "I checked all the inns, hotels, and otherwise here in town. Nothing under the name Sarlo or anyone else relevant." Jack waved futilely at the serving girl. "Anything from the guards, Daelyn?"

"I chatted with a few over lunch. They don't seem to have any leads on this morning's mayhem." Jack looked away, rubbing the back of his neck. "There are plenty of other travelers in town today, so we don't stand out more than anyone else. Nobody seemed to know who Walsh was either. I am guessing he doesn't … or… didn't live here in town." She sat back, folding her arms under her breasts. Tim felt suddenly flush again. She does that on purpose, he thought.

"Anyone get anything on this Kalush fellow?" Jack asked no one in particular. Tim suddenly sensed a feeling of alarm at the table. Uglor's eyes grew to twice their normal size. Tim spun around in his chair. "What…" Jack began. As Jack's voice trailed off, Tim decided that if he were to make a list of ten things that he least expected to see in the hotel lobby behind him, in order from least expected up, he would rank what he saw about a number four. (This did, however, assume the ruling out of completely absurd things like a one-legged man painted blue and red with feathers sticking out of his ears carrying caged toads.)

Kudakaan looked around the lobby for a moment before he saw the four of them staring back at him with their jaws hanging open. He had a filthy bandage wrapped sloppily once around his head, his clothes were dirty and torn in a few places, and he was missing his travel pack, but aside from that, he carried himself with all of his usual arrogance. He walked casually over to the table, pulled up a chair, and sat. Jack was the first to shake off the surprise.

"Uh. Hi," Jack said, eloquently. Kudakaan nodded a greeting and waved the barmaid over. She nodded back and waved. *Oh, fine, we have been sitting here for ten minutes without so much as eye contact, and this guy walks in off the street and gets served right away.* Tim made a note never to come back to this place again in his life.

"Are you okay? We thought you were dead," Daelyn added. Kudakaan turned to her, brushing a strand of hair from his eye.

"Do I look dead?" The hair fell back across his forehead. Jack opened his mouth to respond, no doubt sarcastically, but apparently thought better of it. After a moment, he went on.

"So," Jack said. Kudakaan looked at him blankly. "So, what happened?"

"I escaped."

"I see." He shared a confused look with Daelyn. "How?" Jack's voice held an edge. He clearly did not know what to think at this point. It occurred to Tim that it was possible that things may get ugly.

"I appealed to their avaricious nature," Kudakaan responded.

"Again?" Jack was obviously not satisfied.

"It worked, didn't it?"

"What worked? What the hell are you talking about? Are you going to tell us what happened back there or not?" Jack was nearly shouting. Daelyn shifted in her chair slightly as if expecting to need to move suddenly. Uglor put his fists on the table and stared at Kudakaan, like a large dog staring at a strange cat. Tim decided he would rather not be on the opposite end of such a look. Just as Kudakaan was about to reply, the barmaid came over to the table.

"Can I get you fellas something?" She spat out the words without thinking, as someone who has said a thousand variations of the same thing. Jack took his gaze from Kudakaan for only a moment.

"Come back in a minute." His voice held a steely edge.

"C'mon, I'm busy..." she slumped her shoulders as she spoke, turning to really look at the table for the first time.

"I said come back later." Jack's demeanor left no room for argument. Uglor had not moved. He sat stone-like in his chair, staring at Kudakaan, flexing his fists unconsciously. Jack glared at her with fire in his eye. Daelyn had slipped her hand into the fold of her jacket and darted her eyes back and forth between the two men who stared at each other across the table. The barmaid looked helplessly at Kudakaan. He nodded slightly, and she backed away, clearly worried.

"That was rude," Kudakaan stated. Tim felt the tension drain from the group slightly.

"We are still waiting for an explanation." Jack sat back in his chair. "You take us into a mountain full of Trolls…" Tim looked around the room to see if anyone might be overhearing the conversation. In this part of the country, Trolls were not just ordinary citizens. Things could get even uglier if the townspeople thought Trolls might be following this group of unfriendly strangers. Jack went on. "… Assuring us that it was clearly the best way to get to this town. You get smacked in the head with a log, dragged away, and the four of us barely make it out alive. Who knows what happened to Lena, Qaz, and Corelan? They could be dead for all we know." As he spoke, he stabbed his finger toward Kudakaan for emphasis. He was beginning to raise his voice. "Now you show up out of the blue and expect us to accept, 'I appealed to their avaricious nature' and go about our merry way?" Tim looked at Daelyn, who was sharing his concern, then glanced over to the bar where the serving girl had gone. She was whispering to a fat man in an apron, likely the proprietor of the establishment, and pointing at their table. Not good.

"I can understand your feelings," Kudakaan spoke in a very calm and even tone. "I was going to fill you in more once we were in a more private situation, but you don't seem inclined to wait." Kudakaan smiled as if speaking to an angry child. Way to be diplomatic.

"You could have said that up front," Jack replied. His voice dripped contempt.

"Either way." Kudakaan shrugged. Jack opened his mouth to retort when Daelyn interjected.

"Company," she whispered. Tim swiveled his head around to appraise the aproned fat man. He approached the table with another man who had to be at least part Troll himself. The two stopped just behind Kudakaan. The fat man looked right at Jack.

"Is there a problem here?" he asked, folding his arms across his chest. "Cos' if there is, Bartak here will be glad to discuss it with you outside." He gestured with a thumb to the hulking figure behind him. Bartak smiled a toothy grin and cracked his knuckles. The smile was really quite misplaced. Uglor was noticeably larger and more solid than Bartak, and there were five people at the table, and only two asking them to shape up. The innkeeper clearly had an over-inflated sense of confidence in his security man, possibly because neither of them could add, or they were both just plain stupid. Tim suspected a combination of factors was in play. These facts, however, did not stand to improve the already miserable state of affairs. At this rate, Tim suspected, he would never get something to eat.

"Problem?" Jack's demeanor changed in an instant. He was all smiles and goodwill. "Oh, no. I am afraid the lovely young woman misunderstood. I was asking her to return with five heaping plates full of whatever it is that smells so good in your kitchen." He smiled and looked at Kudakaan, inhaling deeply through the nose. "Mmm, that smells good. Doesn't it, my friend?" Kudakaan managed a weak nod. Jack went on. "What is that cooking in there?"

"Uh… mutton," the fat man responded. He was caught totally off guard.

"Mutton. I just love some good mutton. Let's get five plates of your wonderful mutton." Tim's ears perked up. "And some ale. I will recommend to all of my friends that they eat here in this fine establishment of yours. A round of applause for the man in charge, Bravo, good sir!" He stood and started clapping, gesturing for the others to do the same. Okay, now you are overdoing it. Tim thought. Daelyn ventured a weak clap. Not wanting her to feel too awkward, Tim clapped a few times as well.

The fat man, now convinced he was dealing with a madman, simply smiled and nodded, turning away to the duties of the kitchen. He ushered Bartak away as well, who looked sorry that he would not have a chance to be beaten to a pulp by five times his number. As soon as his back was turned, Jack sat in his chair with a scowl. "Dumb jackass…" he muttered. He looked back at Kudakaan. "Well, since I'm buying, is there anything you want to talk about over dinner?"

"I have no idea what got the Trolls so upset as to attack us," he responded. "My guess is they probably intended to kill us all along and were only trying to lure us into a sense of confidence, so we could be trapped in the cave and taken out easier." Jack listened to this carefully, his face unreadable. Tim could sense that somehow Kudakaan's emotions did not seem right for what he was saying.

It was almost as if he were lying, but he seemed to believe what he was saying to some degree. If he was hiding something, then he was a devious man indeed. "As you know, I was injured. I lost consciousness almost immediately. When I awoke, I was being held in a room somewhere in the cave. I managed to bargain for my freedom, using the last of our petty cash and the remaining horses." Jack leaned forward on the table, raising a finger.

"You sold off the other's horses?" he asked.

"Remember, I had no idea if any of you had survived the attack at all. Only by luck did I learn that there were a few horses left. My captor slipped up and told one of his fellows where I could overhear." Jack leaned back in his chair, his face still unreadable.

"Why didn't they just take the money and the horses and kill you anyway?" Daelyn asked. Jack nodded.

"Rock Trolls are very particular about their honor…" Kudakaan replied.

"I see. Go on," she responded.

"As I was saying, according to their code or some such, since I was a captive and not dead, I still had some claim to my own possessions. If they simply took what they wanted from me, they would be mere thieves. If they killed me as a captive, they would be murderers."

"As opposed to earlier when they tried to kill you and take your things at the same time, which would have been what, victory in combat and spoils of war?" Daelyn asked, half sarcastically.

"Exactly," Kudakaan answered flatly, either oblivious to or simply ignoring her sarcasm. Daelyn blew out a short breath, clearly expressing how she felt about that subtle distinction. "This left them in a bit of a bind concerning what they should do with me. They couldn't rob me or kill me on the spot, which left either holding me indefinitely or selling me into slavery or something. They didn't seem to be too keen on either choice, so I thought of buying my freedom, and they went for it. I threw in something about using me as an example of what happens to trespassers, and they were sold. After a few harsh words and a kick in the pants, I was on my way." Tim still felt something was wrong with this story, but it was difficult to concentrate on anything given the painful emptiness in his middle.

"If you didn't have a horse, how did you get here so fast?" Jack asked. "The north road takes two days of hard riding. At best, a day and a half if you cross country. We ourselves just got here today."

"The Trolls released me, so I stayed on the quarry road. A long walk, but at least it was downhill," Kudakaan responded.

"Ahh, the food's here," Daelyn stated, a little too loud and a little too early. The conversations died as five steaming plates of juicy mutton were distributed about the table. Five tankards of cool ale followed. Jack said something in an over-eloquent fashion to the serving girl, who blushed and giggled as she left. The mutton, served with some bland and uninteresting vegetable medley, was absolutely divine. Tim lost himself briefly as he opened peace negotiations with his stomach with this first offering. Jack watched the woman leave, then spoke.

"So, how did you find us?"

"I wasn't really looking for you. I just got into town, and this is the inn I picked to stay in. You were here." Okay, *something* was wrong with that, Tim thought to himself. He clearly sensed some duplicity there, but it was hard to tell more. Kudakaan was a talented deceiver. "I am curious about a few things myself." Kudakaan went on. "Since I am in charge of this expedition, I'll take the liberty of asking."

"Shoot," Jack replied. Tim could almost see Jack putting on his game face.

"How did you know what we were going to do next?"

"What do you mean?"

"You are here, and I never told you what our plans were."

"Before I answer that, does it not now seem like a good idea to maybe share that information in the future?" Kudakaan did not answer, but his eyes narrowed a bit as he chewed a slice of meat. "In answer, you did tell us. Midweek. In Akeela. You said we were going to Devonshire. So here we are." Jack smiled his signature false grin. Tim could sense that Kudakaan wanted to challenge that but hesitated to do so for some reason. He wondered if he knew about the morning's little adventure. Probably not.

"What have you been doing this whole time if you thought I was dead?"

"We were looking for our lost companions, for one. We were driven out toward Akeela, and it was clear there was nothing useful we could do there. Not knowing if anyone else had survived, we came here since it was the last place that we all knew to go," Jack answered. "Between the added travel time of the north road and then a failed search for our missing friends, we've been trying to determine if we could continue our mission, and if we could not, what our next step would be." Kudakaan looked up sharply. Jack continued. "I think the rest of that thought is better finished in a more private environment. Wouldn't you agree?" Jack asked. Kudakaan nodded in agreement. "Well, I should settle up the dinner bill, and since you are broke, I suppose I'll be renting you a room also. I'll expect reimbursement," Jack added. "If there's nothing else, I might further suggest that we all get some sleep. And since you smell like hell, no offense, maybe a bath." Jack sat back, sipping his ale with only the slightest grimace.

"My thoughts exactly," Kudakaan responded. A crumb of a smile wrinkled his lip. "We meet in the lobby at first light. I need to resupply, and we have some business here in town before we move on." Kudakaan spoke a bit more firmly than was necessary as if to reaffirm his position as leader of the expedition.

"This is probably a topic for tomorrow's discussion," Daelyn began. She glared at Jack as if warning against challenging her suggestion. "…but we should really think about what we are going to do, if anything, about the missing members of our party."

"Yes, excellent. Everyone mull it over, and I'll hear your thoughts tomorrow," Kudakaan answered. "Also, bear in mind that we have no cash flow and may not be able to rectify that for a while until we can arrange something with our employer. It may be necessary to divert some time from our primary task to regain some capital." Tim saw Jack physically choke on his response. Slightly impressed by Jack's ability to remain quiet, Tim stood.

"Well, if that's it for tonight, I'm off to bed," Tim spoke, having finished his dinner. And to get a bath before you dirty up the tub, he addressed silently to Kudakaan.

CHAPTER EIGHT
FIRSDAY
1ST OF CYNDDUM

Daelyn rolled her eyes and steeled herself for another Kudakaan vs. Jack verbal showdown. She glanced over at Tim, who had actually gone so far as to sit down on a nearby bench. He had pulled out a heel of bread to munch on, apparently expecting this to take a while. Perhaps sitting was a good idea. This *could* take a while. A cool breeze blew down the street, striving to wrest dominance from the warm late afternoon sun. This part of Devonshire seemed to have been built all at once by the same unimaginative architect. The buildings were flat rectangular brick boxes stacked in a neat row, perpendicular to the main street running through the center of town. Either the mastermind behind this block had overestimated Devonshire's potential for growth, or business in a general sense had taken a recent dive. The upper floors of the building beside yesterday's crime scene seemed deserted, its broken windows either darkened or boarded up completely. Foot traffic in this area was sparse, especially compared to the bustling market streets a few blocks away. If any part of Devonshire had Underground connections, this was it.

"So, you are saying you have no idea what happened here." Kudakaan put his hands on his hips as he spoke as if scolding a child.

"That is exactly what I am saying. I can say it a fourth time if you think it will help." Jack smirked as if trying to suppress laughter, which only seemed to enrage Kudakaan more. She suspected that reaction, rather than actual amusement, was the purpose of the smile. Kudakaan gestured behind himself toward the building that once contained Walsh's office. They had spent a good portion of the day wasting time sitting around at the hotel while Kudakaan was out 'investigating.' That had driven Jack absolutely mad. He had plotted and discarded nearly a dozen strategies for every possible scenario Kudakaan might present upon his return. They had even tried to come up with a plan to rescue their missing comrades (assuming they were still alive), but every scheme involved somehow returning to the Troll cave, a move which, no matter how you looked at it, was dumb at best. In the end, it was once again decided that nothing could be done, and Qaz, Lena, and Corelan would have to fend for themselves.

She herself had taken nearly all day to compose another report to her employer as she kept getting interrupted by Jack with another 'theory' or by Tim, who was just bored. The report didn't really touch on her primary objective, but she had made no significant progress on that front, so the omission was logical. She filled the report with details on their encounter with Walsh and Kudakaan's return from the dead. She remembered that she still needed to find a drop location somewhere in town before they left.

"You had no idea that our contact here had been murdered?" Kudakaan stated. "In a town this small, a man is killed, another is missing, and you have heard not a single word?" Kudakaan looked around the street to see if anyone was close enough to hear their conversation. "You can't play the fool with me anymore, Jack. I know you are a clever man. I don't believe for a second that you stumbled into town and stood around twiddling your thumbs, waiting for instructions to fall into your lap." Kudakaan shook a finger at Jack and glared down his nose at the shorter man. "I am ordering you to tell me what you know about what happened here."

"Didn't the policeman say he was shot through the neck with some kind of arrow?" Jack leaned on the brick façade of the building behind him. Kudakaan grimaced, barely containing his anger.

"That is not what I asked you," he managed to growl.

"Sure, I heard that somebody got killed. How am I supposed to know anything else?" Jack explained. "You leave us in the dark, dangling in the wind, and we just arrive in the town we only *think* we are supposed to be in, and you expect us to just intuitively know what is happening behind the scenes?" Jack gestured helplessly. "I mean, c'mon, how the hell are we supposed to know anything at all here?"

"Don't start with that. Only a handful of people knew that we had business here in town at all, and of those people, I am looking at the only ones who were here when the murder took place."

"First of all, you don't know that for a fact, and secondly, who says it had anything to do with anything?" Jack looked at Daelyn for support. Don't look at me, she thought. Jack went on. "Maybe he just got robbed or something. I don't know."

"You don't believe that any more than I do."

"Hey, your boss said himself that he has lots of enemies and that probably some are on the inside. Maybe something happened with that. Or maybe, what did you say his name was, Walsh? Maybe he got so tired of being left in the dark all the time, he shot himself in the neck." Kudakaan took a step forward, clenching his fists. Uglor did likewise. Kudakaan glared at him but remained silent. "I just don't see how we are supposed to know anything, especially with you and your ultra-secret need-to-know policy." Jack turned away. "Tim is the psychic here, not me. Ask him." Tim looked up, slightly indignant over being dragged into this squabble. Kudakaan raised an eyebrow.

"Tim?" he asked.

"I would have to get inside to get any vibes. Since we can't do that…" He looked as if he had a list one hundred items long of places he would rather be.

"Let me try one last time to get us in. I need to get a look around inside the office regardless." Kudakaan stormed off towards the dingy brick structure. Once she was sure he was out of earshot, Daelyn turned to Jack.

"What's your plan now, slick?" She addressed him with just the right amount of Toctilian lilt and a sideways look. Behind him, Tim had risen to his feet and was brushing crumbs from the front of his shirt. Jack took a deep calming breath. She could see tension in the corners of his eyes and the set of his jaw. The breeze made a rush at a nearby oak, its rustling leaves producing the only calming sound she had heard all day. She turned to look. The large oak stood in the center of the street, surrounded by a small island of dirt, bricked off from the road by someone who apparently thought the tree was worth saving. They had underestimated its root structure, though, and over the years, the brick ring closing it off from the street had cracked in several places. The foliage, for the most part, was still green. Dots of faded yellow on the leaves near the ends of some of the branches were present, and though today was the first day of Autumn, it seemed that summer would still reign for a while yet.

"Well," Jack began. "I am hoping he is now sufficiently motivated to talk his way past that dumpy-looking town guard at the front door. She looked across the street where Kudakaan was busily talking to the guard and gesturing toward the building. "My guess is, though, that he is going to have to show some coin." Sure enough, a moment later, Kudakaan was digging in his pockets and looking around warily.

"I was referring to the general situation," she corrected. "There is a chance he is going to find out what happened." She found it odd that she didn't care as much as she thought she should. Maybe because she was already in three or four lies deep, it was becoming just too much.

"I want to get in there to look around as badly as he does. We didn't exactly get a good chance to look around the first time. I am hoping to see something, anything, either before or at the same time he does. Hopefully, that will give us an edge." Tim perked up at that last comment.

"He is almost certainly going to ask me what I sense." Daelyn saw Jack's mind engage and race ahead. "I was thinking…"

"Okay, here is your story…" Jack cut him off. Kudakaan was completing his transaction across the street. "Just make it sound like somebody attacked him, there was a colossal fight, and the attacker got away." Kudakaan was now heading back. He would be within earshot in seconds. "Close enough to the truth."

"How do I…" Tim sputtered.

"Wing it," Jack whispered as Kudakaan waved them forward. Daelyn put on her best disarming smile and strolled toward the building in which yesterday (thanks in no small part to Jack's crack-brained decision to lie to the fellow) she had shot their only lead. The guard met them just inside and reluctantly led them through the business on the bottom floor to the staircase in the back. The business appeared to be part warehouse, part retail showroom. It wasn't clear if they sold cloth, clothing, or both. Large bolts of material were stacked unceremoniously against a wall or leaning in a corner. It was dim, quiet, and dusty in the room. Here and there, an article of clothing was on display either as an example or for actual sale. The wrinkled, balding, and squinty shopkeeper glared sharply at them as they passed through; his thoughts, while clearly unfriendly, were otherwise unreadable.

Jack made it a point to face the other direction as they walked by. Daelyn felt a surge of apprehension. Even though Jack insisted no one saw him enter the building yesterday since he had entered through the back door (and she was relatively confident of the same concerning herself), if anyone had a chance of recognizing them, this shopkeeper was the one. Her training with the Underground suggested she consider "taking care" of him as a precaution. She shuddered and looked away. She was no murderer. The shopkeeper frowned and disappeared through a door in the rear of the room.

The guard hefted his sagging and overworked belt occasionally, carrying himself with stooped shoulders and hanging his head as if the sheer effort of traveling across a room was too much to bear. He led them to the stairs and opened the door with a key hanging from a chain at his waist. He turned to the group without really looking at anyone but Kudakaan.

"You got five minutes. Any longer, and I am hauling you out." He shouldered past them roughly on his way back out to the street. Daelyn unwillingly noticed that he reeked of onions. Once they were relatively alone, Kudakaan turned to them, addressing the entire group.

"Uglor, I want you and Daelyn out in the hall as lookouts. If that guard comes back, I want to know about it as soon as you do. Tim, I want you and Jack in the office with me to look around." He looked at each person as he addressed them as if daring them to challenge his word. When no one did, he turned on his heel and slipped quietly up the stairs. As they reached the top of the stairs, Daelyn gestured for Uglor to stand at the end of the hall, where he could see all the way down the stairs. He obliged without a word. One other door fed into the hall, but the dust and cobwebs that had collected in and around the corners of the doorframe suggested that the room had been abandoned for quite some time. She took position right outside the shattered doorframe to Walsh's office, where she could see both Uglor and the three others in the room. She didn't want to miss any of this.

Before entering, Kudakaan gestured for everyone to stay back as he examined the scene. The door, hanging precariously on its shattered frame, creaked loudly and threatened to fall completely off as he poked the hinges lightly with the point of his dagger. He silently went around the room, taking careful note of everything. The papers from Walsh's desk swirled around his ankles as a slight breeze blew in through the shattered window. He stopped and lightly fingered a gouge in the back of Walsh's chair, noting the position of both the damage and the chair itself.

Daelyn was a little unnerved, as Kudakaan's face was totally unreadable. There was just no way to tell what he suspected. Jack leaned on the wall opposite the room, looking for the entire world as if he were a bit bored, but she could see him scrutinizing Kudakaan's every move out of the corner of his eye. If he was nervous, he hid it well. Tim stood in the middle of the hall, his head slightly downcast, with a far-off look on his face. She suspected he was trying to get some impression from Kudakaan. Glancing down the hall, she could see Uglor diligently looking down the stairwell, essentially ignoring the drama in the next room. She found herself trying to think of an excuse to string her bow. Her attention snapped back into the room as Kudakaan spoke.

"Interesting." He crouched on the ground beside the large stain on the floor that marked where Walsh had breathed his last. The still loaded crossbow was still lying on the floor where it had fallen.

"What?" Jack asked casually. Daelyn could feel the muscles in her neck grow tighter.

"Well, this is the way I see it." Kudakaan stood and sat on the edge of the desk. "Quite contrary to what Devonshire's finest have led us to believe, there is quite a bit of evidence here." Jack pushed himself away from the wall and stepped forward to lean on the broken doorframe.

"Good. What do you have?" he asked, still portraying an image of only mild interest. Daelyn was sure everyone could hear her heart pounding in her chest.

"Not enough yet," Kudakaan answered. "Tim?"

"Sir?" Tim responded.

"Could you take a look around and tell me if you get anything?" he requested.

"Sure." Tim entered the room, went straight to the chair, and sat in it. Kudakaan took a step back into the corner to give him space. Tim closed his eyes and felt the chair's arms with his fingertips. "How long did, uh, what's his name, have this office?" Good question, Daelyn thought.

"Walsh. About a week." Kudakaan responded flatly.

"That explains the weak vibes." Tim opened his eyes. "I think I have a feel for him, though." Kudakaan took a step forward as Tim rose from the chair.

"Explain."

"Well, a psychic can sense the energy that people give off. We sometimes call it 'vibes.' This energy rubs off on the things that a person touches, like this chair. The longer the contact, the stronger the vibe. If he had been using this office for months or years, I could get a much stronger impression of his particular feel. It is sort of like the way a bloodhound gets someone's scent."

"Everyone has a different feel, then?" Kudakaan asked.

"Exactly. I need to know which vibes are his so I can tell more about what happened here. Also, the way a person felt when they laid down the vibes can affect the way it feels to the psychic." Tim stepped around the desk.

"Interesting," Kudakaan replied. "Continue." Tim knelt beside the large bloodstain in the center of the room.

"Something that is very personal to an individual, like blood, hair, or even a signature, gives off stronger vibes." He reached his hand out over the stain, hesitating slightly before he touched the floor. His face twisted slightly, and he quickly withdrew his hand. "This may not be much of a surprise, but this is where Walsh died." Kudakaan circled around the desk.

"And this?" He indicated a second set of bloodstains beside the desk. Tim stepped closer and repeated the process.

"Someone else. Can't be sure, but I think he is still alive." That last comment was for Jack, Daelyn thought. Tim stood and looked around the room. He touched the stain on the couch and crossed the room to run his fingers along the broken windowsill.

"What do you think happened?" Kudakaan asked Tim. He had a look on his face as if he were trying to entrap the psychic. Tim looked straight back at him.

"It seems like Walsh and this other man got in a fight. Walsh was killed, and the other man fled, wounded. Possibly through the window."

"Jack, anything to add?" Kudakaan asked.

"Well, if I was forced to speculate, I would say our unknown assailant kicked in this door and took a shot at Walsh, probably with a traditional bow," he answered. "I say that because the police indicate he was shot by an arrow, not a crossbow bolt." He stepped into the room. "I am guessing he missed his first shot, or it would have ended there. That explains the nick in the chair." Jack crossed the room to stand behind the desk. He looked at the chair and pantomimed jumping out of it. "Walsh possibly dove off this way to avoid the arrow. He might have knocked over the papers in the process, which would explain that." He stood in front of the couch. "It is hard to tell what happened next." He looked at Kudakaan as if having a sudden thought.

"Did Walsh have any assistants or help of any kind?" Daelyn was worried that Jack might be overdoing it a bit. If he had a too elaborate scenario already thought out, Kudakaan might suspect something. She looked at Kudakaan, who was as unreadable as ever.

"Yes. A bodyguard. Grimmley," came the response.

"And you haven't heard anything from this bodyguard fellow since you've been in town?" Jack followed.

"No."

"Well, as long as I am speculating, I suppose – Grimmley was his name? – Grimmley came in right around then. I say this because Walsh had to load his crossbow and move into the center of the room to get killed, which doesn't make sense – he wouldn't have time unless his attacker was distracted." Jack reenacted crossing the room to stand where Walsh was shot. "Yeah, I guess the bodyguard came in right then and fought with the attacker and wounded him, or maybe they wounded each other. Who knows? That explains the bloodstains here and here." He pointed at the stains Tim had said were someone else's. "My guess is Walsh was loading up his crossbow during the fight." Jack crossed the room to stand in front of the window. "Something, or possibly someone went through the window, we can see that. Maybe even your Grimmley fellow, though that doesn't explain where he is now."

"I see. Go on." Kudakaan leaned against the wall in the corner of the room, watching Jack reenact the imagined struggle. Daelyn sensed he suspected something. What he suspected, she could only guess. Her fingers strayed closer to the throwing knife, which was tucked beneath her cloak in the small of her back.

"Well, at some point, your Walsh guy came out from behind his desk with his crossbow loaded. Shortly after that, he got pegged in the neck." Jack indicated the floor where Walsh fell.

"If your assailant was by the window, why would Walsh circle the desk to shoot him? Why not shoot him from over there?" Kudakaan pointed across the room to the chair behind the desk. Jack twisted his mouth as if in deep thought. Don't overdo it, Daelyn thought.

"Hmm. Good question." Jack circled back around the desk and began to walk back around as if retracing Walsh's steps. "The only reason I can think of to cross out here is…" He looked around, pointing an imaginary crossbow. As his gaze fell on the door, his eyes lit up. "He was looking out the door or the window. The only reason to step out into the room." Kudakaan shot a look toward the door. "Okay, new theory," Jack began. "The bodyguard came in, or maybe was already in, fought with the assailant while Walsh loaded the crossbow. There was a break in the fight, and Walsh shot the attacker who fell through the window. Walsh reloaded and came over to look out. A second assailant then came through the door and shot Walsh."

"What about Grimmley?" Kudakaan asked.

"Maybe he went through the window first. That would explain the assailant standing by the open window." Jack sat on the corner of the desk. "Or, maybe after they shot Walsh, they captured Grimmley and dragged him away somewhere."

"All this seems consistent with the facts, although highly speculative. Tim?" Kudakaan looked at the younger man.

"None of it is in conflict with what I am sensing. I can't get that much detail, but based on what we have, the theory is as good as any other." He shrugged.

"Daelyn?" Kudakaan shifted his gaze to the corner of the doorway where she stood.

"I don't even have an opinion." She raised her hand in a warding gesture. "He is dead. Let's move on." Kudakaan smiled slightly.

"I agree." He opened his satchel and produced a tooled leather document case. Kneeling to the floor, Kudakaan began to gather the papers that were strewn across the floor. Daelyn saw Jack's jaw clench as Kudakaan collected the pages and dropped them into the leather pouch. Jack stepped forward to assist, but Kudakaan waved him away.

"You think those might be important?" Jack asked, not to be deterred.

"Possibly," Kudakaan answered flatly.

"Maybe we should take a look at them," Jack suggested.

"I will." Kudakaan smirked. He crossed behind the desk and opened a drawer. He poked around in the drawer for a moment before shutting it and moving to the next. Jack slid over around the desk as well.

"So… what are we looking for?" he asked. Kudakaan paused for a moment, considering how much information to share. Daelyn could tell he was choosing his words carefully.

"Walsh, I am told, had made some progress on our problem from this end. I am looking to see what I can learn." Jack shot a look at Tim, darting his eyes quickly to the leather document case.

"What was his role here, specifically?" Jack asked Kudakaan.

"Who, Walsh?"

"Yeah. Was he like an information collector or what?"

"I suppose that is a sufficient description," came the response. Kudakaan knelt to open the bottom desk drawer. Somewhat cautiously, Jack asked the question that had been lurking in Daelyn's mind for some time.

"So, how many other folks are working on this? I was led to believe we were the only ones." Kudakaan stopped what he was doing and stood slowly. He looked around the room. Three pairs of eyes were fixed on him. Jack moved to sit on the edge of the desk, knocking off a small stone, probably a paperweight, she guessed, as he sat. It fell to the floor and rolled over to the wall, hitting the baseboard, making a decidedly hollow sound. Jack perked up and turned to look. He traded a look with Kudakaan, who stepped over to the wall.

"Sounds hollow," Tim stated, giving homage to the god of the obvious. Jack knelt beside Kudakaan and knocked on the baseboard. Daelyn took a step closer as well but could not see around the other men.

"There's a seam here," Jack offered. He knocked on the baseboard again a few inches past the seam from where the stone had hit, and it sounded as solid as a wall should. Kudakaan tapped the same spot the stone hit. Definitely hollow. Jack pulled out a knife to pry the board open, but the wood popped off in Kudakaan's hand. As Jack slid his blade back into wherever he had it hidden, Kudakaan reached into the small space that had been revealed, pulling out a small envelope. Both his and Jack's eyes sparkled. These two don't get along because they are too alike, she thought, shaking her head. Men.

Uglor, standing in the hall, cleared his throat loudly. Everyone stood and spun, facing the door. A fraction of a second later, Uglor poked his head through and pointed back toward the staircase. Daelyn heard the shuffling footsteps that indicated that their visit here was finished.

"C'mon down, folks. You're done," the guard bellowed from the bottom of the stairs. Apparently, climbing the stairs to speak to them required too much effort. Jack looked at Kudakaan as if to say this topic was far from closed. Daelyn, for once, agreed entirely.

The five walked back to *Ingrid's Inn* in relative silence, maintaining an illusion of taking a relaxed stroll through the small town. As they arrived at the inn, Kudakaan headed toward his room. Everyone else followed. Kudakaan's room was small, like all the rooms at *Ingrid's,* and was nearly the mirror of her own room. A small lumpy bed was shoved into a corner with a short chest of drawers at its foot. A rickety writing table was in the opposite corner, and between them, a dirty window with poorly done glass panes was badly concealed behind a faded and mostly ineffectual curtain. Jack followed Kudakaan right through the door and sat on his bed. Tim and Daelyn followed a bit more hesitantly behind.

"Won't you come in, please," Kudakaan commented sarcastically. Uglor, still out in the hall, closed the four in the room, standing just outside the door.

"So. What have we got?" Jack asked politely. Kudakaan's hand drifted unconsciously to the pocket where he had placed the envelope.

"I haven't reviewed anything yet," he responded.

"We know. How about looking right now?" Jack spoke from a seated position, but he seemed to completely control the situation.

"I don't feel inclined to examine any material at this time. You may leave my room now. All of you." Kudakaan's voice held an edge that warned his patience was nearly through. Tim shifted uncomfortably, looking as if he had not intended to participate in forcing a confrontation.

"Then how about answering my question from earlier?" Jack stared at Kudakaan as he spoke without blinking.

"What question was that?"

"We were originally told that we were the only ones working on this project…"

"That was never said."

"It was implied. Pendor said he couldn't trust any of his own people. That's why he hired us." Jack stood and leaned on the wall.

"What are you getting at?" Kudakaan asked.

"What I am getting at is this." He pushed off of the wall and took a step toward Kudakaan. "This mission is a joke. We have been completely in the dark from day one. Now, it is quite evident that someone is willing to kill to prevent this mission from coming to a close. I, for one, will not take a step further on this until I am satisfied that you have told us everything pertinent to our job." He folded his arms defiantly. Daelyn got the distinct feeling that a line was just drawn in the sand. Kudakaan responded in a much calmer tone than she expected. He opened his leather writing case, and after shuffling through it for a moment, he pulled out a sheet of parchment. He extended it to Jack.

"Here." Jack's eyes narrowed slightly as he took a step forward to take the paper from the other man.

"What is this?"

"The contract you signed. It legally binds you to follow my orders. The language is quite specific." Jack opened his mouth to respond but was cut off. "The way I see it, you have two choices. Either do as I say or don't. If you don't, that constitutes a breach of contract, your employment will be terminated, and you forfeit half of your retaining fee, payable to me immediately." Kudakaan paused, giving Jack a chance to respond. Jack was reading the contract over carefully.

"Jack…" Tim began, but Jack waved him silent as he handed the contract back to Kudakaan.

"Now, I am ordering you to return to your rooms, all of you. Meet me in the lobby in the morning. We will ride to Elrynth at first light. Goodnight." He slid the contract back into the case and folded his hands. "Or you can pay me two hundred and fifty silver right now." Kudakaan pasted a sarcastic smile on his face as he awaited an answer.

"If that's the way you want it, then so be it," Jack responded. He turned toward the door. "Just remember, this is your choice." The setting sun threw a golden light on the room through the open window, casting a hard shadow across his face. He turned without further word, opened the door, and stepped out into the hallway. Daelyn did not like the tone in his voice.

"Well. That could have gone better," Tim offered. The gods of the obvious were surely going to bestow a blessing on Tim this evening. He smiled and offered some words of polite parting before leaving the room as well. Daelyn waited a moment, listening to the sounds of retreating footsteps in the hall before she spoke.

"Do you have a moment?" she asked Kudakaan.

"Certainly." He leaned back on the desk and twitched the corner of his mouth in a way that some might dub a smile. She took a deep breath before she spoke, still not sure if she should.

"I have some concerns." She picked her words carefully. If he suspected that she was digging for information, she might as well join Jack's 'I am never going to get what I want' club. Kudakaan stepped over to the door and peered out into the hall. Apparently satisfied, he closed the door gently before responding.

"What is on your mind?" he asked. His voice had softened considerably.

"Well, there is this whole thing with Jack..." She noticed his eyes flicker across her body as she stood at the foot of his bed.

"He just has a problem with authority. I wouldn't worry." He sat back on the desk and smiled a bit more. She realized this was going to be easier than she had thought. She sat on the end of his bed and looked up at him. Men get a kick out of that. It makes them feel in control.

"Well, our guy here in town just got killed. I am worried that somebody knows what we are up to and has sent an assassin after us." For once, the false Toctilian accent could work in her favor. Toctilian society was still a little old-fashioned. Women in that part of the world tended to rely on the men in their lives for security and, in many cases, everything else. Playing up that side of her "heritage" put Kudakaan in the role of the protector, which made him confident and hopefully careless. She let her eyes and posture say just how truly worried she was about this mystery assassin. He swallowed it whole.

"You shouldn't worry. The fighters in this group can handle any attacks."

"Even the best fighters can be killed by an arrow from the rooftop…" she offered. He smiled. It almost appeared genuine.

"I wouldn't worry. Even if someone is tailing us, which I doubt, they couldn't know enough to justify a direct move against us. We are safe as long as we keep a tight lid on our intelligence findings," he huffed. "Something Jack does not seem to grasp."

"That makes me feel better," she responded. Which was true, but not because of anything Kudakaan had just said. She could see that she had planted a seed in his head that there actually was an assassin, thereby pushing him further away from suspecting one of them.

"Anything else?" He smiled again in a smug way as if enjoying the role of the protector.

"You did mention that we were running low on cash and that we might need to divert some energy toward replenishing our reserves. Is that something we should be concerned with?" She leaned forward a bit more to allow him a brief view down the front of her blouse before she stood. The effect was not lost.

"I, uh, no. Not at all." It was all she could do not to smile. Sometimes it was too easy. "I am going to send a letter by carrier pigeon to our employer to solicit more funds. It shouldn't take more than a day or two to hear a response. By then, we should be in Elrynth." She let out a huge sigh of relief.

"Well, I am going to have a nice hot bath, and then I'm off to bed." She said that so he would have something besides their last conversation to think about.

"I am glad I could help." He crossed the room to open the door for her. "Goodnight then," he said. She smiled, pressing her fingers to her mouth.

"Goodnight." As she heard the door click behind her, she dropped the simpering frightened woman routine and mentally began to finish her report. This was getting interesting.

* * * * *

"You are certain Kudakaan said, Devonshire?" Qaz asked for the fifth time.

"Yes. And Corelan agrees, don't you?" Lena responded. Corelan muttered what could have been an affirmation. She sighed deeply. As charming as he thought he was, Qaz could be a royal pain in the neck.

"Then how do we know which hotel to start with?" Qaz looked around the dark street as if expecting the Answer Fairy to leap from behind a building and start flinging knowledge all over the town. It seemed the fairy had retired for the evening.

"We don't," she answered, filling the void left by the overdue fairy. "I am just too tired to deal with it tonight. Seeing as we spent most of yesterday running in circles through the woods riding double on stolen horses trying to evade people who, until Corelan got involved, were our friends. And then after you got us lost…"

"I did no such thing!" Qaz responded indignantly.

"You did," she insisted. "Next time, we ASK for directions." She ground her teeth, struggling to restrain herself from launching into another tirade.

They had indeed spent the rest of the previous day riding in the wrong direction on the wrong road with a small group of angry bandits hot on their heels. Qaz had the bright idea of trying to cut through the forest to rejoin the main road and lose the bandits simultaneously. Against her better judgment, she had agreed. Night fell on them in the middle of dense forest and rendered them as lost as they could be. They had, however, also lost the bandits, as Qaz had repeatedly reminded them in his own defense. This morning, they continued to stumble blindly through the woods and eventually stumbled across a road, which none of them could identify, and given the way the roads wound through this rough country, relying solely on cardinal direction was useless. They came across a farmhouse, and Qaz had nearly thrown a fit when she suggested they ask their way, citing that he knew his way around and they were on the right path.

They were not. Once they found themselves in a charming town by the name of Beaufort, it was painfully apparent that they were well out of their way and had wasted at least half of the day. After asking directions in Beaufort and easily finding the correct road, both she and Corelan had taken turns berating him on their return trip (which incidentally had been along the same road) to such a degree that Qaz had lost his usual good temper and began a ten-minute shouting match which had left them both hoarse. Corelan had quietly complemented her restraint as she held her tongue when they passed the same farmhouse on the way back. Now Qaz had the gall to insist that they had not even been lost…

"Well, I apologize if our pointless day trip to Beaufort did not serve to energize me for a thorough search of Devonshire tonight. I hope you can forgive me." Lena glared at Qaz as she spoke. Corelan looked innocently up to the stars overhead as if he heard not a word. "This hotel is as good as any." She finished with a raised eyebrow, waiting for either another inane question or denial of the obvious truth. Instead, he dismounted and led his sorrel mare toward the stable's rear entrance. Corelan also hopped off of the horse they shared and took a few steps toward the front of the inn.

"I am going to go up front and let…" He shot a look at the inn's wooden sign hanging from an iron chain above the doorway. "…Ingrid know she has three more guests," he offered. "Don't want her thinking thieves are rooting around in her stable."

"Qaz, why don't you go with him? I'll take care of the horses," she spoke as she eased out of her saddle. Qaz nodded in affirmation and trotted over to Corelan. As the two of them ambled around to the front of the building, she pushed open the rear door of the inn's stable. She shook her head in disgust. She had been too preoccupied with saving their collective necks to really get into Corelan's reasoning for starting another fight and, at this point, she was too tired to care. She had not fully recovered from her own battle with the Troll, and today's exertion was beginning to take its toll.

Although Qaz's magic healing had mended her wounds physically, as he had warned her, there was still going to be some residual fatigue. She methodically pulled their meager provisions from the horse's back, noting as the stolen canvas bag hit the stable's dirt floor with a loud chink, that she had never gotten the opportunity to put on her armor. She had also rolled her gambeson into a filthy ball a few hours ago, relenting to the heat of the afternoon sun. It was that, or fall from the saddle from exhaustion. She brushed some of the day's dust from her overlarge and filthy tunic, which proved to be a more symbolic gesture than a practical one. This shirt was terminally soiled. It needed to be mercifully put down. The stable was quite dark; one lone lantern hung from a chain spanning the stable's width, connecting two narrow haylofts that ran the length of the structure over two rows of stalls. The corners were lost in shadow. She stepped over to the lantern and reached up to key it open a bit more. She reminded herself to dim the lantern back before she left. It didn't usually pay to have a large flame burning where you kept your hay. She moved back to brush down her dapple grey gelding. The horse whickered faintly as she gently brushed some of the day's exertion out of its rough, shaggy coat.

"Yeah, I know, you didn't ask to be here either," she offered to the beast. She realized that this was perhaps the first time she had ridden a horse without knowing its name. "What is your name anyway?" she asked it softly. The horse turned a big black eye to her as if preparing an answer. She spun around instinctively as the door to the stable opened. Kudakaan entered the stable from the street, leading a dun colored horse that she did not recognize behind him.

"Lena," Kudakaan spoke as if expecting her. "Are the others with you?" he asked without a hint of emotion. Still acting as if he were still the general of their little army, Kudakaan stepped further into the stable and led his new mount into one of the stalls. He closed the gate to the stall and waited patiently as she overcame her surprise. A moment passed as she thought of and rejected a dozen courses of action, most of them involving bloodshed.

"What did you mean, gift?" she asked. A cold edge gave her voice a dangerous quality that Kudakaan could clearly sense. She took a step forward, loosening her sword in its sheath with her left hand. To her left, a stout wooden door that presumably led into the inn was hanging partially open. Kudakaan stepped across the stable to close it, leaving them in the weak light of the lone lantern.

"What are you talking about? I asked you if…"

"I heard you. What I asked you, though, is what did you mean when you said 'gift'?" She fought to control the anger building inside of her.

"You lost me," Kudakaan replied, peering into a dark corner of the stable.

"When the Troll King was questioning you about why you were late to the meeting, and you told him that Daelyn and I were gifts. What did you mean exactly?" She got to see for the first time what Kudakaan looked like when he was utterly astonished.

"What? How…"

"I believe you said, 'slaves and objects of pleasure' or something of that sort, did you not?" She felt her hand drifting to her sword hilt. "And what of the gold? Did you not promise them gold for something?" She took another step forward. His demeanor changed completely in an instant. He was suddenly relaxed and good-natured.

"Did the Trolls tell you I said that? You should know better than to…"

"I heard it myself. As did Qaz. And Corelan." She planted herself firmly in front of him, glaring into his dark eyes with a fiery gaze. "You have some explaining to do. Right now." With that, she folded her arms and awaited his pleading session. Perhaps she should have, but she did not expect him to lunge at her.

He grabbed the collar of her tunic with both hands, wrenching sideways to throw her to the ground. The overlarge nature of her clothing bought her just enough time to shoot her right foot out to stabilize herself. Their hands grappled as she tried to pry open his grasp. For a moment, she wondered at his response, but that thought vanished as the single-mindedness of combat took possession of her. With a larger and stronger opponent grappling with her, she would never be able to draw her relatively long sword. She needed enough distance for only a moment, and they both knew it.

The two struggled briefly, neither gaining any ground. If she began to get a grip on his hands to pry them off, he would throw her off balance. He would try to throw her to the ground, but the tunic was too loose. After a moment, the fabric of the tunic began to tear. He pushed forward, shoving her back violently into a wall. He released his grip with his right hand and drew it back to punch her. She whipped her fist outward first, catching him with a glancing blow across the chin. With her feet flat and her back against the wall, she couldn't hope for her punch to have more than a momentary stunning effect. Her strike bought just enough time to turn away from the force of his punch, which skipped off of the side of her head as he twisted around with the momentum of his missed hook, losing his balance. He stepped forward to stabilize himself, pulling her off of her feet with her shirt collar, which tore free, coming off in his hand. She fell face down to the stable floor.

She scrambled to a crouch, attempting to draw her sword and face her assailant. Just as the tip of the blade cleared the scabbard, he tackled her, bearing them both to the ground again. She fell on her back, Kudakaan landing on top of her. Somehow, she managed to keep hold of the weapon. The wind rushed out of her lungs. He grabbed her sword arm with both hands, immobilizing the blade. She tried to reach her dagger, but her left arm was pinned to her side by his knee. She struggled to free her sword arm, but he had locked onto her wrist and was attempting to pry her fingers open. She twisted the length of the sword over her head as if she meant to pivot the blade and somehow cut him with the tip, with her hand still held firmly in both of his. It became immediately apparent to both of them that there was no chance of this tactic being effective, and Kudakaan smiled slightly. In response to her movement, he leaned forward more to gain control of her wrist and push the sword further away from them both. As soon as she felt his weight shift, she lifted both of her knees, pushing him further forward. He released his grip with one hand, shooting it forward to the ground to keep from tumbling forward. As his weight shifted further forward, pinning her sword hand to the ground, his weight came off of his knee, freeing her left hand. She snatched her dagger free from its leather sheath on her thigh, stabbing Kudakaan in the back of his leg as he scrambled to gain his balance.

With a roar of pain, Kudakaan dove away, hitting the ground in a roll and coming to his feet several yards away on the opposite side of the stable. Lena stood slowly, re-sheathing her dagger after wiping it clean on the remnants of her tunic. She brought her sword to bear in a defensive position as Kudakaan shifted his weight slightly, testing his injured leg. Their eyes locked across the stable turned battlefield. She concluded that Kudakaan was either a traitor to their cause or that they had been hired under false pretenses from the very beginning. Either way, there was little reason to pursue a discussion of his position at this point. He had committed himself to this course of action; that much was obvious. She would have to see it through.

She ventured a step closer. Kudakaan stepped to his left, not limping nearly as much as she had hoped. His expression was grim and committed. He sidestepped a touch further to buy some time. Suddenly, he lunged toward the stall housing his new horse, and before she could move to intercept, he pulled a length of wood from the corner. With a dreadful realization, she recognized his iron-bound weapon. A black horse with a charming white patch between its eyes poked its head forward from the recesses of another stall to see what was going on. The animal's eyes rolled around with nervous energy, responding to the violent thrashing in the stable. Much more of this, and one of the animals may panic. She shoved the thought aside as she rushed forward with a curse to intercept him before he could bring his weapon to bear. After only a few steps, she knew she was too late. She skidded to a halt in the center of the stable.

With a renewed air of confidence, Kudakaan stepped forward to meet her. He tested his injured leg again. His face betrayed no expression, but his bearing indicated that the wound would not hinder him much. No advantage there. She had never before fought an opponent who used a staff and who had any real training. Her instructors had covered the subject briefly, touching on the staff's advantages of speed and reach. Mostly they had told her to try to avoid such conflicts. A fat lot of help that was. She would have to rely on the greater damaging effect of her sword to win this fight, using fast thrusting attacks rather than a slower slash or chop. Theory was useful, but she acutely felt her lack of experience in this type of combat.

He stepped forward, striking toward her head. She shifted her guard and deflected the blow. She moved to thrust the point of the blade toward his chest, but he was already pivoting the staff to attack her knee. She dropped her guard low and barely caught the attack. He whipped the staff around and smashed again toward her head, using the staff's length to stay well out of the reach of her sword. She lifted her guard and deflected the attack, but there was no opening for a counterstrike. He whipped the staff in a tight circle, stepping back into a defensive position. His face still was smooth as stone. She admired his concentration, noting that a lesser opponent would be tempted to gloat at this point. Kudakaan was all business.

Without moving an inch closer, he slid his rear hand to grasp his weapon at one end, thrusting the opposite end of the staff toward her head. She nearly fell backward, deflecting the blow. He took a half step closer, still remaining well outside of her reach, and thrust again, this time toward her knee. She jumped backward to avoid the strike. Her mind raced, searching for a way to neutralize his advantage. Recalling her fight with the Troll at the riverbed, she backed further into the stable, underneath an overhang supporting a surplus of hay. He shot a quick look to the ceiling, knowing his ability to move the staff overhead would be hindered. After a moment's calculation, he stepped forward cautiously.

She ground her foot into the soft dirt of the stable floor, hoping to be able to rush in with his next attack. He slid his hand forward, grabbing the near end of the staff and whipping the opposite end around in a vicious head-level smash. She lifted her blade to parry the strike but then checked her counterattack, as the length of his weapon now stood directly between them. There was no opening. He proceeded with another swooping attack, striking again on his outside with the staff fully extended, leaving no room for counteraction. Her position under the eaves of the hayloft kept him from attacking repeatedly, but she had no opportunity to counter. She hesitated to move any further back. That would bring her dangerously close to the horses that were already getting spooked by the violence in the barn. She had no desire to risk being kicked to death by a skittish horse. He attacked again. She gave more ground. He was steering her slowly toward the corner where she would have no more ground to give, and he would very likely be able to pick her apart. An idea dawned on her.

With his next sweeping strike, she laid into his weapon with her block, meeting the attack head-on and striking full force with her blade, aiming below the iron-bound end. The staff held true, but she cut a noticeable gash into the wood. Kudakaan nearly lost control of the staff from this unexpected move. She took advantage of this pause to lunge forward, stabbing toward his neck. He lifted the staff, easily brushing aside her blade with the center of his weapon. He pushed the end of the staff toward her head, sliding through his forward hand. She ducked and stumbled out of the way. Kudakaan rolled the staff in his hands, sparing a quick glance to inspect the damage to his weapon. A few more similar direct hits in the same place would most likely split the wood. Kudakaan tilted his head in a way that could almost be seen as an approving nod.

He leapt in, suddenly thrusting the end of the staff repeatedly, attacking with sudden quick jabs. She tried to counterattack against his weapon as before, but his stabbing motions gave no opportunity for her to make solid contact. Part of her wondered how much more noise it would take to get anyone with ears to wonder what was happening in the stable. Surely someone has to have heard something by now.

Kudakaan's next attack made glancing contact with her left shoulder, knocking her off balance. She rolled away from the strike to absorb some of the force, inadvertently releasing the hilt of her sword with her left hand. He whirled the staff in a flat circle over his head, crouching as he did so, to make room overhead for a wide strike toward the back of her knee. With only one hand on her broadsword, she could scarcely hope to block the enormous force of such a strike, so she leapt straight up in the air, hoping to let the attack pass beneath her. Kudakaan adjusted the angle of his attack at the last moment, just managing to catch the heel of her boot, pushing her feet out from under her. Instead of trying to rescue her landing, she pivoted in midair, slashing downward with her blade toward the nearest target - Kudakaan's hand. He pulled his hand back, releasing the staff, and it fell to rest on his hip between his leg and body as he crouched. Her sword cut again into the wood moments before she landed with her full weight on the length of the staff. Prevented from release by Kudakaan's crouching body, the staff bent noticeably as Lena's weight drove into it.

She heard a light splintering sound as her body bent in an unnatural position over the wooden staff. Her sword skittered out of her hand as she thudded into the ground. Kudakaan lifted his end of the staff, levering Lena away from where her sword lay in the dirt of the stable floor. She heard another slight cracking noise and hoped it was the staff and not her ribs making the sound. She stood, unconsciously rubbing her injured ribs as she pulled her dagger from its sheath. Kudakaan ventured a smile now as he flipped her sword away with the end of his staff. It landed several paces away near the door to the stable. It may as well have landed across the ocean.

She looked around the stable. She was now quite near the corner that she very much did not want to be in. She had nothing with which to parry his attacks. But she was not without hope. She lunged sideways to position herself behind a thick wooden beam supporting the hayloft. Kudakaan thrust his staff forward to deny her this bit of meager cover. She planted her feet as if to jump back away from the attack, but instead, she leapt forward into the path of his weapon. Dropping her dagger and grabbing hold of his staff with both hands, she flung her entire body weight against the length of the shaft. The staff was forced into the post, and Kudakaan locked his arms around his weapon to prevent it from being wrenched out of his hands. As she had desperately hoped, the staff gave way with a loud splintering crack, breaking over the support post. She hit the ground hard with the broken end of Kudakaan's staff clutched in her hands.

As she rolled to face her opponent, he leapt into the air with a roar of anger, stabbing downward with the jagged piece of wood that remained in his hands. With horror, she realized she could not move fast enough to block the strike. The attack caught her in the center of the belly. She felt the wood tear through her flesh and bite into the soft earth beneath her. Her eyes widened in shock as she realized she was fatally wounded. Kudakaan growled wordlessly as he ground the jagged wood into the dirt. She screamed as a wave of fiery agony ripped through her body. He crouched over her and whispered.

"Slaves and objects of pleasure. My words exactly." His gloating was cut short as Lena jammed the other end of his broken staff into his throat. The jagged wood ripped his flesh open wide, and he staggered to his feet, clutching the ragged wound. Blood poured between his fingers like a river as he stumbled toward the door to the hotel. He took another step and fell to one knee. He turned to look at Lena with a burning fury as if he meant to incinerate her with the force of his stare. She reeled from the impact of his gaze and squirmed, triggering another deluge of pain from her wound. She let out another weak scream. He tumbled forward and was still.

She stared at his motionless form for a moment, waiting to join him in death. The moment passed. Another moment passed. Still no death. She heard muffled shouts and footsteps from within the hotel. She supposed if she were going to survive after all, that she had best get someone's attention. She tried to yell for help but taking a deep breath sent waves of pain through her. She let out a frail squeak instead.

* * * * *

Jack looked his large friend in the eye. "Ready?" he asked. Uglor nodded in assent. "Okay, go!" With a loud crash, Uglor burst into the stable, his axe ready and eyes wild. He looked around the stable and, after a moment, waved his hand. Jack stepped in cautiously, followed by Qaz and Corelan. He scanned the scene rapidly, gesturing toward the door to the outside. Uglor moved quickly to stand guard. Kudakaan was lying face down in the dirt in a pool of blood far too large to be anything but lethal. Lena lay on the ground several paces away, pinned to the earth with a large, broken stick. Jack turned to Daelyn and Tim, who stood just inside the hotel. "Watch our backs. Don't let anyone in." Jack looked at Qaz and simply pointed to Lena. Qaz rushed to her side and began to minister to her wounds. Jack was trying to contain his anger. The more he saw, the more he began to suspect what had happened. He turned to Corelan, who had produced another one of his tiny cigars from somewhere and was reaching for the lamp. Jack snatched the cigarette out of his mouth.

"Hey," Corelan protested unenthusiastically. Jack lifted a finger in a gesture of warning. He was not in the mood to deal with nonsense. He knelt beside Kudakaan. Dead. He checked his wrist for a pulse, just in case. Nope. Dead. Jack stood.

"Does anyone have half a clue what just happened here?" Jack's voice had a fiery tone, letting the others know that he wanted answers and wanted them now. Corelan cleared his throat.

"It looks like bandits just killed our guide," he offered. Jack leveled his gaze on the other man.

"What did you just say?"

"Bandits killed our guide," Corelan answered, gesturing to Kudakaan's body.

"Bandits?" Jack repeated. He was not sure if Corelan had turned stupid or was presuming that everyone else had instead.

"Yes. Awful thing, bandits." Corelan deftly retrieved his cigarette from Jack's startled hand and lifted the lantern from its perch on the chain.

"I don't see any bandits." Jack turned to look at Tim and Daelyn as if seeking confirmation. Out of politeness, Tim ventured a quick look around the stable.

"That's what you can expect from bandits." Corelan lifted the glass cover from the lantern and lit his absurd little cigar. The puff of light from the leaf lit his face momentarily. Corelan looked Jack dead in the eye and continued. "Bandits are a sneaky lot."

"I see. Bandits. Of course." Jack shrugged as if it were now obvious that this had been the work of some clever and sneaky bandits. "Qaz, how is she?" Qaz looked up from crouching over Lena's prone and bloody form.

"She ain't happy, but she will live." He hesitated for a moment, stifling a grin. "She is going to need a new shirt too." Lena cuffed him weakly on the back of the head.

Jack turned to Uglor, who was peering through a knothole in the stable's outer door. "Uglor, are we clear?" The huge man raised his hand in an affirming gesture without looking away. Jack turned to Daelyn. "Could you check on the innkeeper? We don't want her disturbing our investigation of these… bandit activities." She hesitated for a moment, then nodded and disappeared inside of the hotel. Corelan brought the lantern over to Qaz as he tended to Lena's wound. Jack administered a quick search of Kudakaan's pockets. Tim stepped into the barn.

"Uh, Jack?" he asked. "What are you doing?"

"I am trying to contain a serious situation." Jack concluded his search, pocketing the other man's room key. "Tim, get his feet." He waved to Uglor. "Would you help Tim stash this meat somewhere in the woods, please?" Uglor nodded and crossed the floor to stoop over the dead man. Tim took another step toward Jack.

"Are you suggesting that we conceal this from the authorities?" Tim asked. Jack raised his brow.

"That is exactly what I am suggesting." He could see that this worried Tim. "Do you have a problem with that?"

"Well…"

"Well, what?" Jack took a breath, trying to remain tactful. "Given that lawmen are a naturally suspicious bunch, they may be inclined to mount an additional investigation into this awful bandit activity. I'd hate for them to get the wrong idea and think that we were somehow involved with this tragedy." Tim did not respond. "We need time to determine the nature of our situation. We can't do that with dead people lying about." He stepped forward, putting a hand on Tim's shoulder. "Get his feet."

"You are suggesting that we commit a serious crime. One that could result in all of us being imprisoned or even hanged." Tim had control of himself but was clearly upset about this turn of events.

"Look, Tim." Jack took another deep breath. This had to be handled decisively. "We are in over our heads. There is clearly something big going on, and we are in the middle of it. It doesn't feel like we can trust Pendor, and even though this town is under the Archduke Dornibyn's protection, we don't know the full extent of that we are mixed up in. We really can't afford to trust the local authorities either." Tim shifted his weight unconsciously. "So, my friend, you need to decide right now. Are you with us, or will you try to go it alone?" Tim thought for a moment. Jack noticed his eyes momentarily took on that faraway look that signaled he was doing his psychic-whatever.

"Let's roll him in his cloak," Tim suggested.

"Good. Please handle that." Jack came over to Qaz. Lena was sitting up now and seemed coherent. The shard of wood that had pierced her abdomen lay on the ground beside her. Corelan stood a respectful distance away, poking around in a set of saddlebags that had fallen to the stable floor. "How are you feeling, hon?" Jack asked her. He silently noted the accuracy of Qaz's diagnosis of her shredded tunic. It was truly indecent.

"Just get me upstairs, and don't give me any of that 'hon' crap. I'm not in the mood." She glared at them both, daring them to let their eyes wander.

"Qaz, if you would please escort the lady?" Qaz nodded and helped her to her feet. She ventured a shaky step and stumbled, catching herself on Qaz's shoulder. Qaz tucked his arm beneath her knees and lifted her off the ground to carry her into the inn. She growled a generic protest but allowed the dishonor. Kudakaan's body had been wrapped in a cloak and hoisted atop Uglor's enormous shoulder. Tim poked his head out of the stable door, and the two vanished into the night. Jack turned to Corelan, who had the stray saddlebags slung over his shoulder and was now kicking dirt over the smattering of blood that Lena had left on the ground. Jack noticed the expression of acute discomfort on Corelan's face.

"I didn't figure you for the squeamish type," Jack offered. Corelan fixed him with an empty stare.

"Don't start with me," he mumbled in a voice almost too soft to hear.

"Sorry. I just…"

"Drop it." Corelan's voice had a cold, dangerous edge. Jack had no idea what was going on in the other man's head. He decided to leave it be.

"Sure." Jack dug a key out of his pocket. "Kudakaan was in room twelve. I'll clean the rest of this scene and meet you there." Corelan took the key and went inside without a word. Jack shook his head to clear his mind. He had been hoping that something would happen to change their situation. Next time he would be more specific.

* * * * *

Qaz handed Jack another cup of tea. It was getting late, and they were all tired. For a moment, Jack almost envied Lena as she slept in the other room. Then he thought of being pinned to the very earth with a jagged piece of wood and revised his perspective. The evening's discussion had started badly, with tempers and egos colliding roughly. Qaz had brewed some exceptional herbal tea (he called it his special recipe), and heads were beginning to cool, both from the calming effect of the tea and from sheer fatigue. Jack could only guess where Qaz had gotten the tea, based on the loose description he and Corelan had given him on their adventures since the debacle at the Troll cavern. He supposed it didn't really matter. They had already swapped cursory stories on who had done what since they had been split up. Jack still felt the need for additional details, but for the moment, broad strokes would have to suffice. It was now time to analyze the data and make some decisions.

"So. Qaz…" Jack began. "How many times in a row can somebody, namely Lena, be mangled and then magically healed?" He needed to know the strengths and weaknesses of their group in order to proceed. Jack looked around at the others who crowded the small hotel room that he shared with Uglor. He himself sat in the corner in the room's only chair. The room had two small lumpy beds crammed into its space, which was begrudgingly shared with a long rickety dresser and a mismatched table. Qaz sat on the corner of the bed nearest to Jack, leaning over to tend to the tea on the table beside them both. He seemed focused and dedicated to the unity of the group.

Daelyn sat on the other bed, leaning on the wall, eyeing the group quietly. Jack guessed she was in this for her own purposes, and if things got any hotter, she might drop out. Tim sat on the edge of the bed leaning on the far wall near Daelyn and currently appeared more than half-asleep. Unless Jack misjudged him, he would likely side with Daelyn if it came to that. Uglor was sleeping in the other room. It was decided that *somebody* should be well-rested as it looked as if tomorrow was going to be a long day also.

Corelan had been strangely silent this evening. He had let Qaz do most of the talking as they caught up – a task well suited to Qaz's particular talents. Something profound was bothering the man, and Jack could not tell what it was. Jack felt himself a fairly good judge of other people's moods, and when Corelan and Qaz had popped in out of nowhere a few hours earlier, Corelan seemed his old self. Now, after Lena's fight with Kudakaan, something was drastically wrong. Jack reminded himself to chat with Tim later to see if his perceptions were correct. Corelan presently lounged on the dresser sipping his own brand of tea from the small pocket flask that never seemed to be empty, despite its regular use. Perhaps it was enchanted…

"Well, magical healing is a tricky thing…" Qaz began. Tim stood suddenly.

"Sorry," he explained. "I am falling asleep here. Go on." He rubbed his eyes and temples, stifling a yawn. Daelyn sat up also.

"I'll get some more hot water." Tim stepped toward the door. He noticed Qaz's almost hurt expression. "I pretty much know how this works."

"I'll keep it short." Qaz looked around the room. The others looked back with polite disbelief. Qaz gave an imploring gesture. "Really, I will." Tim stepped over to the table, retrieved the teapot, and left the room.

"Go on," Jack implored. At this rate, they would be talking until dawn.

"Magical healing of physical wounds by any art is just an acceleration of the body's natural healing process, and that, of course, takes energy away from the body." Daelyn stifled a yawn. Qaz went on. "What I am doing essentially just repairs the rent flesh and broken bones only. Can't do much about blood loss or poisons or infections, not at my level. However…"

"Um, Qaz?" Jack interjected. "Don't tell me about the storm. Just bring in the ship." Qaz looked back at him, abashed. "What is the bottom line?"

"She is going to be tired as her body replaces the energy spent on healing. She needs bed rest and plenty of food. She is going to wake up hungry."

"How long before she is at full capacity?"

"If she can rest all day tomorrow, she should be back to full strength by the day after."

"If we have to ride?"

"Then longer. It depends on the individual. She is strong physically and somewhat willful. That will help." He smiled at his understatement.

"Thank you. You can fill me in later on the details."

"No problem." Qaz spared a wink for Daelyn. She returned a grateful nod and stretched her legs out, massaging circulation back into her thighs. Jack turned his attention to the next item on his mental list. He looked at the others trying to gauge their dispositions. Maybe he should talk to Tim to see if he could learn a few psychic tricks.

"Okay, we seem to be in a tough position, and we have a number of facts," Jack started.

"I say we bail," Corelan interjected. Daelyn looked as if she had forgotten he was there. Jack had hoped to get a little further into his presentation before addressing this topic.

"Why?" Qaz asked, sparing Jack from asking the same.

"It is clear to me that something sinister is going on. We were lied to and nearly killed on several occasions. I feel no personal obligation to honor my end of the contract." He sipped lightly from his flask. Most of his earlier hostility was gone.

"Don't you want to know what is going on?" Daelyn asked. Jack closed his mouth, being spared another question.

"No," Corelan answered.

"Why not?" she asked.

"It isn't worth it. It is all a bunch of crap anyway. Probably some kind of grab for political power or money or something. I don't care." He took another sip. "Kudakaan was clearly willing to kill Lena to protect his secret, whatever it is. There is no reason to believe that Pendor won't try the same, given the opportunity. I don't see a reason to give him that chance, just to find out *which* laws he plans to break. We know he is a crook. Let's leave it at that."

"What about the contracts?" she asked. Jack thought she was showing a rather elevated interest in Corelan's motivations.

"Contracts don't mean anything to criminals," Corelan answered. "We only have a paltry sum of Pendor's money…"

"Well…" Qaz began.

"Be realistic." Corelan put his flask down on the dresser. "He can afford it. We only have a bit of his cash, and we don't really know enough to be dangerous. If we disappear, he will probably be thankful." Corelan made eye contact with each of the others, looking for dissent. He looked at Jack last.

"He doesn't know that," Jack stated.

"Doesn't know what?" Corelan asked.

"Doesn't know how much *we* know. As you suggested, and I agree, Pendor is up to something criminal. For a man in power, that is serious business. If he thinks we are a liability, he will take steps to tie up this loose end." Jack looked around the room to see if his implications were setting in. Just then, Tim returned with a steaming teapot.

"What did I miss?" he asked nonchalantly as he resumed his position.

"Jack was just about to explain why we should continue to pursue this madness," Corelan offered. "Weren't you Jack?" Tim nodded and sat, facing Jack.

"Yes, Corelan, I was." Jack reached over to pour a cup of tea. "Here is the way I see it." He paused to collect his thoughts. "We have two choices. Run or try to see it through. If we take off, we will clearly signal to Pendor that we oppose him. He is more powerful and dangerous than we are. In that conflict, we would most likely lose." Jack paused to sip his tea.

"Only if he felt it was worth his time. Which it isn't," Corelan replied.

"I agree with the first part, but not the second," Jack answered. Corelan swung his knees over the edge of the dresser to sit upright. "Since we do not know the extent of what is going on, we cannot be sure of how far Pendor is willing to go to secure it. Secondly, Pendor does not know how much we know. Tactically, it makes sense for him to assume the worst and act accordingly."

"So, what you are saying is, we are screwed," Corelan responded.

"Not in the least bit." Jack leaned forward. "Our other choice is to stick with it for now. Remember that Pendor does not know what happened tonight. As far as he is concerned, we are still completely in the dark, and Kudakaan really was killed by bandits."

"Your point being?"

"We let him believe that. We continue on as if we still trust him. We gather information until we know enough to decide our long-term course of action."

"Or until we know enough to get killed."

"Only if we are sloppy."

"What about that?" Corelan gestured to the folded pages on the table beside Jack.

"Pendor does not know about that either." Jack leaned back in the chair and folded his hands. Qaz perked up at the mention of the pages.

"I think I was still helping Lena when you guys found that in Kudakaan's room." He gestured to the papers. "Did we decide what that means?"

"We believe it is a coded letter to Pendor describing what happened since his last correspondence." Jack lifted the pages from the table and held one of them up. "It is remarkably thin on specifics and doesn't describe anything that we don't already know. Notably absent are details describing what he did after leaving the Troll cave."

"Do we know when his last correspondence was?" Qaz asked.

"Hard to say. Nothing is mentioned of the events that took place before going to the Troll cave, so I would think the last time he sent a report was in Akeela."

"How do we know that there are coded portions of the letter?" Qaz asked. Jack handed him the letter.

"Some of the phrasing is awkward. Some of it seems pointless or forced. Also, the words are spaced unevenly." Qaz scanned the letter and placed it on the bed beside him. "Daelyn seems to think they are using a template." Jack gestured to Daelyn, who blushed and nodded.

"What is a *template* anyway?" Corelan asked.

"A second page with holes cut into it," Daelyn answered. "You lay it over the top of the first page, and the words that show through are the real message."

"Tim also believes there is something encrypted," Jack added. Qaz looked at Tim.

"I just got a feeling when I held the page," Tim offered. Qaz shrugged.

"So, I assume we did not find the second page," Qaz interjected.

"Correct," Jack answered. "Neither have we found the leather pouch with the rest of the paperwork from earlier today." Jack clenched his teeth in frustration. A lot of answers would be lurking in that pouch.

"Sorry, still catching up," Qaz interjected. "What papers?"

"Kudakaan gathered up all of the paperwork from Walsh's office today, including an envelope that was hidden in a false compartment in the wall. He put the whole stack into a leather pouch, which has somehow gone missing within the last two hours."

"Walsh was the guy Daelyn shot?" Qaz asked. "The guy that was our only lead?" She nodded with a frown. "The guy that only attacked you because you lied to him for some reason?"

"Yes," Jack answered tersely. "That guy." Qaz had already voiced his opinion concerning the meeting with Walsh several times, and Jack had had enough snark for one day.

"Kudakaan kept a journal," Daelyn stated. "Could be useful stuff in there."

"I know," Jack responded, swallowing his irritation with Qaz. "I would love to get my hands on the thing, but it's just nowhere to be found. Maybe he put it in the pouch also."

"Odd," Daelyn commented.

"Okay. Where does that leave us?" Qaz asked.

"I got some interesting tidbits from Walsh during my first conversation with him," Jack answered.

"Tidbits?" Qaz inquired with an arched eyebrow.

"For one, there are a lot more people working on… whatever we are working on than Pendor or Kudakaan have let on. There was Walsh, Grimmley, some guy named Kalush, somebody named Ashe, there is a Captain Sarlo, and Walsh mentioned an undisclosed number of 'guys' who were supposed to handle the Troll plan." Jack counted off the names on his fingers.

"What *do* we know about the Troll plan?" Qaz asked.

"Only what you overheard in the cave."

"So, nothing useful." Qaz shrugged. "Do we have anything we can actually use?"

"This Kalush fellow is staying in Elrynth. We can contact him via the management at the Dewdrop Inn."

"Dewdrop Inn?" Corelan snorted. "I suppose that is somebody's idea of being clever."

"Apparently." Jack smiled.

"I thought it was a great name for a hotel," Qaz commented.

"You would," Daelyn added. Qaz threw a pillow at her, missing by a wide margin.

"What are you thinking?" Qaz asked.

"I say we go to the Dewdrop Inn in Elrynth and ask about a fellow named Kalush," Jack suggested. He looked around the room for support.

"Then what?" Corelan asked.

"I suppose it depends on if we can arrange a meeting and how the meeting goes," Jack offered.

"Seems logical," Qaz commented. "Though maybe we use a different strategy than the one you did with Walsh. Otherwise, I'm for it."

"There are a lot of problems with that," Corelan said.

"True, but I don't see a better option." Jack adjusted his position in his chair. "What about you, Daelyn?"

"I think you are right about running." She yawned. "It would signal that we are afraid of him, and if we are afraid, then he would think we have reason to be. Which to him would mean we know something that we don't. That seems enough reason to kill us." She nodded in thanks as Tim handed her a cup of tea. "We should do something to send a signal that we are harmless. This Kalush character seems our only contact with Pendor. Unless we can figure a way to contact the duke directly."

"I thought about that," Jack said. "I think direct contact may worry him. He specifically told us not to try. This could mean that he stands to lose a degree of secrecy if we start poking around his neighborhood looking for him."

"Maybe that could be helpful, though," Tim suggested. "If he feels vulnerable at home, maybe that would be a good place to start."

"I thought of that too." Jack looked at Tim. "We have no leads in that direction, and therefore no way to know if our efforts would be detected. Fishing around blindly for information can very likely tip him off as to what we are doing – namely something we were asked not to." Jack sipped his tea. "That would send a signal that we don't trust him. Which would end up being the same as if we were afraid of him."

"You sure do think a lot," Corelan commented.

"That is my job," Jack answered flatly. "Where do we all stand?" he asked the group. Qaz shrugged, having already stated his position. Jack looked right at Daelyn. She noticed his attention to her rather than anyone else. She met his gaze evenly.

"I think your plan is good so far. I am willing to give it a try." Daelyn took a deep breath. "One thing, though," she started. Jack raised an eyebrow. "Grimmley could still show up and cause us some real problems." Jack sighed. That was the sticky part. It irked him that he could not see an easy solution to that issue.

"Grimmley was the guy you let get away?" Qaz asked. Jack nodded with a sour grin. It seemed as if Qaz enjoyed aggravating people.

"True," Jack replied to Daelyn. "Tim?" Tim looked up, almost startled. As Tim's eyes refocused, Jack got the impression he was just finishing an attempt to read the others in the room or get their 'vibes' or whatever he called it. Tim smiled back at him as if he had spoken that thought aloud. Damn psychics.

"I'll go with your plan," Tim stated.

"So, Corelan…" Jack asked. Corelan locked eyes with him for a moment. There was still something bothering him, Jack thought. Something that maybe had nothing to do with this discussion.

"I am going to wait to see what Lena and Uglor say. If it is unanimous, then I'll go along with you guys for a bit." He hopped off of the dresser. "I am going to bed." He scooped Kudakaan's room key off of the end of the dresser and went toward the door. "Anything else?"

"I can think of a lot of things, but they can all wait," Jack mumbled through a yawn.

"Then I'll see you in the morning." Corelan slipped quietly from the room.

"I guess all that's left is for us to figure out who has to share rooms since our three newly resurrected companions..." Jack looked a Qaz, "...failed to make reservations." Jack stood and stretched. Sometimes it took too much effort to get people to see reason.

Storm Cloud Rising

Jason Lancour

THE STORY CONTINUES

IN

STORM CLOUDS
BREAK

Book Two of the Storm Cloud series.

With the unfortunate demise of the duke's liaison, the already troubled mission begins to spiral out of control. Growing skepticism and mixed loyalties within the band of mercenaries push them into murky waters as varying personal agendas force each member to question whether to see the contract through or cut and run. As a violent collision between opposing forces looms, no choice seems viable, and the lives of many hang in the balance.

ABOUT THE AUTHOR

Jason Lancour tries to spend a small portion of each day with his head in the clouds. In his writing, he hopes to share with his readers what he has seen up there. Jason finds it awkward to refer to himself in the third person but also finds that is how author bios are generally done. He currently lives in Atlanta, Georgia, where he works in film and television, helping to tell other people's stories.

If you enjoyed reading this book and would be interested in reading more, you are encouraged to visit the website www.jasonlancour.com, where, if you're feeling particularly adventurous, you can sign up for an awesome newsletter. Or, if perhaps you're more into the social media thing, you may find (with varying degrees of engagement) a profile on some of the popular platforms using the handle jasonlancourauthor. In either place, you'll be able to receive updates about future work, writing-related news, inside info, idle ramblings, and perhaps a map or two.